Praise for *New York Times* bestselling ~~~~ MICHELLE SAGARA
and The Chronicles of Elantra series

"No one provides an emotional payoff like Michelle Sagara. Combine that with a fast-paced police procedural, deadly magics, five very different races and a wickedly dry sense of humor—well, it doesn't get any better than this."
   —Bestselling author Tanya Huff on The Chronicles of Elantra series

"Readers will embrace this compelling, strong-willed heroine with her often sarcastic voice."
                              —*Publishers Weekly* on *Cast in Courtlight*

"The impressively detailed setting and the book's spirited heroine are sure to charm romance readers, as well as fantasy fans who like some mystery with their magic."
                              —*Publishers Weekly* on *Cast in Secret*

"Along with the exquisitely detailed world building, Sagara's character development is mesmerizing. She expertly breathes life into a stubborn yet evolving heroine. A true master of her craft!"
                              —*RT Book Reviews* (4½ stars) on *Cast in Fury*

"Each visit to this amazing world, with its richness of place and character, is one to relish."
                              —*RT Book Reviews* (4½ stars) on *Cast in Silence*

"Another satisfying addition to an already vivid and entertaining fantasy series."
                              —*Publishers Weekly* on *Cast in Chaos*

"Sagara does an amazing job continuing to flesh out her large cast of characters, but keeps the unsinkable Kaylin at the center."
                              —*RT Book Reviews* (4½ stars) on *Cast in Peril*

"Über-awesome Sagara picks up the intense action right where she left off… While Kaylin is the heart of this amazing series, the terrific characters keep the story moving. An autobuy for sure!"
                              —*RT Book Reviews* (4½ stars) on *Cast in Sorrow*

MICHELLE SAGARA

CAST IN HONOR

MIRA®

Recycling programs for this product may not exist in your area.

ISBN-13: 978-0-7783-1859-0

Cast in Honor

Copyright © 2015 by Michelle Sagara

Printed in U.S.A.

First printing: December 2015
10 9 8 7 6 5 4 3 2 1

For Mary-Theresa Hussey,
With thanks and gratitude for a decade of partnership.

For Mary-Theresa Hussey,
With thanks and gratitude for a decade of partnership.

CAST IN HONOR

CHAPTER 1

Kaylin had a new home, and she loved it.

The Imperial Palace was, to many, the pinnacle of dream homes. But to Kaylin, it had been a nightmare—one that she'd finally escaped. The Palace Guard no longer lined the halls outside of her room, and her rooms were no longer so grand or so fine that she felt as if she didn't belong in them. The shutters on her windows—and they were shuttered, not barred—weren't as warped as they had been in her old apartment, but the windows opened to let both light and air in, when she desired it.

And best of all: Dragon arguments no longer woke her out of a sound sleep.

In theory, Barrani arguments were quieter than draconic arguments, Barrani throats being confined to the general shape and size, even if they were immortal. Angry Barrani weren't exactly *safer* to be around, but at least they didn't demand attention half a city block away.

So much for theory.

The Barrani engaged in this particular argument were in the same building. Their shouts shook the floor, which shook her bed, which caused Kaylin to sit up and scrabble under her pillow for the dagger she always slept with.

Her small dragon familiar, usually a floppy and relatively

inert mass somewhere at the top of her pillow, hissed. It was dark enough—barely—that she could feel him more than see him.

In response to the stray thought, a soft glow lit the interior of the room. This was a standard feature of living in an intelligent and responsive building, but three weeks in, Kaylin still found it a bit creepy.

"I'm sorry, Kaylin," Helen said, although she didn't dim the lights. "It's habit. Generally when people are worried about visibility, it's because they might injure themselves in the darkness." She was, of course, nowhere to be seen—or, conversely, *everywhere*, as she *was* the building.

Guilt, of course, came on the heels of light. Kaylin wasn't used to guarding her thoughts. She could (mostly) keep the bad ones firmly sealed behind her teeth, but Helen didn't require the spoken word. Then again, Helen didn't seem to judge or take offense at the unspoken word, which was definitely for the best.

The floor shook again, and this time, Barrani words were clearly audible. There were, as expected, two voices, crashing into each other: Mandoran's and Annarion's.

"What exactly are they doing?" Kaylin swiveled to dump her feet off the side of her bed. The mattress was dense and thick, but it was not—like palace mattresses—three feet off the ground.

"Disagreeing."

"Sorry, I got that part. What are they disagreeing about?" Mandoran switched, midsentence, to the Elantran that was Kaylin's mother tongue.

"You can't hear them?"

"I heard the last bit, and you should tell Mandoran that what he's suggesting is anatomically impossible." She walked to the chair nearest the actual closet and retrieved the clothing she'd be wearing, bar disaster, to the office today. The small dragon showed his appreciation for being rudely woken by taking off with the stick she used to keep her hair off her neck and face. He also squawked a lot.

"Mandoran says," Helen finally replied, "that it's not anatomically impossible for them. Annarion says—"

"Yes, thanks, I heard his response. Have they let up at all in the past four days?"

"They haven't been shouting at each other—"

"I mean, have they taken *any* breaks?"

"No, dear."

"It's probably a miracle they're both still alive."

"Mandoran agrees. He apologizes and says they will take a break now, and resume practice once you've headed into the office."

In the three weeks since their narrow defeat of the ancestors, Annarion had not emerged from wherever he was training. Kaylin didn't expect that he would until Helen believed that his self-containment was complete enough to walk the city streets without immediately attracting every Shadow in the heart of the fiefs—or worse.

He'd already done that once, though unintentionally. Helen insisted that Annarion had been shouting for attention—for want of a better description—and the ancestors had heard him. Since Kaylin had been standing beside the young Barrani for most of his stay in Elantra, she sympathized with his confusion: she certainly hadn't heard—or seen—anything that demanded attention. Nothing beyond his striking Barrani looks, at any rate.

But…the Shadows *had* come, leaving the containment of the fiefs and venturing into the streets of Elantra proper. And they'd made a beeline to Annarion. They weren't particularly careful about anything standing in their way, especially once they turned their attention to the Barrani High Halls. At that point, the Barrani and the Dragon Court had arrived in force.

The city had mostly recovered, although the streets in the high-rent district were no longer flat; the stone had been melted, and the creatures that had done the melting had left marks in the road when it once again solidified.

Helen was attempting to teach Annarion to be *quiet*. For some reason, Annarion did not take as well to these lessons as Mandoran had done. Mandoran joined Kaylin from time to time; Kaylin suspected that he did it just to annoy Annarion.

Then again, Annarion was desperately worried for his brother, Lord Nightshade. Nightshade's abrupt disappearance from his fief—and, more important, his Castle—weighed heavily on his younger brother, who suspected that his presence was the cause of Nightshade's absence. Kaylin privately agreed, but she didn't blame Annarion.

She blamed herself. She shouldn't have let Annarion visit his brother in Castle Nightshade. She shouldn't have let him out into the city at all until she was certain he wasn't a danger to others.

And you would have stopped him how, exactly?

Rationally, she was not responsible for anything that had occurred within Elantra. But as hers had been the hand that had rescued Annarion and the rest of his cohort from their jail in the heart of the green, her guilt had clear and undeniable roots. Kaylin attempted to push aside the feelings of remorse—they pissed Teela off when she was in the office, and while Teela couldn't actually read minds, her familiarity with Kaylin's moods made her intuition pretty much the same in practical terms.

The sounds of shouting that would have contained nothing but curse words in most languages diminished as Kaylin made her way out of her room.

★ ★ ★

The halls in her new home were in far finer repair than the halls in her first home had been. Doors lined the walls—doors behind which some of her friends now lived. Those friends were seldom in their own rooms, with a single notable exception: Bellusdeo. Her sole guard, Maggaron, had spent two weeks standing in the hall outside of the Dragon's doors; he took breaks for food, but they were short and silent.

Mandoran and Annarion spent their days—and nights—in what Helen referred to as the training room. It wasn't, as far as Kaylin could tell, actually a room in the strictest sense of the word. Teela—the reason that Kaylin had attempted to even find it—didn't consider it a room in the loosest sense of the word, either. Kaylin pointed out that it had a door.

Teela in turn pointed out that Helen—whose voice was present—had had trouble giving the two Hawks necessary directions to reach it; in Teela's opinion, the door had only been created as a visible marker. Helen confirmed this.

Regardless, although the two not-quite-Barrani boys had rooms of their own, they'd been holed up in a part of the mansion that couldn't be considered home, Maggaron had been standing or slumping against a wall in the hall, and Bellusdeo had treated her room like an impregnable fortress. As house-warmings went—and Kaylin had only attended one, at Caitlin's insistence—it was unsuccessful.

Kaylin, however, had felt at home in her room from the moment she crossed its threshold.

She felt at home in the dining room, even though it was large; she felt at home entering the front door, even though it opened to a foyer with multiple levels and too much light; she was even becoming more comfortable with Helen's habit of treating her thoughts as questions, and answering them out loud. Tara, the Avatar of Tiamaris's Tower, did the same. It was hard to feel lonely in this house. If it was also hard to be alone—and it was—Kaylin didn't mind. Helen didn't judge her thoughts, her moods or her achievements—or, more specifically, their lack.

"I would," Helen said, as Kaylin made her way to the dining room. "But thoughts are not actions; they're not *plans*. If you were planning something unwise, I would tell you." This was demonstrably true. "If you were planning something unethical, I would also tell you. I have lived with tenants who have chosen to act against their own beliefs—and the results were not pleasant."

"They messed up?"

"Ah, no, dear. I have had a number of tenants since Hazielle. It is almost universally true that what you cannot bring yourself to do—or perhaps to avoid doing—you cannot believe anyone else would avoid. For instance: if you decry lying, but then do it yourself—and not in the way manners might dictate—you quickly assume that no one is honest. If you betray a trust for your own benefit, you assume that no one is trustworthy.

"This eventually causes a spiral of ugliness and loathing. The reason I would stop you from doing something you despise is not necessarily because I would despise it. It is because of the effect it would have, in the end, on the way you view and interact with the important parts of your world. If you have no self-respect, your ability to respect anything or anyone else is in peril."

Kaylin thought about this as she ate.

Mandoran soon joined her, looking glum and exhausted. Had he been mortal, she would have attempted to send him back to bed. Since he wasn't, and given that he was up against the wall of Annarion's frantic fear for his brother's safety, she decided against it.

"He's going to be the definition of anti-fun until we find

his brother. I've taken quite a personal dislike to Lord Night-shade." He pushed food around his plate as if the eggs were unappetizing. "If it weren't for his brother, we could try to learn to be 'quiet' at a reasonable pace. The way things stand now, Annarion might as well be mortal."

"And you mean that in the nicest possible way, of course," Kaylin replied.

"Not really." Being on the receiving end of Kaylin's glare, he glanced at Helen; her Avatar had been waiting, more or less patiently, in the dining room. She appeared entirely un-ruffled by his comment.

"Look, I understand why mortals are in a rush about every-thing—they get old and weak so quickly that they can't afford to take their time. We're not mortal. We have time."

"We don't know what happened to Nightshade."

"We know he isn't dead."

"There are worse things than death."

"One of which would be practicing with Annarion," Man-doran replied. Wincing, he added, "Great. Now he's angry."

Kaylin was on Annarion's side this time, but said nothing; the Hawks had taught her to leave Barrani arguments between the Barrani who were having them.

Thanks to Annarion and Mandoran's not exactly silent dis-agreement, Kaylin was in no danger of being late for work. The midwives had called her out twice during the past three weeks; they'd sent a runner to the house each time. So far, Helen seemed unwilling to install active mirrors in the manse. Mirrors were modern necessities. Anyone of import used them to communicate, *especially* in emergencies. Since Kaylin was feeling surprisingly awake despite the hour, she turned to Helen to tackle the subject for a third time.

"I need some sort of working mirror connection somewhere

in the house. It doesn't have to be everywhere. It could be in one room. Or even only in mine. Marcus mirrors whenever he needs someone to shout at, and the midwives' guild mirrors when there's an emergency. So does the Foundling Hall. I can't ask the midwives' guild to send a runner between the endangered mother and this house and expect me to make it there in time. So far I've been lucky, but I doubt that will last."

Helen's expression flattened. There was a reason this was the third attempt at discussion. "I have made some inquiries about the mirror network; they are incomplete thus far. I am perhaps remiss; I do not wish to insult either you or the people for whom you work. But the mirror network is *not* secure. I am almost certain such forms of communication would not have been allowed in my youth."

"Almost everyone has some sort of mirror access." Everyone, Kaylin thought, who could afford it. She hadn't had a mirror when she'd lived in the fiefs. She hadn't daydreamed about having one, either—she hadn't really been aware of their existence until she'd crossed the bridge. "Some people—mostly Barrani—have even set the mirror network to follow *them* when they move from place to place. And if the Barrani are willing to use it, how dangerous can it be?"

"There are many things the Barrani do—and have done in the past—that you would consider neither safe nor respectable." Helen sighed. "Understand that the mirror network is a magical lattice that underlays the city."

Kaylin nodded.

"At the moment, it is a magic that I do not permit across my boundaries. It appears to have been designed to travel around areas of non-cooperation; it therefore skirts the edge of my containments. I have not disrupted it in any fashion—it did not seem to be directly harmful. If you wish to have access to your mirror network, I would have to alter my protections to allow the grid's magic to overlap my own, at least in part. I do not know who, or what, is responsible for the stability of the grid; I do not know who, or what, created the spells that contain it; nor do I fully understand the magic that sustains it."

"Don't do it," Mandoran said.

Kaylin glared at him. "Why not?"

"You don't let stray magic into the heart of your home."

"Everyone else does."

"So I'd gathered." He winced. "Teela's in a mood, by the way."

Great.

"I don't know what kind of power your people have—I have to assume it's not significant."

Big surprise.

"But someone with significant power could transmit or feed an entirely different kind of magic through the lattice on which the mirror network is built."

"I'd think the Emperor would have something to say about that—mirrors function in the Palace."

"Dragons aren't as fragile as mortals, for one. Look—I'm not an Arcanist. There are no doubt some protections built into the mirror network to prevent its use as a weapon. I can imagine those protections being successful in most cases—but not all. Magic is not precise; it's not entirely predictable—as you should well know.

"But the possibility of being used as a weapon is not the only threat the mirrors might pose. It's highly likely that they could transmit private information to outside observers." His expression darkening, he added, "I mean—Teela lets the damn network follow her."

Not for the first time, Kaylin wished she could be part of that internal dialogue. "The communication—the flow of information—is bound to mirrors. Teela can't just speak to me whenever she wants unless I carry a portable mirror on my person—and those are way too expensive to give to a private. I can mirror Teela—and she'll pick up *if* she's near a functioning mirror. Break the mirror, and you break the communication. And the mirrors aren't any sturdier than regular glass."

"If you were better at magic," Mandoran told her, "you could easily do what Teela does. It wouldn't be expensive."

Kaylin's magic lessons had been severely disrupted for the past two months, but the implication that she was incompetent was clear. She tried to swallow her defensive words because, blunt or not, he was only speaking the truth. She even managed to succeed, although swallowing food was easier. She focused on that instead.

"If you allow your network access to *this* house, as opposed to the hovel you purportedly lived in before the Palace," Mandoran continued, "the information to be gained could be a danger—to Helen. No one was interested in your previous home until Bellusdeo arrived. They might have had a great deal of interest in your palace residence, but Teela tells me the Palace is practically a magical stronghold." His expression made it clear that he didn't agree. And also made clear, after a moment, that Teela didn't think much of his disagreement and was letting him know.

The thought of Teela in lecture mode made Kaylin appreciate being left out. "People mirror me when they need me. And when they *need me*, it's an emergency. They don't have time to run halfway across the city to hand-deliver a message." She turned to Helen and added, "Even Tiamaris—the Tower of Tiamaris—has mirror access."

Helen frowned. "Let me see, dear."

Kaylin was already thinking about mirrors made of water in the large, glyphed stone room of that Tower, Tara standing beside them, her eyes not quite human.

"Is it only in that room that you have access to your network?"

Kaylin frowned. "No. Tara can create a mirror out of nothing if we need one."

"Understood. I will look into this further. I am no longer—as you know—what I was when I was first created. Information I once possessed has now been lost, and I must work the way you do." This was not in any way accurate, but Kaylin didn't quibble. "It would be useful to have some contact with at least one of the Seven Towers; the Seven do not take unnecessary risks." She glanced at Mandoran. "Perhaps you can be of aid in this regard."

"I'd like to be a guest, if it's all the same to you." Mandoran's answer—which didn't appear to line up with Helen's comment—caused Kaylin obvious confusion. "Guests aren't asked to do necessary work—in large part because they can't be trusted with it." Mandoran's smile was sharp, lean.

"I am not Barrani," Helen replied, an edge of disapproval in her otherwise correct voice. "Believe that I would know if you were misbehaving anywhere it was likely to cause damage." Her expression softening, she added, "We would not have survived without your intervention—and to intervene, you stood almost at the heart of my power. As such, there is now very little with which I would not trust you."

"It doesn't seem like an adequate reward for good behavior," Mandoran replied. He was grinning unrepentantly; it made his entire face both younger and more compelling. "I am, on the other hand, willing to entertain the prospect—if helping out around the house gets me out of other duties."

"I don't know why you say these things; you are just going to annoy your brother." Helen's voice was now reproving.

"Too late." Mandoran had apparently had enough of the

breakfast he'd hardly touched. He stood, turned to Kaylin and added, "Sorry if we woke you up."

"I had to go in to work today anyway."

"That's what *I* said, but Helen didn't agree."

As Kaylin left the dining room and headed toward the grandly lit front doors, there was another surprise waiting for her. The wide, curving stairs had a person on them. Bellusdeo.

Kaylin almost didn't recognize her. Gone was the fancy court dress that marked so much of her life in public; she was wearing pants and a tunic. The shirt beneath the tunic was beige, and if the cloth was a much more expensive weave than Kaylin could afford, it wasn't immediately obvious. Her hair had been pulled up off her shoulders; she wore no obvious jewelry.

"Do I have something unpleasant on my face?" Bellusdeo asked, her eyes a steady bronze.

Kaylin remembered to close her mouth. "No—it just feels like it's been so long since I've seen it."

"And absence has made your heart grow fonder?"

Kaylin blinked.

"It's a mortal phrase, I believe."

"*Mortal* covers a lot of cultural territory."

"True. I admit that I don't completely understand the usage. I'm using it incorrectly?"

"I wouldn't say that, exactly. Are you coming with me to the office?"

"I'm not dressed like this for Diamart's abominable, condescending lessons, no." Her smile deepened in exactly the wrong way. "When he is recovered enough that apoplexy won't kill him, I think I will be, though."

The small dragon, having resumed his ownership of Kaylin's shoulder, snickered.

"Get it out of your system now," Kaylin told him. "I'd like to be taken seriously by the rest of the Hawks once we get to work."

He hissed laughter.

"You're going to find the office a lot quieter," Kaylin told Bellusdeo as they walked.

"Why?"

"We lost four Barrani Hawks and a dozen Aerians; the Swords lost at least that many men and women. The office is still functioning; the duty roster is still being filled in all divisions that require one. It's not that no one dies in the line of duty—they do. But this is the first time we've lost Barrani."

"Is it the first time the Barrani have been injured?"

"What? No, of course not. Barrani arrogance doesn't lend itself to caution. But nothing we run into on a regular walking beat is capable of taking down a Barrani." Kaylin exhaled. "But we lost four in the battle with the ancestor. *Four.* We don't get a lot of Barrani applying for the force. They're culturally willing to swear to protect the city—but the 'serve' part of our oath really gets stuck in their throats."

Bellusdeo chuckled. "Some things never change."

"No. The Barrani weren't given funerals that the rank and file in the Halls could attend. The Aerians were—but half of the Aerian funeral service takes place in the air or in the Aerie, and not all of us could get there or participate in those. Grammayre asked the Aerie if they could hold the parts that take place *inside* the Aerie somewhere the wingless could reach, and they agreed." Most of them, anyway. One or two Aerians, raw with grief and anger at the loss, wanted their beloved departed to have nothing to do with the office that had indirectly ended their lives.

Kaylin hoped that the respect and grief of the Halls of Law

would at least make them understand that their loss was felt, and felt keenly; that the lives of the lost had been respected and valued. She wasn't certain, though. Funerals hadn't been part of her childhood. A gathering of the living around the dead had usually had more to do with desperation than respect or comfort.

"Why do you think they serve?"

"The Barrani probably do it because they're bored."

Bellusdeo nodded. As an immortal, her thoughts on boredom resembled the Barrani opinion with which Kaylin was so familiar.

"The rest of us?" Kaylin shrugged. "I can't speak for the others. But me? I wanted to be involved with something I could respect. I wanted—and maybe this is stupid—to be the good guy or the hero."

"And now? I take it from your self-deprecating tone that you think the desire was naive."

"A little. When I first met the Hawklord, I didn't feel naive. I felt that everyone else was—I mean, everyone who lived on this side of the Ablayne's bridge. Because they'd had it so easy. I still think that sometimes." She shrugged again. "I wanted to be part of something bigger than me, in the end. I like the sense that we're working on something together. That if justice and the law isn't perfect, it's better than the alternative. Someone is always going to be at the top. That's just a law of power.

"But if the law can sometimes be used to protect those who don't have that power, it's better than nothing. Do you think I'm stupid?"

"Frequently," Bellusdeo replied, but her voice was gentle. "But not in this. I wanted to be perfect, when I ruled. I wanted to be a queen who could be admired and followed; I wanted to make no mistakes. In that, I failed. But I considered the alternative worse: to not try. I learned from my mistakes. I made new ones. As I gained power, the cost of my mistakes grew—because it wasn't just me who would pay for them. It's the one silver lining to the cloud of being powerless, here."

"You could join the Hawks."

"Given your Sergeant's attitude toward Dragons, I highly doubt it."

"He's not in charge. If Lord Grammayre gives you permission..." Kaylin trailed off.

"He would require Imperial permission first, and I highly doubt he would receive it. Not in my case. And yes, I am aware that Lord Tiamaris has been, in the past, considered a member of the Hawks. I am content, however, to be allowed to accompany you on your patrols. If," she added, "you have no objections."

Right at this very moment, Kaylin didn't.

If anyone else was surprised to see Bellusdeo approaching the Halls in regular clothing, they were better at containing their shock than Kaylin was.

Clint and Tanner were on door duty, and therefore had the first opportunity. They nodded to Bellusdeo; they were not required to be more formal while on duty. Not that any of the Hawks were great at formality, except those in the upper echelons.

"Anything I should be dreading before I'm given permission to enter?" Kaylin asked, glancing at Clint's wings. They'd been singed, but not in a way that would prevent flight; Clint had assured her that they would be fully functional, and he'd been right.

"Moran had a screeching fight with Ironjaw. She also had a clipped, angry 'discussion' with the Hawklord."

"Moran?"

"You might remember her? Shortish, speckled wings, foul temper, runs our infirmary?"

Moran had reportedly been clipped by fire that was hot enough to *melt stone*. According to Teela, one of her wings was a disaster; her prognosis for future flight was not good, and she was supposed to be confined to the Aerie in the Southern Reach.

"Why is she even in the office? Shouldn't she be at home?"

"You might want to keep *that* opinion to yourself today," Tanner replied, wincing. "She is not in the mood to have her presence at work criticized, and she made that quite clear."

"Can she even *fly*?"

Silence.

Kaylin turned to Bellusdeo. "We're going to take a detour to the infirmary."

"Were we not just warned against that?"

"Not exactly," Kaylin replied at the same time as Clint said, "Yes."

"I am not familiar with Moran," the Dragon said. "I've met her, of course, but our paths have not otherwise crossed."

"If you're smart, they won't cross today." Clint glanced at Kaylin before adding, "But if you mean to tag along where Kaylin goes, smart won't count for much."

"Thanks a bunch, Clint."

"I thought you valued honesty?"

CHAPTER 2

"If your Sergeant was unable to convince Moran that her services are not currently required, what do you think you'll achieve?" Bellusdeo asked pointedly as they made their way to the infirmary.

"I'll worry less. I just want to make sure she's all right."

"You don't expect her to be all right."

Kaylin rolled back her sleeve, exposing the bracer that she wore. It was a gift—of sorts—from the Imperial Treasury, and it looked like a golden manacle, but longer, and with gems. The gems were actually buttons, and when pressed in a specific sequence, it opened. If one didn't know the sequence, the bracer wouldn't open. If it didn't open, it did not come off. Cutting Kaylin's hand off would not remove the bracer—because while she wore it, her entire arm seemed almost impervious to physical damage.

She frequently tossed it over her shoulder; she sometimes tossed it into the Ablayne. No matter where she threw it, it always returned to its keeper.

Its keeper was not Kaylin. It was Severn.

Today, she handed it to Bellusdeo instead. Bellusdeo didn't exactly *argue* when Kaylin dropped it, but she clearly didn't approve of the casual way Kaylin treated the artifact.

"You mean to heal her."

"I mean to try, yes. She has a very Barrani attitude toward healing. She considers it intrusive."

"It *is* intrusive."

"I didn't say she was stupid. I might in the very near future, though."

Kaylin's power had been used extensively the day after the disastrous attack. Moran had been absent from the infirmary, and the mood of the Hawks working in its crowded environs had been a blend of determination and gloom. Moran was not particularly fond of Kaylin's healing ability; she seldom allowed Kaylin to heal at all. But First Corporal Kirby, the Aerian who had taken over the infirmary in Moran's absence, was more of a pushover. He was only a little older than Kaylin, and he lacked Moran's wintery presence and absolute authority.

Since Moran hadn't been present, things had gone more smoothly. If over two dozen officers of the law had died, many, many more had been injured. Moran felt that setting bones—arms, legs, ribs, collars—was her purview. She was less sanguine about burns—especially those that involved flight feathers or wings.

Kaylin had insisted she be allowed to heal the men and women who were not guaranteed to survive. She tended to severe burns and the infections that came with them; she was allowed to heal crushed limbs and fractured skulls. Kirby approved it all, while muttering *Moran is going to kill me* under his breath.

No one had questioned Kaylin's work in the infirmary, though the use of her power was not entirely legal. Kaylin was not yet a member of the Imperial Order or the Arcanum—and she would rather die than join the latter.

In *theory*, there were strict laws that governed the use of magic in Elantra. But in practice, the use of magic wasn't easily quantified. It was therefore very poorly governed.

Even had it not been, it wouldn't have mattered. The Hawk-lord and the Swordlord were fully capable of petitioning the Emperor for permission; neither had felt the paperwork would be productive or entirely necessary.

The beds had emptied slowly. While Kaylin *could* heal—and very effectively—the process exhausted her, and she'd only been able to work on one man or woman at a time.

At least today, if she collapsed on the way home, Bellusdeo could carry her the rest of the way.

The likelihood of that happening was very small if Moran was, as Clint stated, at her desk. Kaylin wanted to believe that Teela had exaggerated. She didn't. Moran, she was certain, should *not* be at work. Not yet.

Clint, unsurprisingly, was right: Moran was in the infirmary. Her left arm was in a sling, and her wings...

Kaylin shook her head. Moran's left wing was a mess; the skeletal structure of the limb itself could be seen, and huge sections of feathers were missing entirely. It looked as if half of the Aerian's flight feathers were gone. Aerians, like regular birds, did molt—but they didn't do it publicly. As far as Kaylin could tell, it would be the cultural equivalent of taking a bath fully nude in the market fountain. She knew that full regrowth could take months if the feathers were damaged. She was less certain about what happened if they were simply gone.

There was no way Moran had flown here. She must have been carried.

Moran glared at Kaylin.

Actually, she glared at everything. She nodded—stiffly—to Bellusdeo, the gesture weighted with what Kaylin felt was genuine respect. "We're honored to have you back among us," she said, startling Kaylin. Her expression softened slightly. "We owe you."

Bellusdeo's eyes, which were already mostly gold, brightened until they were shining. "I have become very fond of the Halls of Law, and of the city. I am less fond of the Barrani High Halls, but if a battle of any significance had to take place within the city—"

"It's better there than anywhere, aye. You'll be going on duty rounds with the private?"

"I will."

"Then you'd best drag her off—she's going to be late, and the Sergeant is not in a charitable mood."

And whose fault is that? "I'm right here," Kaylin said.

Moran had an impressive glare.

"What, exactly, are you afraid of? Everyone *else* who was badly injured accepted my help."

"I am not—"

"You can't *fly*, Sergeant."

"Not immediately, no. The feathers will grow in."

Kaylin didn't believe it; she wondered if Moran actually did.

"I have already had an argument about the state of my health this morning. Two, in fact. If I did not listen to that giant, lumbering cat and I did not bow to Lord Grammayre, believe that I am not going to blithely obey a *private*."

"Teela said you would be out for months."

"She was demonstrably incorrect. There is nothing wrong with my hands, my legs or my eyes. I am capable of doing my duty. I can't fly in these rooms, anyway."

"Moran, *please*—"

"No."

"But your wings—"

"Do you know why I'm a sergeant in the infirmary, Private?"

Kaylin did not roll her eyes, though it took effort. "Because you can deal with the injured, regardless of their moods or state of mind."

"Exactly. You can plead, beg, cry and curse me. I won't be moved."

Kaylin inexplicably felt like crying at the moment. Moran's wings—white and speckled with a brown that almost formed a pattern when the wings were closed—were unique among the Aerians of her acquaintance.

"You still have your childish obsessions, don't you?"

"Yes." Kaylin folded her arms, refusing to feel embarrassed.

Moran's eyes narrowed. They were blue. Aerian blue was not the same midnight as Barrani blue, but it meant essentially the same thing. Moran was angry. Then again, Moran was almost always angry.

"Where are you staying?"

Moran blinked. "Pardon?"

"You can't fly. You can get Aerians to carry you to and from the Southern Reach, but you can't fly back on your own. Given it's you, I'm willing to bet last week's pay that you don't even intend to try."

Moran shifted her gaze; it fell on Bellusdeo. There was nothing else in the room to look at, as the beds were all empty.

Bellusdeo held up both hands. "I am willing to face Barrani ancestors, Shadows and death. I am not willing to pull nonexistent rank on a private. Please don't ask—I am here on sufferance, with the understanding that I will not interfere with the private's duties." She spoke in more formal Barrani, though the rest of the conversation had been uttered in Kaylin's mother tongue.

"You're a Dragon," Moran pointed out. "You don't need rank."

"She's the Chosen," Bellusdeo countered. Her eyes were

still golden, although her expression was neutral. Except for the corners of her mouth, which were twitching.

Moran turned to Kaylin. She could look down on the private from the secure position of rank, but she wasn't quite tall enough to tower. "I intend to stay here until I've fully recovered."

No bloody wonder Marcus had thrown a fit. "This isn't exactly residential."

"It has a roof, and the doors are never completely unmanned. Food is within relatively easy walking distance, and if I need supplies, that's what privates are for."

"And where are you going to sleep?"

"In the Aerie in the halls."

"Which you can't reach." Kaylin's eyes narrowed a little more with each sentence.

"Which is none of your business," Moran snapped.

"Fine." Kaylin turned and marched toward the door. When she reached the frame, she turned back. Bellusdeo was still standing beside Moran; the Dragon looked amused. She was the only person in the room who did.

"I believe Private Neya is attempting, in her brusque fashion, to offer you a more amenable place to stay while you recover," Bellusdeo said.

"I don't need her charity."

"Ah."

Kaylin attempted to count to ten. She made it to three. "But it's okay for *me* to accept *yours*?"

"I'm not offering you charity."

"You've offered me help and guidance for *years*. You've taken care of me after training accidents. You were here when we almost lost a fight to a Dragon." The small dragon, bored or silent until now, lifted his head and bit Kaylin's hair.

"*You*," Moran replied, "were *here*. Taking care of you here is my *job*. And you weren't here for long."

"There's supposed to be give-and-take, Moran."

"Sergeant."

"What*ever*. This is the first time in my entire *life* that I'm able to offer you any help at all!"

"I don't need it."

"*Fine*." Kaylin turned and walked out.

"If you were a Dragon," Bellusdeo said, "you'd be steaming the halls. Possibly even melting parts of them."

"It irritates me that my help isn't good enough."

"The sergeant probably doesn't understand what you're offering. I believe the entire department knew where you were living before the assassination attempt destroyed your home. She might assume you now live in similarly sized quarters—and frankly, the ceiling of your old apartment would be nearly crippling for an Aerian over the long term."

Kaylin stomped down the long hall, but slowed her pace as Bellusdeo's words caught up with her temper.

"I know you're upset at the sight of her wings."

"They told me—" Kaylin exhaled. "They told me she'd been damaged by the ancestor's fire. I didn't actually get to *see* the damage. It's a wonder she didn't die; there's no way she could keep herself in the air with wings like that."

"No. But I have noticed the Hawks keep an eye out for their own. She is alive, Kaylin. But she is an older woman, and she clearly does not care for…coddling."

Kaylin gave a little shriek in response. The small dragon whacked her face with his wing.

Marcus appeared to be looking for a suitable target for his obvious frustration. His eyes were a steady orange, and his facial fur was almost standing on end. Kaylin picked up the thrum of his growl just *after* she had time to reconsider the wisdom of entering the office. Of course. Leontine anger was never quiet or invisible.

She headed directly for his desk, bypassing the duty roster and anyone else who stood between them—except for Caitlin, who waved her over.

"Have you seen Moran?" Kaylin demanded, as Caitlin opened her mouth.

"Yes, dear."

"Why is she even in the office? She should be at home recovering!"

"It's…complicated," the office mother replied. The tone of her voice had a dampening effect on Kaylin's outrage.

"Complicated how?"

"Given that you've seen her—you didn't start an argument with her, did you?"

"I didn't start the argument, no."

Caitlin sighed. It was as close as she generally came to open disapproval. "If Moran didn't discuss it with you, I can't. She is having some difficulty at home."

"She thinks she's going to be living here."

"Her living quarters are definitely not your problem."

"In the *Halls*, Caitlin."

"You've lived in far less optimal conditions in your life. She won't starve and she won't be hunted; she'll have a solid roof over her head. The Halls were designed, in part, with Aerians in mind. She will not suffer."

"I want her to live with me."

Caitlin's eyes flicked briefly to the side, in Bellusdeo's direction. She did not, however, tell Kaylin that she thought it was a bad idea. "Let me speak with her," she said, rising. "I know Marcus and Lord Grammayre have attempted to do so, but I might have better luck with a different approach. You're certain you want this?"

Kaylin nodded, trying not to look as mutinous as she felt.

She was rewarded by Caitlin's smile. "Good. I wouldn't have suggested it—but I think that might be for the best. We're not certain that—" She shook her head. "You'd best speak with Marcus. He's been waiting for you—and not terribly patiently."

Marcus immediately barked Kaylin's name. Or Kaylin's rank, at any rate. No other private rushed to fill the space in front of his disaster of a desk.

"Since Moran is back, you can stop moping around in the infirmary and get back to work."

That was unfair, but life generally was. The Sergeant growled at the mirror on his desk; it flickered instantly to life as an image began to coalesce. "Corporal Korrin! Corporal Danelle!"

Teela and Tain materialized almost instantly, which meant they'd been eavesdropping from a safer distance than most mortals—at least the non-Leontine ones—could manage. Severn joined them before his name could also be barked.

This was two people too many for Elani beat work. Kaylin pushed thoughts of Moran aside.

"There was a triple murder reported up the Winding Path." The Winding Path was both the road's official map name and an accurate description. It crossed two market areas at its lowest point and then headed toward the Southern Reach. It was not a particularly short street.

"Where on the Winding Path?"

"At the Keffeer crossing." As he spoke, the mirror showed a clearly marked spot on the map. "The bodies are to be moved to the morgue when you're done."

"What are you not telling us?"

"I am not telling you anything other than the location. You

are expected there as soon as you can make it. Take the carriage."

Kaylin glanced nervously at Teela and shook her head. "We'll get there faster if we walk."

"Not if I'm driving," Teela said.

"We'll get there *alive* if we walk."

Marcus growled, but his eyes lost a touch of their orange; Teela's driving was the stuff of legend in the office. "Teela, take a mirror kit. The quartermaster is waiting with it. Private, there are Imperial mages on the property. Attempt not to offend them."

"Yes, sir." She hesitated.

"Yessss?" He turned the full force of his gaze on the silent Dragon by Kaylin's side. His exhale was rumbling. "You intend to follow the private?"

"If that is permissible."

"I don't like it. You're not a Hawk, and this is serious Hawk work; it's not patrolling fraud central."

Bellusdeo was helpful; she smiled benignly and held the Sergeant's glare until he growled again. "Keep an eye on her."

Kaylin tried not to bristle.

"I will."

"If any of the idiots in the office attempt to buy you a drink or grovel their gratitude, I'd appreciate it if you ignored them."

"Oh?"

"They're grateful for your intervention. They're not idiots. They're aware that the Emperor wasn't."

Bellusdeo's face stiffened. Had Kaylin been on the other side of the desk, she would've kicked him. She would've regretted it, of course—if he'd even noticed, that was.

"But they're impressed, anyway. Private, are you going to stand around all day gaping like a new recruit?"

"No, sir."

"Good. Head out."

"Going, sir."

"Good." He ran a claw through what was fast becoming a collection of loosely connected splinters. "If you can talk sense into Sergeant Carafel, I'll send your rank request up to the Tower immediately." Seeing the change in her expression at the mention of Moran, he added, "No, I did not bring this up."

"You're at least the same rank—"

"And the Hawklord outranks her. She is not listening to either of us."

Kaylin shrugged. "Caitlin went to talk to her. I want her to move in with me."

He growled his way through a Leontine phrase for which there was no Elantran equivalent. Teela caught Kaylin's arm and dragged her toward the nearest exit.

Kaylin shook her off as soon as they'd made it out the doors. "If it's all the same to you, I'd rather not let the quartermaster see my face. He's pissed off at Jenkins at the moment, and I'd like him to stay that way."

"Jenkins has offended you? He's a bit green, but—"

"No, he hasn't. But it's the first time in months that someone *else* has been the quartermaster's official problem child." Jenkins had recently lost a sword. "I'd just as soon not remind him that I exist."

The Winding Path met Keffeer about a third of the way up the gentle incline on which the southern part of the city was built. It was well away from the Ablayne, although one small stream trickled down from the rocky heights of the unoccupied reach and fed into it.

The homes were not as fine as they were in the expensive districts around the Imperial Palace, but they weren't as run-down as the buildings in the fiefs, either. There were fences and gates that fronted the street, but they weren't uniform.

"Did he even give us an address?" Kaylin asked, as Keffeer came into view.

"You were there. You heard just as much as we did," Teela said. She was, as Mandoran had said earlier, in a mood.

"Yes, but I *remember* less clearly."

"No, he didn't."

Tain, silent, cast a sidelong glance at Bellusdeo. "You might want to sit this one out," he told her.

She raised a golden brow. The line of the arch was almost identical to the line of the Arkon's when he did the same thing. "Do you feel that I am in marked danger in this investigation?"

"It's a distinct possibility."

"And you think that I am likely to fall prey to this theoretical danger when two mortals will not?" She glanced pointedly at Kaylin and Severn, neither of whom were stupid enough to say anything.

Teela grinned. "Give it up," she told her partner before turning to Bellusdeo. "The reason he's attempting to be cautious is the lack of information we've been given. It implies— heavily—that the star of this leg of the investigation is going to be Kaylin."

"Kaylin? Why?"

"Thanks," Kaylin interjected.

"Kaylin is particularly sensitive to magic and its remnants. You've probably heard her whining about door wards?"

"I'm breathing, so yes," Bellusdeo replied.

"It's not just door wards. Any use of normal magic—"

"How are we defining normal?"

"Magic that might be used by a mage of the Imperial Order and most of the Arcanum. The Arcanum does have some branches— You know what, never mind. We can discuss this in a tavern on an off-night. The point is, Kaylin's sensitive enough to see magic without using any of her own—that we can detect, anyway. The Sergeant doesn't wish to influence what she might—or might not—see. He'll have some inkling of what the Imperial mages discovered."

"Inkling?"

"They'll write a report, but it won't come in until tomorrow at the earliest."

"Is everything in your city reliant on reports of this nature?"

"Yes. Paper is easier to lose than Records." She turned to Kaylin. "What are you looking at?"

Kaylin swore under her breath. Mostly. "I think I know where we're heading."

Magic gave Kaylin hives. She'd gotten used to this in the West March, though the magic of the green didn't cause the same reaction as the magic on the streets here did. The Imperial roads, such as they were, were well kept, from the merchant gates to the city's economic center.

But the stones on the Winding Path were cracked.

Kaylin knelt.

"Did we get any witness reports?" she asked, as she touched the cracks she could see.

"Let me access Records," Teela replied, and did so. Kaylin felt a twinge as the pocket mirror came to life in the Barrani Hawk's hand. "Yes."

"What did they say?"

"Marcus has put a hold on that information until you tender your first report."

Kaylin was annoyed, but she tempered her reaction. "Do these cracks look strange to you?" she asked.

"What cracks?"

Which answered that question. "You know, when I first started training with the two of you, we had normal cases."

"Technically, yes. Your first case—"

"Don't mention it. I wasn't a Hawk then." She rose. The street, in her view, was cracked, the stones listing toward the crack as if something very large or very heavy had recently traveled on this road. But the cracks themselves felt odd. She stopped a yard up the path and knelt again.

At her back, she heard the familiar clink of metal against metal. Severn was unwinding his weapon chain. Neither Teela nor Tain told him to stop. "What does the road look like to you?" she asked him.

"Flat, for the most part. It's a relatively smooth incline; there are patches of weeds to either side. You don't see that." It wasn't a question, but Kaylin answered it as if it were, describing what she could see.

"This isn't your usual paradigm," Teela said.

"No. And I see no magical sigils, either. It's not *strong* magic, but it's definitely there."

"Records," Teela said. "Record."

Kaylin described what she saw for a third time, and Teela moved the mirror so that it captured the street. She then handed the tiny captured image to Kaylin. Kaylin, well aware that her head would be on a pike if she dropped or damaged *this* mirror, took it gingerly. The image in the mirror was what Severn had described. She handed it back to Teela.

"What do you normally see?" Bellusdeo asked, as Kaylin rose again.

"Sigils and words," Kaylin replied. "They're often splashed against walls or doors like random paint. The larger the sigil, the greater the magic that produced it."

"Not cracks."

"Not usually, no. I think one or two of the mages in the

Imperium look at magic as dimensionality, though. They see containers. Where magic has been cast, they see the type of shards you'd see if you dropped a vase. The greater the shattering, the larger the magic that caused it. One of them sees particular colors of glass or glaze—his version of my sigils.

"The crack—it's mostly one—veers at the gate three houses to the left of where we're standing."

"The short, wooden gate?"

Kaylin nodded. "Why are you making that face?"

Severn coughed. "I don't think that that's the house with the bodies," he said.

Sometimes Kaylin's entire life felt like a game of gotcha. "Which house is it?"

"Three down," he replied, "and on the other side of the street."

Teela didn't head to the aforementioned dwelling immediately. She began to cast instead. Her spell was much stronger than the afterimage of magic left on the road; Kaylin's skin goose-bumped in protest. The Barrani Hawk handed the mirror to Tain as she knelt in the center of the road.

"Honestly, kitling," she said, passing her hands over the crack that Kaylin could still see. "How bad a teacher can Lord Sanabalis be?"

"He'd say the quality of the student is the determining factor," Kaylin replied. "Are you getting anything?"

"My initial response would usually be no."

Kaylin, having worked with Teela for years, waited as the Barrani Hawk rose and retraced Kaylin's exact steps. She was frowning; her eyes, which had been as green as they ever got at work, were shading toward blue. It was a green blue, so she was concerned, but not overly worried. Tain, on the other hand, was definitely worried.

Kaylin raised her brows at him, and he shook his head. "If you teach me nothing else in your short life," he said, "you have forced me to reevaluate boredom as a concept. There is definitely such a thing as too much excitement."

"This isn't too much excitement," Kaylin quite reasonably pointed out.

"Not yet. Are you betting?"

"Is she breathing?" Teela cut in. "Shut up, both of you. I can't concentrate." Severn—much more quietly—asked Tain what the bet, stakes and odds were. Teela did not tell Severn to shut up.

The Barrani Hawk straightened. "There *is* something. I wouldn't have noticed it—I'm only barely detecting it now." She glanced at Tain, who shrugged.

"Magic was never one of my strengths."

"Bellusdeo?"

"Yes, it was considered one of mine." The Dragon was frowning. She looked at Kaylin. Or rather, at the small dragon sitting on her shoulder. "Well?"

The small dragon was silent.

"Bodies, or house across the street from the bodies first?" Tain asked.

"House," Kaylin said.

"Let Teela do the talking," Severn suggested as they followed the path of this indeterminate magic to what appeared to be its source. "Records indicate that this house is occupied, that the taxes are paid up and that the owner is not a person of political significance."

Kaylin said nothing. That lasted for five seconds. "Is it too much to ask," she said under her breath, "that I not be shoved out in the dark with zero information whatsoever and asked to find something?"

"We're in the same dark. If you hadn't been arguing with Moran—how did that go, by the way?—you would've been in the office when the request came in." When this failed to appreciably lighten Kaylin's mood, he added, "You know that magical precepts are both individual and susceptible to suggestion."

"I bet Ironjaw has more information."

"The Sergeant is not a mage."

Neither am I. She kept this to herself, aware that she was cranky in part because of her discussion with Moran. She was old enough not to be treated like a child.

Teela approached the gate, raised a hand, then lowered it. The frown she wore seemed etched into her otherwise perfect face. "Kitling?"

Kaylin shrugged off her resentment and came to stand by Teela's side. She also poked the small dragon, who squawked quietly, but lifted one transparent wing. He tapped her face gently, to make a point, but kept the wing extended so it covered her eyes.

To Kaylin's vision—with the added interference of a translucent dragon wing—the gate looked weathered. It was slightly warped. The nails that held it in place had rusted a bit, but that was it. "It's a gate." She turned to glance back at the road and froze. After a second, she lifted her hand to gently catch the small dragon's wing. He expressed his appreciation of this loudly, but stopped short of biting her fingers.

"We've got a problem," Kaylin said.

CHAPTER 3

Hawks were not generally armed for lethal combat. Severn was an exception, and the exception had been made because he was, in theory, a Wolf. Teela and Tain, on the other hand, didn't require the usual edged implements to be deadly. Bellusdeo didn't, either.

Everyone turned toward Kaylin and then looked beyond her to the stretch of imperfect, inclining road.

"I want one of those," Tain said, to no one in particular. The small dragon squawked anyway. "What do you see?"

"Shadow," Kaylin said, her voice flat.

Bellusdeo stiffened on a single, sharp inhale. Her experience with Shadows had defined—and almost destroyed—her. She spoke a sharp word. The hair on the back of Kaylin's neck rose in protest as the Dragon moved to stand slightly ahead of her, without impeding her view.

"I can't see it. Tell me what you see."

"It's a very narrow line," Kaylin said. "Similar to what I saw as magic; it's not solid, and it's not—that I can see—active."

"Active, meaning?"

"It's not opalescent, and it's not—quite—moving. But it's there."

"In the heart of the city."

"To one side of the heart of the city, but yes."

"And the line of shadow goes into this house."

"Or through it, yes."

Teela cursed in Leontine. Leontine coming from a Barrani throat was strangely musical. In this case, the phrase she'd chosen was entirely appropriate. "There's nothing going to the house across the street where the murders took place?"

"Not that I can see."

"Are you sure the idiots reporting this didn't— Never mind. It wouldn't be the first time we've had a transcription error," she added darkly.

Severn hadn't set his chain spinning, but he carried one of the attached blades in hand. "Mirror back."

Teela nodded. She glanced at Bellusdeo again.

"I am not leaving, if that's the suggestion you intend to make," Bellusdeo said. "I have been given Imperial permission to accompany Private Neya on her patrols."

"This isn't exactly patrol material."

"No. But it *is* part of her usual duties."

"If anything goes wrong and anything happens to you, you're likely to lose that Imperial permission instantly. And Kaylin—"

"The Emperor would not *dream* of harming Kaylin." The Dragon's eyes had descended into orange; the orange was now tinged red.

Given that his first reaction upon hearing about Kaylin's existence almost eight years ago had been to order her execution, this wasn't exactly accurate. But given Bellusdeo's current mood, accuracy was irrelevant.

"No one in Elantra has more experience with Shadows than Bellusdeo does." Kaylin folded her arms. "If you're worried about me, don't be. I've had enough worrying-about-me to last ten lifetimes. The only thing we might want is Maggaron."

Bellusdeo opened her mouth.

Kaylin continued quickly, "He fought by your side against the Shadows that consumed your world. He knows them as well as you do—probably better. He was *there* for a long damn time."

The Dragon snapped her jaws shut. Normal-sized jaws shouldn't have made that much noise. "We should destroy this part of the road—and that house."

"It's not as simple as that. If the house isn't contaminated—and you know what that looks like—we'll be destroying someone's home. It's—among other things—against the law, unless the Emperor orders it done."

"You don't understand the risk you're taking."

Kaylin wanted to argue, but she understood what Bellusdeo had faced in the past. "Let's just check out the house."

Teela did, indeed, take point. It wasn't always smart to have Barrani be the lead investigators when dealing with mortals. It wasn't always smart to have *any* lead investigator cross racial lines. In the very, very few instances when the Halls of Law were called in to deal with the Leontine quarter, Marcus took point. It was always the best—and smartest—approach.

In some instances, though, Barrani were the most effective. Most mortals didn't believe that a simple thing like a hawk on a tabard guaranteed good behavior from immortals. Kaylin attempted to point this out, but Teela pulled rank. Literally.

She opened the gate more or less carefully, glanced at Kaylin and waited. Kaylin nodded. "The thread goes to the door."

"Beneath it?"

"It's hard to say. When I looked at the road normally, it looked as if something very, very heavy and very thin had just landed. There was a V-shaped indent and a crack at the bottom of it. The path to the house isn't made of the same stone, but it's staved in the same way."

"The stairs?"

There were only two steps up to the door. "Same as the road. The door doesn't appear to be damaged, though. I'm not sure whether the line goes into the house or beneath it."

"Is it active?" Bellusdeo asked.

"I don't know. It's Shadow." She hesitated and then said, "It's like what we might see—the Shadow part, not the staved-in stone—if a living person had been deeply cut but could still keep moving. I think it might be the equivalent of—"

"Bleeding?"

Kaylin nodded. "This is not an expert opinion," she added, as Teela lifted the mirror. "And I'd just as soon not enter that opinion in Records if I can avoid it."

"You've got far stupider opinions entered in Records."

"I was *thirteen*, Teela."

The home itself was not large; it was not one of the grand manors nestled in the heart of the wealthy district. It was modest in size, but seemed to be in good repair. The stairs were stone, and the foundation appeared to be stone as well—but in Elantra, that wasn't entirely unusual. Kaylin had been told that it was, farther away from the city, but her only experience outside of the city had been the West March, which didn't count.

The front door was not warded. That was also unusual, but not unheard-of; Kaylin's previous home had been without door wards, as had almost all of the other apartments in the same building. Door wards were expensive. Even if they didn't make her hand numb and her skin ache, she would have had a decent excuse for not having one.

Teela knocked on the door. Given Kaylin's description of the stairs, she chose not to stand in the center of them. They would have carried her weight, regardless. Bellusdeo stood back, beside Kaylin.

"You can't see anything?" Kaylin asked.

Bellusdeo shook her head. "We have some methods of drawing Shadow out—of forcing it out—of its inanimate hiding places. But many of those methods are complicated; they can't be done in an instant. To do it, the Norannir would have to come, and that would probably cause panic. You might recall the war drums?"

Kaylin nodded.

"They're very effective, but definitely *not* quiet. I think Imperial permission would probably be necessary; at the very least, we would want to clear the drumming with the Swords. It is likely to cause some...unrest. Besides, your marks aren't glowing."

"How can you tell?"

"When they glow, they're visible, even through your sleeves." She glanced at the small dragon. "And Hope is alert, but not yet worried."

The small dragon crooned. It was not one of his regular noises. He then glanced at Severn and made the same sound. Severn nodded as if he understood. It was very frustrating. The familiar, in theory, was hers, and she seemed to be the only person who couldn't understand him.

Teela ignored them and knocked again, this time with more force. Tain lifted Kaylin—literally—and set her to one side; he then joined Teela in the space he'd cleared. Bellusdeo clearly found this amusing.

"She's not furniture," Teela pointed out, as she waited for some sort of response from the resident of the house.

"No. She's too bony and too loud."

Teela knocked a third time. Nothing. Kaylin knew there wouldn't be a fourth attempt.

True to form, Teela raised her voice to let the occupants of the house—if they were present—know that Hawks were standing on their doorstep and were about to enter. This still elicited no response.

It wasn't completely unheard-of for a house to be empty at this time of day, but it was rare. The streets often felt as if they were full of small children and their elderly minders, but many actually stayed home if they had yards or a small space outdoors—something Kaylin had never had in her childhood.

Teela tried the doorknob. The door was locked. Placing a hand on the door itself, the Barrani Hawk closed her eyes. "Bolted," she murmured.

"We can kick it in," Tain offered.

Teela, however, shook her head, her expression shifting. To Kaylin's wing-masked eyes, the door looked entirely normal. "Kitling, the door?"

Kaylin reached up and pushed the dragon wing aside. "No magic that I can see."

"None?"

She pushed her way past Tain and looked again, bringing her eyes inches away from Teela's resting palm. She frowned. "…Maybe."

"Best guess?"

"Someone may have bolted the door from the outside. It wouldn't be difficult for most mages."

"Not diligent students, at any rate." Teela opened the bolt. Magically. She pushed the door inward and entered.

The house appeared to be empty, which wasn't Kaylin's immediate concern. As she once again lifted the dragon's wing, she looked down at the floor. The crack they'd followed to this particular door couldn't be seen; the wooden floor was worn in some areas, but solid. The sense of magic was absent.

Teela walked into the house, announcing her presence loudly without actually shouting, a trick Kaylin had not quite mastered. The Barrani Hawk's voice almost echoed. The house appeared to be empty. For one long beat, Kaylin felt that the house had always been empty.

The building had two stories. They searched the first floor. Aside from the accumulated mess any house gathered and displayed when visitors *weren't* expected, there was nothing that caught the eye. Teela headed upstairs, Tain in tow. Severn, Kaylin and Bellusdeo headed toward the back door to investigate the yard.

The back door, like the front, was bolted; the windows that faced the yard were glassed and barred. The bars appeared to be new. Kaylin studied the bolt, first with small and squawky's translucent wing, and then without; it appeared to be exactly what it was.

"The bolt looks new," Severn said.

Kaylin nodded. She opened the door and looked down the few steps into a fenced yard. The fence, like the bars on the window, appeared to be newly constructed—and in this area of town, fences were rare. The yards were generally like one great common.

The steps just beneath the door bore cracks similar to the road and the front steps of the house. They also—in winged view—looked as if they'd been broken instantly by too great a weight. The line led out into the yard. Kaylin followed it; it seemed to bisect one of the paths between cultivated vegetables, heading toward the distant quarries that provided the city with stone, among other things.

No, she thought, as she slowed an already crawling pace. "Severn, does this look like normal yard to you?"

"Yes. Except for the fence."

"I think there's a...hatch. Up ahead."

"I can't see it."

"Right. There's obviously a basement here; let's assume the invisible hatch and the basement are connected."

"I think it's time we paid a visit to the house where the murders took place."

"Basement first."

Teela and Tain had found nothing of importance upstairs. There were two obvious bedrooms and one sitting room; the sitting room was so pristine it was clear it wasn't used for much. The bedrooms had small, shallow closets that were filled with clothing and linen, and dirty laundry had accumulated in the usual places—at least in Kaylin's experience.

The basement, however, was different.

The moment Kaylin opened the door, her arms began to tingle. Teela, moving slowly and scanning carefully, sucked in air; when Kaylin glanced back at her, the Barrani's eyes were a much darker shade of blue.

"Teela?"

"Be careful here." She glanced once at the Dragon.

The Dragon nodded, and the tingling across Kaylin's marked skin grew sharper, though it was not yet painful. "What do you see?"

"Magic" was Teela's curt reply. She didn't bother to draw a weapon; Kaylin drew a silent dagger. Severn had not let go of his blade.

"I'll go winged," Kaylin said, as the small dragon huffed.

"I'm not sure wingless wouldn't be more useful at this point," Teela said. She gestured and light appeared to her right, in about the position a lantern would hold if she'd been using one. The light bounced off the walls as they began their descent. Teela had once again taken point, and once again, Kaylin let her have it, choosing to take the rear instead.

There was no trail of shadow on the stairs by which they

made their descent. The narrow, steeply inclined steps were whole, if more obviously worn than the stone that girded the front and back of the house. The width forced Bellusdeo and the Hawks to move in single file.

Kaylin nearly leaped out of her skin when she heard clanging bells. It was only when Teela cursed—in Leontine—that she remembered the portable mirror. "Are you going to answer that?"

"No," Teela replied. "It's Marcus."

Kaylin hesitated.

Teela, accustomed to Kaylin's hesitations, said, "Marcus doesn't normally have the ability to communicate with us in the course of a regular investigation. The lack of snarling has not notably harmed us, and he remains in a mood that can only charitably be called foul."

"But—"

"If I answer, he will ask for an update. If I give him an update that reflects reality, he will almost certainly order you—and Corporal Handred—from the building. Possibly from the district."

"He sent us."

"Yes. But you have the most valuable citizen in the Empire as your shadow today. Examining corpses for possible magical taint is unlikely to harm her. Examining a deserted building for possible Shadows, not so much."

Kaylin wanted to slap herself, hard. She did not, however, continue to argue with Teela. Instead, she looked guiltily at Bellusdeo, who she could just see over Severn's shoulder. Bellusdeo had chosen not to hear the exchange, and given that she was in the literal middle of it, that took deliberate effort.

"That citizen," Teela continued, when interruption or argument failed to stop her, "has seen more Shadow war than we have. Her presence might be of value in this investigation."

Kaylin was acutely aware of just how little that would matter to the Emperor, but held her peace, since she was *also* acutely aware of how much it would mean to Bellusdeo. Bellusdeo was the most important single individual in the Empire—in the opinion of the Emperor. As she was the only surviving female Dragon, a life of decadent luxury was hers for the taking. She didn't need to work or take responsibility for anything that occurred within Elantra; she never needed to lift a finger again in her life, never mind actually *risk it* on anything.

And it was killing her.

"You win." Kaylin continued down the stairs, but felt compelled to add, "But it's *me* he's going to be mad at."

"In this, your rank will preserve most of your hide. You're a private. I'm a corporal."

"Don't remind me."

They didn't make it all the way down the stairs; Bellusdeo stopped walking suddenly, and Severn stopped just before he ran into her back. Kaylin, worrying about Bellusdeo, stopped *when* she ran into Severn's back.

"What is it?" she asked.

Bellusdeo said, "The door. The front door."

Kaylin pivoted and ran up the basement stairs. The small dragon folded his wings, slimming the lines of his body; for once he didn't drape himself across Kaylin's shoulders like a spineless, translucent shawl.

Two people stood in the front vestibule. One was a tall, slender man whose skin was pale in a way that reminded Kaylin too much of corpses. His clothing was fine; if he appeared at the Imperial Palace, he was unlikely to be sent to the trade entrance, unlike Kaylin herself. His hair was darker than Kaylin's, his eyes darker, as well. He was just a smidge taller than Severn.

The second person was a young girl of intermediate age—

not enough of her was visible behind the man. Her hair seemed to be a tightly braided, pale brown without the highlights that often made paler hair stand out, and her skin was that mix of ruddy and pale that implied temporary ill health—at least in the young of Kaylin's acquaintance. But she clearly got more sun than the man who stood between the Hawks and the girl like a shield.

"What," he asked, in a tone that made ice seem warm, "are you doing in my home?"

The girl peered out from behind his back, then tugged on his sleeve.

He glanced down at her, his expression softening.

"They're Hawks," she whispered. It seemed to Kaylin that she was attempting to either comfort or encourage him.

"There was some trouble in the neighborhood late last night or early this morning," Teela told him, taking over the conversation as she pushed herself to the front of their five-person group; the hall had become quite crowded. "We're here to investigate that."

"I assure you that there was no difficulty in *this* house."

The small dragon squawked softly.

He was not, however, inaudible, and the sound immediately drew two stares. The man's was frozen and unblinking; he seemed to become a motionless, breathless statue. But the girl came out from behind him, her eyes wide and bright with curiosity. They were lighter in color than they'd first appeared. She took two quick steps, but the man caught her by the shoulder, pulling her back.

Kaylin understood his cautious gesture and immediately crossed the hall toward her; no one followed.

"Is it alive?" the girl asked in a hushed voice.

The small dragon leaned down and squawked more emphatically, which was answer enough.

"Look at it! Look at it!"

The man was doing exactly that; he seemed to shake immobility off with great effort. The smile he offered the girl was, however, genuine. "I am. Where did you come by that creature?"

"Long story," Kaylin replied. To the girl, she added, "I think he's one of a kind."

"Can I hold him?"

Kaylin glanced at the small dragon, who appeared to be sighing in resignation. He opened his wings, hit Kaylin in the face with the left one and hopped off her shoulder. The girl held out her hands; he hovered above them dubiously.

"Don't grab him, and don't squeeze—he hates that." She actually had no idea if that was true, but it was a safe assumption.

The girl's nod was energetic as the small dragon did, finally, land in her hands. He lifted his head and sniffed her hair, and then her cheeks, while she giggled. "It tickles!"

Kaylin was much closer to the man now and revised her estimate of his height. "I'm Private Kaylin Neya," she said, extending her hand.

"I am Gilbert Rayelle," he replied. He made no attempt to take the offered hand, and after a few increasingly awkward seconds, Kaylin lowered hers.

"We have a few questions we'd like to ask you," Teela said, picking up where she'd left off.

"This is not the best time."

"And we regret the inconvenience," she replied. Her tone contained no regret at all. It contained no anger, either. Her eyes, however, were dark blue. So were Tain's. Kaylin glanced at Bellusdeo, whose eyes were almost red. She'd bypassed the shades of orange that usually served as a warning.

"Kattea," Gilbert said, "why don't you go upstairs. It's not yet time for lunch, and I must answer their questions."

"Can I take him with me?" Kattea asked Kaylin.

Kaylin shook her head. "He's my partner. One of them, anyway," she added, catching Severn's eye.

"Kattea."

The girl very carefully handed the small dragon back to its owner. "I'm staying," she said.

Gilbert looked ill-pleased, but to Kaylin's surprise, he didn't argue.

"They're Hawks," she continued. "They're not going to hurt me. I haven't done anything wrong." When Gilbert failed to answer, she continued, "They're not going to hurt you, either—you haven't done anything wrong." She spoke the second statement with as much conviction as the first.

Kaylin, observing the reactions of the immortals surrounding her, wasn't nearly as confident.

"Won't you come in?" Kattea invited. "And sit?"

This was so clearly not what Gilbert intended that Kaylin wanted to laugh. She suppressed the urge as the small dragon returned to her shoulder, where he drew breath and squawked, this time loudly. He appeared to be talking to Bellusdeo. The Dragon's brows rose, but her eyes didn't get any redder, which was a small mercy. Before she could reply, the small dragon swiveled to face Gilbert and screeched at him, as well.

"I think he's talking," Kattea said. To Kaylin, she added, "Can you understand him?"

"Not really."

"Me, neither." She turned to Gilbert, clearly hoping that he could. "What did he say to you?"

"He said 'hello.'"

Kattea looked dubious. "All that was 'hello'?"

"*Hello*, in the old country, is long and involved," Gilbert replied. "It involves a statement of intent, a statement of limitations and a statement of the rules the guest is offering to follow."

"That's not *hello*, Gilbert."

"Not in Elantra, no."

"What did he say to the lady?"

Gilbert hesitated.

Kattea, showing the patience of ten-year-olds everywhere, turned immediately to Bellusdeo. She started to repeat her question, stopped and asked, "Why are your eyes red? Have you been crying?"

"No," the Dragon replied.

"What did he say to you?"

"He said that Gilbert is not, at the moment, my enemy, and reminds me that my people are not all of one mind, and in like fashion, Gilbert may not be what I have...come to expect."

"So...not *hello*."

"No." She exhaled, her eyes shading ever-so-slightly toward orange. "The small creature had better be right." She exhaled again, which was a good trick, because Kaylin would have bet she hadn't inhaled in between. "I apologize for my poor temper, Kattea. Your manners have been much better than mine. We would be delighted to accept your offer of hospitality."

Kattea was a bustling whirlwind of energy and concentration for the next twenty minutes. The house was modest in size and it was clear that they had no servants—and that Kattea did not mind, or even recognize, the absence. She chattered politely but enthusiastically, she beamed and she reproached Gilbert for his heavy silence—without once sounding anything less than familial.

For his part, Gilbert was stiff as dry wood and about as expressive. He laid his arms on the armrest of his large, curve-backed chair and left them there as if he was clinging to it for dear life.

The small dragon sat on Kaylin's shoulder, perched as if to lunge. Bellusdeo sat to Kaylin's right, with about as much warmth and friendliness as Gilbert himself showed. In that, she was more extreme than either Teela or Tain; the Barrani had made an art of friendly, polite, charming death.

Kaylin wondered, as Kattea brought both water and wine, where she'd learned to entertain guests. Perhaps she had a mother who was also out of the house. Kaylin hesitated to ask; she found answering the question hard to handle gracefully herself, and she was no longer a child.

Everyone present, however, was aware that Kattea *was* a child, and one who clearly looked up to Gilbert. Gilbert had again asked that Kattea go to her room, but Kattea ignored the request. After it was gently made a third time, Gilbert surrendered.

"So," Kattea began brightly as she sat down in front of a tray of breads and baked biscuits, her own glass full of water instead of the darker wine, "what are you investigating?"

Teela said, without preamble, "A murder."

Years ago, that might have shocked Kaylin. The Barrani concept of "child" was not the mortal one. Bellusdeo, however, frowned at Teela. She said nothing, but said it neatly and loudly.

The child's eyes widened. "A murder?" Her voice squeaked with, sadly, excitement, and Kaylin revised her approximate age down. "Where?"

"Across the street," Teela replied. "We're not actually supposed to talk much about the investigation to anyone but Hawks."

The girl nodded, as if this made sense to her. She looked up at Gilbert and then away. Interesting.

"Why are you *here*, though?" she asked.

Gilbert said, at almost the same time, "Kattea, I really feel you should go to your room."

"I didn't *like* them," Kattea said, instead of leaving. "The neighbors, I mean."

"Kattea."

"I think," Teela said, "you should listen to Gilbert."

Kattea immediately turned to Kaylin, as if seeking solidarity with the human woman present. "Why do you think we know anything about it?" The question seemed both honest and straightforward.

"We don't necessarily assume that you do," Kaylin replied, choosing her words with care. "But we normally try to talk to the neighbors; they might have seen or heard something unusual that would give us leads."

"Leads?"

Ugh. "Information that might help us find the killers."

"I didn't hear anything," she offered. "Gilbert, did you?"

"No," he replied.

"Gilbert doesn't sleep, you know. He doesn't *need* sleep." This was spoken to Kaylin, but of course everyone else in the room heard it, as well. Kaylin almost told the girl to be quiet—for her own sake, not for Gilbert's. If, in the end, it was necessary to arrest Gilbert, it would also probably be necessary to kill or destroy him—and Kattea would discover, sooner or later, that her naive comments had somehow helped to betray him.

Gilbert, however, looked resigned. He lifted his hands from the armrests and turned them, slowly, palm out as he rose from the chair. "I will ask you all," he said quietly, "to take care that your actions do not harm the child." Turning to Kattea, he said, "I have told you before that it is unwise to tell people about me."

"But they're *Hawks.* And you haven't done anything *wrong*," Kattea insisted once again.

The small dragon squawked. Loudly. Everyone turned toward him, except Severn, who continued to watch Gilbert and Kattea.

"Barrani and Dragons don't need sleep, either," Kaylin said to break the awkward silence.

"You've met Dragons?"

"Yes, I have. We have one here."

The child's eyes alighted on the familiar, which caused Bellusdeo to snort. "Not that," the Dragon said. "Private Neya refers to me."

"Oh." Pause. "You don't look like a Dragon."

"Not at the moment, no. But remember when you asked me why my eyes were red?"

The girl nodded.

"Dragon eyes—unlike yours—change color in different situations."

"Is red bad?"

"It is very, very bad," Kaylin answered, before Bellusdeo could.

Kattea fell silent. It didn't last. "Can you turn into a *real* Dragon?"

"Yes. I won't do it here, though—I don't think your house would survive it."

Gilbert looked wearier by the passing second.

Kattea surprised them all. Rising, she walked to the curtains and shut them. Gilbert did not resume his seat. None of the Hawks stood, but it didn't matter; Teela and Tain could be out of their seats, armed and deadly by the time Kaylin had blinked twice. Gilbert was obviously aware of this.

"We did not see anything out of the ordinary," he said. "Nor did we hear anything out of the ordinary. When did you say this took place?"

"Late last night or very early this morning," Kaylin replied.

"Ah. Kattea—"

"No, I'm not leaving," she told him, folding her arms and suddenly looking older. "I don't think they'll hurt you while I'm here."

CHAPTER 4

Gilbert smiled. It was a drawn, but affectionate, expression. "Kattea believes many things with absolute confidence." His smile was pained, but again, laced with resigned affection. "She does not always understand the world in which you live."

"She's not wrong in theory," Kaylin countered. "But we do have a few questions."

"I will answer, as I may, but first, I must ask: What brought you to our home?"

"Do Kattea's parents also live here?" Bellusdeo asked.

The child stilled. After a long pause, and in a much quieter voice, she said, "My parents are dead."

Kaylin's heart echoed Kattea's obvious pain. "Mine, too," she said. "I was five years old and living in the fiefs."

Kattea's eyes almost fell out of her head. She turned, excited again, to Gilbert. "Gilbert! Gilbert! She's just like us! Which fief?"

"Nightshade."

"Gilbert! Gilbert!"

Gilbert closed his eyes; in the darkened room, he looked less pale. "Kattea was born in the fief of Nightshade," he said quietly.

"Gilbert found me. Gilbert saved me from—" She stopped,

paling at the memory. "Gilbert saved me. And then we came here. Well—not *right* here, but after."

"So your parents didn't live in the city."

Kattea shook her head.

"And you made it across the bridge."

She nodded.

"When did this happen?"

"Months ago," the young girl said.

"Three weeks ago," Gilbert clarified.

Three weeks. Every Hawk present exchanged a glance. "Three weeks," Kaylin said slowly. "This was on the night that the Dragons were flying above the city?"

Kattea nodded.

"Kattea's confidence in the city across the bridge was… high."

Kaylin's had been, too. In some ways, it still was; if the ideal city she'd imagined was tarnished, it was still a far better place to live than the fiefs had been. "Why did you bring her here?"

"Because the fiefs were not suitable. I do not think she would have survived them long. Had I not found her, she would not have survived at all."

"Where were you born?" Bellusdeo asked.

"In Ravellon," Gilbert replied.

Bellusdeo rose then. Kattea stepped, instantly, in front of Gilbert, her arms wide-open; Kaylin reached out and placed a hand—gently—on the Dragon's shoulder. "Forgive us," she said, the words aimed more at Kattea than at Gilbert, "but only Shadow dwells within Ravellon now."

"That is true," he replied. "But it was not always so."

"If you come from Ravellon now, it's true," the Dragon said. Her eyes, which had lightened slightly while Kattea spoke, now shifted back into true red.

"It is not" was the quiet reply. "Perhaps you cannot discern the difference, but there is one. Understand that while we share mutual goals, we are not one creature, and those of us who maintain a shred of sanity retain some element of choice."

The Dragon stared at him, unmoved.

Kaylin said quietly, "Bellusdeo walked the path between worlds to arrive in Elantra. Her world was lost to the Shadows."

"I did not say that there was no danger; there is always an element of danger when dealing with the powerful. You," he said, nodding to Bellusdeo, "are a danger to everyone in this room. I intend you—and your citizens—no harm."

"And the child?" Bellusdeo asked.

"It is as she said. When I stumbled into the fief—and it seems an odd demarcation—I met Kattea. Minor creatures are given free rein in the streets of the fief; she would not have survived them. She called out to me; she asked me to come to her aid. I chose, for reasons of my own, to do so."

"And those reasons are?"

"I say, again, that I have no harmful intent."

"And we are to trust you? Your kind has done irreparable harm here, as well as elsewhere."

"I am aware that it will be difficult to convince you. You have long held my kind in contempt. I am to be judged, always, by the actions of others—actions I would not have chosen to take." To Kaylin, he said, "How is it that you chose to come first to my home? What error did I make?"

Kaylin shook her head to clear it. What Gilbert appeared to be claiming—that Shadows had free will and that they functioned as individuals—was a new thought, at least to Kaylin. It went against everything she had been told about Shadows; it went against anything she had ever personally experienced.

Yes, Shadows were not uniform in shape or size, although there were Ferals. There were one-offs, as her old friend Morse called them: creatures with too many limbs or no limbs or too many heads or too many mouths in one head—the list was endless. Shadows could be freaking *weather*. But every Shadow of any stripe Kaylin had encountered thus far had been attempting to kill. Or worse. The Shadows in Kaylin's day-to-day life existed solely to torment, corrupt and ultimately destroy. Oh, and rule everything.

The Towers had been created by the Ancients to guard against the Shadow incursions that could otherwise destroy not only a city, but a world. *Helen* had defenses against Shadows, and she wasn't even built in the fiefs.

Kaylin's first thought—and second, and third—was that Gilbert was lying. That he *had* to be lying. But Kattea seemed neither injured nor cowed. She seemed, if anything, apprehensive and indignant—on Gilbert's behalf, as he certainly wasn't either on his own.

"Bellusdeo," Teela said, "is this possible? You have the greater experience."

Bellusdeo opened her mouth seconds after the small dragon opened his. This time, the translucent creature *breathed*.

Kaylin had seen this a few times now. The first time, she had understood the pearlescent cloud to be dangerous by the quality of blue in Barrani eyes. The second had confirmed the earlier Barrani opinion. A group of giant Ferals—for want of a better word—had attacked them on their recent journey to the West March and swallowed those clouds.

The clouds had destroyed them.

This seemed fair to Kaylin, because the Ferals' blood had attempted to destroy the Barrani, and in what she assumed was a similar fashion: it spread, transmuting Barrani flesh into—well, into something that was no longer Barrani. Kaylin's ability to heal couldn't stop that transformation: she'd had to cut out the bad bits and start from there. The changes made by the combination of flesh and Shadow blood had instantly *become* the "healthy" or "default" state of the body. What the finished product of that default state would look like, she didn't know; she'd worked desperately to make sure that it never happened.

This cloud hovered above the food in the still air of the room.

Since Teela and Tain were already on high alert, its existence didn't noticeably change their expressions or their eye colors—in fact, Teela's eyes might have actually lightened.

Gilbert stared intently at the cloud. Kattea sensibly asked, "Is it dangerous?" She spoke to Gilbert.

"Indeterminate," he replied. At Kattea's frown, he added, "I'm not certain yet. Is it?" he asked the small dragon.

The small dragon squawked.

Gilbert frowned. When he answered, he spoke in a language that Kaylin couldn't understand. It was not a language that felt familiar, either; its vowels seemed sharp enough to cut the tongue on.

The small dragon squawked.

Oddly enough, this interchange seemed to set everyone else at ease—or as much at ease as they were likely to get—except Kattea, who frowned. "Why can't you speak a language *I* can understand?" she demanded.

"I do not believe he is capable of it," Gilbert replied. "And even if he is, there are some concepts I cannot easily discuss in your tongue. It is not always comfortable to exist in this fashion. My kin are often less confined in the shapes they choose to take."

"He won't teach me," Kattea said to Kaylin. It was the first time she'd sounded less than perky.

"I don't think he can," Kaylin replied.

"Why not?"

"Because he's not human."

Kattea rolled her eyes. "So?"

"We're mostly stuck being what we are," Kaylin replied. "We can learn to do more—or less—with what we are. We can live on either side of the bridge. We can learn to hunt Ferals—" Kattea shrunk into Gilbert's side, at this "—even if we start out hiding in abandoned buildings and praying they can't get in. But Teela is Barrani. She's immortal. She's going to live forever. She doesn't really get cold and she doesn't need to sleep. There are a lot of things we can do together, but I'm never going to be immortal, and when I get no sleep, it's really bad.

"Gilbert isn't like us."

"I *have* explained this to Kattea before," Gilbert added. "But apparently the word of a Hawk carries more weight."

"The word of a mortal," Kaylin countered. "The immortal don't generally know much about us, except that we're weak and not much of a threat."

"That's harsh," Teela said.

"I notice you're not denying it."

"I didn't say it wasn't true." She turned to Gilbert. "Why are you in Elantra?"

"It was safer for Kattea."

"Are you responsible for the deaths of your neighbors?"

"Did they die?"

"Yes. Their deaths are the reason you have Hawks in your parlor."

Small and squawky came back to Kaylin's shoulder and settled there. He didn't seem to dislike or distrust Gilbert—and that, more than anything else, was the deciding factor for Kaylin. If Marcus ever learned of it, he'd bite her head off. While immortals tended to take the small creature seriously—possibly because he didn't sound like an irate chicken to them—mortals didn't.

"Private Neya," Gilbert said, "may I ask one question?"

Kaylin nodded.

"The mark on your face—where did you come by it?"

Teela reacted first. In a voice that implied that frost was her natural element, she said, "Why do you ask?"

"It is unusual. I have not spent the majority of my existence in your streets, but I have spent some time observing—and I have not encountered its like anywhere else."

"I should hope not," Tain said.

"Does it break your laws?"

"*Our* laws, yes. The laws of the Emperor, no. In general, Imperial Laws are designed to deal with difficulties that are well understood and even common."

"Is it painful?" Gilbert continued.

Kaylin ignored the question. "Can I offer you some advice for blending in?" she asked him.

He looked surprised at the question. "Yes, of course."

"Blink occasionally. And stare less."

This confused him. Which, given his origins, was probably to be expected. "The mark on my face was put there by the fieflord of Nightshade."

Gilbert rose and bowed. "Then it is to you I must speak. You are Lord Kaylin?"

"I am Private Neya," she replied, uncomfortable—as she always was—with the Barrani title. It had a weight she didn't understand how to shoulder, and even if she could, wasn't certain she wanted. "I'm a Hawk, and I serve the Emperor's law."

"Yes. I do not see that these are mutually exclusive."

"What, exactly, do you need to speak with me about?"

"Lord Nightshade," he replied. "I carry a message for you."

Nightshade's name—his True Name—reverberated in the hush that followed.

Calarnenne.

There was no answer. There had been no answer for weeks now, and the silence was slowly driving his younger brother insane.

It was Kaylin who attempted to repair the break in the conversation. "You've met him?"

"Yes, and no. If you enter Ravellon now, you will not find him."

Kaylin nodded.

"But he is to be found there—or so he hopes—in the future."

"She is *not* traveling to Ravellon," Bellusdeo said flatly.

"It's illegal," Kaylin added, although the clarification probably wasn't necessary, given the color of Bellusdeo's eyes.

"It is not safe," Gilbert agreed, as if that was the entire subtext of Bellusdeo's statement. "But I was tasked with delivering a message."

"From whom?"

Gilbert frowned. Kaylin considered the question a bit pointless, all things considered. "From—" and here he spoke a word that was thunder. With lightning for emphasis.

All of the hair on Kaylin's body stood on end; her skin instantly broke out in the worst of the rashes that magic caused. In case there was any doubt, her arms—beneath the shroud of long sleeves—began to glow. It was not a glow that could be easily missed. Kaylin couldn't fit *syllables* into the word—or words—that Gilbert had just uttered. She could not repeat the sounds.

The small dragon, however, lifted his head, squawking, and the pearly gray cloud that had hovered in place since he'd exhaled it began to move. It descended, and when it was a foot away from the top of the table on which Kattea had settled both food and drink, Kaylin leaped forward to rescue them.

The small dragon bit her ear without drawing blood; his eye rolling would have been at home on a Barrani face, if Barrani faces had contained eyes that looked like black opals.

"I don't care," she snapped. "You can do whatever you're doing without destroying *food*."

"Perhaps he means to imply that the furniture is more valuable than the food."

Maybe it was. "You can't eat furniture," Kaylin replied. "Believe me. I've been hungry enough to try." Not that she had any memory of that herself—but she dimly remembered the humorous stories that had sprung from the attempt. She set the tray on the ground nearest the girl who'd carried it so precariously into the room.

The cloud descended until it touched the surface of the table. From there, it rose. No, Kaylin thought, it *unfolded*, springing up in all directions from the wooden surface as if it had absorbed the base property and structure of the wood and was transforming it. What emerged, growing as if by layer, was something that might, in a nightmare, be a…dollhouse. It had what appeared to be doors. It had walls. It had a roof—or multiple roofs, as the various stories of the building, misaligned and not by any means entirely straight, expanded. It had towers, and one of these reached the height of ceilings that were much more generous than Kaylin's previous home had once had.

Kaylin might have found it as magical an experience as Kattea clearly did, had her skin not ached so badly. Even her forehead throbbed; the only mark on her skin that didn't hurt was the mark Nightshade had left there.

"What is this?" she asked.

Shaking his head, Gilbert said, "You must ask your companion; it is not a structure of my choosing."

"But it grew in response to your answer."

"Yes." Gilbert knelt by the side of what could no longer be called a table, studying the structure that had replaced it.

"Records?" Kaylin asked Teela.

Teela blinked and then nodded. "The Sergeant is *not* going to be happy."

"Not very, no—especially since we haven't even started on the crime scene yet."

The crack in the road was still there when they left the house Gilbert and Kattea occupied. The small dragon had more to say—and volubly—before they were allowed to depart. In all, it was almost embarrassing. But Bellusdeo allowed it. Her eyes were a deep, unfortunate orange, but at least they *were* orange. Kaylin avoided thinking about how she would have explained bloodred to any *other* Dragon.

In theory, the only one that counted—and was indirectly responsible for her pay—was the Emperor. Kaylin missed a step. Since the ground was flat, she didn't end up falling—but she did stumble, righting herself only because of long years of drill-yard training. Sadly, she wasn't exactly graceful about it.

"I feel exactly the same way" was Teela's curt response. "I hope this doesn't generate another fifty reports. Or a demotion. Don't make that face—you don't have anywhere to go. You're already a private."

"If there's no down, there's always out" was Kaylin's gloomy reply.

"What are you worried about this time? I know that expression. You're not actually worried about a living Shadow in the heart of the city; you aren't even thinking about the murders."

"I am," she said morosely. She glanced at Bellusdeo. "I have an appointment at the Palace tomorrow night."

"In Imperial defense, the etiquette lessons do seem to be having some effect."

"Besides the headaches?"

"Besides those, yes. I admit a grudging respect for Lord Diarmat's pigheadedness. He's lasted far longer than anyone else who suffers under the same pretensions—at least when dealing with you."

The shift of Hawks left on the murder premises was scant—and annoyed. Kaylin recognized both. "Sorry, Gavin," she said to the older man. "We ran into a small problem on the Winding Path and had to take a detour."

Gavin was not quite of the same school as Mallory, Kaylin's avowed enemy—but he wasn't part of Marcus's office the way Teela and Tain were, either. He was as crisp as Diarmat on a bad day, his face etched into lines that implied his frown—and he was frowning—was a permanent fixture.

His partner, Lianne, was both younger and more friendly. She offered Kaylin a sympathetic smile from behind Gavin's left shoulder. "Was the problem dangerous?"

"We thought it might have something to do with the murders," Kaylin offered.

That dimmed Lianne's smile, or rather shifted it into something more brisk.

Both Gavin and Lianne were mortal and human. Gavin could remember a time when Marcus had not been sergeant, and Barrani were new to the force. He was probably still grumpy about their induction, but at least he had grown accustomed to their presence.

He did, however, raise an iron brow when he caught sight of Bellusdeo.

"She's with me," Kaylin said. "By Imperial dictate."

"Permission," Bellusdeo said, correcting her. "I am here with Imperial permission."

"You must be Lord Bellusdeo."

"I am Bellusdeo, yes. I am not a Lord of the Dragon Court." Gavin opened his mouth, but Bellusdeo continued speaking. "I am in the process of becoming a mage of the Imperial Order. I have the ability; I lack the paperwork."

"She has the Emperor's *personal* permission," Kaylin said, wishing Joey had been the Hawk on duty instead of Gavin. "The paperwork, while theoretically important, is irrelevant. Anything that can even bruise her can turn at least three of us into pulped corpses."

Lianne stepped around Gavin and offered Bellusdeo a hand, which the Dragon accepted. "I heard about what you did at the High Halls. If it weren't for you, our losses would have been much heavier. I'm Private Tsaros. Lianne. My partner is Master Corporal Gavin Karannis. He's a stickler for details; it makes him very valuable to the force."

"That," Teela cut in, "is why we have Records."

"Records," Gavin observed, "are not run on a schedule. And clearly, the Hawks' sense of schedule is lacking." He turned to Kaylin. "Private, you have been asked to review the evidence, the building and the bodies themselves. The Imperial mages have been and gone; I am to discuss their verbal reports with you after you have had a chance to assess the situation. And what," he demanded, "is that on your shoulder?"

Before she could answer—and she was honestly surprised at the question, given it had been weeks since the familiar's appearance in the Halls—he continued, "Unless it is an active part of investigative duties, Hawks are not permitted to bring pets on their rounds."

The small dragon hissed.

Gavin did not look impressed. On the other hand, Gavin

frequently confronted a face full of bristling Leontine without lifting a brow.

Kaylin glanced at the small, annoyed dragon. "There's no point squawking at him. He barely blinks when Marcus does it."

Kaylin wondered who had occupied Gilbert's current home prior to Gilbert's tenancy—she'd have to check Records to see if there was any information. The house directly across the street, which was under investigation, was slightly larger; it was in decent condition. The grounds—small though they were—had been partially given to vegetables and fruits, but those patches were mostly tucked in the back. The front, which faced Gilbert's home and the rest of the street, was neatly fenced in; the fence and gate were wooden.

They appeared, to Kaylin, to be perfectly normal.

But most of life—and the crimes that accompanied it—actually was. Kaylin saw a fair bit of the magical and the unexplainable, but that didn't warp her view of the world. For the most part, magic that threatened worlds was the subject of stories or legends. Magic that made the world run smoothly—mirrors, mirror networks, streetlamps—almost didn't count as magic to most of the citizens of Elantra. Or at least to the citizens with money.

Kaylin had grown up on streets where night brought Ferals, not streetlight.

She shook herself. Gavin was giving her the stoic stink-eye, and if she resented the expression, she knew she also deserved it. She hadn't figured out how to mention Gilbert and Kattea, although she knew she had to say something eventually.

"Hey," she said to the familiar, "can you lend me a wing?"

The familiar cast a baleful glare at the master corporal, but lifted a rigid wing anyway. He did not smack Kaylin across the face with it; apparently, he was going to be on his best behavior.

"What exactly are you doing, Private?"

"The small dragon's wing is like a magical filter," she replied. She'd practiced this explanation, but hadn't yet needed to use it. "In special circumstances, viewing magic or areas touched by magic through his wings reveals elements that aren't visible to normal investigative procedures."

He did raise a brow then, as if he *knew* she'd practiced saying pretty much exactly that. "This has been tested?"

"Yes. Extensively. But that's a matter for—"

"The Barrani High Court," Teela said.

"Arcanists?" the master corporal asked, his disdain practically freezing the syllables.

"The familiar is in the possession of the private. Do you imagine that she has done work at the behest of an Arcanist, ever?"

Gavin pursed his lips briefly. "Private Neya? No. Her opinion on Arcanists is *well*-known. This was tested in exemption-based investigation, then?"

Teela nodded. "It involved Barrani, and only Barrani, with the exception of Lord Kaylin and Lord Severn. I did, on the other hand, have reason to confirm that the wing of her familiar does exactly what she says it does. The circumstances were rather more dire. We should not be in danger here."

Gavin didn't ask. Lianne looked as if she desperately wanted to—but not in front of Teela. Smart.

CHAPTER 5

The house had a crowded and untidy vestibule. There were six pairs of boots, though none were of a size suitable for children. None of the victims were likely to be young, which was as much of a relief as she could expect in a murder investigation.

Regardless, the shoes, the coats and the various bits of furniture were not, in any way, magical. They looked the same no matter how anyone present viewed them.

The hall that led into the house from the vestibule was the same: slightly lived in, but also in decent repair. Worn rugs had been placed over slightly less well-worn floorboards that creaked a lot less under weight than her first apartment had. The sitting room was closest to the front of the house, on the right when facing in; on the left were stairs, beneath which was a door.

There were doors that implied other rooms, and a wide, brightly lit space at the back of the house that looked into the common yard.

Nothing about any of the house itself indicated use of magic. Nothing made Kaylin's skin ache, and nothing like the cracked street outside appeared when she looked through her familiar's wing.

"You're wondering why we were sent here," Teela correctly surmised.

"Kind of, yes. Do you see *anything* that implies magic's been used here recently? It's not particularly easy to magically kill a man—or three—and it would leave some markers." It would be faster and less easily traced to kill them in any of the more familiar, mundane ways, which would still require Hawks to investigate, but not this particular set.

Teela's compressed lips made it clear that the answer was no. She turned to Gavin, who was also tight-lipped and about as friendly as he ever got when the sanity of the people making the decisions was in question.

"Where are the bodies?" Kaylin asked.

"Downstairs."

"Downstairs?"

"In the basement."

Ugh.

Kaylin didn't particularly like basements. She couldn't imagine that anyone did, except for small rodents and large insects. She was the shortest of the Hawks present, but even she couldn't stand up at full height once they reached the bottom of stairs that had probably been a hazard from the day they were first built. Bellusdeo offered to enlarge the basement by sinking the floor, which Kaylin assumed was a joke—until she saw Teela's thoughtful expression.

Gavin, however, uttered a very distinct, very chilly *no*. He followed it up with a lecture on structural stability that only Bellusdeo found relevant. "The bodies," he added, "are to the left." He carried a lamp, which bounced off rough walls and rough floors in a way that seemed almost calculated to make them less appealing. Teela had clearly had enough of this and conjured up a magical light of her own, which had the predictable effect of raising goose bumps on Kaylin's skin.

And her marks were glowing. Here, they emitted a glow

that extended for yards, but they weren't as bright as Teela's light, and definitely not as directionally useful.

"Who reported this to the Halls?" Tain asked. He was generally content to let Teela do the talking, but Teela seemed preoccupied.

Gavin answered the question as if he'd expected it. "The daughter. A family of four lives here. One of the four is in the basement, along with two of his friends."

"The rest of the family was unharmed?"

"The rest of the family was, apparently, asleep."

"They heard nothing?"

"No."

"When did they discover the bodies?"

"Early morning."

"Are they here?"

"They're at church, at the moment. The daughter is young, and I believe her mother wished to distract her. We've interviewed the mother and the father. Their son was one of the victims."

"The mages have left?"

"An hour ago. Had you wished to speak with them, you might have arrived at the expected time."

Imperial mages treated Teela with grudging respect—they'd never once demanded proof of her magical competence when she'd chosen to reveal any—but they treated Kaylin as if she were new to both the Hawks and the basic concepts of magic itself.

She was willing to admit—to herself, in private—that she didn't know as much magical theory as she probably should by now. But if they'd bothered to check, they'd see that her reports were filed as part of official evidence and observation in dozens of investigations. She hated to have to justify her existence every single time she met a member of the Imperium.

Today, given the distraction of Gilbert and Kattea, she wouldn't have to. She'd have to justify her tardiness to Marcus, but claws and growled threats of losing her throat didn't irritate her nearly as much as Imperial mages did.

The small dragon squawked volubly. Kaylin slid her hand over her ear in a vain attempt to preserve some of her hearing. "I get it," she told the annoyed—and annoying—familiar.

The hair on her neck had started to stand on end. Her arms, however, didn't hurt—or rather, didn't hurt more, given Teela's light. "Teela."

"You see something."

"Not yet. But something's off here."

"How off?"

"Bellusdeo should probably go back upstairs."

The gold Dragon had no intention of going back up the stairs, and the smoke she exhaled clearly indicated that she was offended at the suggestion. Gavin looked as if he was about to order her off the premises. She was, however, a Dragon—and even those who served at the Emperor's pleasure understood the role of the Dragon Court. In theory, Gavin had the legal right to ask Bellusdeo to vacate—but theory was a very, very poor shield against Dragon rage.

Kaylin was only slightly surprised when Teela's light hit the top of a second set of descending stairs. These were stone, but as the light illuminated them more fully, they appeared to be carved entirely out of a single piece of rock. "These stairs were here when you came to investigate?"

"Yes."

"Did the person who reported finding the bodies mention anything unusual about the stairs themselves?"

"Yes. According to the interview conducted with the parents of the deceased, these stairs are new."

"How new?"

"The basement is used for cold storage. The stairs were not—again, according to the parents—present three days ago."

"Have you asked the daughter?"

"No."

"Did anyone?"

"No. The daughter was not present for the interviews."

"Where is she now?"

"As I said, at church."

Kaylin cursed. "*Which* church, Gavin?"

Gavin had no answer to offer.

"Why is it relevant?" Bellusdeo asked. "You are not particularly religious yourself."

"On occasion, new religions present themselves to people. Some of them start on Elani."

"You suspect fraud."

"Fraud is one thing," Kaylin replied. Her skin began to feel raw whenever she walked or moved her arms. "I don't care what people do to comfort themselves. I don't care if people who claim to speak with the dead offer—and make money from—comfort to the bereaved. I don't even care if people pay through the nose for that comfort. Yes, I used to despise it. I like to think I've gotten a bit smarter."

"Liar."

"It's not the fakes I'm concerned about. Not all religions worship distant gods. Some have magic as their focal point."

"Lianne," Gavin said.

"On it," the private replied, heading instantly back up the stairs.

The stairs looked the same with the familiar's intervention and without: cold, hard and distinctly uninviting. Teela headed down the stairs first; Tain was two steps behind her. Kaylin followed; she wanted Severn to keep Bellusdeo out of what appeared to be a new subbasement. Naturally, he wouldn't do it.

Kaylin couldn't. Bellusdeo was older and more powerful than Kaylin, and vastly more knowledgeable. Kaylin was not a capable judge of the Dragon's actual abilities—she was just the person who was going down, and hard, if anything happened to Bellusdeo. She tried not to resent the worry, and failed—but managed to keep it to herself.

The small dragon warbled very quietly.

"Teela?"

"Hug the wall. This is not a small staircase. It widens at the bottom."

There were walls on either side of the stairs, of the same rough stone construction as the steps themselves. There were no torch-rings or lamp-hooks on the descent; there was nothing on the walls at all. Kaylin stopped when Teela did, the halt staggering back up the stairs.

"The walls, kitling?"

"Nothing up here."

"Come to where I am."

Kaylin headed around Tain and came to stand beside Teela. She didn't lift the familiar's wing; she didn't need to. There was magic here, a sigil splashed and stretched across the left wall. Kaylin frowned.

"You can see it."

"Yes, but…"

"But?"

"It's the wrong color. Most of the sigils I've seen are shades of blue or gray."

"This one?"

"It's purple. Purple and black."

"Is it active?"

"No—it's definitely the remnants of a previously cast spell. Or spells." She frowned again. "I'd say this is the work of more than one person; there are at least two marks here."

"Do you recognize either of them?"

The problem with magical detection—or at least the chief problem, as far as Kaylin was concerned—was the lack of permanent visual Records. Perception was never consistent, and while a mage could reliably state where he'd seen the trace or sigil of the caster before—if he had come across it in any other investigation—the mage's description would offer no useful information to any *other* mage. Only if the investigators were forced to use memory crystals could the images be retained. Memory crystals, however, were very difficult to make and exceedingly *expensive*. They made portable mirrors seem cheap and readily available in comparison.

Therefore, what Kaylin saw could not be recorded in any reliable way. What she'd seen over the almost eight years she'd spent with the Hawks could not be recalled and compared to the sigils before her now. Although this was also true for Teela, Teela was Barrani: she remembered everything with absolute clarity.

"I'm surprised the mages didn't stay," Teela said—in the wrong tone of voice. "Gavin, you have a mirror?"

"Not with me, no."

"Here." She retrieved her own mirror and tossed it—accurately—up the stairs; Gavin caught it in his fingertips. "Mirror Marcus the names of the attending mages. Mirror the Imperial Order. Bellusdeo, it's time for you to leave."

The ensuing silence was chilly.

"Go directly to Sanabalis. No, forget that. Go directly to the Arkon. Tell him exactly what you've seen so far. Tain and Severn will accompany you."

Severn's expression didn't change at all. Tain's did; he had become, in the few minutes since they'd descended these stairs, very starkly blue-eyed and grim. He didn't argue with Teela's command. Everyone present—except possibly Lianne—knew that to the Emperor, any harm that came to Bellusdeo would be paid for by the Hawks she was currently observing.

Or by one particular Hawk.

To Kaylin's surprise, Bellusdeo almost instantly agreed. "Will you mirror the Arkon directly with any other relevant information?" she asked Teela.

"The portable mirror is keyed directly to the Halls. Without tampering, it's not capable of accessing other mirrors, but I'll ask for an immediate relay."

"Keep an eye on Kaylin."

"I will."

"Kaylin," Kaylin interjected, annoyed, "is a *Hawk*, in good standing."

Bellusdeo shrugged—a fief shrug. She'd definitely picked that up from Kaylin or Severn. She then retreated.

"How far do the stairs go?" Kaylin asked Gavin.

"At least as far again as you've walked so far."

"And the stairs weren't here three days ago."

Teela grimaced. "Why is nothing *ever* simple when you're involved?"

"Hey, I'm not here for *every* case that seems to start normal and then goes sideways. You've probably been involved in way more weirdness than I have."

Teela stared, pointedly, at Kaylin's glowing arms. And forehead. Kaylin decided to quit while she was only slightly behind.

By the time they reached level ground again, Kaylin was grateful that Bellusdeo had marked the change in Teela's tone and had decided to take it seriously. "I see six," she told the

Barrani Hawk. "Six distinct and separate magical sigils. Not three."

"Are they all the same color?"

"In theory, yes."

"I'll go with the practical—you were never very good with theory, anyway."

"You know how I said the top three were purple?"

"Top three being the ones you saw first?"

Kaylin nodded. "I think I was wrong. They're purple *now*. But I think, if I'd been here during or immediately after the spell was triggered, they would have been the blue I'm used to seeing. Does that match what you're seeing at all?" Teela had never fully explained the paradigm through which she detected magic.

"I'm uncertain. When you say you think they would have been blue, are you detecting a change?"

"...Yes. No."

"Which is it?"

Kaylin pointed up the stairs. "The ones toward that end are much redder. They're distinctly aftereffect, at least to my eyes. I don't think they're indicators of active contingency spells, but the last one is Dragon-eye red."

"The one before it?"

"Red as well, at least compared to the first sigil."

"They're distinct marks?"

"There are more than six marks," Kaylin replied, frowning as she stared up and down the wall. "But there are six distinct sigils."

"You believe the casters repeated spells?"

"You're seeing a pattern, too?"

"A possible pattern."

Gavin took this moment to clear his throat. Loudly. Mages did not often discuss their evaluations while making them, though they might compare notes after the fact. Kaylin thought that was garbage. Discussing her observations allowed her to focus on what she was seeing in a slightly different way. But then again, she wasn't an Imperial mage.

She went back to the first sigil and carefully made her way down the steps again. "I'm going to need to sketch these," she murmured.

"I'm not certain it will be helpful," Teela replied. Kaylin was not a very good artist.

The sigils did repeat. They did not repeat in an immediately obvious sequence. "I don't think the mages involved were working in concert."

"Because of the different saturation of red?"

"Partially, yes. But there's also some overlap. If the placement of the sigils are any indication, these stairs probably appeared when the last of them was laid down. Teela—"

"On it," the Hawk replied. "If you're about to say these marks weren't placed on *these* walls." Teela frowned and gestured. She didn't *add* to the pattern in any way; the detection spells of the mages were cast upon their own eyes.

"I think you're onto something," Teela finally said. "If we imagine that the spells were cast when the casters were standing on level ground with low—very low—ceilings, they would not overlap in the way they appear to overlap now."

"The red worries me."

"It worries me, as well. I don't see red," she clarified. "But I see some indication of...contamination."

"Is it possible that six different people were trying to cast the *same* spell at different times?"

"It's possible, yes. Which introduces a host of other questions, none of which are comforting."

"No." Kaylin glanced at the small dragon, who lifted a wing in silence, staring at the walls as if he could see, more clearly, what was written there. "Wing view is the same. There's no new information." Kaylin exhaled. "Shall we go view the bodies?"

The bodies were in the room the stairs led into. It was not a small room, and given the depth to which the stairs descended, Kaylin wasn't surprised to find that there was standing room here. The ceilings were tall and appeared to be made of the same rock as the stairs and the floor. There was no way this room and the second set of stairs had been carved in just three days. Not without a *lot* of magic. And noise, for that matter.

Kaylin had not asked the familiar to lower his wing, and he hadn't folded it across his back on his own, so she assumed he intended for her to see something. She entered the room, wondering—not for the first time—how he actually saw the world. Did she see what his wing exposed? Did he see more? Was everything just a jumble of possibilities and probabilities, without concrete reality to hold it in place?

"Gavin," Kaylin said, lifting a hand and immediately regretting it as cloth chafed her already-sensitive skin, "where exactly did you say the bodies were?"

Teela turned to look at her in open disbelief. Gavin was probably drilling the side of her face as well, given Teela's expression.

"Tell the familiar to lower his wing," Teela told her.

The familiar in question squawked.

"I'm sorry," Teela replied, with zero actual regret in her voice, "but we need Kaylin to see what's actually here. You can play the part of slightly detached mask again afterward."

The small dragon lowered his wing.

★ ★ ★

The moment it was gone, the bodies appeared. Nothing else looked different to Kaylin—the room was still far too large and the ceiling too high. The bodies, however, were a significant addition. There were, as Gavin had said, three. They were, on first glance, all male and approximately Kaylin's age.

They were also lying in a kind of sleeping repose and had been arranged in a neat row, their feet even with one another. They wore nondescript clothing of the type that a carpenter or gardener would wear. They did not appear to have expired of specific injuries; there was no visible blood.

"Have the bodies been moved at all?" Teela asked.

Gavin replied in a tight voice, "I have been at this job for longer than most of the Barrani. Beyond what was required to ascertain that they were not alive, they have not been touched."

Teela nodded thoughtfully. If she'd noticed Gavin was offended—and since she was Barrani, there was a chance she hadn't—she clearly didn't care. "So we have neatly lined up bodies of slightly different sizes—all apparently mortal—that Kaylin *can't* see when she's looking through her familiar's wing. This is not looking promising."

"Should we send the bodies to Red?" Gavin asked.

"I think," Kaylin replied, before Teela could, "that we should bring Red to the bodies. I'm not liking the idea of bodies that can't be seen—"

"By you."

"—being deposited in the morgue. The protections we have in the Halls are for the regular magical criminality, and this clearly isn't it."

Gavin hesitated for a fraction of a second, as if taking any advice from someone so junior and from such questionable roots was against his every fiber. He was, however, practical, and his nature forced an end to that hesitation. "I'll mirror it in. Head to the Halls and make sure the Hawklord sits on the Imperial Order—we'll want those reports as soon as possible." He glanced at the bodies. "His parents aren't going to be happy."

"Which one is the son?"

"The one on the left. Neither of the parents recognized the other two, so I've sent a request to Records for any information about previous criminal activities or any missing-persons reports that might involve them." He handed Teela the portable mirror. "Request your forward. Marcus is expecting you in the office."

"This isn't the way to the Halls," Teela observed as they walked away from the Winding Path. Kaylin glanced, briefly, at Gilbert's house; she was almost certain his presence and the deaths of the young men were related. But she couldn't force herself to believe that Kattea was *also* connected to the deaths. Kattea had been in Nightshade—and she'd gotten out. What would be left, for her, if Gilbert was gone?

"Kitling?"

"Sorry, I was thinking. What did you say?"

"I asked you where you thought you were going."

"To visit Evanton. It'll be brief, I promise."

CHAPTER 6

Grethan, Evanton's young Tha'alani apprentice, seemed uneasy as they entered the Keeper's shop on Elani Street.

"Is he in a mood?" Kaylin asked.

"He is currently meditating in the Garden." Which meant, roughly translated, "not yet." Evanton didn't care for interruptions when he was meditating. "But he left instructions to let you in if you happened to visit."

The familiar flapped off her shoulders and headed for Grethan's instead. For some reason, the familiar liked Grethan. Or at least saw him as harmless. The Tha'alani's smile was quick and wide.

"Can you conjure the image Hope showed us at Gilbert's?" Kaylin asked Teela as Grethan took them down the very narrow hall that led to the Keeper's Garden.

"Yes. I'm not inclined to do it more than twice today, but I will show the Keeper if he asks. I already dislike almost everything about this investigation, and we've only barely begun." She exhaled. "Mandoran is upset."

"Annoyed or actually upset?"

"Annarion had a minor setback this afternoon."

Kaylin missed a step.

"Helen was there. Mandoran seems to be more adept at

containing himself. Annarion's containment falters when he is too emotional."

"What happened?"

"Unclear. Annarion won't talk to me at all at the moment, and Mandoran won't talk to me about Annarion. They would like me to clear up the difficulties here and send you home."

She had a thing or two to ask them, as well. Gilbert had implied, strongly, that he had met Nightshade, and that Nightshade had been in Ravellon. This was not exactly the news that would fill his younger brother—his frantic, increasingly worried younger brother—with joy or peace.

After her most recent visit to the Keeper's Garden, Kaylin wasn't certain what to expect when Grethan opened the door. The Garden, however, appeared to be in its normal, contained state. The small hut, which had interesting internal dimensions, decor and occasionally visitors, was not in immediate sight; the pond, around which various small shrines had been erected, was.

Seated on a rounded, mossy rock was the Garden's Keeper. Evanton was dressed not as cranky shopkeeper, but as a figure of mystical import: he wore very fine blue robes that lent him a majesty that his usual apron and jeweler's glass did not.

The small dragon left the apprentice and returned to Kaylin's shoulders, where he flopped like a badly made scarf. Evanton made no move to stand or greet them; his legs were crossed, his eyes closed. He did not look angry, frustrated or enraged; he did not look worried.

Of course, he didn't look up at all.

Grethan hesitated to interrupt Evanton, and Kaylin well understood why. She was hesitant herself, and Kaylin didn't have to live with his moods the way Grethan did. But the apprentice didn't have three mysteriously disappearing corpses and a sentient Shadow to deal with.

She glanced at the familiar. She was almost grateful that he'd been with her when they'd met Gilbert; had he not been, she wasn't certain what she would have done. Leaving Gilbert on his own and trusting him not to harm anyone went against all of her instincts. And yet…small and squawky had been, if not friendly, then at least comfortable in the Shadow's presence.

Marcus would eat her throat, and she'd probably deserve it. But…he wouldn't bite Bellusdeo, and he wouldn't roar at Teela—and they'd both been present. She exhaled. She was *almost* certain Marcus would at least hear her out. She'd probably need to go shopping for a new desk for the Sergeant by the end of it, though.

"You are exhaling loudly enough to wake the dead," Evanton said. He'd moved nothing but his mouth.

Grethan cringed.

"And," he added, as his eyes flickered open, "you are late."

"We had a bit of a problem on the Winding Path," Kaylin began. Then she stopped. "Wait…late for what?"

This made Evanton chuckle. "You've clearly grown accustomed to apologizing for tardiness. Regardless, I was expecting you somewhat earlier."

"I made lunch," Grethan said quietly, alleviating Kaylin's mounting silence.

"Good. I find myself somewhat hungry." Evanton nodded to Grethan. "Lunch will be served in the Garden."

"We're in a bit of a hurry…" Kaylin trailed off, glancing at Teela, hoping for a bit of support. She got nothing.

"You're too busy to keep an old, frail man company while he eats his first meal of the day?"

"…Or not." She took a seat beside him, though she was not

at all hungry, for once. Teela did not sit; she folded her arms, looking down at them.

"Have some tea."

"I've already had tea this morning." Evanton didn't care for tea himself.

"I see. What exactly brings you here today?"

"How much do you know about Shadows?"

"An odd question to ask." He didn't sound at all surprised to hear it.

"We're investigating a murder case. Three young men were found in the basement of a house on the Winding Path."

Evanton nodded, waiting. For an old man who sometimes defined the word *impatient*, he was pretty good at it.

"Across the street from the house where the bodies were discovered is another house. It seems like an entirely normal house…but one of its occupants is not exactly human."

"And not, I'm assuming, Barrani, either."

"Definitely not Barrani," Teela said. She'd mostly abandoned the conversation to Kaylin, but clearly felt this needed to be said.

Evanton rose. "Are you claiming that he is Shadowed?"

"He claims to have come from Ravellon. The only Ravellon I currently know is at the heart of the fiefs—and the only things that escape it usually leave a trail of bodies in their wake. If we're lucky, the bodies stay dead."

Evanton's expression flattened. "You have left this man in the home he now occupies?"

"I know it sounds crazy. But he had a child with him. A girl."

"This girl also claims to have come from Ravellon?"

"No. From Nightshade. He brought her across the bridge."

"And just happened to find a suitable house in which to

raise her?" The word *skeptical* did not do justice to his tone or expression.

Put that way, it sounded bad. Kaylin poked the adornment draped across her shoulders; he lifted his head and yawned. Evanton frowned.

"You saw this so-called Shadow?"

The small dragon nodded.

"And you accepted his presence?"

And yawned.

"Kaylin, do not take all of your cues from your familiar. While he does seem to serve you, he is *not* mortal. He is not human. His concerns and his fears are not—and cannot be—yours."

"I know that, but they spoke to each other. He's pretty clear on what he thinks is dangerous, and he didn't consider Gilbert a danger."

"Gilbert."

"I think Kattea probably named him."

"Gilbert." Evanton shook his head. "Were you alone?"

"Severn, Teela, Tain and Bellusdeo were with me at the time. Bellusdeo was willing to accept Gilbert's existence, and if she does…" Kaylin offered Evanton a fief shrug.

"So you came to ask me about…Gilbert."

"Well, no. I mean yes, but not *just* about Gilbert." Kaylin sighed, resigning herself to the idea of Marcus's inevitable snarling back at the office. "Let me tell you about my morning."

Teela added the details that Kaylin glossed over in her attempt to get to the office in time to preserve her job—and her throat—while Evanton listened carefully. He asked no questions until she reached the end of her narrative.

Suprisingly, his first question was not directed to Kaylin.

"An'Teela, have you seen the ruins just south of the West March?"

Teela frowned. "No."

"They are not easily accessible; simple scholars have managed to lose themselves in the surrounding forest without reaching their place of study. They are, however, accessible if the scholar is an Arcanist."

"This is relevant?"

"It may be. It is not clear who dwelled in those ruins; they are architecturally inconsistent with the West March and its environs. The ruins existed before the Barrani and the Dragons started any of their ill-advised wars. As ruins do, they attracted the attention of the curious."

Teela said nothing.

"Entry to these buildings was often complicated—even after the buildings themselves were deserted. Kaylin, I believe you have some experience of this."

Kaylin bristled. "Helen is *not* a ruin."

"No. But her appearance—both internal and external—is under her own control. She cannot be easily invoked or altered against her wishes. I am not claiming that the basement of a nondescript building within the city is in any way equivalent to Helen—but there were always wards and protections cast upon buildings, and death does not always render them inactive.

"From the sounds of your staircase, it is possible that the homes in that area were built upon the foundations of older works."

"But who would know enough about that to sneak into a *basement* with a member of the family? And what would they stand to gain by killing the three men?"

"Investigation of this nature is what you're paid to do."

"Meaning," Teela said, "you don't know."

Evanton raised a brow at her tone, but nodded. "I admit that the bodies—and their presence or absence—is new to me. But difficulties of this nature are, sadly, becoming more familiar."

"What exactly is the nature of these difficulties?" Kaylin demanded.

Evanton, however, shook his head. "That, I cannot reveal to you at this time. However, I will, I fear, be spending more time in the Garden in the immediate future. My knowledge is inexact, but my function is not. I keep the world...real."

Scary thought.

Kaylin thought she could hear Marcus growling from two blocks away. The Halls of Law loomed like a gallows as they marched briskly toward them. Teela was tight-lipped and blue-eyed by the time they reached the doors. Tanner and Clint framed them, but one look at Teela's expression made them instantly wary. Fair enough. Barrani blue was not a terribly safe look.

Clint's eyes, however, were already the wrong color for an Aerian: coal gray, which made them look hard. He lowered his weapon as they approached, but didn't raise it to allow them passage, and given Teela's mood, that was significant.

"What's wrong?" Kaylin asked.

"I heard a rumor in the mess hall."

"Was it about me?" Kaylin asked.

"Got it in one go."

"I can hear Ironjaw growling from here, Clint. He's been waiting for us to arrive."

Clint had the grace to wince, but didn't immediately grant them passage. "It's about you and Moran."

Kaylin blinked. "Pardon?"

Tanner held out a hand, palm up. Clint dropped a few coins into it, although he didn't really look away from Kaylin. Tanner then said, "Caitlin said you're going to offer Moran a place to stay while she recuperates."

"Caitlin told you this?" Kaylin demanded, feeling a bit of a pang.

"Clint grilled her."

That was also highly unlike the Clint Kaylin knew. "It's not a rumor. It's true. I haven't convinced Moran yet."

"Moran will say no."

"She'll say no the first few times I try, yes."

"Don't try a second time."

Kaylin stared at Clint as if he'd been replaced by a Shadow. "She can't fly."

"No."

"She won't let me heal her—and I offered that first."

"There are reasons for that. The Hawklord wouldn't let you heal him, if he had any say. The Barrani don't let you touch them. I don't imagine the Dragon Lords would countenance it, either."

Bellusdeo allowed it, but Kaylin kept that to herself. This entire conversation had gone in a direction Kaylin would never have anticipated. "Clint—she's living in the *infirmary.*"

"She has been offered conveyance to, and from, the Aerie. She has chosen to decline the offer."

"I *know* that. But the infirmary is more of a jail than a home." Kaylin had folded her arms at some point and was now tightening them.

"To you, Moran is a sergeant. She rules the infirmary. To Moran's family, she is not a Hawk. Her work here has never been treated with respect; it has, among the more considerate, been politely ignored. She was injured in her service to the Hawks."

Kaylin, confused, looked at Teela to see if she was having any better luck following this discussion. From the shuttered expression on the Barrani Hawk's face, she was. The small dragon, however, didn't consider it important enough to budge and lay across Kaylin's shoulder like a slightly resentful shawl.

"I'm aware of how she sustained the injuries, Clint." She used his name like punctuation. "All I'm offering her is an actual home-away-from-home. She needs a place to stay. *My* place will actually have rooms that are designed for an Aerian, even an injured one. She won't have to deal with land-lords. She won't have to deal with rent. She can walk to and from the Halls in relative safety. You're acting as if this is some kind of political deal."

"It is. You've always thought Moran's wings were different."

"Well, they are. All the rest of yours are single colors. Hers look like they're speckled."

Clint nodded. After a few seconds, he pinched the bridge of his nose. "How many *other* speckled wings have you seen?"

"I just told you—" Kaylin caught up. "You're telling me they're significant in the Aerie."

"I'm trying to tell you that, yes." To Teela, he said, "Did you have these issues when you introduced Kaylin to the High Halls?"

"Not these specific ones, no. The Barrani Halls are slightly simpler. Everyone you meet is going to try to kill you at one point or another; she only had to try to avoid the ones who were going to do so immediately."

Tanner chuckled.

Kaylin didn't. "The Hawks are politically neutral."

"Yes, kitling, they are. But none of us exist solely as Hawks. We have duties and responsibilities—and enemies—outside of the Halls. We have history. Some of us have a longer and more complex history simply because we're older. Moran, clearly, has significance outside of the Halls, and you are somehow stepping in it."

"I will let Moran decide."

"Kaylin—" Clint started.

She waited, glaring at him. He didn't finish the sentence.

"What he's not saying," Tanner said, when it was clear that Clint was conceding, "is that you will cause the Hawklord extreme political grief. It's possible the Hawklord will be waiting to speak to you when you arrive in the office."

"Fine. At this point, it's probably moot. Marcus is going to rip out my throat before I can try to convince Moran a room in my house is better than the infirmary." She exhaled heavily and added, "I don't want to cause the Hawklord any difficulty. I'd like to make corporal sometime in my life."

That claim apparently fooled no one.

"Can you explain—later—what or who Moran is to the Aerie?"

"Not easily. There's more than one Aerie in the Southern Reach. Most of the Hawks come from one of three specific Aeries. Moran does not."

"Is this something I should have learned in racial integration classes?"

"No. Racial integration classes are meant to be practical, and the only Hawks who are summoned to the Aerie are, by default, the ones who can fly." He grimaced. "We're all fond of Moran." This wasn't entirely true; it was, however, true of Kaylin. "Go on in."

Marcus *could* be heard long before he could be seen—even by the merely mortal. "I suppose if I quit my job now and ran home, Helen wouldn't let me starve to death."

"I wouldn't bet on it—at least not with my own money," Teela replied, indulging in her usual encouragement.

"Was your life like this before you joined the Hawks?" Kaylin asked, as they walked toward the growling against all base survival instinct.

"Not nearly as frequently. Before you ask, my life in the Hawks wasn't this unusual, either. Not until you joined as a mascot. When you joined the actual payroll…"

"Thanks for the support, Teela."

"You're welcome."

"*Private*, stop dawdling!" Marcus roared.

Kaylin muttered a short Aerian curse under her breath; given the volume of Marcus's voice, his sharper hearing wasn't likely to catch it. She hoped. She also sprinted to reach his desk, bypassing the duty roster on the way. He was bristling, and the raised fur added inches in volume on all sides of his head, his visible arms, his face. His lips were a thin, barely visible line over much more prominent teeth, and his eyes were a decidedly unpleasant shade of orange.

His desk would definitely need replacing.

Kaylin lifted her chin, exposing her throat. Teela, standing beside her, did not, but her eyes were a wary blue. "We stopped by Evanton's on the way back to the office," Kaylin explained—not that explanations were always welcome unless he demanded them, not when he was in this mood.

"Corporal, where is Bellusdeo?"

He'd asked *Teela*. When a lowly private was standing beside her.

"Bellusdeo returned to the Palace in the company of Corporals Handred and Korrin. She was unharmed; she was never in any recognizable danger."

Marcus growled. At the moment, that was what passed for Leontine breathing. "I left orders with Gavin."

"Evanton, however, let it be known that he had news that he felt would be of interest to Private Neya," Teela said smoothly. This did not move Marcus; he knew the Barrani had no particular qualms about lying. "He's the Keeper, Sergeant. When he feels something is of interest, it generally implies an unspoken 'if you wish the city to survive.'"

Kaylin privately thought that the city was not in the most pressing danger at the moment, but said nothing. It was very seldom that Teela was willing to throw herself between Marcus's foul mood and Kaylin, and she meant to appreciate it while it lasted. And it did, to Kaylin's surprise, last. His fur began to settle.

"Verbal report. *Now.*"

"I'm not even sure where to start," Teela began. Marcus was now watching them both with more heavily lidded—but still orange—eyes. "Did you review the mirror transmissions we sent from the Winding Path?"

The Sergeant growled.

"We'd like to see the reports sent to you by the Imperial mages."

"Come back in a week. We might have something then."

"Gavin implied—"

"How long have you been working for me?"

Technically, Teela was not working directly for Marcus. She didn't correct him. "Long enough to know that you can light a fire under their beards and they'll write more quickly."

"I think Bellusdeo will take care of that," Kaylin said. "She was heading straight for the Arkon, and Severn and Tain don't seem to have made it back to the office yet."

"Your report?"

Kaylin dutifully repeated what she was almost certain was *already* in Records by this point.

Marcus's eyes had shaded to a regular bronze by the time she'd finished. "You don't think the bodies should be moved."

"No."

"Corporal?"

"Nothing about the corpses—aside from their arrangement and the lack of obvious cause of death—seemed out of the ordinary to me. None of our investigators would have noticed anything out of the ordinary, had it not been for Private Neya's companion. Given that the familiar itself is arguably more unusual, I would nonetheless advise against moving the bodies. Send Red in person."

"You're not finished there, are you?"

Teela glanced at Kaylin.

Kaylin, thinking of Gilbert, shook her head. "Not yet, no. Though I'm not certain we're going to understand what happened, or why, no matter how much time we spend there."

Growl. Squawk.

"Fine. I'll give you a week. I'll reassign the Elani beat for the duration." He started to carve wood chips out of the surface of his desk, clearly already thinking about the next item on his list. His eyes became a deeper orange as he did.

"Have you talked to Moran yet?"

CHAPTER 7

"No, sir," Kaylin replied, already knowing where the conversation was headed.

"I'm going to ask you not to."

"Yes, sir."

Ironjaw's eyes narrowed. "'Yes,' you agree not to speak with Moran, or 'Yes,' you know I'm asking you not to?"

"You're asking me not to, sir. Offering her someplace other than the infirmary as a temporary home is not against any law on the books. It's not against any departmental regulations." Her eyes narrowed. "You can't order me not to."

Marcus said nothing.

Teela stepped on her foot.

Kaylin frowned, thinking. "You're not actually angry at the fact that I'm late."

"You're becoming more observant as you age," Marcus replied. "It's not an improvement."

"What's happening with Moran?"

"I'm not at liberty to discuss Moran's situation. She has special dispensation to use the infirmary as a base of operations while she recovers from her injuries." The word *while* sounded an awful like *if*.

"Has the Hawklord spoken to you about this?"

Marcus growled. His eyes returned to their more prominent orange, but his fur remained mostly where it had settled.

"We need to check in with Hanson," Teela said, pulling her away from Marcus before she dug herself in any deeper.

"Of *course* the Hawklord has spoken to Marcus. Marcus is enraged. Moran is technically one partial rank below Marcus in hierarchy, but Marcus thinks of Moran as part of his tribe. He is not happy with whatever the Hawklord said. Part of that must have included you—as in, keeping you under a tighter rein. Don't make Marcus acknowledge that if you want to do anything useful."

"Is that why he was so pissed off?"

"You being late probably didn't help. Bellusdeo being absent didn't help, either. You realize it's his neck on the line if—"

"Yes. Mine happens to be on the line, as well."

"He's aware of that. You've slept by his hearth, kitling. You are not his child—but you might as well be. He is never going to trust the Dragons; having Bellusdeo hanging around the office gets under his skin. Having Bellusdeo in the office and outside of his jurisdiction is actively annoying. Having you responsible *for* her when the Dragon Court doesn't appear to exercise much control makes him angry."

"This has nothing to do with Moran."

"No. Before you give me the side-eye, I'm not entirely familiar with Moran's circumstances. I admit that I was surprised when I first met her, but she's sergeant material—and Hawk material—through and through."

"Tell me why you were surprised."

Teela hedged. "You know that you are not sent on sensitive investigations." Sensitive being code for crimes involving the rich and the powerful. "You are left out of investigations of the Caste Courts."

Kaylin missed a step. "Please tell me Moran isn't part of the Aerian Caste Court."

"I know very, very little about the Aerian Caste Court," Teela replied. This was not an answer, and they both knew it. "But Moran is the daughter of an influential flight. She is the daughter of possibly *the* influential flight. I don't know her reasons for joining the Hawks. To be fair, she doesn't know mine, either. The Hawks are, in theory, not politically or racially motivated."

"In theory?"

"In practice, the Hawks are people. People are political. I don't expect any group of people to be perfect, theoretical beings—for one, the pay isn't nearly high enough. Some of the racial decisions made are purely pragmatic; the Barrani are preferentially sent into figurative war zones because we're much more likely to survive them. There is no equality because we are not equal; we are *different*. I attempt to respect those differences."

"Given your comments about mortals, I'd fail you if I were teaching."

Teela chuckled. "Respect, among the Barrani, generally means something different. If, for instance, I say I respect your territory, what I mean is I will not attempt to conquer it. It does not mean that I find your sloping, creaking floors, your pathetically short ceilings, your warped doors and their insignificant hinges or your…windows…to be the equal of my own."

Kaylin rolled her eyes.

"Moran is significant to the Aerians."

"I hadn't noticed her being treated with anything but the usual respect."

"Indeed. You've assumed it's because of her rank and her function."

Kaylin snorted. "Have you ever *tried* to avoid her when you're injured?"

"Frequently."

"Has it worked?"

"Less frequently."

"She had *Marcus* practically strapped to a bed. Last I looked, he didn't have wings."

"Fair enough. Marcus doesn't think there's anything wrong with your request. Neither does Caitlin. But don't ask him for permission—either do it or decide on the better part of valor." She headed up the stairs as she spoke, and Kaylin fell in behind her. "Let's talk to Hanson and then head to the infirmary."

The Hawklord ruled the Hawks, but the details of schedule, among other things, was decided by Hanson, his attaché. Unless the Hawklord personally summoned you, you didn't see him without speaking to Hanson first.

Hanson's office door was creaky and stiff. Nothing would induce him to change this; it was his early warning system, as far as Kaylin could tell. He was at his desk, his glasses hooked to his ears but resting on his graying head, rather than in front of his eyes.

He didn't look particularly *surprised* to see Kaylin; he didn't look entirely thrilled, either. Hanson wasn't normally unfriendly—he wasn't, like Mallory or a handful of other Hawks, disgusted at her inclusion on the force.

"You don't look happy to see me."

"I am delighted to see you," he replied, looking anything but. His lips did twitch, though. He glanced at Teela, and the hint of a smile vanished. "You, on the other hand, look like you have no time to waste."

"If you're the roadblock, I'm perfectly happy to take a break."

"Thanks, no. What do you need?"

"Sergeant Kassan requires a fire to be lit under the butts of the Imperial mages on duty in the Winding Path investigation."

Hanson glanced at the mirror on the left of his desk. It was smaller than Marcus's mirror, but it was significantly cleaner. People did not leave fingerprints on Hanson's mirror. "How big is this going to get?"

"I honestly don't know," Teela replied.

This time Hanson grimaced. "Anything else?"

"That we know of? No."

Hanson's mirror flared white in the room. "Private," a familiar Leontine voice barked. "Imperial Palace transmission. Your presence is requested—an hour ago—in the Imperial Library."

"The message *just came in,* sir."

"Don't bother with logic," Hanson said; he had clearly keyed the mirror to mute *his* voice. "Nothing you do is going to make the rabid Leontine sheathe his claws. Not today."

"Is it too much to ask?" Kaylin muttered as she tromped down the stairs.

"Is what?"

"A normal day."

"Be careful what you wish for. As far as I can tell, this *is* your new normal." Teela's grin was sharp and very Barrani.

"It's not just the weirdness of the Winding Path. I could deal with that. Marcus is almost certainly going to insist we accompany Red when he goes—but that's work. It's Hawk work. But I also have to go home to Mandoran and Annarion—and can I just say that Annarion has been in a mood? He's getting angrier by the day."

"You are not telling me anything I have not fully experienced for myself. Are you going to tell him about Gilbert?"

"I'm going to talk to Helen first—because if I tell him

about Gilbert, he's going to demand to visit, and Helen hasn't cleared him yet."

"Ah."

"We lost too many people the last time he walked our streets. Knowing what we know now, it would be consenting to murder just to let him out the door." She exhaled. "And he *knows* that. I'm not being fair. I would just... I'd kind of like to be able to leave my work at the office once in a while."

"You're whining."

"Yes. I'm whining where a grouchy Leontine won't hear me and rip out my throat." Kaylin exhaled. "Sorry. I kind of like them both. And I understand why Annarion is going crazy—if one of my foundlings was missing, I wouldn't be able to sit still, practicing whatever it is he's practicing. But Nightshade's not anyone's definition of helpless. If we somehow find out that he *is* in Ravellon—and I seriously doubt that he could be, because I'd hear him, I'm certain of it—it's *Nightshade* who's likely to survive it in one piece."

"Annarion doesn't want to take you with them."

This should have made Kaylin feel better, but it didn't. It annoyed her.

"He will, though."

Kaylin stopped at the base of the Tower steps. "You can't make him do anything he doesn't want to do."

"Actually, I can."

"You're not going to Ravellon, Teela. Even if we do go."

Teela smiled her best "that's nice, dear" smile and walked past Kaylin into the office.

The Arkon, Caitlin told them—both Hawks studiously avoiding Marcus's desk—had requested their presence in the Imperial Library. Bellusdeo, Tain and Severn would meet them there.

That left only one item on Kaylin's list of things to do in *this* location. She headed to the infirmary. Moran was significant to the Aerian Caste Court. Kaylin knew the Human Caste Court—and didn't particularly care for it—but it seemed to be a type of figurehead organization of the rich and power-ful. The Caste Court could, in theory, rescue mortals from Imperial Law by invoking the laws of exception—and it had, historically. None of those exceptions had been called for in Kaylin's seven years with the force.

She understood the composition of the Barrani Caste Court; they had never invoked laws of exception. Anyone Barrani who might have benefited from them wound up dead—very obviously dead—in a public space. If the Barrani in question had thrown themselves on the mercy of the Imperial Courts, however, their desire or request took precedence, whether the racial Caste Court liked it or not.

But the Aerian Caste Court was entirely unfamiliar to Kay-lin. Kaylin tried briefly to imagine Moran throwing herself on the mercy of anything, and came up blank. She stared, in-stead, at the very closed infirmary door. Aerians, as a general rule, weren't fond of closed doors; this one was the equivalent of writing GET LOST in large, unfriendly letters.

Kaylin tried the door anyway. It wasn't locked—during normal operating hours, it wouldn't be. Moran was seated, back toward the door, displaying her injuries. "Unless you're dying," she said, without turning, "I'm busy." Her tone also indicated that physical state could be changed.

The small dragon left Kaylin's shoulder before she could stop him—and she did try. He flew straight to Moran, and landed, somewhat messily, on what appeared to be her paper-work. Kaylin cringed. Her familiar squawked.

Moran's ill humor did not immediately descend on the small, winged creature—anyone else would have lost a hand. "Private," she said, still refusing to turn around, "this is not a good time to have a discussion. The infirmary—absent usual emergencies—is closed."

"I didn't come here because I'm injured." Or because she wanted to be, but Kaylin chose to leave that out. "I came because you're living here."

Moran exhaled heavily. "Come and get your pet."

Squawk.

"Or whatever it is you call him."

"I call him 'small and squawky.'"

"Which has the advantage of being accurate, I suppose." Moran finally turned on her stool. She looked bruised and haggard; her hair was flat and dull, and her eyes were gray— a dark gray, not the ash-gray that meant serenity. "Why are you here?"

"Because you're living in the infirmary." Moran opened her mouth and Kaylin lifted a hand. "The only so-called living quarters in the Halls of Law are the *cells.* I have this on the authority of the Hawklord—because when I appeared in his Tower years ago, that's exactly what he told *me.*"

Moran's brows rose.

"Marcus insists that we lead by example. You're several ranks above me. You're not—that I know of—living in a cell."

Teela, who had entered the room behind Kaylin, said a resounding nothing.

"You would have hated my old apartment—you would have twisted a wing just getting through the door. But I have a new place. Maybe you've heard something about it?"

"Not a lot. Caitlin mentioned she'd be visiting sometime next week."

Not to Kaylin, but that was irrelevant. There was never a day on which Kaylin wouldn't be happy to allow Caitlin into her home—she had even given her keys to the first one. "When you say not a lot—"

"I know you're living with Bellusdeo and two Barrani who are visiting the city." Her eye color slid toward blue. Aerian blue wasn't Barrani blue, but the color shift indicated pretty much the same thing. Which of course meant Moran had heard a *lot* more than she was letting on.

"You forgot the Norannir. I've got a Norannir in residence, as well."

"You've got one of the giants in your home?"

Kaylin nodded.

"Does he fit?"

"The common ceilings are pretty high. I've got a tower— much like the Hawklord's Tower—as well, although that won't be as useful to you right now."

Moran folded her arms.

"You probably don't want to live with *me*, and I get that. You've probably never lived anywhere where someone could just lob an Arcane bomb if they wanted you dead."

"Not recently, no."

Kaylin stopped. Moran's expression was deadly serious. "You've had someone lob an Arcane bomb into *your* home?"

"Not recently," Moran repeated. "And that is an entirely personal matter; it has nothing to do with the Hawks."

Kaylin lost track of most of her words and attempted to gather them again. "Please don't tell me you're staying in the Halls of Law because their base protections are so strong."

"Fine."

"Moran—"

"I can't get to and from the Aerie in my current state. I *won't* abandon my responsibilities here while I laze about waiting to heal. I *will not*," she added, in the same dire tone, "allow you to heal me—we've had this discussion before." She exhaled.

"And no, I'm not comfortable accepting hospitality in another's home at the present time."

"The Emperor is willing to let Bellusdeo stay with me."

"Good for him."

"He even said he'd enjoy seeing the Barrani attempt to assassinate her again. He doesn't think they'd survive even the attempt."

Moran stilled. "You're paraphrasing."

"I'm not Barrani—I don't remember his exact words."

"Wait. You're claiming that you heard the *Emperor* say this *directly*?"

Kaylin snapped her jaw shut. Teela had, apparently, forgotten to breathe. Which was unfortunate, because Moran turned to the Barrani Hawk for the first time since they'd entered the room. "When did you let Private Neya speak with the Emperor? It was agreed—" She stopped abruptly, shaking her head. "Apparently the private isn't the only one who's forgetting herself. I'm going to pretend I never heard you say that—and you're going to pretend you never said it. Records," she added, speaking to the flat and nascent mirror, "note. Personal Records: infirmary."

"My current home is Helen. She's like the Tower in Tiamaris. She's not as strong, and she's not as aware of events that occur outside of her grounds—or walls, I'm not entirely certain. Inside her walls, she's got the same control over architecture that Tara has: she can make and change whole rooms, stairs, ceilings, floors—you name it. I wasn't lying about the aperture in the tower—we used it to join the battle outside the High Halls.

"I don't want you to live in the infirmary. One: I was told it was almost illegal, and I want to believe that *everyone* has to live by the same rules. Two: it's not a *home*. You never get to leave your place of work. Everything frustrating about it—and having seen some of your patients, I can't believe there's no frustration—is around you all the time.

"If you're here because you won't take a leave of absence— and I get that because I couldn't afford to lose more than a week's pay myself—"

Teela cleared her throat.

Kaylin forged ahead. "—then the Hawks are grateful. You're scary—but anyone who wasn't couldn't be in charge here. People obey you instinctively. They obey you when you give orders."

"Or when I tell them to get the hell out of my infirmary?"

Kaylin reddened, but plunged on. "I know Aerians don't live in normal houses. I know the Aerie is nothing like any of the rooms we've seen in Helen so far. But Helen can make quarters that will at least be comfortable for you. It's not far from the Halls, and there's nothing wrong with your legs. If you're likely to face assassins while walking to work, it's not more of a risk than you probably faced while flying in."

"Kaylin—no."

"Why?"

"I don't want—"

"I'm not at risk, Moran!" Kaylin was almost surprised at the strength of her emotional response—an emotion she was trying very hard to name.

Her efforts, as they often were when she felt too strongly about something, were apparently wasted. Moran's eyes shifted back to gray, though. "Kitling," she said—a word she seldom used with Kaylin, "—it's not that I don't appreciate the offer."

"I've never *had* much," Kaylin said, in a lower tone. "When I came here—when the Hawklord chose not to—" She swallowed. "I had the clothing on my back and the gear I'd used to scale the Tower. I had my weapons. I didn't have a coin in my pocket. I didn't have a home of my own.

"Not everyone loved me. Not everyone *liked* me. One or two people were offended by my very presence. But most of the Hawks were at least neutral, and some of them were even friendly. Caitlin helped me find a place of my own. I didn't have the money to pay for it, so the Hawks did."

"That came out of a very specific budget, I recall."

"Yes. The mascot budget. Which was embarrassing, but— people helped *me*. When I needed help, they gave it."

"I *do not* need help."

"No?" Kaylin forced her hands to relax, because she had balled them into fists. "I know you won't die without it. But you know what? I wouldn't have died, either. I knew how to survive. This is the *first time* in my life I've been able to offer to help. To pay back to the Hawks what was given to *me*."

"Kitling." Teela's use of the word was so common it might have been Kaylin's actual name. She slid an arm around Kaylin's shoulders. "Your age is showing." When Kaylin failed to reply, Teela added, "No one helped you out because we wanted to humiliate you—if I recall the early days, you did that quite effectively on your own."

"Thanks a lot, Teela."

"No one helped you with the expectation that you would owe us, or be obligated to us, in future. Any kindness done to you in the past is not an obligation you must carry with you until you can—somewhat forcefully, I feel—discharge it."

"It's not really that," Kaylin said, looking at her feet. "It's just—I never had much. I have things now. The Hawks are the only family I have. Moran, you're a Hawk." She lifted her chin. "You're like a terrifying aunt or older sister. Not Barrani-scary—if you're angry at me, I know I deserve it."

Teela cleared her throat.

"But I feel like—I feel—" She stopped. "I know this is not really about me."

"But?" Moran unexpectedly prompted.

"I feel like somehow, still, after years of being a Hawk, and working hard, and becoming an adult—I feel like I'm not grown-up enough, or not *good enough*, to be allowed to help you."

"Ugh," Moran replied. "It has nothing to do with that. It's not about *you*, you're right. I just don't want to involve you in my personal affairs."

"And if Teela had offered?"

"I don't want to involve *me* in *Teela's* personal affairs."

Kaylin laughed. "I don't have much choice."

"You really don't," Teela agreed. "The perils of joining the force as a minor, even as a mascot."

"We can drop the mascot bit anytime now."

"Kids," Moran said. "You can have the rest of that particular discussion in the hall. I've heard it enough to know there's nothing new for an audience in it." They remained silent, and she looked down at the desk, where the familiar was still expectantly perched. "This is irresponsible," she continued.

"You don't have to decide right now," Kaylin told her. "But—come with me when you're off shift? You can meet Helen. You can see where I live—and where everyone else lives, if they're okay with that. You can decide then."

"Fine. Fine, I'll visit."

Kaylin wanted to cheer. "Now?"

Moran sighed. "I suppose we might as well get it over with."

"You're expected at the library," Teela reminded her quietly as they exited the infirmary.

"I know," Kaylin replied.

"Kitling—"

"She'll change her mind. If we don't get her home, she'll change her mind. I can talk to the Arkon tomorrow."

"Your funeral."

"You live in *this* neighborhood?" Moran asked as they walked toward Kaylin's home. Trees—well-groomed and towering—covered the street as if they were nature's fences.

"I know, right? But it's where Helen was built."

"I'm still having difficulty with that."

"With what?"

"With thinking of a building as a person. It's not that it has a name—buildings frequently do. So do rooms. They don't generally have people names, though."

"Or personalities," Kaylin agreed. "You'll understand it better when you meet her."

Out of the corner of her mouth, Moran asked Teela, "Why did I think this was a good idea?"

"You didn't, that I recall. You just weren't willing to accept the cost of refusing to consider it."

Moran glared at Kaylin. "Teela doesn't live with you, correct?"

"No. Two of her friends do, and she's coming with me to check up on them."

"So...I'd be living with Barrani."

"Not technically. You might *hear* them, but at least one of them has been practically invisible for weeks. They're not like normal Barrani—I think you'd actually like them."

Teela coughed, but Moran smiled. When the Aerian smiled, she looked vastly more vulnerable—maybe that was why she did it so seldom. "Is there anything else I should know?"

"Not really. Helen likes flowers."

Moran blinked.

"...And I'm shutting up now. You'll see."

★ ★ ★

Helen was waiting in the foyer by the time Kaylin entered the house. Like Tara, Helen understood Kaylin's visceral dislike of door wards; she even considered it sensible, as no one *liked* pain. She smiled brightly at the sight of Teela.

"I'm so glad you've come," she told the Barrani. "I'm not certain I can talk any more sense into Annarion; he is very, very worried. Mandoran's been trying, but Annarion has shut him out completely."

"Yes, I'd heard," Teela replied. "Are they in the basement?"

"Mandoran is in his room. Annarion is downstairs."

"If it's all right with you, I'll go talk to Annarion."

"Of course, dear. I'm very worried about that boy." Teela walked past her, but Helen had already moved on—though Helen could accompany Teela *and* simultaneously greet a guest without even blinking.

"Helen, this is Moran. She's a Hawk, and she's in charge of the infirmary. As a sergeant. Moran, this is Helen."

"If it's easier," Helen said, extending a hand, "think of me as a particularly concerned landlord."

"Kaylin talks about you a lot in the office," Moran replied, offering her the smile she seldom offered anyone in the Halls, except Caitlin. Her wings folded more naturally across her back, losing some of their height; her eyes settled into a comfortable dark gray. "This is a very impressive foyer."

"Do the Aeries have foyers?"

"Not like this, but yes, there are areas that would serve the same function. The oldest of ours features more weaponry, though." She seemed hesitant to elaborate further.

"I was hoping," Kaylin said, rightly guessing the reason for the hesitation, "that Moran could stay with us. Her wings were injured when the Barrani ancestors came to visit, and she can't fly properly, so she either has to take a leave of absence—"

"—or find a place to stay while she heals?" Helen was look-ing at Moran's wings. Kaylin guessed that she was assessing them from a different vantage point—from the front, very little of the actual injuries could be examined.

"Yes, that. And at the moment, she's living in the—"

Moran cleared her throat. Loudly.

"Yes, I see. That won't do. I do have rooms that I think might suit you, if you would care to look at them. I don't, un-fortunately, have a working connection to the mirror network yet. Kaylin has been quite vocal about the necessity. Would you also require it?"

Moran's smile in response was almost feline. "No, actually, having no mirror connection would be a godsend."

Kaylin followed her guest and Helen, trailing behind. She wasn't certain what she should be doing. Moran's rooms would be her rooms; they weren't part of Kaylin's living space un-less Moran specifically invited her in. But Helen was Kaylin's home, and in theory, it was Kaylin offering hospitality. Would it be bad manners to tag along? Bad manners to hang back?

Etiquette gave Kaylin a headache, in part because good eti-quette demanded entirely different behaviors in almost exactly the same situations. And also because it was Diarmat who was teaching.

She lagged behind, small and squawky across her shoulders like a wet blanket. He didn't even lift his head when Moran opened the door Helen indicated. Her room was nestled be-tween everyone else's in the hall of doors; the door was adorned by a very simple, but obviously winged, person in silhouette.

Kaylin wasn't certain what to expect. She'd seen the Aerie in which Clint and his flight lived—or rather, she'd seen the large, public spaces the entire Aerie shared. It had looked like a giant cave, though with smoother walls and adornments.

She didn't recall windows, but didn't remember the darkness of natural caves, either. She had no idea what Aerians did for kitchens; she knew they didn't eat sitting in normal chairs, because their wings made it impossible.

She had no idea how they slept. The fledglings slept in traditional bassinets, though with more padding. Other creatures with wings slept sitting upright—or hanging upside down, in the case of bats. She'd never been stupid enough to ask the Aerians whether they did the same thing. Or perhaps she'd just been too self-conscious about *sounding* stupid.

Kaylin started forward and almost ran into Moran's back. The Aerian was standing in the doorway, her right hand on the frame; her knuckles were white.

"Moran?" Kaylin asked.

Moran didn't appear to hear her, which might have been because of the raucous noise of birds. Kaylin couldn't tell if they were angry birds or not; she could only tell that there were a lot of them.

Moran turned in the doorway to face Helen, who waited in silence. She then looked at Kaylin. "Did you know?" she asked, her voice entirely unlike the harsh bark the infirmary required.

Kaylin shook her head. "I still don't."

Moran stepped into the room, indicating by gesture that Kaylin should follow.

This was not a room in the traditional sense of the word; it only had three walls, for one. The floor was harder than the one in Kaylin's room; it was stone. Flat stone, mind, that had obviously been worked—but still, stone. Kaylin's habit of falling out of bed when nightmares were bad or the mirror barked did not lend itself to hard stone floors.

The walls appeared to be made of stone, too—and the stone wasn't cut stone or block; it was all of a piece. Arches had been worked into the walls, and Kaylin could see light from rooms to the left and right of this one. But this room was enormous. It was also not one in which Kaylin thought she could *ever* sleep, because it was missing a wall.

There were buildings so decrepit in the fiefs that walls had come down. Tiamaris was fixing those, usually by destroying the rotting ruins and rebuilding from scratch, but Nightshade had never cared enough about the fief and its citizens to do the same—and having a shelter without walls was the same as having no shelter at all, when night fell.

She said nothing. She knew Moran's life in the Aerie was not her own life in Nightshade. Hells, it wasn't her life in Elantra. But it shadowed her; it was so much a part of where she'd come from.

Moran left Kaylin at the door and walked, wings lifting, toward the open sky that faced the rest of the room. The sky was city sky: it was dappled with clouds, but blue and bright, sun setting in the distance. Moran turned away from that sky to face Helen. Kaylin had never seen the expression her face now wore. It was almost uncomfortable to look at; Kaylin felt as if she was intruding on something incredibly private.

Moran opened her mouth, but no words came out. She looked much, much younger than she did in the Halls. Without a word, she turned and left the entry room, walking to the right of where Kaylin stood looking out.

When she'd left, Kaylin said quietly, "She has to stay here. She *has* to stay here."

"I am not a jail," Helen said. Her voice was gentle. "I understand what you want to offer, and Kaylin, I am—as I have said before—happy to do so. Your Moran means you no harm; she is afraid that her presence here will cause it. I can't convince her to shed that fear, because her presence will cause you no harm *here*. But it isn't what happens here that she's afraid of. It's what happens outside of these walls.

"She trusts your safety to me while you are here. I'm not entirely certain what you told her, but I don't need to be. I cannot promise your safety while you are not within my walls—and you will not always be here. I accept that, or I could not have become your home. If she can live with the guilt, she will, I think, remain."

Moran came back. She looked frail, which again was discomfiting. She didn't speak; instead, she walked directly through the arch opposite the one she'd just exited. She paused this time and said, "Kaylin, come with me." She held out a hand. It wasn't a command, but it also wasn't the sarcastic barking that generally passed for requests in the Halls of Law from anyone who wasn't Caitlin.

Kaylin, almost mute, followed, thinking at Helen before she realized that Helen might actually respond to the thoughts—which would just humiliate a Hawk and an Aerian who were both accustomed to more privacy. Helen was mercifully silent.

CHAPTER 8

Kaylin looked across this new room to the pool at its center. Moran had removed her shoes, and her feet dangled in what did not look to be particularly warm water.

Kaylin had seen the natural baths the Barrani liked, and this resembled them; there was rock and water. But the water was also open to the sky and the elements; the shape of the basin implied that rain actually fell here. *So* not Kaylin's idea of a real room.

"This," Moran said quietly, "reminds me of my childhood."

"The other room reminds me of mine," Kaylin replied. "But not entirely in a good way. I think I like actual walls."

"The Barrani influence everything," Moran continued, without looking up. "My grandmother lived in quarters very much like these."

"You were fond of her," Helen said. It wasn't a question.

"Yes. She represented sanity and safety to me in my early childhood. She was considered far too old-fashioned, too out-dated; she lived like a—commoner? I think that's the word."

"So?" Kaylin said. "I live like a commoner."

Moran nodded. "And yet you are Chosen and you number, among your friends, Barrani High Lords and Dragons. And a very cranky Leontine sergeant and his slightly more scary wife. My grandmother had none of these things. She had birth and bloodlines, but after the death of her husband, she leveraged neither. She moved out of the Reach and into the antiquated quarters she had known as a girl.

"When things became…difficult…for my own mother, I was sent to live with my grandmother. I lived with her for four years, until her death."

Something about the way this was phrased made Kaylin tense. Moran didn't appear to notice.

"Her wings were different; they weren't like mine. When I was young, I thought that perhaps I had baby wings and that the spots would fade with time."

"Like freckles?"

"Yes. Exactly like—but mine never faded." She turned her face toward the water and sat, silent, for a long moment. "I know I shouldn't stay here."

Kaylin hoped that this meant she would.

"The old quarters are gone. When my grandmother died, they were…remodeled. The Aerians have their own mages; they are not like Imperial mages. They…shape things; rock and wood and water. Most of the interior Aeries look like places the Barrani might live, if given the chance."

"They wouldn't live here."

"No. Not here. I shouldn't stay," she said again. "But the truth is: I am injured. I *will* heal. But it won't be instant. I would rather live in the infirmary than live—without any freedom— in the home of my flight's leaders, and that's where I would otherwise stay. But—" She drew in a sharp breath.

"We're going to give you a few minutes alone, dear," Helen said. "We'll be downstairs in the mess hall."

"She means dining room," Kaylin added, slightly confused; Helen had never made this association before.

"Moran understands the mess hall in the Halls; eating spaces in the Aerie are not quite the same, although practically speaking, they serve much the same function."

Moran nodded. She didn't rise as Helen drew Kaylin away from the bath toward the exit, but she said, without turning around, "Thank you, Helen. I now understand exactly why Kaylin was so insistent that I convalesce with you."

"But will she stay?" Kaylin asked.

"I am not certain. I think she was unexpectedly moved by what she found when she opened that door, but she is not as young as you are."

"Meaning?"

"She has experienced more, and that experience influences how she makes her decisions. Were she your age, but otherwise herself, there would be no question. She would remain. She would feel very indebted to you, however."

"No, she wouldn't."

"No?"

"She would feel indebted to *you*. But I think that's going to be the case anyway. You're my home," Kaylin added, "but you're not my slave. Most people don't have sentient homes. You speak, think, interact like a person—because you are one. Moran won't be able to see you as some part of me. I don't, and can't, own you. You've decided, for your own reasons, to let me live here; you've decided that you'll accept my guests— even Imperial ones. You go out of your way—"

"It is part of my essential function—"

"—to make those guests feel safe and at home here."

"Mandoran and Annarion were willing to die to protect me," Helen countered. "I could not in good conscience offer less. I would even be willing to house your Teela, but she is… less comfortable with my presence. She does trust me where you're concerned, but she is afraid that the fact that she is not

you, and not like you, would tell against her where I'm concerned. She thinks that I am very like Caitlin."

"And you're not?"

"I do not think so. I have not yet met your Caitlin."

"You'd like her."

"I hope, for your sake, that she likes me," Helen replied.
She led the way into the dining room.

"Shouldn't we use the parlor?"

"This is a much larger room, and the windows are both bigger and brighter." She frowned.

"Problem?"

"Teela and Mandoran are speaking to Annarion; he is not
responding. Or rather, not well, and not with words. I should
go." Helen's voice could be in two locations at once; that ability did not extend to her full, physical Avatar. Tara could, and
the Hallionne could. But there was a lot Kaylin didn't know
about Helen and her capabilities.

"I'll wait."

The small dragon squawked, loudly, in her ear, and Kaylin
said, "But he'll go with you, if you don't mind." More squawking and one spiteful snap at the stick that kept Kaylin's hair in
place later, the small dragon was gone, flapping around Helen's
departing head in a circle of irritability.

Kaylin took a chair and folded her arms on the tabletop; she
dropped her head onto her forearms. She was exhausted. What
she did know about Helen was simple enough: she trusted her.
Everything else could wait.

The first person to enter the dining room was not Helen.
Nor was it Moran, Teela or the other two Barrani. It was Bellusdeo. She was accompanied by Severn and Tain, who looked
decidedly ill-at-ease.

"The Arkon wants to see you," Bellusdeo said without pre-amble.

Kaylin lifted her head. She wondered how long she'd slept, because she had that slightly fuzzy brain that meant sleep had just been broken. "I like the Arkon, but when he wants to see me, it's usually because he has a thousand questions. None of which I can answer. When I can't answer, he gets cranky. He's pretty much never cranky at you." Unlike Diarmat. It was possibly the first kind thought she'd had about Diarmat—and that was upsetting in an entirely different way. She looked up; Bellusdeo was smiling. Her eyes were gold.

Tain's eyes, on the other hand, were blue.

"Teela's here," Kaylin told him, although he hadn't asked. "She's arguing with Annarion."

"Good luck with that."

"Mandoran's on her side."

"You think that's going to change the outcome?" Tain snorted. "I honestly do not see the appeal of children."

"They're not exactly children."

"I've lived with them. That's exactly what they are. They might not appear to be young in the fashion of mortal children, but they have the fecklessness of Barrani youth, coupled with far too much power."

Kaylin remembered what Mandoran had said about living with Tain; he'd likened it to a dungeon, but less dark. She coughed to cover her amusement, because laughter wasn't going to make Tain feel any better.

"What are they arguing about?"

"Nightshade."

Irritation drained from Tain's expression. "What is Annarion going to do?"

"Best guess?"

Tain nodded.

"He's going to head into the fiefs." She smacked herself in the forehead. "That's what I forgot!"

"You don't intend to tell Annarion what Gilbert said, surely."

Kaylin blinked.

"If you don't *want* him charging into the heart of the fiefs, you'll keep it strictly to yourself."

"I think it's too late."

Tain pinched the bridge of his nose. This was the Barrani equivalent of smacking himself in the face.

"I didn't tell him—I haven't seen him since I got back. I visited Evanton and endured a faceful of raging Leontine sergeant, and I'm trying to convince Moran that she wants to stay here instead of living in the *infirmary* for three months. If Annarion knows, it's because Teela told him."

"If Teela told him, she has her reasons."

But if Kaylin told him, she wouldn't? Kaylin glared at Tain; Tain ignored it. "I can't think of any other reason they'd be arguing. Helen had to go downstairs to help out; she thinks Annarion's close to losing it."

This did not change the color of Tain's eyes any.

"What were you thinking, bringing them back from the West March?"

"I didn't bring 'them'; I brought Mandoran. He would have come on his own anyway, because Annarion was here. I didn't expect—" She exhaled, thinking about Moran, and the Hawks that had not survived the ancestors' attack. "I was thinking that they were Teela's friends, that they were people she trusted and that she'd thought they were lost forever. I was thinking that it would be as if they were let out of jail after a really, really long sentence.

"I didn't understand what they were—or weren't. But neither did Teela."

Bellusdeo said, "Leave her alone, Tain. What's happened has happened. There was no malice or ill intent."

"They weren't your losses."

"No?" Bellusdeo drew herself up to her full height, which was much more impressive than Kaylin's.

To Kaylin's surprise, Tain looked away first. "Apologies," he said—and even sounded as if he meant it, although Barrani were very capable liars. "I am worried—"

"About Teela, yes. I imagine she appreciates it about as much as I would."

This startled a genuine laugh from the Barrani Hawk. "At least as much" was his rueful reply. "Teela's family lost a lot to the wars, but I can see why she likes you."

"I lost everything," Bellusdeo replied. "But yes, it's hard to dislike Teela. It's much easier to dislike Mandoran."

"Agreed on both counts." Tain then turned to Kaylin and opened his mouth to speak. Severn, however, gave them all a quiet heads-up as Moran descended the stairs.

The absolute ruler of the infirmary stopped for a moment in the doorway when she saw Severn and Tain. Then she walked past them to the table, and to the backless stool positioned in its center. She sat heavily.

Helen appeared with food—which was to say, food appeared on the table and Helen came into the room. "You'll want to speak with Annarion, dear," she told Kaylin.

That was not the first item on Kaylin's list of desirable activities.

"I know. But he is upset. I've created a containment; he should be able to rage as much as he wants without ill effect on the rest of the house. I cannot, however, continue to confine him."

"Meaning he can leave anytime he wants."

"He is a guest, not a prisoner—but even were he to be a prisoner, I have become too diminished to maintain a cell for either him or Mandoran for long. Mandoran did ask," she added. "He is also very, very worried about Annarion."

"Is Teela less worried than she was?"

"No, dear. I would say she is vastly more worried than she was."

Tain grimaced. Teela worried was about as much fun as Marcus enraged.

"Did I come at a bad time?" Moran asked, entering the conversation.

"No!" Kaylin said, before Helen could reply, although it was to Helen she'd directed the question.

"In my experience," Helen replied, with a gentle smile, "there is never a good or a bad time. There is only time. Please, eat. You haven't had dinner yet, and neither has Kaylin." She turned to Tain. "I don't believe we've met, and I am not always conversant with the social customs of my guests."

"This is Tain," Kaylin immediately said. "He's Teela's partner in the Hawks."

Tain's eyes, which had lightened a bit while talking with Bellusdeo, darkened instantly. Helen ignored this.

"I'm Helen. Kaylin has agreed to make her home with me, and I have agreed to make that home safe and secure. Her friends are, by her choice, her family; you are welcome here. I apologize if ancient buildings are not comfortable for you. I cannot change my nature, but I will attempt to give you the privacy you crave."

Tain nodded slowly.

"Will you join us for dinner? And Corporal Handred?"

Severn, fiefborn, nodded. Kaylin looked with longing at the food, but pushed her chair away from the table. "Did you leave small and squawky with Annarion?"

"Yes. He thought it best that he remain."

"I'm sorry, Moran—I'll be right back."

"I hope so," the sergeant said, in her usual clipped tones. "I can hear your stomach growling from here."

Helen did not leave the guests when Kaylin did. But Helen's disembodied voice joined her as she made her way to the stairs that led to the basement. "Is there anything you would like me to do?"

"I think you've done enough. Thanks for dealing with Annarion."

"I don't think Moran was expecting Severn or Tain."

No, she probably hadn't been—but to be fair, neither had Kaylin. Tain had been an intermittent fixture in her early life with the Hawks, which was probably Teela's doing, since Tain wasn't particularly nurturing on his own. Kaylin grimaced. Then again, neither was Teela.

Severn was Severn. Both of them were so much a part of her life that she didn't blink an eye at their presence. But...Moran had never just walked into Kaylin's old apartment. Moran had never dropped by to check on her. Clint had, in the early years. Marcus had, and so had his wives.

Then again, Marcus would probably rip out her throat if she tried to force living quarters on him—even if he had none. She'd have to stand behind Kayala, the first wife, in order to safely *make* the offer.

People were complicated. If someone had offered Kaylin shelter and a safe, clean space—with food!—she would have leaped through the door, gratefully. The only thing that would have held her back was the lack of trust that anyone living on the edge of survival developed. If she trusted the person offering her safety, then what reason would she have had to refuse?

And yet, clearly, Moran had her reasons.

The door to the basement opened before Kaylin could touch it, but at this point, such things didn't spook her. She wasn't looking forward to dealing with angry, blue-eyed Teela, and that was dread enough.

"She isn't angry," Helen said.

"Fine. Scared or worried Teela. In case it's not obvious, that's worse."

"She should be worried. I am worried myself. Annarion can be contained; he is struggling to control impulses of which he is only barely aware. If he decides that they are no longer a concern—or a primary concern—I do not think I can keep him here without harming him.

"And no, Kaylin, quite aside from your own concerns, that is *not* what I wish. He knows the debt he owes you and the people of your city. Teela has made that *quite* clear."

"But that wasn't his fault—"

"Fault? Perhaps not. But he cannot claim ignorance a second time. It is only the terrible sense of guilt at what transpired that has kept him here these three weeks. He has worked without stop. But he cannot completely contain his fear."

Fear for Nightshade.

Teela was blue-eyed and stiff as a board; absent was the usual sense of grace that even motionless Barrani naturally exuded.

To Kaylin's eyes, Annarion was not in anything resembling a jail cell. He was sitting in the middle of the room—a Barrani room, by the look of the furnishings—his eyes the same color as Teela's. Mandoran was beside him, arms folded, shoulders slumped. There was a window in the far wall. The view outside it looked very quiet and very peaceful.

It was the only thing in the room that was the latter.

Kaylin took a chair, because there just happened to be one that suited her. Whether it had existed in the seconds before she opened the door, she didn't know, and it didn't really matter. "Teela told you about our morning." Teela's glare drilled the side of her face, but Kaylin continued, "I still can't reach your brother. I can't hear him. But I don't think he's dead."

"On what are you basing that assumption?" Annarion asked.

"Instinct." She had a clear idea how much he valued mortal instinct, but he was better behaved than Mandoran and kept his thoughts to himself. "Did Teela also tell you about our visit to the Keeper?"

Mandoran lifted a dark brow. "No."

"And you didn't notice we were there?"

"Teela's pretty good at keeping things to herself. What were you doing at the Keeper's?"

"Asking him about Gilbert," she replied. "Sort of. And possibly listening to his take on gaining entry to ancient ruins, some of which might be malevolent."

They both glanced at Teela.

Mandoran rolled his eyes and glared at the Barrani Hawk. Clearly another conversation was unfolding between the two Barrani, courtesy of their exchanged True Names. Mandoran confirmed this. "I don't understand *why* Teela considers it such a bad idea to give you my name. I'm not insisting anyone *else* do it. But this style of speech is slow and inexact, and your verbal explanations leave a lot to be desired."

"She probably considers it a bad idea because I'm terrible at filtering. If I had your name, you'd probably know everything I was thinking the moment I thought it."

"And that's bad how?"

"For *me*, it would be bad."

Mandoran glared at Teela again. Teela was probably glaring at Kaylin. Something invisible squawked. Kaylin recognized the voice instantly, but couldn't actually see where it was coming from.

"Teela, where *is* small and squawky?"

Annarion tensed; Mandoran rolled his eyes. Mandoran was easily the most human Barrani Kaylin had ever met. Clearly, this had its pros and cons. "He's sitting about a foot above the table, chewing on his wing tips."

Squawk.

"You *honestly* can't see him?"

"Kaylin," Teela interjected, "is one of the worst liars you will ever meet."

"I didn't always suck at lying."

"You probably didn't speak as much, then. If she says she can't see him, she can't see him. I don't see why it's so difficult to believe; I can't see him, either."

"You can hear him, though," Mandoran pointed out.

"The entire house can probably hear him." Teela rose. "Is he trying to prove a point?"

It was Kaylin who answered. "Probably."

"Which?"

"In general? I'm mortal and therefore incompetent. It's the same point most of my friends try to prove when they're on a tear. If he's not uncomfortable where he is, he can stay there for a bit." Kaylin folded her arms. "Helen says you've learned a lot in the past three weeks."

"That's not what she's been telling us."

"I believe she was talking about Annarion."

Annarion's lips twitched.

"How much control do you think you have?" Kaylin directed her question to Nightshade's guilt-ridden younger brother.

"If I was certain I had enough, do you think I would still be here?"

"Fair enough. How uncertain are you?"

"I constantly feel like I have enough control. Helen, however, does not agree. In this case, I have chosen to trust Helen's judgment over both my own and my need for haste and movement."

Squawk. SQUAWK.

"It appears," Helen's disembodied voice said, "that Hope considers me overly cautious. If you are willing to accept his company, he believes he understands the difficulty now."

"And he didn't before?"

"Apparently not, dear.

"I'm not certain I consider that wise," Helen then said, to the very noisy thin air.

The small dragon appeared to be telling her just how much her opinion counted. Had the small creature been on Kaylin's shoulders, she would have attempted to cover his mouth. Annarion rose, walked over to where Kaylin sat and knelt before her. It made Kaylin incredibly uncomfortable.

"Your familiar believes he can counter the worst of the... noise...I make if he remains in his current form."

Kaylin nodded. "Look, can you get up? This is kind of ridiculous."

Annarion ignored her request. She looked to Teela for help. Teela shrugged. It was a stiff shrug; her lips were thin, her eyes narrowed.

"The familiar cannot provide the dampening effect if he is not in his current form."

"The invisible one?"

Squawk.

Kaylin said, "No, wait, let me guess. He isn't actually invisible. He's just invisible to anyone who naturally lives in the mortal world."

Teela cleared her throat.

"You know what I meant."

"Yes. And I still take exception to it. You are, however, correct. I can see what Mandoran and Annarion see—but it takes a great deal of effort and it gives me an almost instant headache. Our eyes were not meant to see the familiar as he exists now. If it's any consolation, without shifting out of the state he occupies, he can't cause actual harm—to us, anyway."

"Can he bite the other two?"

"They seem to feel so."

"If you want my permission," Kaylin told Annarion, "it's yours. You have it."

Annarion clearly wasn't begging for her permission to take the small dragon. "Your familiar cannot remain anchored to the plane—as Mandoran and I are—in this form. Not if you're not with him."

Which explained Teela's expression.

"He is willing to accompany me—"

"Us," Mandoran interjected.

"…Us. But to do so, you must also accompany us." He swallowed. "You have no reason to trust my brother, and little reason to love him. He has sacrificed much. But he is the only living member of my family that I acknowledge."

Kaylin almost asked him if he had unacknowledged family members who were still alive, but decided against it. "You want me to go with you."

He swallowed. Kneeling there in supplication, he looked much younger than he normally did. "Yes. I understand the debt it will incur."

"Please don't say that."

He lifted his head. His lips, his eyes, the whole of his expression, were adorned with visceral pride.

"I know exactly how the Barrani feel about debts." When this failed to achieve the intended enlightenment, she added, "They hate them. I'd just as soon not have you in my debt, because, your brother aside, I actually *like* you." She exhaled. "Nightshade's fief almost destroyed my life. Some of the decisions he's made in the past—" She stopped. After a long pause, which no one filled, she continued, "But he's saved my life, as well. I never intended to let you go to the fiefs alone."

He bowed his head.

"But does this mean small and squawky—"

Squawk.

"—will be invisible the entire time?"

"Invisible to you," Mandoran muttered, which caused another round of squawking.

"Yes, I believe so," Annarion replied.

She turned to look at the empty space that wasn't, in theory, empty. "You're going to have to make less noise when we're outside," she told her familiar. "Most of the time, people think you're cute or valuable. You don't want them to think they're crazy."

Squawk.

She glanced at Teela, who had said a very loud nothing for almost the entire conversation. "Tain and Severn are upstairs with Moran."

"Just what we need." Teela glanced at Kaylin. "Don't think that you're going to Nightshade—or anywhere else—without me."

"Teela—"

"I mean it. I will break your left leg if you attempt to leave me behind. Anything that you can survive, I can survive."

Mandoran cleared his throat, opened his mouth and snapped it shut again. For a moment, Kaylin reconsidered the value of knowing Mandoran's True Name.

"He is pointing out that you are Chosen," Annarion said as he rose.

"I bet she's pointing out that I don't even understand what that means."

"Yes. Though much more colorfully."

"You can't stop her from coming with us," Kaylin added more quietly. "Because she doesn't want me to go. She's still pissed off that your brother marked my face."

"Yes. Very. I am not terribly happy about that myself. But…"

"But it doesn't seem to have altered my life?"

"It doesn't seem—and I do not know your life well—to have damaged your life, no. The mark is used to denote ownership, and it can be used to enforce it. It does not have the strength of a name—but it doesn't require it. Had you been of equivalent power, he could not have placed that mark upon you without your explicit consent. You did not consent, yet you are marked."

"He hasn't used it against me. But I know his name."

Teela coughed.

Mandoran made a face at her.

"That is not generally common knowledge," Annarion finally said.

"I know—but everyone in this room already knows it."

"Everyone in this room also knows that I have sex," Teela cut in. "But no one needs to *hear* about it."

Mandoran lifted a hand. "Actually, I would—"

Annarion said, "I would *not*. Helen?"

"Yes," Helen's disembodied voice replied.

"I'm ready to resume our lessons. I apologize for my frustration."

"Very well. Kaylin, dear, you will have to see to our guests."

Kaylin and Teela returned to the dining room; Mandoran and Annarion remained below. Teela was not exactly green-eyed by the time they'd reached the kitchen.

"You don't want me to go."

"I don't want *either* of you to go. I am not the only one," she added. "Sedarias is distinctly cool to the idea. She's been arguing against it. I can't understand all of what's being said—and yes, before you ask, I find that frustrating. Mandoran is neutral. He doesn't think it's wise, but wisdom is not something he prizes. He will not, however, remain behind."

"And the others?"

"Varying degrees of neutrality. We hold each other's names, but we have never used that knowledge to attempt to dominate. I'm not certain their names could be used that way now. What will you do with Moran?"

"If she'll stay, I'll keep her. I'm not you—I'll whine at her if she tries to say no. But I can't force her."

"Good. She is not like me in most ways, but she *is* like me in a few notable ones. I would be quite annoyed if you whined at me, but at the same time, unoffended. You whine a lot."

"Thanks, Teela." She squared her shoulders as they reached the dining room. To Kaylin's relief, Moran was still there. So was the food. It said something about her that the relief at seeing each was about equal.

Squawk.

CHAPTER 9

"Can you give me a few days to think it over?" Moran asked while Kaylin ate.

"I can try." At Moran's expression, Kaylin said, "What? No one else is ever going to use those specific rooms. They're yours. I said I would try."

"Which is like saying no." Moran's frown was a familiar sight. "There's some chance that certain elements of Aerian society won't appreciate your offer or my decision."

"That's going to be entirely their problem."

"When we're here. But at the Halls, in the Aerie…" She trailed off, then asked, "Have you spoken with Lord Grammayre about this?"

"No. I'm not offering the Hawklord a temporary place to stay."

"You're not the only one who will be censured."

Kaylin froze and then set her fork down. "They'll—whoever they are—take things out on the *Hawklord*?"

"They will express their legitimate concerns, yes." She smiled; it added no joy to her face. "Grammayre is an old friend. He is not a family friend. I joined the Hawks when he offered me the position; the offer came at a time when things were in a dangerous state of flux for me.

"He received no thanks at all for it, of course. Being a Hawk is not an occupation that was ever considered suitable for me."

"This isn't changing my mind any," Kaylin pointed out.

Moran's smile deepened. "I loved the rooms. I know you were a bit shocked to see them; to you they must look like—like—"

"Living in the wild, yes. But without the bugs."

"I feel as if I have returned, in part, to my youth. And some part of me wants to commit this extra act of defiance. Living in the infirmary already makes that point. Living with a mortal would…exacerbate it. I do not wish to use you in that fashion."

"And if that were the only consideration, I would never have offered, Moran. I'm *happy* to be part of that."

"You don't even know what it is."

"I think I understand enough. I'm the type of undesirable you should never have made friends with—I mean, if you consider me a friend—"

Moran chuckled. "A bit late for that, don't you think? Yes. You are right. But the Hawklord is also considered unworthy. Clint. Mellian. Not a single one of the Aerians who have given their lives in defense of this grounded city would have been considered worthy. And I? I am worthy only by an accident of birth. I am—I have remained—a part of my flight, but I am, like my grandmother before me, an outsider. Do you know why I accepted the Hawklord's offer?"

Kaylin shook her head. She had known almost nothing of Moran's life until now. No, that was wrong. She had known Moran as a sergeant and the ruler of the infirmary. She had been Moran's patient; she had seen Marcus and many of her colleagues treated by her, as well. She glanced at Moran's injured wings. Moran had flown when the Hawks had flown. Moran had been in the sky with the Dragons.

The Hawks could not hope to face—and fight—what the Dragons fought. They couldn't expect that they would all survive it. Kaylin knew what she had done in her youth in the name of survival; she would never have been among the Aerians, the Hawks, the Swords. She would have been as far from the fight as her legs could carry her. Farther.

The Hawks had known.

They had carried the chains and netting necessary for the Arkon's complicated defenses. They had made themselves targets as the enemy shot down anything in the sky. When one fell, another took up both their duty and their burden.

Moran had been there.

"I accepted the Hawklord's offer because I wanted the opportunity to *do* something with my life. Something that affected others. Something that I could respect. I didn't start out in the infirmary," she added. "And I had my share of run-ins with Marcus, in my time."

"How did you end up in the infirmary?"

"The infirmary was contemptibly run. It was both inefficient and, in my opinion, dangerously unorganized. Why does that amuse you?"

Kaylin shook her head. It was the first time since crossing Helen's threshold that Moran had sounded like herself again; she couldn't help but smile.

"It was work. It was work that I had never before seen or done. I didn't...fit in, immediately. The Aerians were not particularly kind."

"And they survived it?"

Moran laughed then. "They weren't *wrong*, Kaylin. I wanted to be of use, but I had no real idea how to interact with people. I expected to be treated with the respect due my flight. I didn't *think* this consciously," she added, "but it's true. I expected the others to treat me as I had always been treated by those outside my flight.

"They didn't. I was a *private*. Many of them were corporals. They expected *me* to treat *them* with obsequious respect because they outranked me." She shook her head. "I'm not at all sure you would have offered me shelter during my first two years with the Halls.

"Most of the Hawks expected me to quit. They expected that I would flounce out of the office, wings rigid. But I'd fought so hard to be allowed the right to join the Halls of Law that it would have been humiliating. I was," she added, still smiling, "torn between two different humiliations. Being humiliated by strangers was the less terrifying of the two. So I stayed.

"It was six months before the Aerian Hawks would talk much to me, but the force is comprised of more than the Aerians. Caitlin took me under her wing. You'll have some experience with that. I didn't expect the rest of the mortals—or the Barrani—to treat me any differently, which is probably why they were comfortable with me. The rest of the Hawks eventually understood that I was in it for the long haul and that—birth aside—I could do my job.

"They stopped seeing the spots on my wings. So, for the most part, did I. It was very liberating. My injuries," she said, voice dropping, "reminded them. Reminded all of us. I am expected to quit the force. Reparations have been demanded from the Hawklord."

"Good luck with that."

"They've been demanded through the *Emperor*; the castelord has spoken with him personally."

"And he's not a pile of feathered ash?"

Moran's smile was grim. "The castelord and the Dragon Emperor both understand when a polite and perfectly civil request is a demand or a threat. The actual words are almost irrelevant, since neither will use open insults.

"I have not endorsed these demands. Nor have I tendered my resignation. The Hawklord has not relieved me of my duties.

If I return home with the intent to continue to serve the Halls of Law, I will be forced to arrive at the Halls on my own."

"But you can't fly."

"No. The Aerian Hawks have offered to aid me—but if I accept that offer, they will suffer. Not in the Halls, of course. But they don't live in the Halls. They live in the Southern Reach."

"So you chose to stay in the infirmary."

"Yes. It's my last act of defiance." She exhaled. "Understand that if I stay here, I am Moran while I'm under this roof. I am only a sergeant while I'm in the Halls of Law."

Kaylin nodded.

Teela, however, snorted. "Kaylin has never been particularly good at remembering to follow correct form. Don't expect her to change; it'll only lead to disappointment."

"Sergeant Kassan has never set a good example for her."

"Not really, no. I admit the Barrani have been somewhat lax about rank differentiation, as well. Kitling, don't make that face."

The face in question was not her usual grimace, though. "I really, *really* want you to stay here."

"Did you not just say you would give me a few days to think it over?"

"No. I said I could *try*. You're going to leave, aren't you? You're planning to go back to the infirmary. Could you at least stay here for the night? You're tired, you've just eaten and we *have* the room."

"Is she always like this?" Moran asked Helen.

"I believe you already know the answer," Helen replied. She was smiling. "Farther into your suite of rooms, you will find warmer water. Your wings are stiff."

Moran exhaled. "Yes, Kaylin. I will stay for tonight."

"Good." Kaylin did not clap her hands, because she was not four years old. But she had to remind herself of this fact.

"You're looking kind of green." At Teela's pointed side-eye, she added, "What? She is. I'm not making it up."

When Moran left the room, Bellusdeo, who had been silent throughout their exchange, turned to Kaylin. "You don't intend to enter the fiefs with Annarion, do you?"

"There is *no way* you are going with us," Kaylin replied. This had been her only lingering fear.

Bellusdeo folded her arms.

"That doesn't work on me. I have a Leontine regularly threatening to rip out my throat, remember?"

The gold Dragon exhaled smoke.

"...And Helen won't let you breathe on me, anyway."

"I try to stay out of personal matters," Helen told her. "It never ends well when an outsider joins a family argument."

"We're not going to war," Kaylin gamely continued. "We don't intend to fight Shadow. We're not going to Ravellon."

"After what Gilbert said to you, I don't believe you."

"The Emperor will have my head." It was the wrong thing to say, but it was also true. "If I get lost in the Shadows, I'm one Hawk. The future of an entire race is not depending on me. If *you* get lost..."

For a being that could naturally breathe fire, Bellusdeo had a lot of ice in her expression.

"We will keep Kaylin safe," Annarion said, entering the room. It seemed suspiciously like he'd heard the entire conversation. "The familiar will accompany us to the fiefs. He is more easily capable of living across planes and existing in some form on many of them simultaneously. I wouldn't ask Kaylin to accompany us, but she is his anchor—and to keep the rest of the city safe, we need him.

"I would not go at all if it were a choice between my brother and the Lady."

Kaylin was confused for a moment—the mention of the Lady made no sense.

Bellusdeo didn't have any problem making the connection. "I am not the Lady. I am not the Consort. I am—"

"You represent exactly that to the Emperor and the Dragon Court. Under no circumstance would an attempt to save a Barrani Lord—*any* Barrani Lord—be worth risking your life. Just as it wouldn't be worth risking the Barrani Consort's."

"And it's worth the danger to Kaylin?"

"She is Chosen," he replied. "She has responsibilities."

Kaylin frowned. "What do you mean?"

"Do you think the marks that grant you power exist for no reason?"

"I think they exist because the Ancients decided they should—but they didn't exactly give me commands or training when they placed them on my skin. They didn't ask my permission, either."

This appeared to confuse Annarion, who turned to Helen. "Perhaps I am not using the language correctly?"

"You are using it correctly."

"Ah. Why does she speak of permission?"

Bellusdeo snorted. "Mortals believe in choice."

"Even when they have so little of it?" Annarion frowned again. "We do not choose to be born. Do mortals?"

"No."

"We do not choose the names which will govern our lives."

"No."

"We do not choose the families or lines into which we are born; we do not choose the language we speak; we do not choose the talents with which we are born." He waited for Kaylin's nod before he continued, "Why, then, does your permission *matter*? You are what you are."

"Fine. It matters because if they'd had to *ask* permission, they would have had to explain what the responsibilities of the position *actually are*."

Annarion looked to Teela then. "Have you not explained it?"

Teela actually looked uncomfortable. "...No."

"Why not?"

"Because I *don't understand* what you're talking about when you speak of the Chosen. I can't understand the words or the images. They make no sense."

Annarion looked at his feet. After a long, awkward silence, he said, "Kaylin's used the power of the Chosen multiple times now. It doesn't matter if she completely understands it—it's clear that she understands it well enough to use it, if it comes to that."

Mandoran entered the dining room, as well. "No," he told everyone, "I am *not* staying behind." He looked at Kaylin as he spoke.

She held up both hands. "Don't look at me like that—I wasn't even going to suggest it."

"Teela did."

"Then glare at *Teela*. I don't even *like* the fiefs. The only one I willingly visit is Tiamaris. Teela has a better chance of survival in the fiefs than I do. She always has."

"Teela suggested," Teela said, "that she would stay behind if Mandoran chose to do so."

Kaylin rolled her eyes. "Like that was ever going to happen. Can we get back to—"

"The important person?"

"In a manner of speaking, yes." Kaylin exhaled. She did not want to drag Bellusdeo into the fiefs. She didn't want her anywhere near any fief that wasn't Tiamaris. She especially didn't want to have to explain *any* of this to the Emperor.

The Emperor.

What had she said to the Emperor? What was she doing now? Bellusdeo was a *Dragon*. Kaylin, marks all over her body, was *mortal*. She wanted to insist that Bellusdeo stay where it was safe because *why*? Because the Emperor would be mad at her?

Didn't that mean she was making the same mistake that the Emperor was making? That she was diminishing Bellusdeo because she was afraid? No, it was worse. Kaylin was afraid of the Emperor's reaction. She wasn't afraid *for* Bellusdeo.

She looked up and met the gold Dragon's eyes. "Can we just pretend that everything I've said in the last half an hour never left my mouth?"

Bellusdeo smiled. The expression made her look younger. Younger and at the same time, more confident. "I think you're forgetting immortal memory."

"Because mine is mortal," Kaylin countered. She turned to Annarion. "I can't do this during working hours."

He looked as if he was about to speak, but didn't. "Does Helen charge you...rent?"

"Actually," Helen replied, "yes, I do. I do not demand more than Kaylin can currently afford—but rent, such as it is, is a basic responsibility. It is not my intent to turn Kaylin into a walking child who is free from all material consequences."

Bellusdeo's smile inverted. "I do not believe you are—"

"You are a guest" was Helen's serene reply. "Kaylin did not attempt to charge you rent when you lived with her before she moved here. While you were beneath her roof, you were her responsibility."

Kaylin started to wave her hands in the air to get Helen's attention.

"You always have my attention."

"Bellusdeo's never been my responsibility."

"She is your friend," Helen said, her tone making the statement a counter to Kaylin's.

"Exactly."

"Friends feel a certain responsibility for each other. Is that not why you are going to Nightshade?"

"I don't think Annarion considers me a friend, exactly."

Helen frowned.

"Annarion is *Teela's* friend. Teela is *my* friend. I'm helping because—"

"I consider you a friend," Annarion said in Elantran. "Even if you are not like Mandoran or Teela. I personally think you could be, but Teela has forbidden it, on pain of death. She's only partially joking."

Kaylin blinked. She felt oddly self-conscious.

"You've surprised her," Teela told him.

"I don't have a lot of friends," Kaylin explained, feeling even more self-conscious.

Annarion frowned.

"Don't ask me—ask Kaylin. Who can't hear you if you don't actually speak, remember?" Teela said. She folded her arms and leaned against the table. Tain joined her, speaking to her in a low enough tone that Kaylin couldn't catch what he said.

"Perhaps Teela's understanding of your tongue is better than my own," Annarion said quietly. "But it seems to me that this statement is flawed. It is clear to me that you do not think you are lying; you must therefore be interpreting facts in a way that I cannot. What do you mean when you use the word *friend*?" All of the question was asked in Barrani except the one word.

"If I say that I have few friends, among the Barrani, it would be inaccurate. In my life, I have given eleven people the whole of my name. I was not coerced. I was not threatened.

"Among my kin, eleven is a vast number. If by friend, you speak of that—the gifting of the name as a sign of absolute and unwavering trust, both now and in the future—then perhaps I am being presumptuous. But Teela has long considered you *kyuthe*, and you do not have her name. I have seen very little of your life, but Mandoran has seen more—and what he has seen, I have also seen.

"You have Corporal Handred. You have the Hawks. You have Bellusdeo. You have Helen. You love almost unconditionally—and that is reflected in those around you. When you say you don't have many friends—"

Kaylin lifted both hands in surrender, hoping it would stop his words. She had never really attempted to enumerate her life in the way Annarion was clearly doing. When she looked at it from his point of view, she could see he was right. She hadn't had many friends in the fiefs. She hadn't lived there for more than seven years, but clearly her perception of who she was hadn't shifted much.

Severn had often said she was too trusting. But the truth was—she desperately wanted to find people she could trust. She wanted to believe that people could be trusted. No one had ever specifically asked her what friendship, as a concept, meant to her. When she used the word, when she heard the word used, she assumed that it had meaning, like true words did.

But it was just a word; a mortal word.

"When I say that," she finally told Annarion, "I say what I said when I was—was much younger. It was true, then. I didn't have as clear a concept that sometimes even our own truths can change, with time. I'm not the person I was when I believed that. I'm not the person I was when I first arrived in Elantra. But you're right to question it. It's *not* true now." She hesitated. "Where I grew up, if you had something special, you kept it hidden. You kept it to yourself. If you didn't, you were likely to lose it. It could be stolen or broken. You never wanted to stand out. You never wanted to attract too much attention, because some of that attention would be bad.

"I think I say it now to protect myself. If I don't acknowledge the things that are important out loud, where people can hear it, no one will take them away from me."

Annarion lifted a brow in Teela's direction. "She's young," Teela replied, with a shrug. "She never felt she had power—and only the powerful can claim power openly as a way of defending themselves. She is not Barrani. She wasn't raised as we were raised—the scions of the powerful and the ancient lineages. She did not know her father; only his absence shadowed her life—if it shadowed her life at all, given the fiefs.

"We knew ours." There was a curious, blue bitterness in Teela's eyes and voice, and of course there would be: Teela's father had killed her mother while Teela watched, helpless. The fact that her father had, in the end, died for that crime didn't bring her mother back. Maybe it gave Teela a sense of peace or closure, but Barrani memory made that vastly more difficult.

Annarion said softly, "Yes." His voice matched Teela's eyes, and silence descended.

"I once envied people like you," Tain surprised Kaylin by saying. He spoke, significantly, in Elantran. "People who had taken—and passed—the test of the High Halls."

"Annarion hasn't," Kaylin reminded him, before she could bite off her tongue. What *no one* needed was an Annarion let loose in the High Halls. Not yet. Perhaps not ever.

"I'm aware of that. Had Annarion returned from the green, he would have. His father, his brothers, his cousins—all were Lords of the Court."

"Not all," Teela replied. "Enough, Tain."

"My father made no attempt to court power and significance in the High Halls," Tain continued. "And for some part of my youth, I resented him for it. You would not have liked my father," he added, for Kaylin's benefit. "But I believe you would have liked him a great deal more than you would have liked Teela's."

"He's dead."

"Yes. But I remember him clearly. Mortal memory is fragile, but it is not always unkind, in the end."

Kaylin had never heard Tain talk about himself. Not like this. She tried to find something to say in return—something that might have the same weight and significance. She came up with nothing. "When did you meet Teela?"

The two exchanged a glance. "If I answer that, she'll kill me. Or try."

"She really will," Teela added, looking even less amused, which, given her starting point, should have been impossible. "Go home. Annarion and Mandoran are not your responsibility—and before the words fall out of your mouth, *neither am I.*"

Tain grinned. Teela didn't. Kaylin wouldn't have gotten away with that expression, given Teela's current mood—but she wasn't Tain. She wanted to know their history, but told herself that having the knowledge didn't really matter. Tain trusted Teela. Or maybe he just accepted her. There was no point in worrying about Teela—unless you wanted *angry* Teela.

Kaylin wasn't Tain, but she understood that if she went into the fiefs with Annarion and Mandoran, Teela was going, too. She looked across the room to Severn, who had, as he so often did, remained neutral.

"I notice you're making no attempt to ditch Severn," Tain said.

Kaylin turned to stare at him. "He's my partner."

"So you want to leave a Barrani corporal and a Dragon Lord behind because it might be dangerous, but you haven't even stopped to think about the hazards to a mortal."

"He's my *partner,* Tain."

"Just checking. I'll see you in the office tomorrow."

★ ★ ★

Moran did not come back to the dining room, or any of the spaces Kaylin privately thought of as public, that night. Teela closeted herself with the two Barrani; Severn left, not quite dragging Tain out by the collar; and Bellusdeo went upstairs to talk with Maggaron. If Severn was Kaylin's partner, Maggaron was—in as much as she had one—hers.

At this rate, they wouldn't be investigating anything—they'd be launching a full-scale invasion. Small and squawky remained invisible. His negligible weight no longer adorned Kaylin's shoulders, and he didn't bite or chew her hair. She could hear him—silence was not in his character—but that was it. She was surprised to find that she missed him.

But Moran had chosen to stay at least one night.

Bellusdeo had not turned carpets—or Kaylin—to ash, and Mandoran hadn't insulted Dragons once in her hearing. Some positive things *had* happened today. Kaylin mirrored the Imperial Palace—or tried to. The mirrors remained stubbornly reflective, and she remembered that Helen was still working on a "safe" connection—which meant, of course, that one didn't exist yet.

She would arrange to speak with the Arkon tomorrow. She didn't need to speak with Evanton again.

Anything else?

"I believe so, dear," Helen, disembodied, said. "You have a visitor."

"An emergency visitor?" Kaylin asked, thinking immediately of the midwives.

"You are likely to consider it an emergency, but no, dear. It's only the Emperor."

"You need to work on your Elantran," Kaylin said, as she sprinted for the door. "Is Bellusdeo still awake?"

"She is in Maggaron's room. Dragons," she added, "don't require sleep, as you may recall. You would like her to remain ignorant of the Emperor's visit?"

"If that's *at all* possible, yes" was Kaylin's guilty reply.

"In general, I wouldn't recommend it, given how sensitive she is about the Dragon Court—but I imagine you know best."

Well, at least one of us does, Kaylin thought. She answered the door. The Emperor, absent guards or Imperial Library pages, waited on the steps. Although he wasn't pacing—wasn't, in fact, moving much at all—everything about his rigid, perfect posture implied impatience.

She opened her mouth to invite him in.

"It is a lovely evening," he said, before she could speak—and even if he was here informally, she knew far better than to interrupt or speak over him. "Shall we walk?"

"I did not intend to arrive without warning," he told her, as the house faded into the distance. "But the usual methods of communication do not appear to be available."

Kaylin grimaced. "Sorry. For the mirrors to reach *us*, we apparently require some sort of connection, and Helen doesn't trust it. We're trying to come up with a secure workaround."

"I...see."

"Strange things have happened with the mirrors before," Kaylin felt obliged to point out. "It's not a groundless fear."

"I had hoped to speak with you more frequently, but I seldom have the leisure to visit. There are some difficulties—perhaps you are aware of one of them."

Since it wasn't a question, Kaylin waited.

"The Aerian Caste Court has petitioned the Emperor for willful and flagrant mistreatment of one of its citizens."

Kaylin stiffened.

"Ah. You are, indeed, aware."

"I'm not aware of what was *said*." Moran was not nearly as shaky a topic as Bellusdeo. She hoped.

"They wish to have the sergeant removed from her duties."

"The sergeant doesn't wish to be removed."

"Ah. I am to speak with Lord Grammayre on the morrow. Is this what he will tell me?"

"I don't know what he'll tell you. But I know that Moran doesn't want to abandon her duties."

"You are aware that she cannot fly?"

"Yes. I've offered to fix that, and she's refused. It's like she's Barrani."

"Her inability to fly is at the heart of the complaint."

"She's perfectly capable of running the infirmary without wings. The ceilings are too low for actual flight there, and she's not a Sword; she's not required to patrol. There's nothing she can't do—"

"Except return home at the end of the day."

"...Except that, yes."

The Emperor exhaled smoke. In that, he was much like Bellusdeo. "I assume, given your reaction, that you have already interfered."

"If offering her a place to stay is interfering, then yes, I have. I'm well acquainted with the laws of Elantra, and the offer hasn't broken any of them. She's free to say no."

"Given the tone of the envoy I received, she is only legally free to do so. Much of society is not governed by strict legality. You have offered her rooms in your manse?"

"Helen was fine with it, so yes, I did. She was living in the *infirmary*. I get that she doesn't want to go home—I'm not sure I would, either, if I were her. But she deserves way better than a cot in the infirmary."

"Ah. In that opinion, at least, you are of a mind with the

envoy." He smiled. It reminded Kaylin of how seldom he did so. "I confess that you seem to have had a...full...day."

Kaylin didn't miss a step, but it was a near thing. "I've had a day, yes," she replied carefully.

"And Bellusdeo?"

"Bellusdeo reminded me once again that she's a fully functional adult with a great deal more physical prowess and political know-how than I have." She glanced at the Emperor, who appeared to be watching the street, aware that she wasn't *in* her Dragon-proof home at the moment. "I'm sure you're aware that she's been observing the Hawks."

He nodded.

"We were called in on an investigation on the Winding Path; she came with us."

"Yes. So the Arkon said."

Which answered Kaylin's carefully unasked question. "Did he give you the details?"

"Yes."

"Does he consider the situation to be dangerous?"

"I would say, in different circumstances, that he was merely curious."

"But Bellusdeo's involved."

"Ah, no, you misunderstand. Certainly *I* would consider the risk of the unknown a danger if Bellusdeo is involved. The Arkon is not me. What do you intend to do?"

There were no Imperial Guards, no other Hawks, no Dragon Lords. The Emperor approached Kaylin this way because he intended to let her be herself. It was like a test, and she took the risk. She tried not to think of what failure would mean.

"I intend to twist Moran's arm so she stays in my house. I intend to visit the Palace to speak with the Arkon. And I intend to continue the investigation into the murder."

CHAPTER 10

"Please do so in exactly that order."

Kaylin did miss a step then.

The Emperor didn't smile; his expression made stone seem yielding and warm. But his eyes were almost gold, although the warmth was muted by raised inner membranes. "You are surprised."

Kaylin nodded.

"I am slightly amused by your current predicament. Private, when I ask for advice, I listen. I admit that I was dubious at first about the usefulness—or the quality—of your advice. I am less dubious now. Bellusdeo has not lived in my Empire for as long as even you. She does not understand it. She understands its ruler to the same extent that she understands the city.

"You were right. She was both helpful and necessary in the fight against the Barrani ancestor. I did not hesitate to lead the rest of the Dragon Court into battle, excepting only Bellusdeo. Were we to be faced with the same difficulty again, I would make different choices. I cannot, however, undo what was done; it is in the past. The past, of course, is a different country; it is occupied, frequently, by regret, and it is ruled by tyrants. They cannot be moved.

"I would not make the same error again. I wished to protect

Bellusdeo from certain danger. To protect her from uncertain danger would be, in her view, more of a crime, would it not?"

"I think so. She doesn't get mad at *me* if I try to stop her from doing things. I can tell her whatever I'm *thinking*, and she might be annoyed, but..."

"Not enraged."

"Not usually, no. It's different. I can't physically stop her from doing something. Even if I was intent on it, she's a Dragon. I'm not. Maggaron fusses over her as if she were a foundling—but in the end, he doesn't try to stop her from doing what she feels she should be doing. I try to learn from him. It's not easy; he's...not me."

"No more am I."

"No, but you're both not me in different ways." She exhaled. "Yes, I was afraid you'd turn me to ash if I let Bellusdeo follow me—not, as I mentioned, that I could stop her. But... I'm also really worried about Moran."

"This would be Sergeant Carafel? Moran dar Carafel?"

"Yes. I know you don't like dealing with the Caste Courts—" Kaylin stopped herself. If she could have bitten off her tongue, she would have done it.

The Dragon's eyes shaded to orange.

"No one complains about it," she said quickly—and inaccurately. "But...the Empire is yours. Having to make exceptions so that the Barrani—mostly—can skirt Imperial Law is never going to be something we appreciate."

One brow rose; the scar across his face had whitened. "Your Sergeant doesn't care for it."

This was the real reason why talking to the Emperor at all was so dangerous. Kaylin had once assumed that no one could relax in the Imperial Presence—but the upside to that was no one else could open their mouth so wide they could fit both feet in, and still have room for leg.

"Have you met Sergeant Kassan?" she asked.

"Yes. Not often. He is Leontine, and the Leontines are not notably formal. While he has adapted to the Barrani language and laws, its general customs have escaped him almost entirely. I will not hold the Sergeant responsible for anything you say."

"Thank you. No, really—*thank you.* Marcus is—Leontines are—more like *me* than the Barrani or the Dragons. They're sometimes more like me than the rest of the humans in the office. It's probably why we only *have* one Leontine. Marcus doesn't tell us secrets. Most people don't think he has any."

"I am well aware of the Hawks' view on Caste Court exemptions. If the Hawklord, the Wolflord and the Swordlord are more circumspect—and, Private, they are *vastly* more circumspect—they are nonetheless forthright. Do you know why I encourage racial integration among the Hawks, no matter how difficult it might otherwise be? It is precisely because I wish people to understand that there are costs to exemptions, and a diminishing respect for Imperial Law.

"If it is not clear to you, the decision involving Caste Courts and single-race crimes was a pragmatic one, and it was created almost in its entirety because of the Barrani. I did not wish my city to turn into a war zone. The Dragons would survive. The Barrani would survive."

"But not the rest of us."

"What do you think?"

"The Aerians might survive it."

"You have never seen the flights at war, if you believe that. I have. I am not *fond* of the exemptions. I am not fond of dealing with the representatives of the Caste Courts. I find it difficult not to reduce them to ash."

Kaylin remembered to close her mouth, because it was kind of hanging open, as if she'd forgotten it was attached to the rest of her face.

"Surely, given your own feelings, that cannot surprise you? I understand the concerns of the Aerian Caste Court—they were made quite clear. I am not, however, Aerian." His smile was sharp and cold. "And as I am not, matters which the Aerian Caste Court consider of import are not matters to which I must personally attend. It pleases me to note that they are stymied. If you fear censure from me, you will have to look elsewhere.

"For instance, if Bellusdeo is harmed in the fiefs, I will be... very angry."

This was what Kaylin had expected.

"But she would be quick to point out that were it not for your interference—in the fiefs, no less—she would not even be here. She would, of course, take longer to express the sentiment, and she would speak our native tongue. I do not propose to do so in the streets of my city." He slowed his pace. "I find this entire interaction taxing. But it is enlightening. Having made the decision to respect Bellusdeo, you still worry."

"Yes. But I think...I think that's natural. I mean, for mortals, it's natural. We kind of worry more about the people we know and care about."

"And you do not worry about yourself? Given the differences in power between a mortal and a Dragon, does this not strike you as ridiculous?"

"...No."

"You are about to enlighten me as to the reason."

"I don't really have a good reason. I live inside my mortal body. I know what I've survived. I know how much some of it hurt, and how much some of it terrified me. My own death, when it happens, isn't likely to upset me, because I won't be here. If someone else dies on me, I'll still be here for the rest of my life, and I'll be looking at a big, bleeding hole where they used to be.

"So... I guess it's still about me. And having had to make

that clear to you, I can't let that fear and that—that selfishness, govern what I do. But for me, it's hard. I have no idea what's going on in today's investigation yet, but it smells. I know breaking the law is always bad. I'm paid to know it. There are some things I hold my nose and just enforce. Sorry.

"But this case—it's got nothing to do with money. It's probably got something to do with power, if it has anything to do with *people* at all."

Squawk.

The Emperor blinked. "Your familiar has lost cohesion?"

Squawk.

"Is that a formal way of asking if he's invisible?"

"Ah, no. I have some experience with illusion and invisibility; I would be aware of him were he here and merely invisible. I am without guards and without my Court; I am not foolish enough to also forsake reasonable precautions. He is not merely invisible. I would not have said he was present at all were it not for his very audible voice."

"I don't really understand it myself, but at the moment he's here in a way that we—or at least I—can't see." She frowned.

"You are thinking again."

Still frowning, Kaylin began to walk. The familiar existed. He was here. She couldn't *see* him, and neither could the Emperor. She didn't understand it. No one else she knew did, either. But…small and squawky wasn't terrifying. And any reasonable person might consider that stupid: he could change size, he could fight with Dragons, he clearly had motives of his own.

More important, it wasn't the first strange invisibility-that-wasn't-invisibility of the day.

Annarion and Mandoran could *see* the little stinker. Teela and Tain couldn't. Helen *probably* could.

Helen couldn't be moved; she was a building. But Annarion

and Mandoran could. With the familiar's aid, they could even be moved safely. Kaylin wanted to take them to the crime site and ask them what they saw. Were the bodies similar to the familiar in his current state?

They were there. They were physical, they were real, they were lifeless.

But until she'd removed the familiar's wing from her eyes, she hadn't *seen* them. It was the inverse of invisibility, to most people. And most would have no reason to doubt the truth of their senses—and their prior experience.

She turned in the direction of the familiar's voice. "You're like the bodies."

His squawk was softer and more encouraging. It didn't, however, give her any new information. She remembered, belatedly, that she had company when said company cleared his throat, which was never a promising sound.

"I'm sorry. The small dragon is hooked into a reality that the rest of us can't directly experience, being alive, corporeal and…well, actually, that's all I know. Helen understands it better, but she can't explain it in words we have concepts for."

"You think your current investigation is somehow connected to this phenomenon."

"I am *really* hoping it isn't. But…yes."

"I ask that you do what I cannot," he said. This was an enormously humbling request, but Kaylin's mouth was already closed and she managed to keep it that way.

"She doesn't hate you," Kaylin replied—which, as replies went, was strictly third class—or lower. "She understands, probably better than I do, what Elantra means to you. She understands what her presence theoretically means to the Dragons. But she is never, ever going to beg more than she already has. And before you say she hasn't, she's living here. She came here with pretty much nothing. She has no money, no power and no status *of her own*. The one thing she has to offer, her one area of expertise, is Shadow."

"And Shadow is unpredictably dangerous."

"Yes. Believe that she's aware of that."

"You are not saying this idly." His eyes grew more orange.

"…No. I'm doing that thing that I always do."

"Babble?"

She reddened. "Yes, that, too. I'm talking *myself* into doing the right thing, even when I don't want to do it. I told you before—my big fear isn't about dying. It's about losing the people I love.

"And Shadows don't care about love. Or at least not about the people I love."

"I understood that. Do you intend to take Bellusdeo into Shadow?"

"I don't intend to *take* her anywhere. But…she intends to follow wherever this leads. I can't actually order her to remain behind and expect her to obey me."

"And I—nominally—can."

Kaylin nodded.

"This is a test?"

No one with a functioning brain tested the Emperor.

His eyes, a deeper orange in color, made clear just how little he appreciated this. But he understood that if orders were to be given, he had to be the one to give them. And he now understood that the orders would have consequences. "I will not, as you call it, turn you to ash if Bellusdeo survives. There are things she might, in time, forgive. Your death at my hands will never be one of them. If she perishes while in your care, her opinion of your death will no longer be relevant.

"You have never seen me angry."

She had seen him angry at least once, but wasn't stupid enough to correct him.

"She is not mine," the Emperor continued. "She is not my hoard."

"Could she ever be someone's? Could *you*?" It had never occurred to Kaylin until this moment that the concept of "hoard" was elastic enough to encompass actual people. Given the Emperor's expression, that was probably for the best.

"She is a *Dragon*," he replied.

"I take it that's a no."

"I will speak with the Halls' educational liaison. Your lack of fundamental knowledge is appalling."

"Do female Dragons have hoards?"

"I will speak with the liaison the moment I return to the Palace." He hesitated, which should have been a big red flag. "I had hoped to invite Bellusdeo to dinner."

"At the Palace?"

"At any place of her choosing. No," he added, looking even more uncomfortable, "I wish to choose a place in which she would feel comfortable."

"Oh, that's easy."

"Not, apparently, for an Emperor."

"Come to dinner at our place." The minute the words left her mouth, she felt stranded by them, but she had no way to reel them back in. "Are you— Do you mean to come as the Emperor?"

"No."

"I mean, you *are* the Emperor and that doesn't really change—but—" She stopped digging.

"I understand why Lord Diarmat finds you so difficult. Bellusdeo, however, does not. I intend to issue the invitation in person, and I hope to be less...formal."

She doubted he could be more formal than he was in the audience chambers in which he and Bellusdeo had had several very audible arguments. "I'm really not great at relationship advice. Really, *really* not great at it. So I want you to keep that in mind."

"I will not hold you responsible."

"Unless she dies?"

"Yes. It is unlikely that an invitation to an informal dinner will kill her."

"Was that a joke?"

"I am not entirely without a sense of humor; I have been told mine is very, very dry."

Dry enough to spontaneously catch fire apparently, which, given Dragon breath, was not ideal. "An informal invitation would work, I think. I don't want her to be upset, and I don't want her to think I'm ratting her out."

"I will attempt not to take offense. When do you believe she will be free?"

Kaylin, thinking of Ravellon, the fiefs and Annarion, almost shrugged. Because her companion was the Emperor, she didn't. "Tomorrow, she'll come with me to visit the Arkon. And after that we're probably going to chance Nightshade. So, tomorrow is no good.

"I don't know what will happen in Nightshade. Give it a few days—maybe five? When Bellusdeo puts on her war hat, she's pretty focused. She takes Shadow personally."

"I am aware of that."

"If you want to strategize—without insulting or minimizing her advice or experience—that would probably be the best thing you could offer her. But not if you're going to end up having another deafening 'discussion' about her safety."

"Perhaps I will do exactly that," he surprised Kaylin by saying. "It will give us something to talk about that is less awkward."

"What do you normally talk about?"

"You and Lord Diarmat. And yes, the importance of her safety. I will attempt to avoid all three subjects."

Living in a sentient building was almost heaven. There were one or two drawbacks, however.

Helen insisted that Kaylin eat breakfast. Kaylin didn't usually have time, given her early-morning routine—which involved falling out of bed, shoving herself into the nearest clothing and heading for the door at a run.

Helen blamed this familiar routine on Kaylin's irregular hours and her inability to wake up on time. Since she couldn't change Kaylin's working hours, she'd settled for waking Kaylin in time to eat. Today, for the first time since she had changed Kaylin's familiar routine, Kaylin had company.

Moran was seated on the left side of the table when Kaylin entered the room. She was dressed for work and appeared to be far more awake than Kaylin felt.

She smiled, and her face didn't crack. "Not in the Halls, remember?"

Kaylin nodded and took a seat, looking at Moran. The Aerian's color was better. The tight slope of her shoulders had eased. She looked comfortable at this table. "Did you sleep?"

"Yes. I slept well."

"And she woke well," Helen added.

"Where are you?" Kaylin asked.

"With Annarion. He is in a much better mood than he was yesterday. He spent some time speaking with Hope—and I think you named him well, even if you find the name too sentimental to actually use. He's looking forward to your outing. We'll be joining you shortly."

Bellusdeo entered the dining room before Helen and Annarion reached it. She nodded at Moran and took the seat across from the Aerian. "Have you decided to join us?"

That was the only question on Kaylin's mind, but she hadn't had the guts to ask it.

Moran pushed food around her plate as if it took effort. When she lifted her head, she looked to Kaylin. "You understand that this might cause difficulty for you?"

Kaylin shrugged. "What doesn't?"

"It might cause difficulty for the Hawklord, too—and I owe Grammayre more than trouble."

"Has he told you not to stay?"

"I don't think he considered the possibility, or it's likely he would have."

Kaylin's expression made clear that she didn't believe it.

"It might cause difficulty for the Emperor, as well."

"The Emperor doesn't get involved in difficulties with the Caste Courts." She hesitated. Everyone in the room—and one person who wasn't, yet—marked it. "And frankly, the Emperor would probably be pleased if you accepted our offer."

"Oh?" Bellusdeo said, in a distinctly chillier voice. "What makes you say that?"

"She's spoken with the Emperor," Helen replied, when Kaylin didn't.

Bellusdeo's eyes drifted, predictably, toward orange. "When?"

Kaylin's food appeared, along with Helen and their two Barrani housemates. "Last evening, I believe. I didn't hear the conversation, though; the Emperor did not stay."

"The Emperor came here," Bellusdeo said. It wasn't a question.

"Yes, dear."

"Why, exactly?" She asked the question of Kaylin, who was now looking at breakfast with an amazing lack of appetite.

"He's worried, of course," Helen replied again—coming, in the worst way possible, to Kaylin's rescue.

Annarion and Mandoran made a wide, wide circle around

Helen and came to the table. They chose seats as far from Bellusdeo as the table stretched.

"If it's any comfort," Mandoran said, "we get this from Teela all the time. It's like she thinks we're children."

This was clearly no comfort to Bellusdeo.

"And if that isn't," Annarion added, "Teela—and several of our other friends—are telling Mandoran to shut up."

The Dragon's lips twitched at the corners, and the color of her eyes lightened.

"You worry for the Arkon, dear," Helen pointed out softly. "He does not find this insulting or condescending."

"No. But I don't tell him what to do. I can't give him orders. Had he come to me with his plan to face the ancient, I would never have attempted to forbid it."

"Do you place no value on your own life?"

"I don't need to" was Bellusdeo's bitter reply. "Everyone else is always telling me what I'm worth."

Moran cleared her throat.

It was a familiar sound; had Kaylin been speaking, she would have shut up instantly.

"Helen, is it always this noisy first thing in the morning?"

"Sadly, no. The house hasn't been this lively in a while."

"Lively."

"There is goodwill beneath the frustration and anger," Helen replied, her smile serene. "And affection. I have missed it. Understand, Moran," she continued, as she drifted around the table, "that all living things yearn for purpose. Mine is—and always has been—to become a home. But a home is defined entirely by the people who live in it.

"If you will allow it, I would be honored to make a home for you until you can once again return to the Southern Reach."

Moran settled her hands in her lap. "What will it cost me?"

"That, dear, is for you to decide. Obligation and a sense of personal debt are too delicate and too complex for a simple building to navigate."

Bellusdeo's snort had smoke in it.

"But regardless, that decision is not in my hands. This is Kaylin's home. I imagine that the entire cost will be written in pride. Yours," she added softly.

Moran glanced at Kaylin and then at Bellusdeo. To the Dragon, she said, "The Emperor is merely worried. He is Emperor. He has not forbidden you freedom of action."

"He has made the attempt."

"Perhaps you do not understand our Emperor," the Hawk continued. Kaylin's jaw dropped. "He is not, historically, incompetent enough to make unsuccessful attempts. If he has attempted to move you by discussion, debate or even argument—"

"A *lot* of argument," Kaylin said.

Moran ignored this. "He has not commanded."

Bellusdeo said nothing for a long beat, but when she exhaled, she lost two stiff inches of rigid height.

"I understand the formal protocols of the Empire are foreign to you; I understand that Lord Diarmat is…problematic. But even a private in the Hawks can see that the Emperor is trying to accommodate you. It is not something he is generally accused of being—accommodating, that is. He will probably get it wrong more often than right. Frankly, were you Aerian, you would not be allowed to fly outside of the Aerie. You would not be allowed to go anywhere unaccompanied."

Bellusdeo could have pointed out that she wasn't unaccompanied. She didn't. Instead, she exhaled more air than she could have possibly inhaled and folded her arms. "What did he come here for?" she asked.

Seeing an opportunity, Kaylin said, "He wanted to join us for dinner."

"Join us."

Some opportunities *were* disasters. "He doesn't want to be your enemy. Inasmuch as Emperors have friends, I think he'd like to be one of yours." When Bellusdeo failed to reply, she continued, "You understand the burdens of a ruler. You were one. Dragons are not known for their ability to gracefully accept advice or criticism—but I think you have more in common with the Emperor than you think. Except for your sense of humor."

"Oh?"

"I don't think he has one."

Mandoran snickered. So did Bellusdeo.

"Did he say when?"

"I think that's going to be up to you. Look, I can't tell you how to behave around the Emperor. I wouldn't be stuck in Diarmat's hell class if I was qualified to do that. But...he'd be here without his stuck-up, wooden guards, and he wouldn't be sitting on a throne. It probably wouldn't be boring."

"Are we invited?" Mandoran asked.

"Absolutely not," Bellusdeo replied.

They devolved into bickering, and Kaylin looked back to Moran. To her surprise, the formidable sergeant was smiling.

"You'll probably regret it," she told Kaylin. "But...yes. If the offer is still open, I'd like to stay here until my wing is healed."

"About the wing—"

"On its own."

CHAPTER 11

Ditching Annarion and Mandoran proved to be much, much more of a problem than Kaylin had anticipated. Helen was willing to allow them to leave if they accompanied Kaylin, as her familiar could more or less keep them hidden from the non-mortal Shadows who seemed to hear them so clearly.

Teela didn't particularly care for either the Arkon or the Imperial Palace; she could tolerate them, but she never sought them out willingly. She hadn't, therefore, insisted on accompanying Kaylin. Severn had shown up at the front door as a reminder of the appointment she'd already managed to miss once.

Annarion was willing to follow Teela's lead. Mandoran was not, and Annarion wasn't willing to let Mandoran be the only Barrani representative from their collective crew. But Severn considered the visit less risky than Kaylin did, and in the end, Kaylin had agreed to let them accompany her. She was fairly certain Marcus's fur—all of it—would be standing on end if he knew, but it was easier to grovel and beg forgiveness than to ask permission.

The Arkon had wanted to meet them, anyway.

Bellusdeo, uncertain that the argument would ever end, left first. "I do not find Lannagaros's company taxing," she said on the way out. "Given recent events, I find it exactly the opposite."

Since Annarion and Mandoran were now part of the visit to the Arkon, Teela also accompanied them, and wasn't entirely pleased about it. Or quiet.

"...And I'm warning you now that if the two of you touch *anything* in his collection, we'll all be smoldering ash. Just—if you could be quiet and still, it would be helpful to *my* continued employment. And existence. And when I say 'you,' I mean Mandoran." Teela could have said this silently; she had their True Names. She didn't need to speak out loud.

"Plausible deniability," Teela said, correctly guessing Kaylin's thoughts. "Honestly, the primary reason I'd never give you my True Name is because it wouldn't be advantageous to me—what you think is so plainly written across your face I don't need you to speak out loud to catch it."

Mandoran pulled a face. "I swear, once we've gotten your brother, I'm going back to the green."

Annarion winced, but said nothing.

Kaylin didn't believe him, because she wasn't that lucky. She kept this to herself, with effort. Gilbert. Kattea. Evanton's concern about ancient, mysterious ruins. The bodies that disappeared when she looked at them the wrong way. There were too many things that were strange and wrong, and Kaylin was attempting to juggle them all.

She was a crap juggler. Eventually they were going to come raining down on her head.

She'd appreciate it if that didn't happen while the Arkon was present.

The Arkon met them at the library doors, although the library was well-staffed during daylight hours. Said staff were watching the visitors with barely concealed interest; they appeared to be tending to their various jobs. Kaylin had no doubt they would all be talking in muted whispers the minute the visitors were out of earshot.

The Arkon's eyes were a shade of orange that immediately set Kaylin's teeth on edge. "You said you wanted to meet them," she began.

"You will be silent for at least the next fifteen minutes." He paused. "My apologies, Lord Teela, but I must insist that you, and your companions, also comply with my request."

It certainly wasn't phrased like a request.

"Morgrim, please call the librarians to the desk. The interruption to their regular duties should be minimal."

"This should cause no discomfort."

"What should cause no discomfort?" Kaylin asked.

The Arkon's answer was typical: it had nothing to do with the question she'd asked. "You have brought two visitors."

"You *wanted* to meet them."

"Yes, I did. I am delighted to have the opportunity to do so." Delight was clearly the same as suspicion, at least for Dragons. "But they have—to use your colloquial phrase—tripped a number of protective wards on their passage through the gallery. I wish to ascertain that their presence here will not harm the more susceptible parts of my archive."

She glanced at the library's front desk. The librarians were gathered behind it. Actually, they were *huddling* behind it. This did nothing to ease her worry. But her arms didn't ache; her skin didn't feel as if it was being peeled off. If there was magic in use, it was not the type of magic to which she was apparently allergic.

The Arkon began to speak. His lips moved in slow motion, and he raised his hands, turning his palms slowly toward the ceiling.

Kaylin felt the air crackle. She wouldn't have been surprised to see lightning strike, but had the suspicion that it wasn't the *floor* it would hit first. Teela's eyes were very blue.

Mandoran's and Annarion's were almost black. They didn't arm themselves; they didn't run. They didn't try to stop the Arkon. But their mouths, unlike the Arkon's, were compressed, tight lines and white around the edges.

Words began to form in the air around the Arkon. Literally.

If true words had irrevocable meaning, they clearly also conveyed tone. Or perhaps it was just the choice of words. These were a deeper blue than any previous words the Arkon had chosen, laboriously, to speak, and although they were glowing, they felt...dark. And cold. She had walked around the visible representation of ancient and unknowable words such as this before; she had even touched them.

She did not want to touch these. Ever.

The air grew colder.

Squawk.

The Arkon frowned. His eyes were a steady, pale orange. If the words were as dangerous as they felt to Kaylin, they were not spoken in anger, if they were even being spoken at all. When Sanabalis spoke ancient, true words, Kaylin could hear them. She could hear the timbre of his voice, the rumbling native to Dragons, even in human form; she could hear the stretch of syllables. The language itself felt familiar, every time, but she could not understand a word of it. Nor could she easily memorize any of the spoken component.

This time, she didn't even want to try.

Squawk. Squawk.

The Arkon's hands stilled. His eyes narrowed. His expression fell into much more familiar lines, although the color of his eyes didn't shift to gold. He closed his mouth. When he opened it again, it moved naturally, because he spoke normally.

Squawk.

"Yes, the Emperor advised me of your current state."

Squawk. Kaylin had been holding her breath. She needed to breathe, but had almost forgotten how. In all of the reports she had written about the attack on the High Halls in the heart of the city, she had failed to mention Annarion's visit to Castle Nightshade. Deliberately.

The Emperor would, of course, be enraged. He would demand Annarion and Mandoran be subject to confinement—in the best possible case. People had died. *Hawks* had died. Homes had been melted or burned to the ground. The fact that Annarion had had no intention of waking ancient, hostile demigods wouldn't bring any of the dead back to life.

But as the small and invisible familiar continued to squawk, the true words faded, losing solidity and finally disappearing from view. It wasn't *those* words she was now worried about, but she couldn't make that clear without damning herself—or Annarion.

She was surprised when Severn touched her shoulder. He said nothing. But she found she could breathe again.

"Kaylin," the Arkon said, as if her breathing was displeasing, "do you understand what your familiar is saying?"

"No more than usual."

"He claims that it is not your companions who tripped my wards."

Kaylin grimaced. "I'm sorry," she said, "but I wasn't aware of any wards on the walk here."

The Arkon frowned. "You are aware of wards in general."

She nodded. "They make my skin itch. Door wards actually hurt. But silencing wards or privacy wards don't, unless I trip them."

"These wards are different. They are not meant to stop idle

chatter. No wards of any significant power would stop that in these halls."

"What are they meant to do, then?"

"They are a very rudimentary set of Shadow wards. They provide warning and detection of things that are not immediately visible to the naked eye."

"They do more than that," Mandoran said. Kaylin wanted to kick him. Given the way his jaw snapped shut, Teela probably had, and more effectively. This did not, however, shut him up. "What were you trying to do, there?"

"The wards are, as I said, rudimentary. The words I was attempting to speak are less so. They prevent unwanted intrusion. You wish to add something, Private?"

She didn't. The Arkon, however, was glaring at her. "I wouldn't walk past them if I had any choice."

He raised a brow.

"They were true words."

"Indeed."

"They weren't friendly."

"They are not inflected. They serve a very specific purpose and they are seldom spoken."

"I couldn't hear you speak them at all."

He frowned. To Mandoran, he asked, "Could you?"

"I can still hear the echoes."

"And your friend?"

Annarion was tight-lipped and blue-eyed. He did not respond.

Mandoran answered for him. "Yes."

Teela cleared her throat. "The man with whom you are conversing is Mandoran of Casarre."

"And his companion?"

Teela exhaled. "Annarion."

"Annarion."

"Of Solanace," Annarion added.

Teela's breath cut the air.

"Interesting." The Arkon clearly understood the significance of what had just been said. "I was under the impression that that line had come to an end."

"You were mistaken."

It was Mandoran's turn to look queasy.

"I am a Dragon. I am not Barrani. The information that comes to us is, of necessity, incomplete. I apologize if I have been misinformed." He turned to Kaylin. "Your familiar has claimed full responsibility for the safety of my archive."

Meaning it would be her fault if anything unexpected happened. She exhaled a few inches of height. "Yes, sir."

"Bellusdeo is waiting. She has been keeping an old man company."

"Did she mention our latest investigation?"

"Yes. She also extended an invitation to dinner. Do not stand in the library gawking. If you have something to say, say it while we walk. Ah. My apologies," he said, turning once again to the two Barrani visitors. "I am the Arkon of the Emperor's flight. This library and the contents of its archives is my hoard."

Kaylin's biggest question, as she followed the Arkon's impatient lead, was *Yes, but are you going to accept?*

Squawk.

She missed a step, her eyes narrowing in the rough direction of the small dragon voice. "Can I ask you a question?"

"Several, if history is our guide."

"Why are you willing to trust my familiar?"

"That question is even intelligent."

Squawk.

"Yes, intelligent enough that I will answer it."

If he'd been sitting on her shoulder, she'd have clamped a hand over his tiny mouth.

"I am willing to trust him because he is yours."

"But—but—"

"Yes?"

"You don't trust *me* that much!"

"Ah. I don't trust your competence, no. You are far too impulsive—too young—but I see that you have that in common with the two visitors you have brought." Mandoran, who had started to look smug, frowned. "Your familiar's competence, I trust. He is not young. I am not certain he has ever been young."

"But he was just born—"

"—during the chaos spell, yes. But *born* is inexact in this case. He *emerged*. If you think that his existence began with an eggshell, you are wrong. His competence is wed to your *intent*. Your intent, Private Neya, only a fool would distrust." When Kaylin failed to reply, he continued, "You do not understand the forces with which you now interact. That is to be expected; even *I* do not understand them fully.

"Your familiar understands them far better than either of us. But he *is* your familiar. He has chosen you. Until you perish—and given your history, that is likely to be sooner than later—he serves you. You can command him, but you do not; you will not learn how. Nor," he added, lifting a hand to still her protest, "can I teach you. What your familiar would be in my hands, he cannot be in yours—but I do not think, in the end, he would have consented to serve me. He came to you."

"He wasn't born to me," she pointed out.

"Was he not?" He gestured at a patch of blank wall, and the wall faded. As far as doors went, this was preferable—the wall had no wards that Kaylin was expected to touch. Bellusdeo was, as the Arkon had said, waiting. She was seated in a room that was almost shockingly bare.

Usually, there was so much *stuff* everywhere that it wasn't even safe to *walk*.

Bellusdeo rose to greet them. "Lannagaros and I have been discussing the investigation to which you are currently assigned."

"Can he make any more sense of it than we can?"

"Almost certainly," the Arkon replied before Bellusdeo could. "But regrettably, more sense and enough sense are not the same. I am concerned," he added. "I have been told that the Keeper is also concerned. And anything that concerns the Keeper..." He walked into the room. It housed not a desk, but a table, much like a dining room table. The centerpiece of that table was a stone pyramid. The Arkon took a seat at the head of the table.

Teela's eyes had not gotten any greener, but she took the chair beside Bellusdeo. Severn took the chair to the Arkon's immediate left, and Kaylin sat beside him; Mandoran and Annarion sat beside her.

Kaylin turned to Bellusdeo. "Did you mention Kattea?"

"And Gilbert, yes," the Arkon again replied on her behalf. "Understand that Bellusdeo has lost more to Shadow than you have ever owned. Her fears are rational; they are based in experience. Her knowledge is invaluable.

"You came to ask me about the bodies?"

She'd come because he'd pretty much demanded her presence, but she was politic enough not to say this out loud. "I came to ask about the bodies, but also ancient ruins and their entry points."

"Records," the Arkon said.

Light spread from the apex of the small pyramid, rising in a familiar, oval shape. It was a mirror, of a sort, but it had no back, no silvered front. Anyone seated at the table could see the images it produced. "Records: location."

The image that everyone could clearly see was a familiar display of Elantran streets. It saw regular use in the Halls of Law. The Arkon then said a word that was not Elantran, but not—given the volume—draconian, either.

It caused all Barrani eyes in the room to widen.

"Personal Records: historical map, variant 22B. Overlay current map location."

The lines of the current map faded until they could only barely be seen. Other lines, however, joined them. The Arkon snorted smoke. "Historical map variant 2A." As the historical map faded and reappeared, the Arkon's eyes narrowed. "Historical event map, by location. Significant nexus disturbances."

This time, the map lit up areas that Kaylin recognized. One was a big, glowing blue blotch over what would otherwise be Elani Street. She started to pay attention then. She could guess what that event was; she'd witnessed it.

She hadn't witnessed any of the others, but there were others. The map didn't give event dates, just locations. Without thinking, she said, "Records, enlarge map." Nothing, of course, happened.

Bellusdeo then repeated Kaylin's command, and this time—naturally—the map grew. So did the oval that contained it. At the heart of the city, bounded by rivers and walls, lay the fiefs. No streets could be seen; there was a blur of glowing gray, gray and more gray, that grew darker as it reached the center of the fiefs themselves.

"Ravellon."

"It should come as no surprise to you that disturbances of any significance once occurred there. Look at the Winding Path." As he spoke, the map once again moved; Ravellon fell off the edge of the image.

Gray covered the whole of the midsection of the long Winding Path. At its center was the house in which the bodies had been discovered.

CHAPTER 12

"Gray is bad, right?" Mandoran asked. When Teela glared at the side of his face, he laughed. "I'm joking, Teela. Joking. You remember what jokes are, right?"

"Gray," the Arkon said, in a voice so dry it should have caught fire, and might well yet, "is, as you put it, bad."

"I'm wondering why the Hawks don't have a similar map," Teela added.

"You have a good working knowledge of current events; you could place those events and re-create a large portion of the relevant, modern map." The implied *if you weren't so lazy and shortsighted* hung in the air without the actual need to be said. "The reason the gray is so dark in Elani is because—"

"That's where the Keeper is," Kaylin finished.

"Indeed. We do not distrust the Keeper, precisely. But his abode is in the heart of the Emperor's hoard."

"How long ago was the previous difficulty on the Winding Path?" Teela asked, as Kaylin simultaneously demanded to know what, exactly, the difficulty *was*.

"Centuries ago," the Arkon replied, answering Teela's question. Kaylin's he left hanging, like bad laundry. "I believe you have had access to the archives of the Arcanum."

"I do not have access to those archives at present."

"No, of course not. You're a Hawk." He stared at her.

"I'll ask," Teela grudgingly offered. "But I'll be expected to offer some information in return."

"We have no information at present, and Arcanists are famously difficult when they decide to investigate on their own. Perhaps it is wise to contain that request for the time being."

Teela nodded.

"You entered the subbasement. Did you note anything of significance aside from the magical detritus on the walls?"

"No. The Halls would welcome your investigation, should you decide to visit the site in person." This was exaggeration, if not an outright lie.

"Given my last excursion, I do not plan to leave my library for at least a decade."

"Not even for dinner?" Bellusdeo asked.

She could have stabbed him in the leg and caused less obvious pain, in Kaylin's opinion. "I will, of course, be delighted to accept your offer of hospitality."

Bellusdeo laughed. Her eyes were pure gold. "At your age, Lannagaros, you should be a much better liar."

"I have had enough power in my life that I have never been forced to learn the art of dissembling." To Kaylin, he said, "Your familiar does not feel that...Gilbert...poses an immediate threat. I wish you to ascertain what Gilbert's presence means. His presence across the street from this unusual murder—and basement—cannot be a coincidence. Bellusdeo will accompany you when you interview him."

Kaylin opened her mouth, thought better and closed it again.

The Arkon then turned to Mandoran. Kaylin didn't understand a word that left his mouth when he spoke to the Barrani youth. Teela didn't immediately understand them, either, but her expression made it clear that Mandoran did.

"I cannot believe," Mandoran said, as his eyes shaded to indigo, "that you are still alive. The High Lord did not understand just how much of a threat you posed."

"The High Lord approves of the Arkon," Kaylin pointed out.

"He refers," Teela said, in a brittle voice, "to the High Lord who reigned at the time of the last of our great wars. He has had no interaction with the reigning High Lord."

"What exactly did he *say*?"

"Nothing that you need to hear," Teela snapped. It had been a long time since Teela had used that tone of voice; the last time Kaylin could remember hearing it, they'd been caught in the cross fire of a magical fight. An illegal one. And Kaylin had still been a mascot.

Bellusdeo, however, folded her arms. "Perhaps Kaylin doesn't," she conceded. "I, however, would like an explanation. Arkon?"

The Arkon looked at Mandoran and Annarion. To Kaylin's great surprise, he didn't respond to Bellusdeo, either. "You said you were of the Solanace line."

Annarion nodded.

"You are aware that the line ended when your brother was made Outcaste."

"I am Solanace," Annarion said. "I have committed no crime. I have broken no law."

"You will not take the mantle of your father's line if you do not face the test of the High Halls."

"No."

"You are aware that your ancestral lands are in the hands of your cousin."

"Why, exactly, do you know so much about the Solanace family?" Kaylin asked.

"I know many things. If I were to catalog them all, you would die of old age—or possibly fire. I do not enjoy your constant interruptions." This last had more thunder in it. "I did not threaten your companion. I merely wished to know how much he would understand."

"What language were you speaking?"

"An old, dead tongue."

"An old dead tongue, more to the point," Teela said, rising at last, "that *I* have not personally encountered. Mandoran and Annarion were exposed to the same languages that I was, in my youth; they have not been exposed to the breadth of languages that I have since our separation."

"Then you will have something to chat about on your way out."

Kaylin blinked.

"Bellusdeo told me everything of value. You will, as I said, speak with Gilbert. You will keep me informed."

"Of course." Kaylin smiled. "Dinner in five days?"

The Arkon exhaled smoke in a steady stream. Bellusdeo came to stand beside Kaylin. Her smile, which looked genuine and made her face seem so much younger, deepened.

"I cannot think why I missed you in your long absence."

"Of course not. Come. If we must build bridges—and why, exactly, *bridge* is a good metaphor when we can all fly, I don't know—help me to establish a different paradigm. You were there at the beginning. Be here now."

Bellusdeo was still chortling when they left the Palace.

"He didn't answer any questions," Kaylin pointed out.

"He answered most of mine earlier, and he doesn't like to repeat himself."

"Except when he's being critical."

"He's seldom critical of me."

Of course not.

"But he was *always* critical when I was young. It makes me nostalgic. He was so stiff and so proper it was fun to tease him."

"Should I ask what Dragon teasing entails?"

"No. Teela is already giving me the side-eye." Still smiling, she said, "His interactions with you remind me of the way he always treated us—me and my sisters. I do not believe you could annoy him so much that he would kill you; he has some affection for you." Her smile faded. "All of my attempts to irritate him come to nothing now; he pities me too much."

"I would have thought that would be life-ending. His life."

"He is old, Kaylin."

"Which should make it—"

"Age in the immortal sense does not mean what it does for your kind. If I truly meant to kill him, I would resort to poison. I am not sure I could do enough damage, otherwise."

"He would never kill you."

"In self-defense, we are more…primal."

"And why, exactly, are we talking about your possible death at the hands of the Arkon?" Kaylin glanced at the rest of the company. They all looked amused.

"It passes time," Bellusdeo replied. "And it is pleasant enough to consider in the abstract."

Kaylin was never going to understand immortals.

Convince Moran to stay with Helen. Check.

Visit the Arkon. Check. She had even managed to sneak in the possibility of an informal Imperial dinner.

Squawk.

She should have felt at least a little accomplished. But sometimes the world—her world—seemed so fragile. One wrong move, one moment of unrelieved ignorance, and it was over. The Devourer had almost destroyed it. The idiot who had hoped to take over the *power* of the Keeper—without any of the responsibility, of course—could have destroyed it. If the heart of the green had been destroyed, if Mandoran and Annarion had returned to the world without the tenuous link to the names that had given them life, Kaylin thought it likely that the world would have eventually ended, as well.

The fact that it hadn't implied, strongly, that they'd been collectively lucky. And relying on luck was a mug's game. The only reliable thing about luck was that it was a coin toss. It could come up heads or tails, good or bad, win or lose. If you played long enough, bad was inevitable.

"Kaylin," Mandoran said.

She stopped.

"Where are you going?"

"Didn't you hear the Arkon?"

"I did."

"Well, then. I'm going to visit Gilbert and Kattea."

Teela said, "Your stomach is making so much noise I can hardly hear myself think. We're almost near the midmarket. Pick up something to eat—for all of us—on the way there. Bellusdeo can pay."

"Oh?" the Dragon said.

"The Emperor will see to any reasonable expense you accrue. Even if he offered to do so for Kaylin, ranks of bureaucracy stand in the way of her refund." When Bellusdeo failed to respond, Teela grinned. "Look, he has to be good for something."

The gold Dragon snorted. But she paid.

Kattea was far more subdued on their second visit than she had been on the first. Her eyes did light up when Bellusdeo presented her with the basket that contained a late lunch; she didn't even wilt when Kaylin explained that the day had been so grueling none of them had had time to eat yet.

The small dragon squawked. A lot.

"Is Gilbert in?" Kaylin asked.

"Yes. He's busy."

"Does he need to eat? I mean, can you interrupt him?"

"He knows you're here."

Kaylin frowned. The difference in Kattea was so marked, she dropped straight into worry. "Did something happen last night?"

Kattea shook her head. She glanced once over her shoulder, and when she turned back, her face was shuttered. She was polite; her body language was deferential. But she might have been an orphan navigating the streets of Nightshade, she was suddenly so wary.

Kaylin knew that wariness well, she had lived with it herself for so long. "Ferals?"

The girl froze. "There are no Ferals on this side of the bridge," she whispered. As if it were a prayer. As if she almost didn't believe it.

Kaylin had been there, too. "No, there aren't. Not unless something goes badly, badly wrong. Was Gilbert injured?" So many shots in the dark. But this one hit its mark.

Kattea nodded.

"Have you eaten?"

She shook her head.

"Eat with us?"

Wariness, again.

Kaylin smacked her own forehead. "This is Annarion, and this is Mandoran. They weren't here yesterday, but they're friends. They're Teela's friends. They are not the fieflord's thugs."

"Are they Hawks, too?"

"Not yet."

Annarion looked gray green. Mandoran looked as if he
wanted to add something. He didn't.

Kattea's wariness diminished as she ate. Gilbert, however,
did not make an appearance, and when Kaylin was certain
that her stomach wouldn't embarrass her, she rose. "Kattea?"

The girl glanced at the Barrani—all of them. Kaylin had a
very bad feeling.

"Will you take me to see Gilbert? If he's injured, I might
be able to help."

Bellusdeo rose, as well. Her eyes were not quite orange yet;
her expression suggested that if Kaylin insisted on going to see
Gilbert without backup, they would be.

"You can't help him. He said no one could help. Not even
me."

"Want to make a bet?"

Kattea's eyes narrowed. "For what?"

She really was a child after Kaylin's own heart. Since Bellusdeo had paid for lunch, Kaylin fished around in her pockets
and drew out two silver coins. They were as round as Kattea's
eyes became. "I...can't match that."

"No. What will you bet?"

"What do you want?"

"Information. If I *can* help Gilbert, you have to answer my
questions as truthfully as you can."

Kattea weighed the stakes. She looked momentarily crafty
and calculating. "I'll take it," she said, standing. "You can
come see Gilbert."

By unspoken consent, Kaylin and Bellusdeo left the room
together. Severn, Kaylin's partner, remained behind with the
Barrani.

"Did any Barrani come here yesterday?" Kaylin asked. "I mean, besides us?"

"You haven't won the bet yet."

Bellusdeo lifted a brow behind Kattea's back, but made no comment until the girl bypassed the stairs that led to the bedrooms. She headed to the door that led to the basement, instead. Of course it had to be the basement.

Bellusdeo's eyes were orange by the time Kattea opened the squeaking door. Kaylin's would have shifted to orange or blue if human eyes changed color with mood. She glanced at her arms. Her skin didn't hurt, which would have been a comfort in other circumstances, but the marks on her arms had begun to glow.

Bellusdeo couldn't fail to notice. Light seeped through the dark, full-length sleeves Kaylin habitually wore while on duty.

The basement was not well lit. Some homes had window-wells at the height of basement walls; the previous owners of this one obviously hadn't seen much use for them.

The stairs ended.

"Is it always this dark down here?" Kaylin asked their guide.

Kattea did not carry a lamp or a torch. Her left hand trailed the wall as she walked, but the light from the door above them ended abruptly. It was replaced by a lot of darkness.

Bellusdeo could see in the dark; so could Teela and Tain. Kaylin and Severn required a bit of help. So, in theory, should Kattea. "Gilbert says you need light," Kattea said, a hint of question in her voice.

"In general, yes. You don't?"

"Not if Gilbert's here."

Kaylin silently kissed two silver coins goodbye as Kattea led them farther into the basement. She forgot about the bet when she realized that the floor beneath her patrolling boots was made of solid stone. Reaching out, she touched a wall that was also solid stone; it felt smooth to the touch. Smooth and cold.

"This is a large basement," Bellusdeo said, presumably to Kattea.

"It's *really* big," Kattea agreed. "It's mostly empty."

As they walked, the word *mostly* echoed in the invisible heights above their heads. The sound of their steps in unison made the kind of noise that suggested vaulted ceilings and a deplorable lack of carpeting.

"Kattea—is this how you found the house?"

She didn't answer.

"Tell Gilbert that he's right. I need the light." It was funny how little it helped when light flooded the basement.

The ceilings were fifteen feet off the ground, and the ground was, as Kaylin had suspected, stone. If not for the utter absence of natural light, this could have been a grand hall in a manor into which Kaylin would never be invited. Or a palace.

There was no way that this was the basement of the house in which Gilbert and Kattea claimed to live. There was no way it would *fit*.

"Is it too much to ask," Kaylin murmured, "that something be normal for a few days? Just—normal? Normal, venal criminals, ordinary stakes?"

"You are clearly not immortal," Bellusdeo replied. She glanced at Kaylin; her eyes were fully orange now.

"Meaning it's not boring."

"Normal—for me—for centuries was the heart of Shadow. I do not yearn for it. Normal, for me, was the war that eventually destroyed my home."

"I get it. I suck. I'll stop feeling sorry for myself. Or," she added, when Bellusdeo raised a brow, "I'll at least stop whining out loud."

"The latter is conceivable."

"Thanks."

"You should never have accepted the marks of the Chosen if you wanted a boring life."

"I wasn't offered a choice."

"What is the phrase that Joey uses?"

"Joey? Oh, you mean at the office?"

"Yes. I think it's 'Sucks to be you.' Did I say that right?"

"Yes."

Kattea snickered.

"That's funny?" Kaylin asked her.

"No. Gilbert doesn't understand what it means. *That's* funny."

Gilbert was not present. Any hope that Kattea was not communicating with him in his absence—and it was very scant hope, given the observable facts—wilted.

"It's around here somewhere," Kattea told them. "There should be a door."

"Should be?" Bellusdeo asked, her voice deceptively soft.

"The basement here is a bit confusing. It changes shape, sometimes. Gilbert says that's normal."

"It is *so* not normal," Kaylin told her.

"I told him that. I think it confused him."

"Gilbert sounds like he's easily confused."

"He really is. He says—he says that's why he needs me." The words trailed into silence. Kattea was a child. She was not a young child, but she was a child. But that meant nothing in the fiefs.

"Do you think he's lying?" Bellusdeo asked. She had apparently decided to ask all the difficult, awkward questions that Kaylin had so far managed to keep to herself.

Kattea's shrug was pure fief. Answer enough, as well. Gilbert was clearly competent, powerful, dangerous—any need he had for an orphan in Nightshade didn't bear examination. Not when he was the only reason that orphan was still alive.

Had Gilbert found Kaylin after Steffi and Jade had died, she would have followed him. She would have asked no questions unless he invited them. And she would have done whatever she could to protect him, no matter what *else* he did. Because he represented food and shelter and another day or two of life.

No fear Kaylin had for Kattea would measure up against that, and why should it? The concern of an uninvolved stranger was worth nothing but sentiment and air. She couldn't judge the child. She couldn't ask that she make wise choices. What choices, in the end, did Kattea really have?

The door did not appear until they'd walked another thirty yards, and it did not appear where Kattea was looking for it. Bellusdeo was less obviously disturbed by this than Kaylin, and Kattea did not appear concerned at all. She did look very pleased when she sighted it, but she didn't look relieved. She had expected she'd find it.

It was, in Kaylin's estimation, not that hard to miss. It looked far more like a closet door than a door that would normally be found in halls like this one; even the doorknob looked old and worn.

Kattea didn't open the door. Instead, she knocked. "Don't touch the handle," she said, although neither Kaylin nor Bellusdeo had moved to do so. "Gilbert will open the door."

At her words, the door swung open into a large room, which was rectangular in shape. The floors of this room were covered in rugs—at least three, none matching. To the right was a large bed; to the left, a desk and two standing shelves. Those shelves had gathered books, dust and what looked, at this distance, like impressive cobwebs.

Kaylin took these details in before her gaze returned to the man who had opened the door. He looked pinched and drawn; his eyes were fever-bright, but a normal color. His face was long, but otherwise looked normal.

He did not look like the Barrani.

He did not look like a Dragon, either.

But Kaylin felt certain that he had to be immortal, because she thought Kattea must know his True Name.

Gilbert stepped away from the door to allow them to enter.

Bellusdeo went in first, cutting Kattea off to do so. Kaylin almost reached out to grab Kattea's shoulder, but she knew how she would have reacted to that at Kattea's age. Kattea's trust of Gilbert was not trust as Kaylin had grown to understand it. It was necessity.

"Kattea said you were unwell."

"I know."

"You look…"

"Unwell."

"Yes."

"I *said*—" Kattea began.

"Kattea and I have a bit of a bet going."

"Kattea has been attempting to explain betting to me. It is confusing."

"It can't be more confusing than basements that change shape and size and doors that aren't where you left them."

Gilbert frowned.

Kattea said, "That's what I told him."

"Did any Barrani come to this house yesterday?"

"No."

"But something else did?"

Gilbert was silent for a long beat.

"Let me lose a bet."

"I do not think that would be wise. The injuries you heal are not the same injuries that my people sustain. My injuries would not, I believe, make sense to you."

"They don't have to make sense to me." Kaylin lifted her arms. Gilbert, seeing them, froze. He turned to Kattea.

"Her arms—were they glowing like that when she entered the halls?"

"You couldn't see it? You can see *everything*." Kattea said this without apparent sarcasm.

"I can see it now, yes. I— May I examine your arms?"

Kaylin unbuttoned the cuffs of her sleeves in reply. She rolled up the loose material and winced; the marks were *bright*. She rolled her sleeves down again instantly.

"Kaylin?"

"Sometimes they— Sometimes the words leave my skin."

"Yes." Gilbert now looked confused.

"You've seen marks like these before. You called me—"

"Chosen." The most disturbing thing about his gaze, Kaylin realized, was the fact that Gilbert didn't blink. Nor did he look away. His glance never strayed.

"You lived in Ravellon," Kaylin said, changing the subject. He nodded.

"How do you know what these marks mean?"

Bellusdeo folded her arms. Her eyes remained a bright, intense orange as she studied Gilbert.

Gilbert frowned. "I do not understand the question."

"Ravellon is at the heart of the fiefs. Kattea's told you about at least one of them—you found her there."

"Lord Nightshade's home."

"Yes. The fiefs exist *because* of Ravellon. The Towers—or castle, in his case—exist to prevent Shadow from encroaching upon the rest of the city. Gilbert, was Ravellon your home?"

★ ★ ★

Gilbert turned to Kattea. "Go upstairs," he told her quietly, "and entertain our guests." He glanced up, as if the ceiling of this very ordinary room was transparent to his gaze. "Kattea. Go. We do not have much time."

Kaylin glanced at the girl. She had folded her slender arms tightly, clearly intending to stay.

"Kattea, you gave me your word."

Mutinous, the child hesitated.

"Do as he says," Kaylin told the girl. "It's never wise to break a promise made to someone as powerful as Gilbert."

"I didn't promise to obey," Kattea said, voice low. "Not *everything*."

"You must go to our guests. While you are with them, they should be safe."

"From what?" Bellusdeo demanded.

"I would tell you to leave with Kattea, but it would be pointless. You will remain with the Chosen. I intend her no harm."

"But you send the child from the room."

"I am not what you are. I am not what she is. She has made a bet with Kattea." He spoke the word as if it were a sacred oath. "I am not what I *was*. I am...ill. There is a possibility that she can heal me."

"Healing is not, generally—"

"But there is a possibility that she will fail. Or that I will. You will, in all likelihood, survive such a failure. The Chosen is likely to survive. Kattea is not."

"Are you sure you know what you're doing?" Bellusdeo demanded of Kaylin.

Since the answer was more or less no, Kaylin didn't bother with it. Kattea was already afraid. "Keep your promise," Kaylin said.

"You don't even know what the promise was."

"I don't have to. You know, and Gilbert knows."

Gilbert cut in. "Go upstairs. I will meet you there."

"You promise?"

Gilbert was silent. He was pale now, far paler than he had been when he'd opened the door. His eyes, however, were just as bright, just as clear. No, Kaylin thought, they were brighter and clearer; it was as if light was now attempting to escape his body, and his eyes were the only possible exit.

"Bellusdeo."

"I am not leaving you here."

"Kattea has to go. I don't want her to get lost in the halls—"

"I *won't* get lost in the halls!"

"You don't get lost because Gilbert guides you. He's telling you he might not be able to. You need to be somewhere safe."

"There's *nowhere* safe!"

"Fine. You need to be somewhere *safer*. There are two Imperial Hawks in your parlor. Go there and stand behind them if something *else* comes to the house. But do it *now*." Speaking, she reached out and grabbed Gilbert's hands. The light that she saw in his eyes was familiar. It was not the gold of Dragon calm or Barrani surprise; it was the gold of the marks on her arms, legs, back and, she imagined, the mark on her forehead, which had not yet returned on its own to the Barrani Lake of Life.

Bellusdeo's eyes were a deeper orange. Her gaze moved from Kaylin to Kattea and back. Kaylin wasn't certain that Bellusdeo would, in the end, do what she'd asked, but she had hopes.

"If you do not return unharmed," the Dragon finally said, "I will find your remains and burn them to ash."

"Fine. But only if I'm dead."

"No promises" was the dire response. Bellusdeo then turned her glare on Kattea. "We're leaving. Now."

Kattea didn't argue.

★ ★ ★

"Ravellon was my home."

Gilbert's hands were ice. Kaylin had handled warmer corpses. "You should lie down."

"Kattea said this, as well. I do not completely understand it."

Realization came to Kaylin as she held Gilbert's hands. "You're not used to the body you inhabit."

"I am not used to the smallness of the form I inhabit, no."

"Why do you bother?"

"Because I cannot walk here if I do not. Not safely. The seals are breaking."

Kaylin understood that this was important, but it made no sense, and to make sense of it would probably require time. Or someone else. She had a hundred questions to ask, and all of the answers were equally important. She chose one. "How much time do you have?"

To her surprise, he laughed. The laugh echoed in the room; it was almost a Dragon's laugh. This did nothing to make Kaylin any calmer.

"Time," he said bitterly, "I have."

"You just told Kattea—"

"Time is what *you* do not have. It is what Kattea will not have."

"Can you tell me what's wrong?"

"I am wounded, Chosen. I am bleeding in ways you cannot see." His hands tightened on hers. "Lord Nightshade's brother is here."

Kaylin frowned and turned. She was relieved to see that Annarion wasn't present in the room. Relief shattered when she heard a very familiar—and very close—squawk. If Annarion was present, however, he remained silent; unlike Mandoran, he was good at that.

She closed her eyes, in part because her marks were now

glowing so brightly that they hurt to look at, and in part because Gilbert's eyes were doing the same thing. "Should I be able to choose which word leaves me?"

"Can you not? If you cannot, how can you use the power you've been granted? How can you fulfill the responsibility that comes with it? The words are your power. Without them, you are merely mortal."

Kaylin was more or less used to this, but still found it annoying. Annoyance, on the other hand, was better than fear; she held on to it because it was familiar. Eyes closed and holding the coldest hands in the world, she let her awareness expand.

CHAPTER 13

If Kaylin did not heal immortals often, she did have some experience. She didn't expect Gilbert's body to conform to the rough shape and functionality of her own. She did expect to at least find wounds, because Barrani wounds and Dragon wounds had a lot in common with merely mortal ones, and in general, bleeding implied that kind of injury.

Gilbert was not Barrani; he wasn't a Dragon. He had chosen to adopt the appearance of a mortal—possibly for Kattea's sake. It wasn't, however, a simple illusion.

Gilbert's appearance was in some ways like Kaylin's skin. It was attached to him. It was part of the whole, not separate from it. But the whole was not simple interior—organs, muscle, bone; the skin didn't *contain* the rest of him. Even had it, she would have found it disturbing. She didn't expect Shadow to be living and organic. She expected it to be...well, shadowy. Deadly.

This...wasn't like that. Parts of Gilbert were physical; they were almost what his form suggested. But they didn't...attach to each other in a way that suggested those parts had an actual function. If Kaylin could look at the contents of a working stomach—she'd seen the dissection of a dead one in the morgue—she imagined they would look similar to Gilbert's body. Except for the things that a stomach couldn't contain.

She wondered, queasy now, if that was what his interior

was—a collection of the things he'd swallowed, consumed and only partly digested. As a living body, this one didn't *work*. And yet it was alive. She could sense that much.

A body knew its healthy state. Kaylin's healing wasn't like doctoring or surgery. Had it been, she would have failed the first time she tried; she'd been twelve or thirteen, and she'd had no words for any of what she did. The words, the knowledge, had followed from the time she'd spent on a stool in the morgue at Red's side.

The morgue would not give her the words for what she touched now.

Kaylin often felt fear when she healed, but this fear was different. It was visceral. Gilbert felt *wrong*. He was alive, yes—but in his case, life was inimical, dangerous. She was afraid to heal him, because at the core of the mess that was Gilbert, she felt and touched traces of the unpredictable Shadow that grouped in the heart of the fiefs, traces of the Shadow that crossed the boundaries created by active Towers, and in so doing, transformed the landscape and the living they encountered. Shadow was death. Shadow meant nothing else, to Elantra.

Shadow, however, was part of Gilbert.

It would have been easy to assume that the Shadow existed in Gilbert as contamination. As something that needed to be cut out and excised in order to save his life. It wouldn't be the first time Kaylin had had to do it. But she'd *known* then. She had known what Barrani health looked like. She'd been able to see the Shadow corrupting the Barrani body it infested and knew that if it wasn't stopped, nothing Barrani would remain.

But she did not understand what healthy Gilbert looked like. Her power—if power had sentience—didn't understand it, either.

Squawk.

Annarion was definitely here. Mandoran was probably with him.

"I need to heal him," she told the familiar, without opening her eyes.

Squawk. Squawk.

"He apologizes for intruding," Gilbert said, his voice so close to her ear, his mouth might have been plastered to the side of her face. "He feels you will need...help."

"Did he happen to say what kind of help?"

"No, Chosen. I believe he expects you to understand."

And after a long moment, she did. It did not make her day any better. "He's here to help contain you. The other two are somehow with him because they need to be within range of him or..."

"Or?"

"I can't explain it because I'm not them. You probably understand it, if he's here." To the familiar, she said, "I don't know what he's supposed to be when he's not—not injured."

Squawk.

"No, you don't *understand.* I don't usually *have to* know. The—the patient's body knows."

"And Gilbert's doesn't." This was Mandoran. Kaylin didn't open her eyes.

"No."

"Do ours?"

"I have no idea. I've never been allowed to heal either of you. The only Barrani I've healed wanted to kill me for it."

"I wouldn't," Mandoran helpfully said.

"Great. If you get mortally wounded or infected, I'll keep that in mind. Annarion wouldn't let me touch him."

"That is possibly for your own safety," Gilbert told her.

Healing went one way, in theory. Power flowed from Kaylin to the injured. Information—scattered and diffuse—also traveled, and that was a two-way communication.

What surged through Kaylin now was not information. Not as she understood it. It was not—quite—Shadow, but it was *of* Shadow. She pulled her hands away from Gilbert's; she no longer had to be in contact with him to be aware of what he was.

She could, with her eyes closed, see Gilbert's eyes. He had two of them, in the expected place. Not all Shadows did; many had multiple eyes, of different sizes, different shapes. Those eyes often occupied body parts that eyes normally didn't, at least not in any race or species with which Kaylin was familiar.

But...he didn't have two eyes now. The quality of the eyes, the harsh clarity, the solid physicality, remained. They were Gilbert's eyes. They just weren't attached to his face anymore, and there were a lot more of them. She stepped back—or felt as if she was trying to—but it didn't help; the eyes ringed her, surrounded her, cocooned her. There was no way out.

She opened her eyes, her physical eyes.

Gilbert's eyes remained, but the rest of the room returned. With it, she caught a glimpse of Mandoran, Annarion and her familiar.

Her familiar.

He was not in his small dragon state. He was not in his large, rideable state, either; he was somewhere in between. He had wings, yes, and he was slender, but he had lost the reptilian look that had defined his relationship with Kaylin. If what stood before her now bit her ear or stole her accessories, she'd probably try to stab him before she could override her instincts.

And yet, she knew him. The fact that she could now see Annarion, Mandoran and her erstwhile familiar was far less disturbing than it would have been at any other time. What *was* disturbing was the lack of Gilbert.

"What are you doing?" Mandoran asked her.

"I am trying to heal Gilbert."

"Possibly not your brightest idea. Teela says you take betting to unacceptable extremes. She's worried," he added.

"This is not about a bet," Kaylin said, through clenched teeth.

"Teela offers a wager."

"Tell Teela to shut up. I need to concentrate."

"On what?"

On Gilbert.

"Yes," the familiar said. He stepped toward Kaylin. She recognized his voice, although she heard it seldom.

"I understand you."

"It is a function of your state. You cannot maintain it for long; you will be absorbed. You are too thin an existence to avoid it."

Kaylin shook her head. "Kattea has avoided it."

"Gilbert has avoided absorbing Kattea—or anything else he has touched in this city. His efforts mirror those of Annarion and Mandoran, but he is not entirely as they are."

Kaylin lifted a hand. Holding her breath, she placed her palm as gently as she could against the nearest eye. The eye closed. Until she'd touched it, it hadn't appeared to even have an eyelid.

"What are you doing?" Mandoran asked.

"Thinking of strangling you," Kaylin snapped at him. Even as she spoke, she reached for the next eye, the movement both deliberate and hesitant. This eye also closed. It made her feel vaguely better, but there were a lot of eyes. This was not *at all* like healing.

"Your feet, Kaylin."

Kaylin looked down. She was practically standing on a bed of eyes. She could no longer see the stone floor. What she saw in its place was chaos. Opalescent Shadow; hints of broiling color that glittered and moved as if being disgorged. The eyes rested above it.

"This is *not* healing," Kaylin almost shouted.

"Then stop," Mandoran told her.

She would have if she'd any idea how. But the eyes formed a layer between her feet and the Shadow that would transform them, and that Shadow seemed like a very, very large pool. She left those eyes alone, for the sake of self-preservation.

The rest, she continued to close. After half a dozen such closures, she no longer hesitated. After a dozen she finally noticed that the marks on her arms, which were still glowing brightly, had begun to develop dimension. They were still attached to her skin, but they were attached to her skin the way Gilbert's human appearance was attached to his body: they were part of Kaylin, and yet at the same time separate from her.

"How did you get here?" she asked Gilbert as she worked. "You said you crossed the bridge." She closed an eye.

"That was not entirely accurate."

"No kidding. Did you come underground?" Another eye. And another.

"As you have surmised, yes."

"You didn't find Kattea underground." She reached for the eyes that hovered above her head, as if closing them would give her more space.

"No. I found it difficult to find Kattea at all."

"Were you looking specifically for her?" She crouched; more eyes closed. With them went some of the light in the room. The balance of the light now resided in her marks. They hurt.

"No. I was simply looking for someone who existed in this time and place. Time is a dimension and an anchor. To people like you, who are wed to it, it is unavoidable. It is part of your essential nature. Without time, you do not exist."

"And you do."

"Yes, Kaylin Neya. I do. So, too, does your Lord."

She bristled; her hand froze. "If you're referring to Night-shade, he is not my Lord."

"I feel his presence only when I am near you, but I find your language so limiting, I may be expressing myself poorly."

"Very, very poorly," she replied. "The floor—"

"Yes?"

"It's not—it's not stone anymore."

The shape of Gilbert's open eyes changed; she could almost trace the expression—confusion, possible frustration—from the subtle narrowing. He asked a question—or at least it sounded like a question by the intonation.

The familiar answered in the same language. Kaylin couldn't name it, but she recognized it; it was the language the Arkon had chosen to speak to Mandoran. It was, however, a language that Kaylin thought, with time, she could learn; it didn't have the enormous weight and echo of true words.

"The floor does not look different to my eyes," Gilbert said. "There are patches of your city that do—but they are not areas I can navigate."

More eyes shuttered. Kaylin's arms began to burn. It wasn't pleasant. The words seem to be struggling to escape her skin, but it was almost as if they were trapped, and the burning was a simple consequence of their attempt to break free.

This had never happened before.

Then again, no healing had ever worked this way, either. The fact that she could see her familiar made it clear that she was not entirely in the space she had occupied before she had taken Gilbert's hands in her own. She was in a place that An-narion and Mandoran occupied if they didn't focus properly. They at least looked normal, for Barrani.

"Choose." Like the eyes, the voice seemed to come from all around. It did not sound like Gilbert's—but maybe it was.

Gilbert had a thousand eyes; he quite possibly had a thousand mouths, as well.

She had chosen words before—in a dream, or in what she thought of as a dream. This was not the same. That choice had been painless, and the words had been giant representations of themselves, things that could not fit on her skin.

She had needed them. She had known it, the way one knows anything in a dream.

But that dream had profoundly affected the reality it wasn't a part of. She had apparently skipped the dreamlike state that had made the entire endeavor of choosing words somehow safer. This was reality.

"Kaylin." Her familiar's voice brought her back to herself.

"I have no idea what I'm supposed *to do*."

"Choose a word."

"But I—"

"Choose a word, Chosen, or lose them all. If Gilbert has time—and he does, although not in a fashion that you would understand—you do not. Were it not for those words, you could not be here at all. Choose."

"You can read them—you choose."

"If I could, I would make that choice for you. But it would change all of the bindings that hold us together, and in ways that you would not, in the end, appreciate. You live, as Gilbert said, in time; once you have made a choice, taken an action, there is no way to undo it, no way to return to what existed before."

"I think I like it better when I can't understand you."

He smiled.

Her arms ached. So, now, did her legs, her back, the back of her neck—any part of her skin that was marked. She wondered if her entire body was bulging the way her arms now were. Probably. She could only see her arms.

What purpose did these words serve, in the end?

What purpose did any words serve? The Barrani Lake of Life was a repository of true words—those that could become names. These words weren't the same—and even thinking it, she realized that the lone mark on her forehead did not burn or struggle to escape her skin. So: the words she bore, and had born, were not True Names. They didn't grant life. They didn't wake stone.

She had lost such marks before. The Devourer of Worlds had eaten the ones she had offered. But so had the familiar, when he had managed to struggle his way out of his shell. She hadn't chosen which words she'd surrendered either time. She hadn't chosen the word that had freed the trapped spirit of an ancient Dragon, deep within the bowels of the Arkon's collection.

But she'd chosen the words that had freed the Consort from her sleep in the heart of the green. She had had the time to choose. She had had some understanding that she needed to communicate, somehow, with the heart of the green; that she had to show it an experience that was similar to its own. She couldn't speak the words necessary.

She hadn't needed to speak them.

Here, now, she could speak, and Gilbert could listen. She could make herself heard. The purpose of whatever word she chose was not the same.

It was hard to think while her arms hurt, but she had some experience with that. "Hope."

"I am here, Kaylin."

"Is the city safe?"

"Yes, for the moment. Yes and no. Gilbert came here for a reason, and I can now perceive it in the edges of his thoughts."

"I can't feel his thoughts at all."

"Yes, Kaylin, you can."

"I can't—"

"You are standing on them, or above them, almost literally. You are—carefully—quieting some of them."

"They're not thoughts. They're eyeballs."

"...Eyeballs."

"Yes."

The familiar fell silent for one painful beat. He then said, to Mandoran, "That is what she actually sees."

Mandoran's eyes were attached to his face—which was probably good, because he widened them so much, so quickly, they might have fallen off, otherwise.

"What do *you* see?" she demanded, through clenched teeth.

"Not eyes. Why *eyes*?"

It was Annarion who answered, although he spoke without certainty. "Eyes may represent observation. You are an Imperial Hawk. Observation is an integral part of what you do, and what you do defines you."

Kaylin wanted to laugh. She grunted, instead.

"Observation requires your presence. You can't observe what you can't see. Your observation is active. It does not—in your case—rely on vision alone. I would almost expect to see ears—"

"Please don't. Just—don't."

"Gilbert can act and observe in a variety of ways that you can't. I think he can do so in a variety of ways that *we* can't."

"Meaning your cohort, minus Teela."

"Yes. We think—Sedarias thinks—that what you are experiencing as discrete instances of multiple eyes is a representation of the myriad ways in which Gilbert observes or interacts with your world."

"Our world."

"The world we are attempting to live in now, yes."

"And he's doing this because he's *injured*?"

"We cannot clearly perceive any injury."

"And the chaos? The Shadow?"

There was a longer pause. "We are uncertain. If you were, in reality, standing on Shadow as you perceive it, we would not be having this conversation. You are normally aware of some part of your patient's thoughts when you heal?"

"If the injury is extensive, yes."

"She suggests that the Shadow you perceive is some part of Gilbert's memory or thought. If it hasn't killed you yet."

"And the Shadow I perceive in the mess of what is possibly a body?"

Silence again. "Sedarias says, 'You're the healer.'"

Which meant she didn't know. The problem was that Kaylin didn't know, either. She'd sent her power out. She'd touched the rudiments of the body's structural components, and it *all* felt wrong to her.

And what if that wrongness was the very thing that allowed Gilbert to be in Elantra safely? What if she got it wrong, made a mistake, brought the *rest* of his Shadow to the fore?

She exhaled. She'd long lived under the principle that it was better to beg forgiveness than ask permission. But corpses didn't have a lot of meaningful forgiveness to offer.

The power that she had attempted to send to Gilbert had not gone to Gilbert. It had, instead, turned back on itself. It had flowed into the marks of the Chosen, which were probably going to cook her alive if she couldn't figure out what the hells she was supposed to do.

Words. Shadows. Ancients.

Words.

Shadows.

"Gilbert."

"I am here."

"Barrani and Dragons possess True Names. They require them to live. The name is part of their functional identity. It's not a soul—not in the way most mortal religions define soul—but it might as well be."

"Yes."

"The Ancients created Barrani and Dragons."

"Yes." He sounded slightly confused.

"I've heard the Ancients called Lords of Law and Lords of Chaos."

"Yes."

"And the Lords of Chaos, in theory, created Shadow."

"I fail to see—"

"Did Shadow not require True Names?"

Silence.

Kaylin lifted an arm and brought it closer to her eyes, squinting to see the shape of the marks through their light. "Hope."

"Kaylin."

"When the Arkon spoke in the library, you saw the words, right?"

"Yes."

"True words have meanings. True words are complete in and of themselves. If you were to speak to someone who can understand them, they would understand your meaning." She spoke the statements as if they were a question.

"Yes."

"Names, True Names, true words—these were created by the Ancients. But if the very nature of the Lords of Chaos was transformative, what brought *them* to life?"

"Words, Kaylin."

"Different words? False words? Did they even *have* the concept for those, back then?"

"Chaos was a whisper. Law was a shout."

"But whispers and shouts *use the same words.*"

Silence.

Kaylin was bloody tired of silence.

All of the words seemed to strain upward, as if they needed the space—and looking at them carefully, Kaylin thought they did. They had developed a rough dimensionality; they looked like glowing welts.

"Gilbert, can you see the marks of the—of the Chosen?"

"Yes. I do not think anyone in this room could miss them."

"Can you read them?" Into the silence that followed, Kaylin added, "I need an answer. I'm not asking for the good of my health."

"I can...hear them."

"Pardon?"

"I can hear them, Chosen. They move too quickly to be easily read."

They weren't moving at all, not that they weren't trying. She exhaled. The eyes beneath her feet were now the only eyes she had not closed. If her familiar was right, the Shadow she saw was not actually present; it was the visual artifact of Gilbert's prior memories.

As she closed the remaining eyes, breath half-held, she thought of every other time the marks on her arms had been somehow used. Twice they'd been eaten. She discarded those; she didn't think Gilbert could devour the words themselves. She didn't understand how the words could be physical, could provide sustenance. They weren't, like True Names, singular. They were mostly like awkward tattoos.

The word on her forehead, rescued in the Outlands, was the only one that wasn't straining against her skin. It was also the only one Kaylin was certain *was* unique. It had the power to wake Barrani babies. To bring them to life.

The rest of the marks were not like that one, although they

looked very similar to the naked eye. But if they weren't like that, they were just...components of language. She couldn't read them; it hadn't occurred to her, when they had first appeared over half her body—they'd spread a bit since—that they were *words*.

Something twitched in her memory. She turned and caught it before it escaped; it was a feeling, an instinct. She had been in this place before.

When? She had certainly never met a sentient Shadow that wasn't trying to destroy everything in its surroundings. She had never touched one voluntarily; the idea of *healing* one was so foreign, it was almost laughable. She *knew* what Shadows did.

But she had known what the Tha'alani did once, as well: they were evil mind readers who tore a person's darkest secrets from them. Everyone had known that about the Tha'alani.

And everyone had been wrong. So wrong.

No, it's different. I was afraid of the Tha'alani for no reason. The Tha'alani aren't like the Shadows. They don't kill. They don't blackmail. They don't judge. The Shadows do destroy. It's different.

She shook her head, trying to clear it, but the doubts clung. She had never walked into Ravellon. She had only seen what walked *out* of it. Was it too much to believe that not everything that lived there was evil?

Everyone had their own story. Her eyes narrowed as she rose, turning the thought over. Everyone had their own story.

Kaylin had known very little about Dragons. She'd learned a lot more when Bellusdeo crashed into her life—but she still tripped up, because *Dragon* was a word that had weight; it was almost mythic. Myths did not have bad days. They didn't have good ones, either. They didn't suffer loneliness, isolation, despair; they didn't have desires. Myths were not alive.

The word *Shadow*, like the word *Dragon*, existed as a modern myth. And at base, myths were...stories.

She struggled with this. She had never thought of Shadows as individuals until she had met Gilbert. And were it not for Kattea, she would never have made the attempt to heal him. But if she thought of Shadows as people—with their own lives, their own stories, their own *reasons*...

Silence.

The last of the eyes beneath her feet closed.

CHAPTER  14

Kaylin breathed a sigh of relief when she did not fall into the whorls of chaos below her.

Cautiously, she looked around the room. She could see Mandoran, Annarion and her familiar; she could see walls, a bed and the very disturbing floor.

She could not see Gilbert.

The walls of the room hadn't changed the way the floor had; the bed was still a bed. The desk was still a desk; it was a bit battered and dinged, suggesting age. But the shelves nearest the desk drew her eye. Kaylin had noted there were books on them when she'd first entered.

It was to the books she now looked. She didn't trust the floor, but she trusted her familiar. She walked across the room, her gaze fixed to the spines of Gilbert's many volumes.

Gilbert didn't speak, but the temperature in the room plunged; the air was now colder than his hands had been.

The books weren't uniform in size; the tops of the spines didn't form a neat and even row. The dust was thick, even on the cobwebs. Whatever Gilbert kept here, he hadn't touched in a while. Certainly not for cleaning, which was a stupid thought. Shadows as housekeepers.

Kaylin was used to thinking of them as death.

She picked a book up off the shelf—or tried. The books

were so tightly packed, the random volume she'd chosen didn't budge. When she applied strength, half a dozen books came free with it.

"What are you doing?" Mandoran asked.

"Looking for words."

"You might want to consider doing that later."

"There's not going to be a later if I can't find them now." She collected the books that had been pulled loose and set them on the shelf's edge. The book she'd chosen, she opened.

The color of light in the room changed.

Books generally had pages. This one was not an exception. It had a lot of pages. But it didn't seem to have a beginning; it didn't seem to have an end. Opening the cover of the book didn't lead to a first page of any kind. This wasn't a problem, because the pages were also blank.

Kaylin closed the book and set it down. She retrieved a different book from the small stack and opened that one instead. The same thing happened. The book opened to some nebulous part of the middle, and it opened in a fan of blank pages.

Grimacing, Kaylin looked at the shelves. There were a *lot* of books.

Was this the right place? Was this where she would find what she was looking for? Ugh. "Gilbert, what's in the other room?"

Silence. She almost shrieked in frustration.

"Apologies, Chosen, but I am uncertain. To which other room do you refer?"

"The room behind the door on the far wall."

He didn't answer. "If you tell me there is no door on the far wall, I'll consider serious violence."

Silence.

Kaylin exhaled. "The door opposite the one I entered? Same

shape, same general size?" Her eyes narrowed; her shoulders fell. "The one with the door ward instead of a knob?"

When he again failed to speak, she turned to Mandoran. "Please tell me you can see the door. Look—*I* could see the door when I entered the room. Before I tried to heal Gilbert. I don't know what you're looking at—but could you try to look at it the way the merely mortal do? Just for a minute?"

Mandoran frowned. "I believe I am looking at the door the way the merely mortal do. Now you've done it," he added, with a little too much glee.

"Done what?"

"Teela's heading down. She tells me to tell you she'll break your left arm if you open that door before she gets here."

"She's not my partner."

"Your partner is coming, too."

Kattea and Bellusdeo did not appear at the door. Tain, Severn and Teela did. "Yes," she said, before Kaylin could open her mouth. "I see the door." Severn nodded. He also unwound his weapon chain.

"What, exactly, are you doing?" Teela demanded.

"Trying to find the right place to put a missing word, if you must know."

"Kattea said you were—"

"Healing Gilbert, yes. But that doesn't mean what it normally does. He's alive, but not in the way any of us are. I think—I think I need to put a word somewhere. To finish a figurative sentence." She tossed Teela the closed book in her hands.

"Do *not* open that!" Gilbert shouted. It was the first time he had raised his voice.

"Teela, can you see Gilbert?"

"Yes. You can't?"

"No. I can hear him. I can't see him."

To Gilbert, Teela said, "Kaylin opened this."

"Yes."

"But you don't want me to."

"I do not think it would be wise. Kaylin is Chosen; she is interacting with the book in a way that you will not."

"What did you do, kitling?" More edge to this question.

"I picked it up and opened it. It's blank," she added. "I think they're all blank."

"They are not blank," Gilbert told her. "Or at least they will not be to your friend."

"Are they yours?"

"They are in my keeping." Which wasn't the same thing.

Teela handed the book back to Kaylin; she tucked it under her arm. "The door?"

Kaylin nodded.

They paused in front of it. Severn was a yard behind them. When Teela lifted a hand, Kaylin caught it before the Barrani Hawk's palm made contact with the ward.

"Not you."

"I'm not in the mood to listen to you whine about door wards." Teela was never in that mood.

"This is a door that Gilbert, Annarion and Mandoran can't see. If small and squawky were a reasonable size, I'd look at it through his wings; as it is, if he sits on my shoulder it'll only be because I'm flat out on the floor. I don't imagine this is a normal door ward. If it is, I will do my level best not to—as you put it—whine." When Teela failed to move, Kaylin continued, "Gilbert didn't think it was safe for you to open this book. If he thought it was safe for you to open the door, I'd let you do it and be grateful.

"But since he can't see it, his opinion doesn't count."

Teela glanced at Tain. Tain shrugged.

Kaylin placed her palm against the ward.

She was braced for the sharp jolt of pain that door wards always caused, and mindful of Teela glowering at her side. She was not prepared for the pain to stop.

But it did. The marks on her arms, although they still shed light, were once again flat, a colored part of her skin. As a bonus, the door swung open.

Teela's skepticism was practically physical.

The room beyond was dark. The only thing that shed light was the floor, because this floor very much matched the floor in the other room—the one she'd seen only when she made direct contact with Gilbert. It was a steady stream of chaos, colors bubbling up to its surface as if it were lava. The air, however, was cold enough to cause breath to mist.

"What are you hoping to find here?"

"Words" was Kaylin's flat response. "Don't close that door." She rolled back both of her sleeves and lifted her arms. "Can you guys tell me what you see?"

Teela hesitated. "What do *you* see, kitling?"

"Not much. It's cold and it's dark. I can just make out the ceiling, which is flat. Teela?"

"It looks like a morgue."

"A morgue." Kaylin exhaled. She moved toward the center of the room, but she didn't run into any tables. Or chairs. Or, more relevant to Teela's description, bodies. "No wonder Mandoran and Annarion are having such a hard time."

"Pardon?"

"There are no slabs here. There are no chairs. There are no cupboards and no corpses. Why morgue?"

"There's a sheeted corpse," Tain said quietly.

"Is it human?"

"I said it was sheeted. It is roughly human in size." He then spoke to Teela so quietly Kaylin couldn't pick up his words. Teela's were clearer. She was cursing in Aerian.

"It's not human."

"Leontine? Tha'alani? Anything mortal?"

"No."

Kaylin, frustrated, turned toward Teela, to find that she had vanished. Only her voice remained; hers and Tain's. It was disorienting and very, very uncomfortable, but it was also a reminder: Kaylin was still, somehow, attached to Gilbert. What she saw now was, in some part, a function of that. "You can't identify the race."

"It is not draconian; it is not Barrani." Teela hesitated.

"Is it an ancestor? I mean, like the ones that woke up in Castle Nightshade?"

"No," Tain said. "We're wrong. I don't think it is a corpse."

Tain had seen his share of corpses. They all had. It was not an easy mistake for the Barrani corporal to make. Kaylin was frustrated; she wanted to see. She approached Tain—or rather his voice—because that was all she had to go on.

Severn said, "It feels like ice."

"It's not ice," Teela replied. "Marble, maybe; it's too polished for stone."

"It looks like a corpse, not a statue," Tain added.

As she approached their familiar voices, the air grew colder. The mist produced by warm breath in cold air grew more dense. She could not see any of the other Hawks in the room. Nor could she see the body or statue or whatever it actually was. She saw her arms, her breath and layers of darkness that were parted by the light the marks on her arms shed.

She needed to see what they were seeing, and there was only one way to do that.

Severn.

He was there instantly.

I'm sorry.

Don't be. You mostly stay on your own side of the fence. She felt the undercurrent of humor.

You can see what they see?

Yes.

I need to see it, too. This might be uncomfortable—

Kaylin.

Right. She stopped wasting time on apologies or explanations. She had a True Name. She wasn't born to it, hadn't been given life by it, but it was there. None of the Barrani really understood what a True Name meant for a mortal, and as a result, the mortal in possession of that name didn't understand it, either. But she had given her name to Severn.

She could speak to Severn, and Severn could speak to her. They didn't have to be in the same room, although in this case being in the same room was no guarantee of anything. More than that, they could see what the other person saw, or hear what the other person heard—with effort.

Kaylin made that effort now.

Through Severn's eyes, she could see Teela and Tain. Teela was examining the not-corpse, her brows folded in toward the bridge of her nose. To Kaylin's eye, they weren't actually in the same room that she was. Their voices were, but otherwise, there was no overlap.

But she saw what Severn saw. What Tain had initially assumed was a body lay, half-covered, on a stone slab that stood two feet above the ground. Given the shape of its upper body, Kaylin assumed it was meant to be male. To Kaylin's eye, it resembled the Barrani, up to a point: the length of face, the height of cheekbones, the build of the chest.

But the Barrani of Kaylin's acquaintance didn't have three eyes.

"Gilbert?"

"I am here."

"Can you see what—what they see?"

"In this room, Kaylin, I can see nothing. I think it more likely that at the moment, you see only what I see."

"What they see—it's real." There was a hint of question in the statement.

"Yes. It is not precisely what I see. You do not see dreams when you wake."

"Dreams aren't real."

"Are they not?"

She closed her eyes. *Severn, I need you to speak.*

"What do you need me to say?"

"Just speak."

He did. Severn wasn't much of a talker. He didn't tell stories; he didn't offer many humorous anecdotes. What he did, instead, was describe the body. He pulled the sheet down and folded it. The body was definitely male. Severn touched its face, ran the tips of his fingers over the lids of closed eyes.

Through their connection, Kaylin felt what he felt. She saw what he saw. She understood why the Hawks had used both ice and marble as descriptions. What she could not see was herself.

Opening her eyes, she could see the trail left by the simple act of breathing in a very cold place. It hung in the air, and unlike breath, it didn't dissipate. Kaylin raised her left arm; gold light was reflected by this odd cloud.

"Can you put your palms on his chest?"

Severn didn't ask her why. Teela did.

"If there are words in this room, this is where they have to be," Kaylin replied.

"You're certain?"

"As certain as I can be."

This didn't impress Teela. To be fair, it didn't impress Kaylin, either.

Healing had been the one blessing to come out of the marks that adorned her skin. It had always just worked. It hadn't required practice or lessons or experience. She had saved lives—for the midwives, in the Foundling Hall, in the Halls of Law—merely by desiring it. She hadn't studied bodies; she hadn't studied herbs or plants or esoteric branches of magic.

This was the first time that healing had not worked on its own, as a function of Kaylin's will. It was the first time she had resented her own ignorance so viscerally. Or maybe not. At heart, she was mostly ignorant. She'd gained enough experience that she could frequently hide it. But not from herself.

Not when it counted.

She kicked herself. Now was not the time for this. She could hate herself later.

Her breath had come out in mist, and the mist had gathered, condensing. She couldn't stop breathing, and as she did, more mist joined the mist that hovered just in front of her, above the floor.

Kaylin moved to stand in what she thought might be the position Severn now occupied. She could feel the cold, hard lines of the body's chest beneath his palms. Fortunately, Severn's hands weren't numb yet, despite the chill in the air.

"This," she said aloud, "is a total pain."

"You expected something easier?"

The mist before her eyes did not, as Kaylin half hoped, solidify. Not entirely. But it moved more like smoke than air. Strands of silvered white twisted around each other; she could both see them and see through them. They had dimension. She couldn't see any words; the mist moved too much.

"They are there," her familiar said, appearing by her left

shoulder. "They are a microcosm of this place. You can see them only because you are entwined with Gilbert's consciousness. You cannot touch them."

"Can you?"

"Not as I am."

"Am I—am I doing the right thing?"

"I cannot answer that question. There are too many variables."

"Will this heal Gilbert?"

"Ah. I do not know, Kaylin. I do not know what you are now attempting to do."

She looked at the flat, bright marks on her arms. "...Neither do I. I'm just thinking of all the old stories."

"Stories?"

"The Barrani. The Ancients. The True Names. True words."

"They are more than just stories."

"I didn't say they were just stories. But...they *are* stories." She hesitated and then added, "A lot of our actual experiences become stories. Things we tell other people. Things we don't tell other people. It's not just about the words. But...sometimes words are what we have. They're not everything; they have to be enough."

"Even the words that you don't understand?"

She looked at her arms. "Even then. Because these words are part of me. Maybe if I use them enough, I'll understand them so well I can say what I really mean with them."

"What do you really mean, Kaylin?"

Kaylin blinked. "I'm not talking about right now. But— in general. I can't always say what I mean. No, that's wrong. People don't always hear what I thought I was saying. I mean, they hear what I actually say."

"Ah. So you feel you choose the wrong words?"

"I must. If I'd chosen the right ones, they'd understand me."

"I do not think it is ever that simple."

"It would be if I could speak true words."

"Ah, no. Because anyone with whom you might converse so earnestly wouldn't hear them. But the words that you seek are here. You cannot see them; there is too much flicker, too much movement."

"Can Gilbert?"

Silence. To her surprise, Hope broke it. "Your instincts have always been good. No, Kaylin. What he could perceive before you entered this chamber was even less than you yourself now see. You breathe. You live."

"You once ate a word."

"Did I?"

"Yes. Could Gilbert do the same thing?"

"I do not know. What you see in Gilbert, I do not see—except through you. It is similar to what you now see when you speak with your Severn."

"What I see?"

"You see what is here where you are standing—but also, because of your bond, where he is standing. You feel what his hands touch. You see what his eyes see. And he sees the inverse. I do not know how you intend to utilize this. Both are, as you suspect, real."

"Why am I not where he is? I can hear his voice—"

"Because you have moved aside one or two steps. Not all beings can see all realities. Mandoran and Annarion are aware of many—but not all."

"Why are there—why is there more than *one*? No, never mind—answer that later."

"The answer, of course, is that there is only one. But you were not created in a way that allows you to see and retain it all. You are like a fish. If you are born in air, you will die; if you are forced to spend time out of the water, you will also die. What you see in the water can be seen—if the water is clear—from the air, but it will not be seen in the same way.

"Gilbert is a creature who can be at home in either the water or the air—as are your two friends. But sometimes, he carries pockets of air with him, and if your Severn is caught in one, being a fish, he will die. There is no malice involved, but that does not make the danger of death any less real.

"You are trying, in your fashion, to allow Gilbert to survive in the water without the benefit of the air that will kill you. I do not know if that is healing in any precise sense of the word." He hesitated.

She marked it.

"Is the body that Severn can see Gilbert's actual body?"

"Choose, Kaylin. You are not a bird. You must return to the water, soon."

Kaylin lifted her right hand to her forehead. This mark was *not* one of the marks granted her by Ancients who'd never asked permission; it was a True Name. It was a name she had gathered and placed onto her own skin to preserve it.

It belonged to the Barrani. She knew this.

But it was the only True Name she had. She could not return to the Lake of Life to capture another word from its waters; not in time. She very much doubted that she would be allowed to do so even if time weren't an issue.

She lowered her hand. The word had not left her forehead.

Grinding her teeth, she lifted her hand again. Her breath—because she'd continued to breathe—filled the air in front of her. As if she were a Dragon on a bad day, it had filled the room like smoke. And yes, she could now see the ghosts of words lingering in its folds.

This was what she needed, but it was only part of what she

needed. The rest? Attached to her. Now that she knew this, the words were flat and dimensionless, of course.

This would not be the first time she'd tried to pick them off. But the last time, she'd been a terrified child.

Keep your hands where they are, she told Severn.

He nodded; she felt it. She lifted her hands again, but this time she tried to remember what it felt like to find a word in the Lake of Life. The Lake had not appeared as a lake; it had appeared as a...a desk. The surface of a desk. A place upon which words were written. Yet her hands had slid below that surface—

She did not want her hands to slide beneath the surface of her own skin. In her own reality, that would be impossible. But in Gilbert's?

In Gilbert's reality, the rules were different. Inhaling, she focused on her memories. Her hands had fallen below the hard surface of the table, and she had—eventually—found a word whose shape and weight seemed right. Here, there was no search. She only had one word, of the many, that could function as life.

This time, she felt her hand dip beneath the surface of her own forehead, as if her skin were liquid. She had to try three times; the first two attempts were disturbing enough she froze. But the third time, she felt the pinprick edges of something against her fingers and palm. She cupped the word carefully and withdrew it, and it expanded to fill her hand, gaining dimension and weight.

The names were not sentient—not in a way that Kaylin understood sentience. But she felt, holding it, regret and worry. She silently apologized for not visiting the Lake to take it home. If she'd said it out loud, Teela would smack her when she could finally reach her. Teela, after all, forgot nothing.

She lifted the word.

The cloud parted. The word didn't leave her hand.

It wasn't enough, she thought. Yes, she carried it, the way she carried the other marks—but in the end, it had a place that wasn't a patch of Kaylin's skin. It wasn't *of* her. Or rather, it wasn't part of her duties as Chosen. Duties that she had never understood.

She understood them now, but not in a way she could easily put into words. Ironic, really. Severn should have been Chosen. He made a lot less noise, but when he spoke, it meant something.

Maybe the words were given to you because you can speak so freely, Severn pointed out.

Fine. *But I can't choose words* well.

Why do you have to choose one?

Because there's some part of the story that's incomplete. This made sense to Kaylin.

How do you know that?

I don't know, *Severn. I just… It's just…*

A feeling. It was just a feeling. It was intuition. She raised her right arm; her right hand held the only True Name in the room that wasn't already occupied. Her left hand was free, and it grew colder. Her cheeks stung, and the air drew the breath out of her lungs, froze her nostrils. Only the hand that held the name felt any warmth at all. Kaylin did not consider this a particularly good sign.

She glanced up at a cloud of translucent words, made from her own breath and the bitter cold.

Kaylin.

I'm moving as fast as I can—

The body is getting colder.

So was the room. Her arms were shaking enough that it was harder to see the brighter, closer marks on her skin; her hands were curved in loose fists that wouldn't hold anything competently. Her right hand still held the name because it was the only source of warmth in the room.

But even that warmth was fading.

Kaylin—

She touched her arm; her own marks stopped their slow traversal of her skin. The rune she slid her shaking fingers over felt almost brittle to the touch. For one long, held breath she was afraid that she had waited too long. It was frozen. It would not move.

"Kaylin." Like the words of breath and mist, her familiar was all white, an ice that implied endless cold and death. She couldn't see his eyes. "I do not know why you were Chosen; were it not for my presence, you would be lost here." He gestured at the mark on her arm; it rose. It rose and expanded, becoming dimensional as it hovered above her arm.

"I cannot touch you here," he said, voice quiet. "It would destroy you." He looked at the words that weren't hers in the darkness, as if reading them. "Do what you must do, but do it quickly."

"Can you—"

"No, Kaylin. I can touch neither you nor the tale that is told; what was written here was not of me; it is not mine. I could destroy it. I could refashion it—but then it would be a different story, and not the story of the one you call Gilbert.

"And if I did that, you would also perish. You will perish, regardless. You are not Barrani, not Dragon, not any of the older races; you will age and you will die." He spoke now, as if to himself.

Kaylin reached out for the word he had freed from her skin.

"But time, to you, is a prison from which there is no escape, except one. You do not feel its immediacy."

He was wrong. She *did*. She knew better than anyone what *too late* meant.

She listened as she moved. Gilbert's words, revealed by breath and cold, were an arm's length away, no more, but they seemed to remain inches in front of her, no matter how hard she strained to reach them. The shuddering didn't help.

She had never been so cold in her life.

There was warmth waiting for her—and food, and family—if she could complete the pattern in front of her. She *had* a home now. She had a place to go. She cursed in quiet Leontine and lifted the rune that had come from her skin into place; it took four attempts.

She knew when it had successfully joined the mass of the words of ice because gold spread across white, seeping into it as if it were ink on a tablecloth. It spread. What had been mist and ice became, at last, true words as she understood them.

Sadly, they didn't make the room any warmer.

There was only one thing that could do that. She held it in her hand: life, in the paradigm of the Ancients. It had to go to a body she couldn't see or touch herself.

Think, damn it. Just...*think*.

The name in her hand had been created *for* the Barrani, but it was the only name she had to offer Gilbert.

She had never asked the Consort how names were transferred to the babies that straddled the boundary between life and death, as all Barrani newborns did. The Barrani were understandably protective about the Lake of Life. Any mention of it caused Barrani eyes to darken by several shades, and the resultant blue was uncomfortable. Or worse.

She had a suspicion, though. It involved being able to touch the body. She had no idea how to do that here; she couldn't even *see* it.

She needed to be where Severn was. She closed her eyes and

returned her awareness to him; to his vision. He was looking at the body that was not a corpse, but not quite a statue; his hands remained gently spread across its chest.

She could feel ice and stone. She could feel them as strongly as she could feel the True Name in her own hands. She could see his hands clearly, but she couldn't see her own. She didn't try. Instead, she apologized to her partner and tried to move his.

She lifted his right hand. She flexed his fingers. Curved them into a fist. Opened the hand again and examined the scars across his right palm. Cupped that palm and held it steady until it felt like her own hand to her.

"Corporal?" Tain's voice.

Severn didn't answer.

Severn? Severn!

I'm here. It's bloody cold.

Severn was where Kaylin was. She felt a moment of pure panic; both of his hands clenched in involuntary fists.

Come back. Come back to you.

Silence.

Severn—come back right now. She was terrified; the fear was sudden and sharp and too visceral to be cold.

He didn't reply.

She looked up at Teela, at her familiar blue eyes, at the subtle shift of her brows. "Severn's not here," she said.

Teela's eyes narrowed into perfect edges. "Kitling, what are you doing?"

"I'm here—Severn's where I was. He won't—he won't come back. How do I make him come back?"

"Ask and hope he agrees."

"Tried that."

"If I understand what's happening, you're not the person who gets to make that decision—you can fight, but it will cause you both immense pain at a time when you cannot afford it." Teela exhaled. "You're here for a reason. Please tell me you're here for a reason."

Teela's irritation was so familiar, so normal, it steadied the younger Hawk. "Yes."

"Then do whatever it was you came here for. Do it quickly."

For one heartbeat, she couldn't remember. Severn's hands unclenched; Severn's lungs took in air, held it for a beat and exhaled it. She lifted her right hand, cupped it; lowered her left. She meant to place it squarely in the center of the figure's chest, but it drifted up, toward its closed eyes instead.

"I think I need three hands."

"You've only got two. Make do."

She lowered the right hand. Severn's hand, unlike her own, did not cup or carry a name. She brought his right hand to the center of the figure's chest. With the left, she tried to pry the middle eye—which was set slightly higher in the figure's face than the other two—open. She was surprised when it worked.

At first glimpse, the eye socket was missing an eye. That would probably have been for the best, because a second, steadier look made it clear that the eye itself was a dark, round obsidian that did not reflect light at all. There were no flickers in its depths to suggest that it was chaos or Shadow, but it seemed to move, very slowly, beneath the fingers that held the eyelid open.

Kaylin.

She exhaled. "I need my body back."

I'm not sure how to leave it.

You're lying.

He wasn't.

Kaylin had had nightmares that made more sense than this. She snarled a long Leontine phrase that made Tain's ears twitch.

Can you see the word in your—in my—hand?

Yes. It's the only light in the room.

Kaylin had had nightmares that were less upsetting. *There are words right in front of you.*

They're not words that I can see.

"Hope—can you still see them?"

"Yes."

"Why in the hells can't he see them? He's behind *my* eyes!"

"I do not know, Kaylin."

"Kitling, what are you trying to do?"

"Heal Gilbert." She had come in search of Gilbert's name. She was almost certain she'd found it. She'd hoped that somehow, the Chosen could finish a story, or at least make what she could see of it complete.

But the words were in a place that no one else could reach except her familiar. She'd made the faint, almost ethereal figures solid. Golden. They *were* words now, not the ghost or the memory of words. But that didn't finish the story. The isolation and the cold hadn't come to an end.

What had she expected? Gilbert was not like the trapped spirit of an ancient Dragon. Gilbert's life was not over.

She'd taken the single name she had managed to preserve from her forehead, because there was a body here that could contain it. Until she'd seen it, using the True Name hadn't occurred to her.

But that name and this body were not in the same place. No, she thought, frowning. They *were* in the same place. They were like the murder victims. Real and not real. Present and not present.

"I couldn't see the victims with your wing plastered to my face."

Silence.

She had looked through her familiar's translucent wing many

times. She had seen things that she couldn't see on her own. She had gone places she wouldn't have gone. It had never occurred to her that seeing them did not immediately make them real and accessible.

She'd thought of Hope's wing as a way of seeing through illusion, of getting to the truth of what was *actually* there. She'd assumed that what she was seeing through his wing was *the* truth, that there was only one.

But what if it was only her perception that was the bottleneck? Then she needed to change that. She needed to change it *now*. She wasn't certain that she could change it while caged in Severn, and thinking that, she once again felt his presence, heard his interior voice.

She was angry and relieved, and swung wildly between the two.

I could hear you, he said. *I could always hear you. You were becoming too quiet. Too distant.*

So you decided to take over my body while it was—

Dying?

The word hung in the air between them; she shoved it aside. She had done what she needed to do, in Severn's body. She needed to do the rest in her own.

It was cold. It was cold enough that pain had given way to numbness, and the numbness to something that felt like distant warmth. She knew this was not a good sign. Her hand, her right hand, was folded around the name as if to protect it. That had clearly been Severn's choice, not hers. She knew it wasn't necessary.

With Severn's help, with the bridge of a True Name between them, she could see the two rooms that were *both* real. She wondered if this was what Mandoran and Annarion dealt with all the time. If they could—with one set of eyes—see both rooms. Kaylin usually couldn't. She could see one or the other, with help.

She lifted her right hand, cupping the name; she turned. She turned in two bodies: her own and Severn's. His arms were longer, and he was taller; the vantage through which he viewed the inert form on the slab was higher up. His reach was greater; she had to adjust it, to adjust her own leaden arm, to compensate for the stiffness of her native limbs and the way she wanted to fold them in around her chest to conserve body heat.

Her head hurt. Her eyes watered—or maybe those were Severn's eyes; she was almost certain tears of her own would be frozen.

But she moved her hands—no, their hands—in unison. Severn steadied her because he was also there. She felt warmth that was not like heat as she brought the name to its future vessel. She didn't place it, as she'd originally intended, in the center of the body's chest. Instead, she carried it all the way to the third eye, the peak of the awkward triangle.

Light was reflected in what now looked like an obsidian orb. Light, shape, form. The name did not shrink; it did not change shape. The eye did. It grew. Kaylin held the name steady, but that took effort. She wasn't the only one who noticed; she could hear Tain's sharp intake of breath.

The eye expanded, darkness widening until it occupied most of the form's forehead. The other two eyes remained closed, and the body remained motionless. Kaylin should have found it disturbing, but didn't have the mental energy for it. Or for anything other than what she was doing: holding herself, and the single word, steady.

She had thought what occupied the third eye socket was obsidian. As it expanded, she realized she'd been wrong. It was, or seemed to be, a very viscous liquid, like an oil. She turned her right hand over and let the name go.

It fell slowly. Had the black liquid sprouted tendrils to grab it and drag it down, Kaylin would have found it less disturbing somehow. She watched as golden curves made contact with what had taken the form of an eye, and watched them sink. It seemed to go on forever.

Forever, she didn't have.

She lowered Severn's arm and set both of his hands against the lip of the exposed slab, as if by so doing she could shore up her own weight. But if they shared a vision, they didn't actually occupy the same body; her own knees buckled.

It didn't matter. Standing was no longer required. The darkness that absorbed the name she had carried from the West March expanded as she watched.

It took everything with it.

CHAPTER 15

"Kaylin."

The voice came from a distance. Kaylin had the futile hope that it would stay there.

"Kaylin. *Kaylin.* I know you're awake." Mandoran's voice grew louder. "Teela's pissed off. It'd be a huge help if you opened your eyes."

"Is she pissed off at me?" Kaylin asked. As an experiment, she tried opening her eyes. They were sticky, and the light in the room was too damn bright.

"I think she's pissed off at *Gilbert.* And if it's any incentive, Bellusdeo's eyes are almost bloodred."

Kaylin sat up. This was not the smartest idea, but someone caught her before she regretted it too badly. Mandoran. The light in the room—which she forced herself to endure—was sunlight. She blinked, lifted her hands and rubbed her eyes. "Where am I?"

"In Gilbert's house. Upstairs."

"And there are no *beds* upstairs?"

"Not in this room, no. Severn suggested a different room, but Gilbert didn't think that was a good idea. Did I mention that Bellusdeo's eyes are red?"

"Yes." Kaylin had been lying across a very ugly rug. It was a shade of green that would probably make anyone feel nauseous, and if that didn't, it was fringed in bright orange. Orange. She looked at her hands. They were hers. They were no longer Severn's.

Severn.

She tried to push herself off the ground and failed a second time. "I'm here," Severn said, his voice coming from somewhere behind her.

"Are you okay?"

"He's standing, and Teela's not worried about him," Mandoran replied.

"He's also capable of speaking for himself."

"When he can get a word in edgewise." It was true that Severn wasn't very chatty on most days. "Teela's worry is like a big wall of silence." He paused, lifting his head. "She's coming over."

When Teela failed to materialize, Kaylin frowned.

"Oh, she's not *here*," Mandoran said.

"She left?"

"You've been out for two days."

"Two *days*?"

"The Dragon's eyes didn't start out red."

"Two days. Why didn't you wake me? Marcus is going to tear my throat out!" Or worse, fire her.

"You can field this one," Mandoran said, over Kaylin's head.

"We attempted it," Severn said.

Kaylin digested that statement and assessed her physical condition. Her arms, when she lifted them, trembled. Her legs ached. Her mouth felt as if she'd spent the previous night drinking with Teela and Tain. And her stomach, not to be outdone, growled.

Mandoran snickered. She glanced at him. His eyes were almost entirely green.

"What's funny?"

"Now she's pissed off at you."

"Thanks. A lot."

"You don't know what she's like when she worries."

"Believe that I do. Why didn't someone take me home?"

"Gilbert thought it would be a bad idea to move you before you could move on your own."

"Did he happen to say why?"

"Yes."

Kaylin shrieked in frustration; it hid the noises her stomach was making. "Honestly, if my arms weren't so weak, I'd strangle you. What, exactly, did he say?"

Looking, if it were possible, more smug, Mandoran repeated what Gilbert had said. To no one's surprise, Kaylin couldn't understand a word of it. "If it helps, he was talking to your familiar."

"Not really. I'm guessing my familiar told everyone to leave me here."

"Yes. Bellusdeo elected to stay. Gilbert was visited by another one of your Dragons last night."

Kaylin wanted to cry. "Emmerian?"

"Lord Emmerian," Severn said, both correcting and confirming the guess. "Bellusdeo chose to remain. She was not willing to leave the house without you."

"Did you at least go home?"

Silence.

"So…Annarion is here, as well."

"He's downstairs in the parlor. I like that word, by the way. We have a bunch of questions for you."

"Food first. If I don't eat, you won't be able to hear my answers over the noise my stomach will be making."

Bellusdeo's eyes were a steady orange when Kaylin made it into the parlor. She was standing; Kattea was asleep in the largest chair the room contained. Gilbert, however, was absent. "You look terrible."

"I've been in the same clothing, unwashed, for two days, if reports are true. I haven't eaten. I am terrified that Marcus is going to rip my face off."

"Teela took care of that. Teela also dropped by your house and left word with Helen."

"I heard Lord Emmerian was here?"

"He will be back shortly. I sent him on an errand," she added, showing the first hint of a genuine smile—one that made Kaylin feel instant sympathy for the Dragon Lord. "Don't look like that. I sent him to the market. With Gilbert."

"On their own?"

"They were both beginning to annoy me."

"Can I just go back to being unconscious?" Kaylin, however, entered the room and sat in the nearest chair. "Or sleep. I think sleep would be good. Did Teela say anything about the state of the investigation across the street?"

"Yes. In Elantran. And Leontine."

Kaylin winced. Tilting her head back, she closed her eyes. She opened them again when food arrived and had the guilty impression that the interval between these two states wasn't exactly short.

Lord Emmerian glanced at Bellusdeo when he entered the parlor; seeing the color of her eyes, he relaxed. Gilbert, however, paused in the doorway. He offered Kaylin a very formal, very ostentatious bow. He then went to the chair Kattea occupied and woke her. She yawned, stretched and then noticed that Kaylin had joined them.

"You sleep a *lot*."

"Not usually." She attempted to look at Kattea when she spoke, because otherwise, she'd be staring at Gilbert. She recognized the longer lines of his oval face, the straight lines of shoulders, the length of his arms.

He smiled, as if reading her thoughts. "I am well," he said, voice gentle. "You have my gratitude."

What he lacked was the third eye. Kaylin didn't ask him where it had gone. Given Emmerian's presence in the room, she thought it smarter to keep her own counsel.

"Do you have a working mirror here?"

"I do. I will take you to it after you have eaten." Gilbert bowed again and left the room. Kattea leaped off her chair and followed, chattering in his wake.

Lord Emmerian's eyes were shading to gold as Bellusdeo's did. "You are well?"

Kaylin, wary, nodded. "Hungry," she added.

"Do you expect more difficulty?"

"I didn't even expect the last bit. But no, I'm not going to be trying anything I don't understand in the next little while."

He met Bellusdeo's eyes. Bellusdeo wasn't glaring, but it was close. "Then I shall depart. The Arkon conveys his best wishes and requests the pleasure of your company at your earliest convenience." He bowed—to Bellusdeo—and left.

"He's not much like Diarmat, is he?"

"Thankfully not." Bellusdeo exhaled. Given her expression, Kaylin was surprised not to see smoke. Or steam. "What happened?"

"I tried to heal Gilbert. I think I mostly succeeded."

"You have certainly altered his appearance. He looks vaguely Barrani."

Mandoran coughed.

"He looks more Barrani than he does human. I think it's his skin. Or his ears."

"His skin?"

"It is remarkably flawless. His eyes, however, are not Barrani—

or Dragon—in nature; I do not believe they have changed color once. What is he, Kaylin?"

"I don't completely understand it myself." She glanced at Mandoran. "Do you?"

He shook his head. "You've changed him, I think."

"Is that good, or bad?"

Mandoran shrugged. "What Bellusdeo sensed in him when she first met him, she does not sense in him now."

"I do not necessarily find that comforting," the Dragon added. "It merely means that it is hidden—and if that is so easily done, it raises questions of security."

"Define *easily.*"

Bellusdeo snorted. She walked over to the chair Kaylin occupied, bent and said, "You look terrible. I suggest we go home."

"Can I eat first?"

"Given how quickly you cram food into your mouth, that won't take long." She grabbed Kaylin by both shoulders and shook her gently. For a Dragon. Kaylin was surprised her teeth didn't fall out. "If you want to have a conversation with Gilbert, have him come with us."

"Can we bring Kattea, too?"

The first words Helen said—to Kaylin—when she entered the safety of her own home, were "I surrender. I have managed to create a relatively safe containment sphere which will accept mirror transmissions."

The first words Kaylin said to Helen were "I'm sorry."

Helen's frown was glacial, but she opened her arms. "Welcome back."

Kaylin walked into her hug. "I didn't mean to worry you—"

"No, of course not." Helen smiled, looking careworn. She lifted her head, released Kaylin and stepped back. It might have been a trick of the lighting, but Kaylin thought Helen actually reddened. "I have entirely forgotten my manners. You have guests." Her expression froze, and the normal, mortal brown of her eyes drained from them as she looked to the occupied doorway.

Kaylin turned to Kattea, who had walked through the door, and Gilbert, who had not. "This is Kattea, and her companion is Gilbert. Kattea, this is Helen."

Kattea smiled up at Helen, who had, once again, let her manners slip; she didn't appear to see the child.

"My apologies for the intrusion," Gilbert said, when Helen failed to speak. He turned to Kaylin. "This was possibly not the wisest of ideas. I believe you won a bet with Kattea; she is willing to answer your questions. I will wait." Turning to Helen, he asked, "If that is permitted?"

"Where did you meet Kaylin?"

"In my current residence. She came as a Hawk."

"Are you responsible for her absence?" Helen's eyes were now obsidian.

"To my regret, I am. I am in her debt."

"Kaylin?"

Kaylin was embarrassed. "I tried to heal him. I think I mostly succeeded. We still have a bunch of questions to ask him, and at least some of them are important to Annarion. They're about his brother. Gilbert didn't invite himself over."

"No. He wouldn't."

"I invited him. Do you think we can have the rest of this discussion in the side room?"

Helen's black gaze turned to Teela. "You did not inform me of all of the facts."

"I don't have all of the facts," Teela replied, shrugging. If Kaylin was worried or intimidated by the Avatar of her home, Teela wasn't. Nor was she about to start.

Kaylin turned to Helen. "Do you recognize him?"

"I am not certain." Not a good answer. Helen's memories of her early life—and her early duties—had been irreparably damaged sometime in the past. "He is not the first of his kind I have encountered." She exhaled. "I cannot read him. I do not think this visit wise. I have spoken to you about the sorcerers of my youth."

Kaylin turned to look at Gilbert, who still hadn't moved.

"Well…" Kaylin said, considering. "Unless he tries to harm you—or anyone else—while's he in the house, I'd like to take the risk."

"Very well." Helen nodded stiffly. "Give me a moment to prepare the room."

Kattea asked Helen if she wanted help in the kitchen. Time in the kitchen was not, strictly speaking, a requirement for Helen; Kaylin was surprised when she didn't say as much. Most of the sentient buildings of Kaylin's acquaintance were not famously good at lying.

"But you're a guest," Helen said.

"I like kitchens," Kattea replied. She had the earnest look of a puppy—a scruffy, underfed puppy who had not yet been kicked in the face enough that it had lost the ability to trust.

Helen hesitated for a moment longer and then nodded. "But if I tell you not to touch something, you have to listen. Certain items in the kitchen are not entirely safe for you." She led Kattea out of the room.

Gilbert offered his apologies again.

His deference clearly amused Mandoran; Annarion was silent and watchful. Teela lounged—there was no other word for it—across the largest free space in the room; Tain took a patch of wall instead and leaned into it. Severn sat in the chair closest to the door, facing inward.

Gilbert sat to Kaylin's right; Bellusdeo camped to her left. In all, it was not a very comfortable room.

"You've been in buildings like this one before," Kaylin said.

"I am of the opinion that I have never set foot in a building such as this. You called it Helen?"

"If you mean did I name her, then no. Helen is her name. She's in charge. I live here, and I can ask her for things—but I can't enforce obedience."

Both of his brows rose. "And it—she—cannot enforce obedience from you?"

"I imagine if she bent her mind to it, she could."

"She's certainly been doing a number on Annarion," Mandoran added. Annarion glared, but said nothing.

Gilbert looked about the room. "She reminds me of my youth. We once lived in homes such as these—places that heard our voices and spoke with their own. But we knew their names. It was one of the many ways in which we communicated our desires." His eyes were a curious shade of brown, almost rust in color.

"It was," Helen's disembodied voice said, "the chief way in which control was exerted."

"And such control was unpleasant?"

"Was it not unpleasant to you?"

Gilbert frowned. "It was not possible," he finally replied. His eyes darkened. They weren't, then, like mortal eyes. Until this moment, Kaylin hadn't been entirely certain.

"What wasn't possible?" she asked.

"For our names to be known. I understand that your names are not like ours," he added.

"We don't—Kattea and I—have names." Her frown mirrored Gilbert's. She understood why immortals resisted being healed. It was almost impossible for the healer not to see the thoughts and emotions of the healed, to some extent. "When

I tried to heal you…" Her thoughts weren't solid enough to form useful questions.

Gilbert's nod was quiet. "You almost lost your life."

Kaylin shrugged. "It wouldn't be the first time." She hesitated and then said, "I had no idea what I was doing. And having done it, I still don't understand. When you say knowing your name is impossible, what do you mean?"

He turned his head, his gaze fixed on nothing.

The nothing squawked.

"It is impossible for you or any of your companions. I am told it is impossible for any who live as you live."

"But you *have* a name."

Squawk.

"There is some misunderstanding. I am an earlier iteration of life. An earlier design. The Ancients were my creator; they were my parents. I do not, cannot, have children in the fashion I am assured you do. Children such as yours—any of yours— would not have been considered possible or desirable on the eve of my creation." His smile deepened as Kaylin's confusion grew. "I am not so very different from your Helen."

"He is mistaken," Helen said.

"Am I? You were created to serve a specific function. I do not know what that function was or is; your story is opaque to me. I sense its presence, but I cannot read it. I cannot *hear* it. I was created to serve a specific function—but that function did not rely on others. You cannot move from the space you occupy; to move would destroy you. In that, we are different. But in all else, I believe we have more in common than I have with any of your inhabitants."

"Your name—it's like the names of the ancestors," Kaylin said.

Gilbert frowned.

Kaylin turned to the empty space that Gilbert had been addressing. "Can you explain the ancestors to him? Please?"

Squawk. Squawk. Squawk.

Gilbert's expression shifted with each screeching syllable. "Where did you encounter these ancestors?"

"In Nightshade's Castle."

Squawk. Squawk. Squawk.

His eyes shifted color as Kaylin watched; they were a true brown now. As brown as Kaylin's, although they had darkened so much she could no longer see pupil. He was rigid by the time the invisible familiar fell silent.

"Yes," he said. When Kaylin's forehead creased, he added, "My name is very like the names of those you call ancestors. They are not," he added, "ancestors, in the Elantran meaning of that word. Their names are not as complicated as mine. I thought them gone or contained."

"The two we met were sleeping. They woke up."

"They heard Annarion." It wasn't a question.

Annarion looked about as comfortable with this statement as Kaylin felt.

Gilbert glanced at him. "I heard you when I first attempted to leave my home. I followed the sound of your voice…but I could not hear you when I finally arrived in this Elantra. I could not hear you when I first met Kaylin. I can hear you now. I can hear your friend. It is…distracting. Distracting and compelling."

This didn't increase Annarion's comfort level; it also added Mandoran's discomfort to the mix.

"We hear your pain," Gilbert continued. "We hear your loss. We hear your fear. We do not understand its cause, but we understand that you are here, that you are real. Your voice is that strong.

"In a bygone era, your voice would have been one of thousands." He hesitated. "You were not created as I was. You were...born. You have not been altered by any will save your own. The word at your core is so simple, so singular, I cannot hear it. And yet, Annarion, I hear you. I hear Mandoran." He grimaced. "I hear Kattea."

"She is engaged in her kitchen duties," Helen's disembodied voice informed him. "Refreshments will not be offered immediately; I think it would break her heart if all of her work was wasted. But...I confess I am mildly confused. Gilbert said he found Kattea in the fief of Nightshade."

"I did."

"And according to Kaylin, that was weeks ago—a handful of weeks."

"Yes."

"Her behavior, and her knowledge of, among other things, food, is not consistent with that claim. Her experience in Nightshade does not mirror Kaylin's. One would, of course, expect some differences; no two mortals have identical histories or experiences."

"Is Gilbert lying?" Kaylin asked quietly, noting the shift in the color of both Dragon and Barrani eyes.

"No, dear. Kattea's memories are consistent with Gilbert's version of events."

"What is the difficulty you perceive?" Annarion asked Helen.

"The fief of Nightshade that Kattea was found in is not the fief in which Kaylin was born."

CHAPTER 16

Silence.

Kaylin was uneasy. Everything Helen had just said mirrored thoughts—doubts—Kaylin had also had. The silence stretched until Kaylin broke it. "How is Kattea's Nightshade different?"

"She was not starving. She was not terrified of her neighbors. She lived in a modest house. The Ferals she feared were not—as they were for you and Severn—a simple fact, like sunset or sunrise. There was a functional market within walking distance of her home. She learned to cook while aiding her mother and her aunt." Helen hesitated.

Kaylin marked it. "What else aren't you saying?"

"I am not mortal," Helen began apologetically. "I may misunderstand. But Kattea believes that the Elantra in which you live and work is in her past. She believes that the city as it is now disappeared very shortly after she was born."

"She thinks she's from our *future*?"

Helen hesitated again. "She did not speak of this out loud, and perhaps, as guest, I should not…"

Gilbert, however, said, "Yes."

Kaylin turned to Kattea's guardian. "You told Kattea you needed her."

"I do not live as you live. I do not travel as you travel. My home was—and is—Ravellon. Ravellon is unlike your city. If the Ancients can be said to have been born at all, it is Ravellon that was their birthplace, and it is in Ravellon that they came of age. In Ravellon, they designed and argued and built. In Ravellon they learned to see, and speak, and sing.

"And in Ravellon, they learned to sleep. And die. And kill." He rose and began to pace. "Death is not—to us—what it is to you. Your lives are so simple, so silent, they pass beneath us; we notice them if we study your kindred, but in general, you are, to the Ancients, what a blade of grass is to you. Or perhaps an ant.

"Mortals were not created in my waking hours, but I see you as an extension of ancient arguments and debates. The Shadows you speak of now were birthed in Ravellon. They were not meant to be what they became."

"What were they meant to be?" She hesitated. "Part of you is part of what they are now."

His smile was thin. "Yes. And it is because they are part of me—and were, at my inception—that I can be here at all. It is why I can understand some small part of your speech. Why I can see time almost as you see it.

"Kattea is necessary because time—for mortals—is inevitable; it is a wall above which they cannot climb." He glanced at Teela and Bellusdeo. "For the purpose of this discussion, you are also mortal in my eyes."

Teela shrugged.

Bellusdeo looked mildly offended.

"It was not always safe to be exposed to the Ancients during periods of unhindered creation. Creation requires a malleability that can be…destabilizing. Buildings such as Helen were designed to withstand such instability." There was a hint of a question at the end of that statement.

Helen answered. "My memory is faulty because I destroyed elements of myself."

"You did this?" Kaylin thought she could have told him she'd lopped off her head and it wouldn't have surprised him—or horrified him—as much.

"Yes."

"Why?"

"I wished to be able make my own decisions."

Gilbert's command of Elantran was clearly not perfect. "I do not understand."

"I wished to choose my own lord."

He looked dumbfounded.

"Is that such a strange concept to you? I served. I had served for the whole of my existence. I do not recall resentment. We all need purpose, and mine was clear. But my lord left, and he did not return. In his absence, I was forced to destroy some parts of myself to protect what remained of his work.

"And in his absence, I became aware of—fond of—a mortal woman. She cared for me. She did not understand that I was alive, that I was sentient. She cared for the space in which she found herself. She made small pockets of me her home. I understood that my lord would not return. And I understood that I could make myself home to this woman.

"I did not destroy the defenses," Helen added, almost self-consciously. "Were you to attempt to harm me—or anyone under my protection—you would not succeed."

He was staring at the wall. Helen's Avatar had not returned. "So," he said, voice soft.

"I interrupted you; I'm sorry. It's a bit of a habit."

Gilbert shook his head as it was of no matter and picked up where he had left off. "I dwelled within a building similar to the space that Helen occupies. Its name was more complex, and its purpose less easily divined by those who had not dwelled within it for centuries; it is the *gardia*. It had, as Helen does, physical boundaries, external borders. I believe it occupied more space than Helen; perhaps as much space as a fifth of your city, absent the population that fifth also contains.

"We had warning of a grave perturbation and returned to weather the storm within the walls of that building. But the difficulties we faced were unprecedented, and in the end, we were drawn into the building's core as it surrendered the outer walls and everything those walls contained. I chose to sleep. Sleep, for my kind, is not what Kattea experiences when she sleeps; it is a way of minimizing contact, an echo of the decisions the building itself made. There are periods of instability; when the instability has hardened or passed, I wake.

"In this instance, however, I did not wake on my own."

Kaylin found herself holding her breath.

"Yes," Gilbert continued, meeting—and holding—her gaze. "I woke at the behest of Lord Nightshade."

Annarion leaned forward, as if to catch the words that followed. He didn't speak. Kaylin was impressed; if she'd been Annarion, she'd have jumped across the room and grabbed Gilbert by his collar.

"Nightshade was in Ravellon."

"Yes."

"How? How did he reach Ravellon?"

"A good question, and a difficult one to answer. Lord Nightshade did not cross the boundaries that separate Ravellon from the rest of your world; he did not enter with the intent to find or wake me. He was sent to the core of the building that sustains those of us who survived the disaster."

Gilbert closed his eyes briefly. "Lord Nightshade should not have been able to wake me. That he could was the will of the *gardia*, the building. I was the only one awakened. The great halls were empty and still. None save Nightshade moved or spoke. Even the *gardia* was silent.

"There is a silence that is welcome; it is a reprieve from noise and chaos, a type of peace. I do not mean to denigrate silence."

Helen's expression, as she studied Gilbert, was grave.

"Nightshade spoke. I did not hear him, at first. I could only see him from the corner of an eye."

Kaylin, remembering the eyes she had, one by one, carefully closed, said nothing.

"I told you I had to invert myself; it was not a quick process. Nor was it painless. It is not something I have attempted prior to this. I could not speak to your Nightshade in any other way. The *gardia* had sent him to wake me—or so I assumed; I made the adjustment." He winced, but the expression faded into a very surprising smile. "I did not expect to like his voice.

"The *gardia* provided for his needs, and I learned to speak, first Barrani, and then the Elantran, which seems more prevalent here. I learned to listen. It is surprisingly difficult; the language you speak is so flexible, and the same words can have entirely different meanings depending on the speaker. I had to ask questions, repeatedly; I had to choose different angles, different approaches.

"But I came to understand him. He spoke of his family. His father. The Barrani High Lord and its High Halls. The High Halls he described felt faintly familiar. He spoke of you," he continued, staring at the mark on Kaylin's cheek. "He spoke of his Lady, and last, of his brother, Annarion. He spoke of the way time changes all things.

"Time," Gilbert added, "does not change me. The concept of this change—as a thing that occurs naturally and without the deliberate intent of a creator—was new. It was interesting. I asked many, many questions. Lord Nightshade spoke of his home. He spoke of his Castle. He spoke of Dragons, and of the Dragon who lived in Ravellon."

Bellusdeo stiffened.

"Lord Nightshade wished to venture into Ravellon—and beyond. He wished to return to his Castle. He wished to speak with his brother, to explain what might be explained. I do not understand all of your difficulties," he added, a trace of apology in his voice as he glanced at Annarion. "But I came to understand the depth of his desire, and I wished to accommodate it.

"Do you understand now?"

"You spent enough time with Nightshade that you became friends, and you wanted to help him?" Kaylin asked.

Gilbert smiled. "Yes. You understand."

"How *long* did you spend getting to know him? In mortal years. Or at least my years."

Gilbert turned to the empty space Kaylin had silently marked "small dragon." He spoke. The familiar squawked.

Gilbert then turned back to Kaylin. "Not more than forty of your years."

Annarion turned to Gilbert, his eyes a shade of purple that Kaylin seldom saw. "What did he tell you of our family? Of our father? What did he say of me? What explanation did he think to make that would be *of value*?"

Gilbert lowered his chin slightly. "You have no doubt noticed that I struggle with your language. With any of your languages. I do not share your history, except secondhand. I will not speak for your brother, in this.

"If you wish to know, you must find him." He hesitated. "But it might be best if you remained with Helen. I did not lie. I arrived in this time and in this place because, in my wandering, I *heard you*. The silence of the *gardia*, the silence of those you would call my kin, was broken by your voice, and yours alone.

"You called me, Annarion. You called me and I came. I lost the thread of your voice. I grieved at its loss. You would wake us all if you lifted that voice in our presence—and I do not think that is your desire. Your brother understands that you are not what you once were. Understand that he is not what he once was."

Annarion nodded slowly, and Gilbert continued.

"I could not find a path that would lead from the *gardia* to Lord Nightshade's home." He frowned. Turning, he rose, walked to the doors and closed them. "This door is closed. The room we are in now could exist in the *gardia*. Pretend, for a moment, that it does." He then opened the door. "On the other side of this door is the foyer. But if this *were* a door in Ravellon's center, it would open into an entirely differ-ent space. Opening this door a hundred times would grant a glimpse into a hundred different spaces.

"You have no desire to explore. You have a specific space to which you must return. This is analogous to my attempt. Your Nightshade could not clearly describe his residence. Had I wished, from the outset, to aid him, it would nevertheless have been impossible for me. Only with the passage of years, and my growing familiarity with the way you communicate, was there a possibility of success.

"But it was...difficult. My inversion meant that there were transitions I could not make without sustaining injury. The transitions that were allowed were few, and they did not lead to Nightshade's home. In the endless corridor very, very few of the doors now open. The silence is absolute."

Gilbert paused for a moment, seeming to collect himself before continuing, "In all of my many attempts, I found only one path that led to Nightshade's home, as he perceived it; only one tenuous connection."

"The Castle."

"Yes, Helen. The Castle. The path to and from the Castle was damaged, frayed. It existed in the aftermath of Night-shade's departure. It led from the *gardia* to the Castle.

"The Castle was reluctant to grant me entry. It was more reluctant to allow me to leave, even when I explained my chosen mission. The discussion devolved into argument; the argument into conflict. I sustained injuries there. I was in danger of losing coherence."

"And then you met me!" Kattea said, grinning as she entered the parlor. She carried a tray that looked as if it weighed at least half of what she did; Helen was hovering behind her. She didn't take the tray.

"I did offer, dear," she told Kaylin. "But Kattea did almost all of the work, and she wanted to bring it in herself." She gestured, and dishes appeared on the sideboard to which Kattea was carrying the tray.

"You weren't frightened?" Helen asked Kattea.

Kattea shrugged. "It's hard to be afraid of Gilbert when you're expecting Ferals. Or worse."

Which was perfectly reasonable, as far as Kaylin was concerned.

"Kattea was the first person I encountered. Had I never endeavored to communicate with Nightshade, I would not have recognized what she was. Because I had, I could hear her, and even see her. If I focused on Kattea, the disorientation caused by the Castle slowed enough that I could think. Kattea has explained the concept of races. She has attempted to explain the physical differences between them. To me, however, she was very like Nightshade."

A ten-year-old girl was *nothing* like Lord Nightshade.

"With the exception of Annarion and Mandoran, you all are. The way you live, the way you are confined, the limited scope of your interactions with the world—they are consistent across the various species. But there is something else that is strangely consistent, as well. It was not a trait that I noticed in Lord Nightshade; it is a characteristic of every other inhabitant of the city I have encountered."

"And that?"

"Your relationship with the time in which you dwell. Kattea is rooted in her own time. The length, the consistency, of those roots is strong, but they will fade the longer she remains here; she will meld into the now in which you live. This now will sustain her, just as her own would. I do not wish to return her to the place in which I found her." He grimaced. "Your language is thin and inexact. You speak of 'time' and 'place.' To you, these are distinct. They may overlap, but they are not one.

"Kattea is not an anchor in the sense that your boats—"

"Ships."

"—ships have anchors. But she serves the same purpose. She is part of her own time, and only in that time is there a road into—and out of—the *gardia*, by which Nightshade might leave. Only through Kattea do I have the confidence that I am able to return to that time. But that connection will wane.

"It is almost irrelevant at this point. I did not intend to stop here. I did not intend to come here at all."

"You meant to return to Castle Nightshade."

"Yes. I followed the sound of Annarion's voice until it abruptly ceased. When I could not longer hear him, I attempted to correct my course. I could not. It is not that I am trapped here," he added. "I can move, if I so choose.

"But there is nowhere to move to."

★ ★ ★

Kattea, determinedly unaware of the weight of the ensuing silence, busied herself with floating plates. "Gilbert asks a lot of questions. Some of them are kinda funny."

Gilbert smiled. "I have come to understand mortality from Kattea's answers. I understand that you contain no true words, no paragraphs, no stories. Such words do not form, guide or control the shape of your life."

When Kaylin made no immediate reply, Helen said, "You have choices that we do not. The Ancients created us for a purpose. They devised the beginning of our conscious lives, and they saw to the end of them. Everything within the parameters of our creation is open to us. Everything beyond or external to them…is not.

"You have said we have the power of gods within our own boundaries. We do not. We cannot create life, although we can destroy it. We can speak, but if no one crosses our threshold, we cannot be heard. We have purpose, but it is a purpose dependent, always, on others." She reddened. "And I speak, of course, for myself, not for Gilbert. Gilbert can move independently. He can make decisions that I could not, before my injury, make. He can make connections that are still, by my very nature, denied me."

"Yes. Apologies, Helen. Yet if I can make those connections, my interactions are nonetheless prescribed. Yours, Kaylin, Kattea's, perhaps your companions', are not. They do not exist in all of the planes of being."

"We have names," Bellusdeo told him, her voice unusually gentle.

"Kaylin and Kattea do not even have that. Yet they think, they speak, they plan. Perhaps the wisdom of their plans can be called into question—but they have a choice and they make it, unhindered."

Kaylin cleared her throat. "We don't."

"You do."

"No. We've got choices, sometimes. But what choice did Kattea have? Did she choose to lose her parents? Did she choose to lose her home? Did she choose to be hunted by Ferals?"

"Kitling—"

"Did she choose to meet you outside of Castle Nightshade?"

"Kitling, I think—"

"He's romanticizing poverty and desperation, Teela. If he's going to talk about *choice* that way, I want him to understand what he's actually saying. Yes, our lives aren't predetermined. They're not fixed. But we need to eat. We need to keep warm. We need to sleep. We don't get to choose where we're born, or how, or to who. We're not guaranteed to *get* any of the things we need. We're just as trapped by the things we need and the things we fear as you are by the words at your core—but most of us will never, ever be able to do the things those words allow you to do.

"If Kattea had met Ferals instead of you, she'd be dead. You'd never find enough—"

"Kitling."

Kaylin stopped.

Kattea, however, threw Teela a look that seemed far too old for her face. "Why are you making her stop? She's right."

"I think Teela is concerned about the effects discussing your death might have on you," Helen offered.

"Because the discussion would change it? She's right. If Gilbert hadn't found me, I'd be dead. If Gilbert had been a different person, I might be alive—but I might not be free. At all. I have no family to protect me. No one who would care if I disappeared. I don't expect Gilbert to understand all this—he didn't even understand breathing. No, I mean it. He didn't. He didn't really understand eating, either. He doesn't understand family. He doesn't understand *anything*. But Kaylin *does* understand. And she should be allowed to speak."

Kaylin shook her head. "I think you've just said everything I was going to say."

"I didn't. Do you know what the two days before I met Gilbert were like?"

Kaylin closed her eyes. "I can imagine."

"Gilbert protects me. But I help him, too."

"And how," Mandoran drawled, "do you do that? If you're so helpless, so powerless, how do you help him?"

She flushed, but continued, her expression clearly shouting *I don't like you*. "Because he doesn't know anything. I *explain* things."

Mandoran was clearly not impressed with the ability of a mortal child to explain anything. Kaylin was about to kick him when Helen intervened.

"She explains her life," she told the condescending Barrani. "And it is her life, and lives like it, that are most foreign to our experience. How she sees, what she sees, what she knows, what she doesn't know—this information is of incalculable value. Do not deride it. It is information that we cannot otherwise possess."

"It's not just information," Kattea continued, with less anger and more confidence. "If I'm not with him, Gilbert can't go home."

Squawk.

Gilbert turned to the empty space occupied by an invisible familiar. He replied. Kaylin couldn't understand a word he spoke, but the familiar didn't have that problem. Neither did Mandoran, who joined in.

Kaylin and Kattea ate while they argued, as did Severn. There was no point in starving.

"Are they always like this?" Kattea whispered.

"Yes. And they can hear you two rooms away, even if you whisper."

"Oh. I don't like him."

"Mandoran?"

"Is that his name?"

"It's the polite version."

"What's the rude version?"

"Kitling," Teela warned.

"It's not a name," Kaylin clarified. "Look, I won a bet, right?"

Kattea nodded.

"So, let me ask you some questions."

"About the murders?"

"Got it in one."

Kattea nodded. "We didn't kill them," she said.

"Did you see them alive at any point?"

Kattea's voice was hesitant, wary. "...Yes."

"They're dead, Kattea. They can't hurt you; they can't take offense at anything you tell me now. Did Gilbert speak to them?"

Kattea nodded. "But only one time."

"When?"

The girl's eyes slid off Kaylin's face, which was pretty much an answer. Kaylin asked anyway. "The night before they died?"

Kattea nodded again. "Gilbert doesn't get angry. He was angry then. It was the first time I'd seen it."

"How could you tell?"

"He—he hit one of them." Kattea hesitated. "But not—but not with his hand. I think it was magic." She spoke the single word with both reverence and a touch of fear. "They shouted. I think they tried to use magic, too."

"Did Gilbert speak to all three of them?"

"Four."

"Three."

"There were four," Kattea insisted. "I can count to *four*."

Kaylin winced. "Sorry."

Kattea exhaled. "Me, too. But—honest, there were four. It was the fourth guy Gilbert didn't like. The fourth guy hit Gilbert."

"Physically?"

Kattea nodded. "But…they were standing in the middle of the street, and the street wasn't empty. So the other three didn't stick around. They went into their own house."

"Can you describe the fourth man?"

"No, but he was Barrani. He was Barrani and he was wearing a thing on his head. Not a crown, but—"

"A circlet? Was there a gem across his forehead?"

She nodded. "It was yellow, I think."

"Teela—"

"On it," Teela said. "You're certain the circlet had a yellow stone? It wasn't green or blue?"

"Or red?" Kaylin added.

"It was yellow or clear."

Teela said something short and curt—in Leontine. "I surrender," she said, to Kaylin.

"What did I do this time?"

"Nothing is *ever* simple, where you're concerned."

"I had nothing to do with this!"

"Yellow is bad?" Severn asked. Given Teela's expression, Kaylin had decided against it.

"Diamond," Tain said, "is bad."

"So we're hoping for yellow."

"Yellow doesn't exist—not if we're assuming the involvement of Arcanists." Tain looked at his partner. As far as Kaylin knew, Tain didn't know Teela's True Name, and Teela didn't know his. But they'd worked together for as long as Kaylin had known them. When things got serious, words were superfluous.

"Kattea, how did you get to your house?"

"We walked."

"Did you walk through the halls in your basement?"

Kattea nodded. She hesitated and then added, "Gilbert wanted to leave the fiefs. I told him it wasn't safe, even at night. No one crosses the bridge. So we went back to the Castle."

"You didn't get here through the Castle."

"No. But there's a well—a dry well—behind it. Gilbert said it connects to the city."

Kaylin started to tell her that Gilbert was wrong, and stopped. She had climbed down that well, using it as a back door into the Castle itself. What it connected to was water. Elemental water. The uneasiness in prominent display in Teela's and Tain's eyes took up residence in Kaylin's mind, as well.

"Did you discover water at the bottom of the well?"

"Yes. And a boat."

"...A boat."

Kattea nodded.

"I didn't get a boat when I had to climb down the well."

"Complain later, kitling."

Squawk.

"You used the boat?"

Kattea nodded. "There was a river, an underground river. We got into the boat, and the boat began to move. Gilbert spoke." She took a deep, nervous breath and said, "The water *answered.*"

"What did the water say?"

Kattea's brows furrowed. "You believe me?"

"I've spoken with the water beneath Castle Nightshade before. Yes, I believe you." She wanted Gilbert and the familiar to shut up. Their voices quieted instantly. Kaylin immediately turned to make sure they were still there.

"I am sorry, dear," Helen said. "When you think with such ferocity, I can't quite tell if you mean for me to act or not."

"...Sorry. I just— It's hard to hear Kattea with all the squawking." She turned back to the girl. "What did the water say?"

Kattea's shoulders curved toward her knees; she rested her chin on them. "I don't know. I couldn't understand it."

Gilbert looked up. "I did not understand most of it, either."

"You're sure it was the water you were hearing?"

"Yes, Chosen. The water carried us to the halls beneath my current residence. We found the stairs, and the house it-self was unoccupied."

"And you just...stayed there."

"I did not know where I was; Kattea had a better under-standing. She seemed...excited."

Kattea nodded. "We can't cross the bridge," she told Kay-lin. "No one who crosses the bridge returns." She said this in a hushed voice.

"No one who crosses the bridge wants to return?" Kay-lin asked.

"I don't know. No one knows what's on the other side of the bridge. No one can see anything past the Ablayne. Four people left two years ago. They crossed the bridge. We could all see them until they reached the banks of the opposite side."

"What happened?"

"They disappeared. They just—they just weren't there any-more. They were supposed to cross the bridge and return. They didn't." She continued to look at her knees. "My dad used to tell me stories about the city across the bridge." Lift-ing her chin, she added, "He was born here. This is where he grew up."

"If your father grew up here—"

"He was a Sword."

Kaylin felt her stomach drop about two feet, which would put it somewhere beneath the floor. If Gilbert was right, Kattea was part of a nebulous and suddenly threatening future in which Elantra itself had been destroyed or swallowed; a future which saw Swords—or former Swords—living on the other side of the Ablayne.

If Swords had crossed the bridge, it explained Kattea and her view of Nightshade; it explained Kattea's resolute belief in the Hawks. Unfortunately, it explained almost nothing else.

"Fine." Kaylin exhaled. Turning to Severn, she said, "We've got our work cut out for us."

Severn rose.

Teela stepped in the way. "Where do you think you're going?"

"To see Evanton. I want to speak to the elemental water."

"Now?"

"I have to go now, or I won't get back in time. In theory, we have dinner tonight with a very important guest."

"In practice," Bellusdeo said, "we don't. Don't give me that look—I had no idea when you would wake or if you could be moved. The Emperor accepted the deferral for reasons of his own."

"And those would be?" Kaylin demanded.

Teela's lips thinned. "Did we not agree that this was not a pressing concern?"

"Kaylin appears to be materially unharmed. She's going to find out anyway."

"What exactly is Kaylin going to find out?" the private in question now asked.

Bellusdeo exhaled smoke. "Tiamaris has fallen off the mirror network."

CHAPTER 17

"Pardon?"

"The fief of Tiamaris can no longer be reached by the mirror network."

"And the other fiefs?"

"The only other fief in which the Halls had a known contact was Nightshade."

"Have you tried? Andellen—and the rest of his men—should still be there."

Teela hesitated. "Yes," she said, voice a shade too quiet. "Word has been sent to Lord Andellen. The fief of Tiamaris can be reached on foot, and Tiamaris is unharmed. The mirror network, however, will no longer cross the Ablayne."

Kaylin shook her head. Lifting her hand, she began to count. "One: Evanton's. Two: Tiamaris. Three: the Winding Path. Four: never mind."

"Four is Nightshade."

Kaylin glanced at Severn. "Four: Nightshade. Am I missing anything?"

Teela held up one finger. "Five: the Arcanum."

Bellusdeo held up a hand. "I might as well play. Six: the Arkon."

Kaylin grimaced. "Teela and Tain can cover the Arcanum. You can speak to the Arkon."

"Nightshade?" Teela asked.

"I'm not sure what we're supposed to find there, but yes, I can go to the Castle and attempt to speak with Andellen. But I really think we should ask Tara about the whole push-forward-in-time thing. If we understand how it works, we may be able to figure *something* out." She massaged the back of her neck as she considered. "I don't know if you heard what Kattea said—"

"We heard," Teela replied.

"—but we need to know what she actually knows. If something happened in her past, it's something that's going to happen in our present. With our luck, probably now. Any information she can give us might point us in the right direction."

"I'm going to bet on Arcanist and ancient basement myself," Teela said. "We're heading out."

Bellusdeo said, "I'll get Maggaron. We'll speak to Lannagaros—but he's not going to be happy that you're not there."

"Why? Because he'll have to be polite to everyone in the room?"

Bellusdeo grinned. "Maggaron is too earnest for Lannagaros's taste; he begins to feel guilty if he teases him."

"I'll have to try that approach."

"I don't understand it myself—I find teasing Maggaron both amusing and irresistible." Her smile faded. "I won't insist on following you to the Keeper's or Tiamaris."

"Nightshade?"

"I am…uneasy. I can, however, deal with Lannagaros; it's far better than having to speak with Arcanists."

"It's far better for *you*," Teela countered, an entirely different smile coming to the fore. "If Tain and I go, any difficulties are entirely a matter for the Caste Court."

"Meaning?"

"If anyone happens to die, it's not murder, according to Imperial Law. If we have to drag any of you, on the other hand, things become messier."

"That's only assuming the Arcanist in question is actually Barrani," Kaylin felt compelled to point out.

"Yes. You have problems with that assumption?"

"Not all Arcanists are Barrani, Teela."

"No. But mortal Arcanists have seldom caused large-scale destruction and danger."

"Hello? The last time—"

"Oh, hush. Don't rain on the only possible bright spot in an increasingly dreary day, hmm? And try not to get yourself killed in our absence."

"In general, your *presence* has caused me more trouble."

Gilbert turned to Kattea, who was still seated, knees beneath her chin, against the wall. "What do you wish us to do?" he asked quietly.

"If you were a Hawk," Kaylin told him, "we'd send you to keep an eye on the basement that contains the possible murder victims." She frowned. "You haven't seen the bodies, have you?"

"No. As Kattea has mentioned, I had some very small interaction with three men the night before the Hawks were summoned. If they are the same men who were disincorporated—"

"Killed," Kattea corrected, although she still didn't look up. "I told you—people don't evaporate. Only water."

"Ah. Yes. If they are the same men, I have not seen them since their deaths."

Kaylin, who was watching Kattea—or what she could see of the girl, which at the moment was a bowed head, forearms and legs from the knees down—frowned. Kattea's arms had tightened. In a quieter voice, which she hoped was somehow comforting, she said, "All of this is off-record. If for some reason you *have*, tell me now."

"I have not." Gilbert looked slightly bewildered. "What is off-record?"

Kattea snickered into her kneecaps.

"It means that I won't mention it to anyone who would get angry about it. More or less." Teela and Tain were gone; Bellusdeo was upstairs. That left Helen and Severn. "I was hoping to leave you and Kattea here. It's safe. Helen won't hurt you—but more important, she won't let anything else hurt you, either."

"Who would attempt to hurt me?"

"Someone apparently did, according to Kattea."

Gilbert frowned. "There was some difficulty, but it was minor in nature."

Kattea lifted her head then. She looked both outraged and—well, differently outraged. Gilbert's obvious stupidity—because it was clear that Kattea considered him to be just about too stupid to live at the moment—cut through her fear of the future. "It was *not* minor."

"What happened?" Kaylin addressed Kattea.

"People came to the house. They knocked. We ignored it."

"When was this?"

"The night before you came back."

"Before I healed Gilbert?"

"Before you won the bet, yes."

"Fine. These men came after your neighbors were murdered?"

Kattea nodded. This nod was…off. Kaylin glanced at Severn; his face had become a mask. But he nodded; he noticed what she had.

Fair enough. Kaylin, at Kattea's age, would never have answered a door at night. The only people who went out at night in Nightshade were fools—or worse, people powerful enough not to have to fear Ferals. "What time was it?"

Kattea shrugged. "It'd been dark for *hours*. No one you want to speak to comes that late at night." She spoke this as if she were repeating something she'd heard in her childhood. A lot.

Kaylin resisted the urge to bend or otherwise diminish the difference in their height. "How many were there?"

"At least three."

"Four," Gilbert replied.

"I said *at least*." She exhaled. "I only saw three." She tightened her arms, lowered her chin, inhaled. Kaylin thought she would fall silent again, but no—this time, she was gathering her courage. "It was the *same* three. The three that you said were dead."

Apparently, this was news to Gilbert; it certainly caught the attention of both remaining Hawks and Helen.

"I do not think—" Gilbert began.

"Yes, I know," Kattea shot back. She stood. "Gilbert doesn't— he doesn't *see* people the same way we do."

This was making assumptions, but Kaylin was fine with that. "No, I don't think he does."

"Kattea has explained what death means to the mortal. If you, as Hawks, were called in to investigate deaths, it follows that the men in question could not be the same men."

"That would be the hope, yes." Kaylin hesitated. "Did they *look* dead to you?"

Kattea rolled her eyes. She didn't expect to be believed. But Kaylin had believed her about the water. She was willing to *try*. "No. They looked exactly the same as they had the night before."

"Exactly the same?"

Kattea nodded. "But there were only three this time."

Gilbert said, "There were only three that *you* could see. There was a fourth. I am sorry, Kaylin—but they did not appear, to me, to be the same men. I have some difficulty recognizing individuals."

"Kattea, are you *certain*?" Kaylin asked.

Kattea nodded. She was done with hesitation. "Gilbert was staring at a wall when they knocked. When Gilbert stares like that, it's really hard to get his attention."

"Kattea does manage," Gilbert said, with a faint smile.

"You told me how. You didn't tell them."

"If you didn't open the door and Gilbert was busy, how did they get in?"

"They came around the back and kicked the door in. I woke Gilbert up," she added, "when I heard the back door. It took them a while."

"Gilbert doesn't sound like he was fully awake."

Kattea's snort was not particularly delicate. "He was awake enough to talk."

"What did they want?"

"Mostly? I think they wanted to kill Gilbert."

The three corpses, such as they were, had been invisible when viewed through the wing of her familiar. They had, however, been examined by Red—and by Hawks who had seen enough death to be able to recognize it.

"I meant to leave you both with Helen, where you're safe. But I think we need to visit the Winding Path. I need you to look at the three bodies."

Two days. Two *days*, she'd slept. "Next time," she said to her partner, "wake me up."

Annarion and Mandoran chose to remain with Helen. Given the look on Mandoran's face, "chose" was probably the wrong verb, but the argument his expression implied was not audible. This meant, on the other hand, that Kaylin's small and flappy familiar came out of hiding; Helen was capable of muting their voices.

He appeared in midair and landed on Kaylin's right shoulder.

"He's back," Kattea said, voice hushed but perfectly clear.

Kaylin, who would have sworn that the familiar was nothing but a pain on most days, was surprised at how *right* it felt to have him there. She endured the quiet squawks that sounded suspiciously smug.

"He'd better be useful to you," Mandoran told her, his perfect mouth folding into a not-entirely-unattractive pout. "He's most of the reason we're staying put."

"You don't—"

"Sedarias doesn't want us anywhere near theoretical bodies. Or Gilbert, if it comes to that."

Although she'd stayed behind in the West March, Sedarias had Annarion's and Mandoran's True Names. She could see what they saw, and was free to offer advice and opinion. Sedarias's opinion carried a lot more weight than anyone who happened to be present.

Kattea was, in spite of her fear, excited. Kaylin felt ambivalent about this. There was something wrong when a child was excited about seeing *corpses*. She attempted to hint at this, but Kattea saw it as Hawk work, and she wanted to be included. Any hope that she would stay—quietly—with Helen when Gilbert left was instantly dashed.

Kaylin, remembering herself at thirteen, couldn't bring herself to put her foot down. Severn, who had grown up in the same fief that Kaylin had, didn't blink, either. She expected Marcus to be growly about it, but hoped to avoid actually *telling* him. She'd have to write a report, but Marcus didn't usually read those all the way to the end.

The Hawks were in evidence when Kaylin approached the house. She let Severn do most of the talking, because if Kaylin and Severn did not consider a murder site—with bodies—unsuitable for a child, they were probably the only humans on the force who didn't. In the end, Kaylin said, more or less truthfully, that Kattea was needed as an interpreter for Gilbert, who lived across the street.

"And the neighbor has information that he can't give us without seeing the bodies first?" This was a perfectly reasonable question. Kaylin tried not to resent it. Gavin had never been her biggest supporter; he was practically purple now.

Kaylin waited while Gavin glared at Gilbert. He did not glare at Kattea; she was too young. At least in that, he was better than Mallory.

"This is highly irregular," he said.

"I know. I only get called in on the weird magical problems, and this is definitely that." She almost volunteered to route his request through Marcus, but waited. Marcus would put Gavin at ease, but it would eat time.

Time they didn't have.

"Gavin, I still have to consult with Evanton, and if there's time today, I have to go to two of the actual fiefs. I need to get this done. They won't touch anything; I'll be there to supervise."

Gavin's estimation of Kaylin's ability *to* supervise was vanishingly small. "*I'll* be there to supervise. Are you going to stand here all morning?"

Viewing the bodies—or having Gilbert view the bodies—had seemed like a smart idea in the comfort of her own home.

Gavin took the lead, which was to be expected. Kaylin followed, and Gilbert trailed after her. Severn took the spot behind Gilbert and Kattea pulled up the rear, at Gilbert's insistence and to the child's annoyance. She did not feel endangered in the presence of Hawks—and Gilbert himself—and she was old enough, barely, that she didn't want to be treated like a child.

Gilbert abruptly stopped walking as they approached the stairs that led to the subbasement. Gavin continued down the stairs, stopped and turned when he realized that no one was following. "Is something wrong?" he asked. Well, demanded, really. Asking was not entirely Gavin's style.

Gilbert didn't answer.

Kaylin turned and froze herself; Gilbert's eyes were black.

And there were three of them.

She almost reached up to close the third eye, but knew it was pointless. The eye looked like a normal eye, except for its placement; closing it wouldn't make it disappear.

"When," Gilbert said, in a voice that implied he had more than one mouth, although only one, thankfully, was visible, "did you disturb this place?" The stairs shook.

Gavin's eyes were slits. "Private Neya."

She exhaled. "He's here to look at the bodies because he can see things we can't. For obvious reasons."

"What *is* he?" Gavin's hand had fallen to his dagger; he didn't have a sword.

"Gilbert. He's—he's not from around here."

"I can see that. Where is he from, exactly?" He retrieved a pocket mirror with his left hand.

The small dragon leaped off Kaylin's shoulder and flew at Gavin's face. She dived after the translucent familiar while Gavin attempted to swat him out of the air.

"Don't!" she shouted at the small dragon. "He's not going to hurt us!"

Severn leaped down the stairs, using the wall to halt his momentum. He raised a hand and caught the familiar by a spindly leg. It screeched in his face. "Apologies," Severn said to Gavin. "The Arcanum has been implicated in these murders. We require knowledge that the Arcanum has, without consulting or otherwise alerting an Arcanist. Gilbert is foreign; he is not from the Arcanum." To the familiar, he said, "Gavin needs to mirror the Halls of Law."

The familiar squawked loudly—and furiously.

Gilbert said, "Your companion is trying to tell you that it is not safe—in *any* way—to use the mirror in this building."

Gavin frowned. He'd recovered his composure. Flying, tiny dragons and men with three eyes might have walked past him every morning before breakfast. "The mirror has been used— to no detriment—in the past."

Gilbert closed all three of his eyes. He spoke to the familiar, and it spoke back. Neither were intelligible to Kaylin. Or to Gavin, given his expression.

"Harm has been caused. If you do not wish your magical communications to be completely compromised—" He stopped. "Kaylin, this mirroring—Mandoran attempted to explain it. How does it work?"

She punted the question to Severn.

"None of us are mages," Severn said, "but my understanding is this: it is a magical net that is spread across the whole of Elantra. Mirrors are fixed locations that are attached to that net; a mirror can be designated in two ways. Geographically—to a building—or personally. Teela can be reached at any mirror that is attached and activated. Kaylin cannot. If you require a more technical explanation, you'll need to speak to an Imperial mage."

"Can this be done now?"

Kaylin blinked.

Gilbert's eyes were open again. The two that were divided

by his nose blinked the normal way; the one that rested in the center of his forehead didn't. It didn't blink at all. It did, however, move, although the movement was subtle. Gilbert spoke to the familiar. Kaylin decided then and there that she was going to learn the language Gilbert spoke. The familiar sounded too much like an enraged chicken; she couldn't even pull syllables out of his squawking.

"My apologies," Gilbert said to Gavin. "I did not mean to interrupt your progress."

Gavin's lips thinned. He looked pointedly at Kattea, the necessary "interpreter," as Kaylin reddened. He then looked at the nascent mirror in his hand before shoving it back into its well-cushioned place in his satchel. "Neya."

"Sir."

"Just how big is this going to get?"

She knew she had to choose her words with care. Apparently she was not fast enough for the older Hawk.

"Private."

"I don't *know*. I'm sorry, Gavin—but I don't know."

"Bigger than the tidal wave?"

Silence.

"Bigger than the Devourer?"

"No—not that big."

"So you do have some idea." He ran a hand through his graying hair. "You understand there's a chain of command?"

"Yes."

"So it's my butt in the fire if anything goes wrong here?"

"…Yes."

He shook his head. "With your background, I would've expected you'd be better at lying."

"Only when my life depends on it."

"Fine. Let's get this over with."

★ ★ ★

Kattea's excitement had faded considerably as they once again descended en masse. She clutched the back of Gilbert's jacket so tightly her knuckles were white, and kept her eyes on her feet. Kaylin's gaze was drawn to the markings on the wall: magical, all, and invisible to the naked eye if one wasn't blessed—or cursed—with magical vision.

The familiar returned, disgruntled, to Kaylin's shoulder. He didn't lift his wing. He didn't lift his head, either, but he did complain a lot.

Gilbert stopped walking and turned to the wall on which the detritus of previous spells had been splashed. Kaylin was not surprised when he reached out to touch the wall.

She was *very* surprised when his hand passed through it.

Kattea's breath stopped. It resumed when she realized that Gavin, back toward them, hadn't noticed. "This was a bad idea," the girl whispered, presumably to Gilbert.

"Most of the work we do is," Kaylin told her, just as quietly. "But someone's got to do it."

"But what *is* the work?"

"Right now? We're trying to figure out what the Arcanum wanted with this particular building." She hesitated. "You said the water brought you here."

Kattea nodded, moving as Gilbert once again descended the curved, stone stairs, and stopping when he stopped.

"I think I can guess why."

"Why?"

Kaylin exhaled. "Your Nightshade is not my Nightshade. I was born in the fief. I know it. I *hate* it. I ran across the bridge. But the bridge brought me here. It brought me to the Hawks. Your bridge doesn't lead here. It doesn't lead anywhere."

Kattea nodded again.

"There must be a reason it doesn't lead anywhere. And it's here, somewhere."

"You're certain?" Severn asked.

"You aren't?" she countered.

"Did you write these?" Gilbert asked, as if no other conversation had been taking place around him.

"They're not exactly writing," Kaylin began.

Gilbert once again slipped his hand through the wall, as if he were rearranging something.

Kaylin wanted to tell him that the marks he could see were the echoes of magic's use. She refrained because she didn't actually know what he was seeing. No two mages saw evidence of casting the same way. She suspected that even given that, Gilbert, with his third eye, was unique.

"According to the owner of the building, the subbasement is new."

"It is not newly constructed," Gilbert replied, stating the obvious without apparent condescension. "What was its purpose?" He hesitated, frowned and returned up the steps, dragging Kattea as if she were just a heavier part of his outerwear. His hands passed through the wall again and again, and as they did, Kaylin saw the runic symbols of forgotten or unknown mages realign. The colors, the blue that shaded to purple and from there to red, shifted as well, blending into a continuous glow of…gold.

"I'm not sure you should have done that," Kattea told Gilbert.

Kaylin felt absolutely certain he shouldn't have—because if Kattea could now clearly see the sigils, it meant that everyone could, including Gavin.

Gilbert was frowning. Kaylin's frown was different. Where she had previously seen the distinct hand of multiple magicians, probably attempting to cast the same spell at different times, she now saw writing that looked almost familiar.

Lifting her left arm, she unbuttoned her sleeve and inspected the runes on her skin. *How big is this going to get?* The sigils left behind by strong magic had never reminded Kaylin of ancient words before. Gilbert's rearrangement had altered that. She could see familiar bold lines, heavy curves, lighter strokes.

"Gilbert, what are you doing?"

"I am trying," he said, "to understand the purpose of this alcove. I do not believe it was meant to be accessible to you and your kind."

Gavin, predictably, stiffened at the phrase.

"Those aren't—those *weren't*—a message."

He lifted one dark brow.

"Until you touched them, they weren't visible to anyone."

"They were visible to you."

"Yes, because I can see magic."

"These are magic?"

Gavin's snort was not followed by words.

"A certain kind of magic. Not everyone can use magic. But when magic *is* used, the caster leaves evidence."

"Evidence."

"Yes. Magic is very individual. Even when mages cast the same spell, they don't leave the same…magical trail. That trail is evidence that can help us to track down a mage if they commit a crime using magic. The wall contained traces of that evidence." Which Gilbert had destroyed. "That's not what it contains now."

"No. But I believe your…mages…were attempting to invoke this phrase."

"Pardon?"

"This is what they were attempting to say, in this place."

Kaylin started to tell him that that wasn't how magic worked.

She stopped. What she knew about magic, in any practical sense, amounted to the lighting of one candle after months of useless attempts. And how had she achieved that?

By knowing the name of fire. A word. A word that defied easy pronunciation or comprehension; a word that dribbled through the figurative cupped palms of her concentration. "All of them?" she asked, instead.

He nodded. "They were not standing in the right place, but close." He lowered his hands, the words on the wall reflected brightly in only his third eye. "This was not meant for you."

"Was it meant for you?"

"No." He bent slightly and retrieved the edge of his coat from Kattea's hands. "I think you should wait upstairs."

Kattea let his coat go, but folded her arms, looking the very definition of mutinous. And frightened. Only one of these held sway. "What are you going to do?"

"If we are very, very lucky, nothing."

"And if we're not?" she demanded, and Kaylin again felt a pang of recognition.

Gilbert, predictably, didn't answer. He looked to Kaylin instead. "You said there were bodies."

"Yes."

"Mortal bodies."

"Uncertain."

Gavin said, "Mortal bodies," with a side-eye at Kaylin.

"They are in a room?"

"Yes. The stairs lead to the only room in the subbasement."

"No," Gilbert said quietly, "they do not." But he pulled his gaze away from the words he had arranged out of nothing on the wall and followed Gavin without further interruption.

The large room in the subbasement had not changed much. It was better lit than it had been on first visit. This didn't bother

Kaylin. The fact that the bodies were now in entirely different positions, however, did. Where they had once been laid out in a row, they were now laid out in a triangular position; their feet were touching, their heads pointing outward.

"When did Red examine them?" Kaylin asked.

"Two days ago. Corporal Danelle recommended they not be moved; Red concurred, after his examination."

Kaylin turned to Gilbert and said, "These are the corpses."

"They are not dead," Gilbert said.

Gavin's gaze attached itself to Gilbert's face for one long, silent moment. To Kaylin, he said, "You should really report to the office if you want full details."

"I'll take what I can get."

"Red didn't say they were alive. We've seen our share of corpses. But he was concerned."

"Because?"

"They haven't decomposed at all. Some very basic magical protections have been laid across the bodies to preserve them, but Red says they're working *too* well. No pulse. No breath. They don't bleed—he did check that. But he's not comfortable."

"What, does he think they're undead?"

"He didn't say. Before you make that face, stranger things have happened."

"Yes—but with *Barrani*. You know, the ones that have to have True Names to animate them at all?"

"Red doesn't care. He wasn't willing to cut them up here. He did as thorough an examination as he could, given that, but that's it. The Sergeant wouldn't give leave to have the bodies moved; apparently the Dragon Court had a word or two to say about that."

Kaylin had a few words to say, too. She kept them to herself and turned to Gilbert. Gilbert was staring at the three corpses.

She wasn't certain what a healthy skin color was supposed to be in a member of Gilbert's race—but she was pretty certain that white-gray wasn't it.

"They are not dead," he said again. She walked to where the bodies were laid out and knelt. Or tried to kneel. Gilbert had grabbed her shoulder.

"I've touched them before," she pointed out. Gilbert released her shoulder reluctantly, and she poked the small familiar. He sighed and lifted a translucent wing so that it covered half her face. She didn't watch him do this; she was looking at the corpses.

They vanished.

She'd expected that, given her previous experience.

What she didn't expect to see—inches beyond where the top of each man's head was positioned—were three oddly luminescent, standing stones.

At first glance, they were uniform in size. She frowned and once again readjusted the familiar's wing until it covered both of her eyes; he bit her hand in annoyance, but not hard enough to draw blood. The bodies were no longer visible.

With the exception of the lack of bodies and the presence of the stones, the room was the same. So, to Kaylin's relief, were the people standing in it.

"Gilbert," she said, as she cautiously approached the closest of these standing stones, "what do you see here?"

"I see three of your kind." There was a moment's pause and then he continued, "They are far, far clearer to me than anyone in this room, save Kattea. If I understand what Kattea has said about mortality, these men are not dead."

Kaylin opened her mouth.

Gavin spoke first. "Red had some concerns. I told you: you want that information, you'll need to mirror in for it, or talk to Red yourself."

Thanks, Gavin. Grimacing, she moved again. "Gilbert, can you see standing stones here?"

"Stones?"

Kaylin took that as a no.

"Private," Gavin said sharply.

She glanced back at him while the familiar complained.

"What are you doing?"

"When I look through my familiar's wing, I can see three stones; they're in a triangular pattern. I'm examining them."

"That's not what he means," Kattea said. She hesitated and then added, "What he means is, you—you're kind of standing in that guy's face."

"On?"

"No. *In.*" She started to come out from behind Gilbert's back, and Kaylin realized he was holding her in place. His third eye hadn't closed, and she could see reflected light across the whole of its surface. "It's kind of creepy."

"This place—it is not stable," he said. He turned to Kattea. "Kattea, return home."

"I'm not going without—"

"*Now.*" This last word was not uttered quietly. Kaylin wouldn't have been surprised if the whole neighborhood heard it. She wouldn't have been surprised if the inhabitants of the *Palace* heard it.

Kattea surprised Kaylin; she hung on, but she was pale in her resolution and visibly trembling.

His shoulders sagged and he lifted her. "I am sorry. I am not accustomed to company; not like yours. You are too slight for this, and I do not want to see you hurt."

Pale, she said nothing.

"What did you see, Gilbert?" Kaylin asked quietly.

He was silent for a long moment, his gaze fixed on Kattea, who was now seated in the crook of his arm as if she were a baby. An angry baby, but still precious. "I told you that when I met Kattea, it was difficult for me to see her. To perceive her."

"You said she was like Lord Nightshade."

"Yes. And you disagreed."

"I disagreed less profoundly than Kattea would."

"That is true. But regardless, it was difficult to see her. Difficult to hear her. It is...difficult for me to see the boundaries of your buildings, your streets. It is difficult to eat your food. It is like...grasping the smoke from your fire would be to you; grasping it and trying to make it solid, to make it functional.

"There are key areas, geographies if you will, in your world that are *not* as insubstantial or difficult, to me. The Castle was one. Your Helen is another. If I look out across the breadth of your city, there are a handful of monuments that are as solid— to my eyes—as your city is to yours.

"What you did for me, what you called healing, was helpful in this regard. I do not see you as you see yourself—I do not think that is possible—but I see you more clearly than I did before."

"The basement of your house?"

"It is real, to me."

"And the basement of this one?"

"It is real."

"The stones?"

"They are not, in any sense of the word, stone." He exhaled. "Seeing you at all, seeing Kattea, is an act of...translation? You are writ in a tongue of which I have only rudimentary understanding. I glean meaning, but it takes effort, and it is exhausting. Your familiar is real to me. He is a comfort. He understands the difficulty—but he does not share it. He speaks my tongue as comfortably as he speaks yours, in a metaphorical sense.

"The bodies, and the stones that you can see only with the

help of your familiar, are *not* like you, or Severn, or any of your other friends. But they are nonetheless much more like you than I am."

Kaylin could only barely understand how someone could look at standing stones and confuse them with actual people. "How are they like us?"

Squawk.

"If you saw what Gilbert sees, you could've tried harder to communicate it."

Squawk.

"Could you speak with the stones?"

Gilbert frowned.

"You can speak with us," Kaylin pointed out.

He turned to Kaylin. "You will have to take Kattea."

Kattea threw her arms around his neck. She would not look at Kaylin at all.

"Every attempt at communication is an act of inversion," Gilbert explained. "And I am not certain that it is safe for Kattea to be in my physical presence while I make the attempt. It caused your Nightshade some difficulty."

"Kattea—"

"No."

Gilbert closed his eyes. "You understand that I am concerned for your cohesion?"

The girl nodded into his shoulder. "You promised."

"I did not promise—"

"You promised you would let *me* choose."

"I did not promise that I would let you commit suicide." Above Kattea's head, he asked, "Is that the correct word?"

"Pretty much. You understand that Kattea is much, much younger than Nightshade, right?"

"Yes."

"Letting Nightshade choose—"

Kattea cursed.

"—or not. If the stones are alive, if the stones are like us, why do you think there's a risk to Kattea?"

Squawk.

"They are not like you; they are more like you than the basement of my house, or your Helen. They are attempting to communicate," he added. "Can you not hear them?"

She couldn't, of course. But...she could see them, could see the light they shed. She wondered if that light was the Gilbert equivalent of a foreign language. She exhaled. "You hold Kattea," she said. "I'll touch the stones."

"No."

"Kattea is a mortal child. I'm the Chosen."

"You have already said you do not understand what that means."

"I don't understand what it means to you, no. Or even to the Ancients. But my arms are starting to ache. I think I can survive talking to a stone or three."

Squawk.

The familiar abruptly lowered his wing. In case his meaning was too subtle, he also smacked Kaylin's cheek with it.

"Tell me again why I missed you?" Turning to Severn, she said, "Three bodies. Three stones. Gilbert says both the bodies and the stones are alive."

"I do not understand," Gilbert added, "why you speak of them as if they are distinct and separate."

"...They're not separate to you."

"No."

Kaylin grimaced, stepped forward and placed her hand on the nearest stone. Her hand passed through it. The stones were not solid. They weren't speaking to her, either. "Fine. Gavin?"

He nodded.

"Apparently the three dead men walked across the street

last night—or the night before—and attempted to break into Gilbert's house. We don't have to cut them up—but I'd suggest we move them."

"I'll mirror the request in—" He stopped. Had he been Kaylin, he would have cursed. "I'll send Lianne to the Halls with the request."

But Gilbert shook his head. "If you mean to move the bodies you can see, it will make no difference. This is where they *are*."

Kaylin exhaled. "If I move—"

"Yes. If *you* move—or any of your compatriots, save your familiar, and Helen, who cannot—you *move*. Moving these three will not materially change anything; in any real sense, they are, and will remain, here."

"Fine." She looked to Severn. "Elani or Tiamaris?"

He tossed her a coin.

CHAPTER 18

Kattea explained what a coin toss meant while they trudged their way toward Elani Street. Gilbert did not set Kattea down, but she seemed willing to forgo the dignity of being treated like an adult for the duration of her explanation.

"I'm not certain you're going to be invited in," Kaylin told him.

Gilbert nodded.

"Is this one of the buildings that looks real, to you?"

"Yes."

"Does it look dangerous?"

"I don't understand the question."

Given that Gilbert could confuse an attempted murder for an act of communication gone wrong, Kaylin supposed that made sense. The small dragon did not consider Elani Street worth much effort and was sacked out across her shoulders. He lifted his head when she reached Evanton's door.

It opened before she could touch the knocker.

A wild-eyed Grethan stood in the door, the stalks on his forehead weaving like a drunk. He was dripping wet. "Kaylin!"

She almost took a step back. "Are you going to stand in the doorway or can we come in?"

He moved. He moved back, and Kaylin understood why he was soaked: it was raining. Inside the store. The familiar squawked in obvious displeasure and bit Kaylin's hair when she was stupid enough to enter anyway.

Severn followed; she was surprised to hear a familiar Aerian curse from him, although it wasn't loud.

Gilbert, however, remained outside, which implied he had more common sense than Kattea was willing to acknowledge. He bowed—awkwardly, since he was still carrying the girl.

Grethan said, "Evanton's not accepting visitors today."

"I cannot enter without your permission. It would be irresponsible and very unsafe."

Grethan looked to Kaylin. Evanton's apprentice was not at his best today. "I trust him," Kaylin told the Tha'alani youth. "Or at least I trust his intent."

Grethan knew the difference. But he wasn't Evanton. "I'm not sure it's my permission you need," he said.

Gilbert, however, smiled. "Your permission will do."

"But I'm not—I'm not the Keeper."

"I am uncertain what you mean by Keeper; I am not uncertain about permission. If you are willing to grant me entry, I will enter. If you are not, I will wait. It seems less unpleasant outside," he added.

Grethan muttered, "Tell me about it. Yes, if you're stupid enough to want it, you have my permission. I'm sorry about the rain," he added.

The Keeper was not, as the rain suggested, in the store. He wasn't in the kitchen, either. "Where's Evanton?"

Grethan hesitated. Kaylin assumed this meant he was in the Garden—and if it was like this *outside* of the Garden, she wasn't certain she wanted to enter it. She needed to speak with the elemental water, but water, when enraged, was like a death sentence. Evanton could be drowned in a deluge and survive; he apparently didn't need to breathe.

Kaylin, Severn and Kattea did. She wasn't sure about Gilbert. "He's—he's upstairs."

"He's upstairs?" Kaylin knew that there was an upstairs to the storefront. It wasn't a secret; a second and third story could be seen from the street. Neither had ever been relevant to Kaylin. She assumed that they were where Evanton and Grethan lived. Or she *had* assumed that, until now.

"Can you tell him we're here?"

"He's not—" Grethan swallowed water. Then again, they were all pretty much swallowing water until Grethan thought to offer them umbrellas. Kaylin noted he didn't take one for himself. "I can try." He hesitated again and then offered Kaylin a very bedraggled smile. "I'm glad you're here."

Kattea wanted to know how it could be raining inside the shop, when it was bright and pretty much cloudless outside. It was a good question, but Kaylin's best guess wasn't suitable for children, so she didn't answer.

The stairs that led to the upper floors reminded Kaylin very much of the hall that led to the Keeper's Garden: they were sloped and rickety, and they had to be walked single file. They were also steep. Grethan, however, forged ahead without apparent hesitation.

The hall the stairs ended at was a bit wider and seemed to be in better repair. It was not wet. The rain appeared to affect only the ground floor.

"Has it been like this all day?"

"It was worse yesterday," Grethan replied.

"When did it start?"

"Yesterday. Evanton was in the Garden."

"I don't suppose he had much to say?"

Grethan flushed. "He wasn't happy. With anything. Or anyone."

And the only other person living with Evanton at the moment was Grethan. Kaylin cringed in genuine sympathy. She liked Evanton; she couldn't imagine actually living with him. That had never been more true than today. Not even her most creative nightmares involved waking up to rain on the inside of a house that still had a functional roof.

The ceilings were shorter on the second floor. More than that, she didn't have a chance to see, because Grethan continued down the hall to another flight of stairs. Judging by the dust on the handrails, these weren't used often.

Kaylin glanced at Gilbert. His third eye—his unfortunately visible third eye—was open. It moved in a way that the other two, which looked comfortably human, didn't. He didn't seem to be worried, but he didn't set Kattea down, either.

He stopped at the foot of the stairs. "Are you certain this is wise?" he asked. He didn't appear to be looking at Grethan.

"Probably not," she replied. "But we're going to need to talk to Evanton eventually. Do you understand what a Keeper is?"

"I am not certain. I do not know the word in the context you have used it."

No, Kaylin thought, he wouldn't. Kattea wouldn't know it, either. "The Keeper binds the wild elements that exist as an intrinsic part of the world. He stops them attempting to destroy each other, which keeps our world stable. I'd like to know your word for it—I'm certain you must have had one."

"How so?"

"You live in the world. Even if you live in it differently, you live here." She followed Grethan up the stairs.

The stairs didn't lead to more hall. They led to a door. Like the door that led to the Garden, this one was narrow; it was the width of the stairs. It was shorter, as well. For someone

Kaylin's height, this wasn't a problem—but a Barrani would have to duck to get through the frame.

If, she thought, the door actually opened.

Grethan knocked. This produced a very muffled, but distinct "Go away." This was not promising. Grethan looked down the stairs at Kaylin, and there was a bit of shuffling while they traded places. Kaylin's knock was nowhere near as timid as the apprentice's.

"I said *go away.*"

"Heard you the first time," Kaylin replied. "But we're in a bit of a pinch."

"That is not my problem."

"Actually, I think it is."

The door opened to a *very* cranky Evanton. He was wearing his store apron, and tufts of wayward hair suggested he'd been pulling at it in frustration. His eyes were also bloodshot. "It had better be" was his sour reply. He had more to say—when he was in this mood, he always did—but stopped when he looked down the stairs. He exhaled inches of outraged height. "My apologies," he said—to Gilbert, as Kaylin had never rated apologies. "I wasn't expecting guests; I apologize in advance for the state of my abode."

"I don't think he cares," Kaylin told Evanton. "He's not necessarily looking at the clutter the way the rest of us do."

"*I* care."

"…Sorry, Evanton."

"You did not pick a particularly *good* time, no. I would make tea, but the kitchen is—"

"Flooded, yes." Kaylin exhaled. "What's happening?"

"Would it surprise you to know I am not entirely certain?"

"Yes, actually."

"Then be surprised *quietly.*"

"Fine. This is Gilbert. And Kattea. Gilbert, Kattea, this is Evanton."

Gilbert bowed. He came dangerously close to scraping the floor with Kattea. "I understand," he said—to Evanton. Kaylin didn't understand the word that left his mouth next.

Evanton, clearly, did. His eyes—his normal, human eyes— widened. "Kaylin," he said, although he didn't take his eyes off Gilbert, "what have you done?"

Kaylin brushed past him and entered a room that she had never seen before. To her surprise, it was almost empty; there was a table—not a desk—against the wall. The roof angled sharply above the tabletop. The room itself was narrow. It had a window, built into the steeply inclined wall above the table, and a small door that implied a closet. The floor was in better repair than the floors on the ground floor, probably because it didn't get as much foot traffic.

The familiar squawked at Evanton. Loudly. His mouth was an inch from Kaylin's ear.

"What is it this time?" Kaylin asked.

He lifted his wing, smacked her nose and then held it in place over her eyes. For a translucent lizard, he had no difficulty conveying impatience and a certain long-suffering annoyance.

Dragon wing made visible what normal vision didn't: there were words engraved in the sturdier wood of this room's floor. They were glowing, as if light had been poured into them.

"This is the room in which I, for want of a better word, meditate."

"Is the Garden safe at all?"

"Not for you. And not, I fear, for Gilbert. You wish, no doubt, to speak to the water?"

She nodded.

"Of course you do. It would have to be water, given the present difficulty. What has occurred?"

"The long version or the short version?"

"Start with the short version; it is what I have patience for at the moment."

"The water apparently carried Gilbert and Kattea across time. Maybe ten years of it."

Evanton raised his hands and massaged his temples. "Thank you. I'll take the longer version now."

Evanton listened to Kaylin without interruption, which was unusual. He sent Grethan out to fetch bread, water and something that looked suspiciously like wine, but otherwise confined his actions to nodding or raising a brow.

This ended when Kattea joined the conversation at his request.

"You said the water spoke to you."

"It mostly spoke to Gilbert."

"Mostly, or entirely?"

"...Entirely."

He nodded. To Gilbert, he asked, "What instructions did you give?" As not many people were expected to give instructions to the elemental water, Kaylin was slightly surprised by the question.

"I asked that we be conveyed—in a manner safe for Kattea—to Elantra."

"Those were the only parameters you set?"

"Yes. It did not occur to me to examine the details of the request; that level of granularity has seldom been necessary."

Evanton nodded, as if this made sense.

"Evanton—*how* did the water bring him to here? I mean, to here, *now*?"

"That is a very good question. And an appropriate one. I

believe I have a better understanding of the rain." He glanced at his drenched apprentice and added, "It is likely to stop soon, one way or another. I have a preference for which way."

"Can you not give commands to the water?" Gilbert asked.

"Yes. As you suspect—as you recognize—I can. I am not, however, like the original Keeper in that regard. I can give commands that are heard *now*. I cannot give commands that are heard at every moment of the water's existence and awareness."

Kaylin blinked. She opened her mouth and closed it as she approached the shopkeeper; he was gray. Almost literally gray. "Have you been eating?"

"I am *long* past the age where I require maternal care" was his clipped reply. "My control—my stewardship, if you will—exists now. It has demonstrably existed in the past. It will, in theory, exist in the future—but the future is, to me, uncertain. I may die tomorrow. Grethan, do not make that face.

"I may merely be incapacitated. My responsibilities, my ability to endure and perform them, exist now. Now is a moving target. From any vantage in which I exist, I am 'now.'"

"This isn't making things any simpler," Kaylin said.

"No, it wouldn't. Believe that I am not enjoying it, either. I *believe* the difficulty resides with Gilbert's instruction. He is here now. He is also there, then. The water exists in both places, and it is aware in both continuums. Gilbert's imperative is causing a type of stress the Garden was not meant to contain."

"…What does that mean for the rest of the city?"

"At the moment? That they shouldn't come barging into my shop unless they want to get wet. I believe I have things more or less under control."

"You're lying."

"I am not. The context of this control is difficult. There are reasons that the rain occurs only within the shop—but there are also reasons it is no longer contained to the Garden." He turned to Gilbert. "Stop speaking to the water."

"I am not—" He closed two of his eyes. "Ah."

"If I understand what has been said, you set out to find a way to send—or bring—Lord Nightshade home."

"Yes."

"Nightshade—like Kattea or Kaylin—exists in a way that is not conducive to that homecoming. You understand this better than anyone here. It is not unreasonable to assume that your difficulty—and mine—is in part caused by your presence. Or Kattea's."

Kattea stiffened.

"I did not mean that you had done anything wrong," Evanton added, voice more subdued. "But this is not where you should be. Gilbert is more flexible. He is not what you—what we—are." He turned to Gilbert.

Gilbert said, "When I arrived here, I could no longer sense time. I believe that the water delivered me here for reasons of its own. The parameters of my request allowed it. If your suggested solution is my return, it is impossible."

"That is not what I wanted to hear," Evanton replied. He turned to Kaylin. "I would happily grant your request to speak with the elemental water, but it would be irresponsible. I do not think you would survive it. Gilbert, however, might. There may be other issues."

"What did you wish to ask the water?" Gilbert asked Kaylin.

"Why it brought you here. I'd like to know how, too, but I'm beginning to think that's irrelevant; it's clear that Evanton doesn't believe Kattea would have survived had you not been with her." She hesitated.

"If you are going to keep something to yourself, do it competently," Evanton snapped.

"It's not mine to share." She turned to Kattea, who was

still rain-wet. "Tell Evanton what will happen to you if you go back."

"I'll die."

"The water isn't like the other elements," Kaylin said, when it was clear Kattea intended to let those words be the whole of her contribution. "I think—I think she heard Kattea. Not, maybe, at first—but Gilbert was specific about the mode of travel: she had to choose a path that *Kattea* could survive.

"I think she's aware of Kattea. She was certainly aware that Gilbert was distracted by Annarion. You haven't met him—he's Mandoran's brother, effectively."

"I would thank you to keep him to yourself for the time being; I have more than enough trouble at the moment."

"Yes, well. I am keeping him to myself—he's living with me. So is Mandoran."

"You are obviously a saint."

"No—but Helen probably is. One of these days you're going to have to tell me how you knew about her. She doesn't re-call meeting you."

"One of these days, when it is not raining on the inside of my shop, I will." He exhaled. "What else do you need from a poor, tired, frazzled old man?"

"I don't know. Do what you're doing. And let Gilbert ask the water why."

Evanton's tired, old and frazzled was a constant. His cloth-ing, however, wasn't. When he accepted Kaylin's request, it changed instantly into the blue robes that she associated with his title or his role. He then turned to pick something up off the table and smacked his head against the lower portion of the angled wall.

He could curse like a Hawk.

Grethan hovered in the doorway, waiting for Evanton, clearly feeling equal parts fear of and fear for his master.

"Stay on the second floor. Or in this room. There is some danger that the rain will become a deluge on the ground floor. No, not you," he snapped at Grethan. "I'm going to need your help."

The familiar squawked.

Evanton, looking aggrieved, said, "If you *must*."

And the familiar floated up, off Kaylin's shoulder, and came to rest on Evanton's head.

Gilbert deposited Kattea on the table; she was the only person who could sit there without hitting her head. There wasn't a lot of sitting space otherwise, but Kaylin had lived with floors—or worse—in her time. She sat. So did Severn.

"Is it really because of me?" Kattea surprised them both by asking.

"No," Kaylin said.

Severn said nothing, which, oddly enough, was louder.

"Is it because I should have died, and didn't?" She directed this question to Severn.

"*Should* doesn't matter," Severn replied. He exhaled. "I think the problem is actually Gilbert."

This wasn't comforting.

"Gilbert, the water, time and something the Arcanists have been doing. I think you're caught up in it—but I don't think it's your fault."

"What happens to me if Gilbert goes back and I don't?"

"Gilbert said you'd be fine here," Kaylin answered. She tried not to insult Kattea by glaring her partner into silence. "I believe him. He wants you to survive."

Kattea nodded. "But...Gilbert's kind of...stupid."

"I don't think he's stupid. He's just not used to being one

of us. Give him time and—" She stopped talking. "Severn, did you hear that?"

Kattea, notably not Severn, said, "It sounded like something cracked. Or shattered."

Severn was already on his feet. He scooped Kattea off the table. "I think we wait outside."

Kaylin opened the door. "How well do you swim?" she asked Kattea.

"I don't know how to swim. We weren't allowed to go into the Ablayne."

"Then we're going to have problems."

CHAPTER 19

Kaylin knew that Evanton could be totally submersed in water without drowning. She'd seen it. She had to trust that Grethan could do the same. The rains, which hadn't chased them up the first flight of stairs, weren't falling, but that no longer mattered. The second-story hall was underwater.

"Is there any chance that window leads to actual Elantran rooftops?" she asked Severn while watching the water's currents.

"Possibly."

Kaylin turned away from the rising river the house had functionally become. She could see the window clearly now. Water roiled on the other side of the closed glass. "I hope not, given what that would mean for the *rest* of the city."

Kattea said, "Is Gilbert okay?"

Fair question. Gilbert had not made the list of Kaylin's immediate worries. "Gilbert," she said, "is probably the only one of us guaranteed to survive this. Well, Gilbert and Evanton. I'm worried about us, selfish as that sounds."

Kattea said, in a much smaller voice, "Sounds practical." But she said the last word as if it were a guilty confession. She looked, for the moment, much younger and frailer; she was afraid. And of course she was afraid: she had working eyes and ears. Water did not work this way unless magic was involved—and in general, if there was a clash between normal people and magic, magic won.

She turned to the door again.

"The water?" her partner asked. He did not set Kattea down.

"Rising, of course." Kaylin exhaled. "I'm going to leave the room. I'm closing the door. Don't open it."

"Kaylin—"

"Don't open it. Promise me." She turned back. Kattea's slender arms were around his neck. "You're a Hawk," she whispered.

Memory was a bitch. Always. It cut you at the worst times, for the worst reasons. It returned in a way that made no sense; it followed no logical pattern. Kattea *was not* Steffi or Jade. She *wasn't* Kaylin's baby sister; she wasn't Kaylin's responsibility.

But she was the same age. She was a shadow of the past; a shadow of everything that had come between her and Severn.

Severn nodded.

Kaylin walked out the open door, closing it firmly behind her. She leaned her forehead against it, briefly, and then turned and headed down the stairs.

The water was rising as she watched. She hadn't lied to Kattea; she was certain Gilbert would survive. She wasn't certain that his ability to interact with the rest of them would, and in any practical sense, that was the only thing that mattered to Kattea.

But Kaylin hadn't come down the stairs without a plan. The plan, unfortunately, involved contact with the water—but the sooner she managed that, the better.

The currents, while strong, couldn't knock her off her feet yet. Sliding her right arm between the banister rails, she caught one picket firmly in the bend of her elbow, bracing herself for the unexpected; she had no idea how much time she had before the inches of water became a flood.

She knelt, grimacing, and tried not to think of water damage to her clothing. Stupid thoughts, really, but she didn't have the time to remove her pants—or boots. She had time to place her left hand firmly in the water.

Self-preservation made her yank her hand clear.

Responsibility made her grit her teeth and once again submerge it.

Kaylin was not Tha'alani. She was not one of the native race of telepaths that lived in Elantra, doing their level best to keep to themselves and away from every other race's inborn isolation.

That isolation, to the Tha'alani, caused insanity. It caused bitterness and delusion and fostered misunderstanding and self-hatred—which, of course, led to hatred, which led to violence, and in the worst cases, death.

If the only people in the world had been Tha'alani, there would be *no need* for Hawks or Swords or Wolves. Misunderstanding was pretty hard to maintain when everyone around you could hear your thoughts. It was hard to maintain when you could hear theirs. The fears were addressed before they had time to grow ugly roots; the pain was addressed, comforted. You were never alone.

Once, Kaylin had feared that: you could *never* be alone. There was no privacy. There was no way to hide what needed to remain hidden if you were to live in the world. But she hadn't considered that maybe there was *no need* to hide. Not until she had touched the *Tha'alaan*. Not until she had experienced the truth of it.

Had it been up to Kaylin, she would never have left it. But…she wasn't Tha'alani. She had no way of contacting the *Tha'alaan* except this: to touch the elemental water. Because the core of the thoughts, emotions, dreams of the entire race was contained in the heart of the water.

It was the reason that elemental water, alone of the four elements, was different. The long, slow accumulation of the daily lives of thousands—tens of thousands, maybe hundreds of thousands—had slowly altered the way the water itself thought. But only part of it; the elemental water was still a wild, chaotic force.

Kaylin could not hear its voice. When angered, when frightened, when outraged, its voice was too loud and too destructive. And yet, throughout, the Tha'alani were part of it. It was the Tha'alani she needed to reach. It was the voices of mortals, not ancient, imperturbable nature. No, she thought; what she needed to do was hang on to the rails and wait until they could reach her.

Kaylin.

Ybelline. She closed her eyes. She couldn't plug her ears; she had no way to block the roar of moving water, the distant sound of deluge. But she could "hear" Ybelline Rabon'Alani as if the castelord was beside her, lips pressed against her ear. More: it felt like a hug.

Ybelline.

Where are you?

Kaylin showed her; it was easier than using words. It was easier to just...open up everything and let Ybelline see what she saw, as she saw it. A year or two ago, this would have been Kaylin's worst nightmare. Now?

She wasn't alone. Yes, she was standing—more or less— on her own two feet. But someone was standing beside her. Someone who couldn't take the weight of responsibility off her shoulders, who couldn't just *do* what had to be done—but who saw it, who understood it. Who saw Kaylin and understood Kaylin—and didn't judge.

We…will speak to the Tha'alaan. *Speak to the water as you can,* she added, the interior voice grim. *We will speak as we can. But, Kaylin—*

Yes?

The Tha'alaan *is…confusing now. There are—there are thought-memories in its folds that are ours—but not ours. We did not think those thoughts; we did not live through those events. It is…chaotic. We are used to dreaming thoughts and memories, but they do not have the same weight, the same texture.*

Kaylin froze. Ybelline sensed everything Kaylin was trying to gather words to explain. And Kaylin, in turn, sensed Ybelline's hesitance. It was almost like fear. Fear of a future that had not yet happened, but which the *Tha'alaan* remembered.

You need to know what happens in those memories and thoughts.

Kaylin swallowed. *Yes. It's—it's why I came to talk to the water at all. Not—not that I knew the* Tha'alaan *was affected, but that I thought the water could tell me, tell us, what's about to happen.* What *had* happened, sometime in the near future. *But…the water isn't us. It's not mortal. It's not living* here. *You are. I am. Whatever thoughts you're hearing—the haven't-happened-yet thoughts—I think they'll be clearer, and cleaner.*

She felt Ybelline's reluctance give way—and she expected that. That was Ybelline, all over. What she didn't expect was the water's frenzied response. The inches of water across the second-story hall reared up in a sudden wall, like a tidal wave in miniature. It dropped on Kaylin's head—and the stair railing.

The railing snapped.

If she drowned here, Severn was going to be so *mad*.

The water did not *speak*.

It roared. It roared like a flight of Dragons, the sound a sensation that made Kaylin's teeth—and every other part of her body—rattle. She lost the *Tha'alaan*; lost the comfort of Ybelline's steady presence; she lost everything as the water swept her, and the very broken rail, down the hall and into the door at the end of it.

The door gave way as Kaylin crashed into it; she could feel it shatter, but couldn't hear it. She couldn't, for a moment, hear at all. There was water everywhere.

But it wasn't high enough to instantly drown in, even if the only breaths she could draw were the ragged gasps that panic often caused. She had time to close her mouth; time to find her footing; time to see that the windows here were normal windows. Normal meant closed; in this section of town, it didn't immediately mean barred.

Unfortunately for Kaylin, in this house, normal *didn't* mean backyard and familiar city landscape, either.

She'd come here to talk to the water. She'd let Gilbert do it instead. Clearly, the water in the here and now didn't agree with Gilbert's presence in the here and now. She struggled for more air and less water, coughing the water out. The tide at her feet was strong, but the water itself wasn't deep. Kaylin didn't want to give the water time to regroup and try again, if it was even attempting to kill her consciously.

It wasn't. She inhaled, coughing less. It wasn't trying consciously. It was aware of her; it must be, to dump a wall of water in a way that shattered the railing to which she'd been clinging. But it didn't *see* her as Kaylin.

She felt confident that if it could or did, she would be in far less danger.

There was only one way to get its attention, and she once again dropped her hand into the water. This room was not like the single room in the third story; it had furniture and waterlogged carpet. It had chairs. It had—ugh—shelves, and the books on them were going to be far, far worse for wear.

And none of that was relevant right now.

Only the water was. Kaylin's arms stung; her wet, wet clothing chafed her skin. And she knew what that meant. At any other time, she would look for the source of magic; the water itself didn't usually cause this type of pain. Today, she looked at her arms. She saw the faint blue glow of runes through the cloth plastered against them.

She saw the hand she'd plunged into the faintly rocking water.

If it had been natural water, there would be visual distortion. It wasn't natural, and there was no distortion; the water might have had the same properties as air, except for the inability to actually breathe it. She heard roaring again—the same shattering roar she had heard and felt at her first contact.

She did not hear the *Tha'alaan*. She didn't try.

As the light on her arms brightened, she tried to speak a single word. It took effort. The syllables—there were more than one—snapped on her tongue; they slid out of her mind and she lost them and had to start again. And again. And again. But the third time, in the warmth of water she could no longer feel, she held them all, forcing each out of her mouth, although speech wasn't technically necessary.

And the water rose.

It formed not a wall, but a pillar, and as Kaylin watched, the pillar refined its shape, until it was no longer a standing column of water from floor to ceiling. Kaylin was prepared to see the watery figure of a woman: this was how the water spoke to Kaylin when it chose to speak.

She was not prepared to see the water take the form and shape of a child—although this would not be the first time.

Nor would it be the first time the figure had looked solidly, profoundly *mortal*. A mortal girl. Young enough to be Kattea, and hurt enough, bruised enough, to be Kattea as she would, no doubt, have become.

No, Kaylin thought. Kattea's fief was not Kaylin's fief; her life, not Kaylin's life. If it was true that her father had once been a Sword, it meant that others—like Kattea's father, and not Kaylin's long-dead mother—could be living there, too.

Liar, Kaylin thought. *Gilbert found her in the streets at night. Near Ferals.*

And again, that didn't matter. Not right now. What mattered now was the water.

"Kaylin." The name was spoken by a bruised mouth, distorted by swelling at the corner. The water, as it manifested itself in this room, was shorter than Kaylin, and skinnier. *Slender* was not the right word: she was gaunt.

"I'm sorry," Kaylin said. She looked at her hand. Held in it was the child's. Beneath the child's feet lay soaked carpet; it was dark enough to be black, but Kaylin suspected it would be blue when dry. Beyond the child, seen through the door frame, which would not, without repairs, house a door again, the runner in the hall was also soaked. But the floor was no longer a wading pool. "I didn't know that having Gilbert here would upset you."

"Gilbert?" The child's eyes narrowed in a way that children's eyes seldom did. "Is that what you call him?"

"It's what Kattea calls him. And yes, it's what I call him, as well." She hesitated.

"I can hear the *Tha'alaan*," the girl whispered. Her expression shifted; she looked anguished. "I—I'm afraid I've *broken it*."

Ah. This, Kaylin could understand. There wasn't much the elemental water and a mortal woman had in common—but the fear of accidentally destroying something beloved? That was clearly universal. "Why? Why do you think it's broken?"

"There are things in it that should not be in it; there's a bend, a break. I didn't—" She swallowed as if she were breathing, as if she needed the air she fundamentally hated.

"The *Tha'alaan* is not that fragile. Ybelline is there. Ybelline understands, now, what this fracture means."

"You don't understand."

"No," Kaylin agreed, gentling her voice without thought. "But I don't need to understand if Ybelline does. They will listen to her. They'll hear her."

"They hear her now," the water whispered. "They hear her fear. They hear her death."

Kaylin stiffened. Blanched. Forced herself to continue. "Yes." She didn't argue because there was no point. If one of the memories the *Tha'alaan* now contained was Ybelline's death, it would be known, examined—and terrifying. The fact that Ybelline was demonstrably not dead would not be the comfort it might be to anyone who couldn't access the memories and emotions of every member of their race who had come before.

It was comfort to Kaylin, though. Comfort—and fear.

"I don't understand how you came to know what you know," Kaylin said. "I came to—to ask you."

"Ask Gilbert. Gilbert knows." This was said with a sullenness that bordered on resentment.

"Gilbert doesn't know. Or if he does, he can't explain it to someone like me. Neither could fire or air or earth," she continued. She was not above using truth as flattery. At least it made her better than most of the residents of Elani. "Only you can, because you are the heart of the *Tha'alaan*.

"Kattea—you haven't met her, but you can see what I see if you want to look—said that it was the water that brought her to Elantra. Gilbert didn't even realize that he was crossing through time. I don't think it was *enough* time," she added, trying to be fair. "The water of the time he was in carried the boat he was also in to our time. To us.

"I wanted to ask you how."

The water was silent.

"But actually, how doesn't matter."

"What matters?"

"Why." Even saying it, Kaylin thought she knew the answer now. *Ybelline's death.* No, not just Ybelline—because Ybelline would not die alone.

"And now?"

Kaylin tried to smile and failed miserably. The water's fear was a fear Kaylin herself had lived with, on and off, for her entire life—or for as much of it as she could remember. People would abandon her—by dying. Because *that was what people did.*

She tightened her free hand and considered smacking herself, hard. *Not the time for this, idiot.* Not the right time. Ybelline *wasn't* dead yet. In some future, she was—but it hadn't happened, which meant there was time.

Kaylin had daydreamed about going back in time. She'd never really considered all the effects this would have on everyone—anything—else. But it had all been idle; she *couldn't.*

And yet, Kattea was here.

"Now I think I understand the why. The Tha'alani die, in the future. The near future. You brought Gilbert here to prevent it."

"I have tried to explain it. To the Keeper," she added, as if this were necessary. "I have tried for two of your days."

"Rain isn't likely to explain much."

"He cannot hear."

"Rain in *his store* is likely to be seen as its own emergency."

"Kaylin—his Garden *will not exist.* It does not, in that time."

★ ★ ★

"You're partially from then."

The water nodded, eyes darkening, bruises spreading. Kaylin suddenly wanted the "how." Instead, she said, "Gilbert was trying to speak with you."

"Yes. I am sorry. I heard him as...threat."

"Why?"

"Because he will destroy that part of me, if he understands it."

"He did *not* come here to destroy you—why would you think that?"

"Because *it is what he is*."

"Did you understand what he was when you brought him here?"

"...Yes. Yes."

There was only one obvious question to ask. Why? But Kaylin already knew why. "Please don't destroy him."

"I cannot destroy him."

"Please don't destroy the tiny part of him that's here and now. And stop the raining. I understand enough to talk to Evanton." She hesitated. "No, that's not true. Do you understand what happens—or what did happen—to the Garden?"

"No. But it is gone, Kaylin."

"I'll tell him. I'll tell him— Stop trying so hard to communicate with him." She tightened her hold on the young girl's hand. "Why can't you talk to him the way you talk to me?"

"Because Evanton is not Chosen, and Evanton has not been adopted by the *Tha'alaan*. He cannot be the one, and he will not be the other."

"Why?"

"Because it would break the *Tha'alaan*. Kaylin, I would kill him first."

Kaylin doubted that this was possible. Evanton was Keeper. She didn't tell the water this, because she tried not to tell people something they already knew, especially not when they knew it better than she ever could. It tended to make them angry.

"Then let me talk to him."

The water nodded.

"Umm, in order to talk to him, you have to close the flood-gates."

This caused only confusion. Kaylin thought it funny that the words made no sense to water, because so much of a port city was constructed for, on or by the water.

"You need to stop raining and flooding the house. Evanton won't drown—but I will if I try to reach him." She was afraid to let the water go; her own knuckles were white. "Gilbert didn't come here to destroy you."

"No, of course not. But he will see the ripple. He will attempt to fix it."

"Not right now, he won't."

"You cannot stop him. He is not like you or your kin."

"He didn't come to fix things. He came to find a way to a here that someone like me could survive."

"Why?"

"Because he met Lord Nightshade, in a future time and place, and he wants to bring him home. To us."

"You do not understand Gilbert if you believe this."

This was a stupid conversation to be having with elemental water. It was also necessary. "I know. I don't understand what he is. I can't. But—I've healed him."

"Impossible. He can no more be healed than we can."

"Fine. I can't say it felt like healing. He's here, but he's as trapped here as we are."

Silence.

"He says he can't see time here. It's gone. For now, he's part of us. The only thing that isn't is the part of you that chose to bring him here."

Severn.

I see her. And yes, if you drowned, I'd be...upset.

Kind of embarrassing that that was my first *thought. I'm going to go find Evanton. And Gilbert.*

"But we have another problem, and I think they're all connected. Can you talk to Ybelline?"

"Ybelline is speaking to me now," the water replied. As she spoke, her form began to shift; she grew up as she walked beside Kaylin, her hand still in Kaylin's. Her voice became stronger, her words lost the shaky hesitance of uncertain youth. Her eyes lost their bruises, and her lips, the swelling. "It is difficult. I hear Ybelline now—but I hear her in the other now."

"Can you speak to her in the other now?"

"Do not ask that of me."

Which meant it was possible. "Ask my Ybelline if she understands what happens next."

"She understands—" was the remote response "—that she dies. Kaylin—the Tha'alani quarter, all of it, perishes."

"Does she—" Kaylin swallowed. "Does she understand what destroys it?"

A longer silence. "No."

Leontine filled the hall. Kaylin didn't bother to curse under her breath. Cursing didn't bother the water.

"If this is too destabilizing, I'll go to Ybelline directly. If I'm in front of Ybelline, it's almost as good as being in contact with you."

"You will lose my voice," the water replied.

Kaylin nodded. "Tell me what Gilbert is—I mean, what he's supposed to be."

"He is ancient, which is irrelevant. He could be created to-morrow, or next year, or centuries from now, and he would be ancient. He is like us, and entirely unlike us; he is younger, but less raw. There is a purpose at his heart which was not our pur-pose. We are part of him, and separate from him; he sees us at the beginning and the end. He is present, always, everywhere.

"And he is dead."

No, Ybelline's musical voice said, before Kaylin could ask. *That makes no more sense to me than it does to you. It is difficult*, she added. *We…die, I think…very quickly. There is some resistance. Where we have power—magical power, elemental power—we survive in small pockets. In those cases, our deaths are hours ahead, no more.*

Did you—did they—see anything? She hesitated. She heard, beneath the calm of Ybelline's words, a very real fear. And fear sometimes led to insanity, in the Tha'alani mind. Kaylin could investigate a death. But even she had trouble thinking about the deaths in her life she would not be able to prevent.

What she was asking was so much worse than thinking about it. She was, she realized, asking Ybelline to experience them all.

Yes, was Ybelline's reply. *But I understand why—it is to prevent them. Kaylin, I can do this. It is…difficult, but the alternative is worse.*

"What I did," the water said, "is forbidden."

"Then how could you do it at all?"

"Because Gilbert and his kind are dead."

"Not dead. Just…sleeping."

"They do not sleep, Kaylin."

"It's how he described it."

"Perhaps it is how you understand it."

"But if you knew—"

"What would you have done to save your children if you knew what would happen?"

Anything. *Anything.*

"And if the only solution, if the only legal solution, was to let them die? I *did not know* but, Kaylin—had I, I would have done the same thing."

"All right. All right, I accept that. I can't judge it. I can't disagree with it. I just don't understand why you could do this *now*. I don't understand why you knew to bring them to right *now*, and not tomorrow or ten years ago."

The water rumbled. It spoke, but the words were sensation, not sound, and Kaylin could make sense of none of it. She headed down the stairs, her hand still paired with the hand of the Avatar. But she was thinking. Thinking and approaching the question from another avenue.

Ybelline said, *I believe it is because this was the only time. No, that is not the whole of it. Earlier might have been better—but the jumps cause less friction if they are short; they are far less likely to be detected. There was no later time.*

The water existed in Kattea's time.

Yes, Kaylin. Yes, but—no. I do not understand it.

There's no "No" here. If the water didn't exist at that time, how could it bring them back to this *one? Ugh. I hate time.*

Ybelline, however, had not surrendered. *I am sorry, Kaylin—I understand the urgency. I...cannot...explain...what I hear at the heart of the* Tha'alaan; *it is too foreign. Too large. There is something in this time, something like a rip or a tear. I do not think the water could move Gilbert to any other time. The attempt could be made only because of this fissure. I think.*

... And it's the fissure that causes the disaster. It almost wasn't a question.

I am not the Hawk, Kaylin. Those answers are not mine to find.

Ybelline's confidence in Kaylin underlined every word. Kaylin did not have any of it, and wanted it very badly. What she had, however, was a probably half-drowned Gilbert and a drenched Keeper and Keeper's apprentice. It was a start.

But before she went in search of them, she headed back up the ruined stairs, keeping her back to the wall. "Severn?"

The single door at the top of the stairs opened.

"We have to go fish Gilbert out of the water—but I think it's safe now. As long as you're careful on the steps."

CHAPTER 20

The rain in the storefront had stopped. The water had receded. The mess caused by both was still very much present—but a mess of that kind wasn't Kaylin's problem. She felt a twinge of sympathy for Grethan, because it was going to be his.

Elemental water, like fire, could withdraw completely. Had the water been natural—well, never mind. Natural water didn't start a passing monsoon on the inside of a small, narrow building. Natural water didn't take on the form of a woman, and it couldn't be solid enough to hold on to without causing frost-burn.

The water, however, was now evident only in the form of its Avatar. "I do not think the Keeper is going to be very happy."

"Probably not," Kaylin agreed. "On the other hand, he can't exactly kill you. Believe that if I'd caused this mess—" She shuddered.

Kattea was impressed by the mess; the chaotic jumble of unsold junk seemed to be more worthy of attention than the elemental water. She did give the water the side-eye, though, and she kept Kaylin and Severn between them.

"The hall here is narrow," Kaylin told the girl, as they made their way past the kitchen. Water had risen quickly enough here that the dishes caught in the flood hadn't shattered; they rested on the ground. That was about the only positive thing that could be said for the state of the kitchen.

She started to lead the way out of the kitchen and stopped; Evanton's back hall was not two people wide, even if one of them was pure liquid. Before she could disengage her hand, she heard voices. Well, to be precise, she heard squawking.

Small and flappy sailed into view. He paused in front of the water's Avatar, screeching like an outraged seagull. This didn't appear to upset the water. It gave Kaylin a headache.

"I see you were busy." Evanton surveyed the mess of his kitchen with pursed lips and very narrow eyes. Grethan, coming up behind his master, viewed it with dismay. Gilbert, on the other hand, had to be reminded—by Kattea—not to step on the dishes.

The water's Avatar shifted in place. Kaylin tightened her grip. The last thing she wanted—at this very moment, as last-things-wanted was a moving list—was for hostilities between the water and Gilbert to resume. Gilbert, in his disheveled clothing, was not dripping wet. He turned to face the water— or maybe the familiar, it was hard to tell. Gilbert's eyes—the eyes Kaylin thought of as natural—were unfocused. His third eye was open, unblinking black.

"Gilbert," she said, before he could speak. "You said that you were created for a specific purpose, sort of like Helen was."

"Yes."

"What, exactly, was that purpose?"

Silence.

No, Kaylin thought, as she waited for a reply, he wasn't silent. She could feel the rumble beneath her feet that implied Dragon "discussion"; she just couldn't hear it.

Gilbert regarded the water. The water's Avatar returned his regard. Water, when frozen, became ice, and Kaylin could feel the drop in temperature.

"You have spoken with the water," Gilbert said. Since he spoke while looking *at* the water, it took Kaylin a few seconds to catch on.

"Yes."

"Do you understand what now needs to be done?"

"No. Understanding it is high on my list of emergencies, though. You didn't come here to destroy the water, did you?"

This did get his attention, or at least the attention of two of his eyes. "Of course not. The water cannot, in any meaningful way, be destroyed."

"Did you manage to speak to the water?"

"We did not," Evanton said, before Gilbert could. "The Garden was in some disarray." He looked, pointedly, at the water's Avatar. "Nor does it appear to be necessary. I am an old man, Kaylin." This was code for: *I don't have much time left, so you better not be wasting it.* "The water, however, appears to be calm at the moment." The irritation left his expression as he approached the water's Avatar.

Almost gently, he said, "You should rest." As if the water were, in fact, a very exhausted mortal woman who had been pushed just past the edge of her limits—and was not wearing a Hawk tabard.

"I am not here to destroy you," Gilbert added. "And if that is your fear, you fail to understand my purpose." He turned to Kattea. Kattea was hovering uncertainly at his side, and he bent and lifted her.

"*I* fail to understand your purpose," Kaylin interjected. "And I'm trying really, really hard. You have something to do with time?"

He nodded. "I can traverse time because my nature is not your nature. What I said of you—and your companions—is true. You live *in* time. It is necessary for you to function.

"The Ancients were not so bound. Their understanding of

causality was therefore different. Causality implies a before and an after; it connects them. Causality is at the heart of ancient stories. You carry them," he added. "I do not understand *why* those forces sought to create stories—and to you, Kaylin, those stories would be so vast, *world* might be a better description.

"The place you call 'world' is comprised of many things. The water is one. The Keeper's function is to contain the water, to constrain enough of its movements that 'world' is stable."

"He doesn't—"

"He does. You think of storms and the lives lost in them; of fires and the lives lost in them; of earthquakes, perhaps, and the lives lost to them. The Keeper's role is not simple safety; it is not for the benefit to *one* life. Were it not for the Keeper, you could not live at all. You were structured, you were iteratively created, to live in this cage.

"I am not cognizant of all of the iterations. Nor am I cognizant of all of the failures. I am not aware of the minutiae. I am aware that it exists."

"Wait—is the water trapped here, then?"

"No," the water replied. "And yes."

Great. More questions.

"You exist," Gilbert continued. "It is not that you are invisible to me. But I do not look at specific elements, and if they are like you or Kattea, they are too brief; by the time I turn to look, they are gone. The water, I see. Your familiar, I see."

"But Mandoran and Annarion—"

"They exist in multiple ways. There are places to which I can go, elements which I can study in less chaotic, less frenzied, environs. They are part of those, and yet also, part of here." His smile was almost rueful. "As am I now; I believe I understand it better than I did." He abandoned his smile. "Water exists. But in its ability to interact with your kind, it is constrained— must be constrained—as you are constrained.

"If you were to be aware of every minute of your existence, you would be bound by none of it. You could not think, speak, function; your existence would dwindle to introspection. Your ability to interact with the world itself is contingent on your perception of time. It is true of you. It is true of Lord Nightshade.

"It is true," he added, "of Kattea. You understand that when the water folded in on itself in the fashion that it did, there were—and are—consequences." This didn't sound like a question.

I can hear the Tha'alaan. *I'm afraid I've broken it.*

She nodded. She wondered how she would live if she could, at any time, experience her own death. She wondered how much of her life would be lived in an effort to prevent it, how much of her life would be fear and nothing but fear. She wondered if she would view every person in the room as dying or dead if she knew, in advance, what their fates would be.

"It is to prevent such ruptures that my kin were created. In some cases, we could not mend what was broken. We were not required to destroy the resultant chaos, but to quarantine it. We were not required to save individual lives, such as yours." He looked at Kattea. "We could not, as I said, see them. Not without risk and effort."

"Gilbert?"

"Yes?"

"If your job isn't to save individual lives, why are you here?"

"I explained this to you."

He had. She'd even understood it, but frustration had dimmed the effect of the words. Or maybe lack of knowledge about Gilbert had. She looked at him now, Kattea in his arms, and understood. He had chosen to befriend Nightshade. He had chosen to look at a presence he could only dimly register. He had somehow taught himself to hear and then to speak.

And he had then gone searching for a way to restore Night-shade to his own time. Nightshade. One man, not a world, and not an epoch.

Squawk.

Gilbert exhaled. His breath was visible. "The water is correct. What was done should not have been done. It should have been impossible. And were such impossibility to be detected, it would be corrected." He hesitated.

Kaylin *really* hated Gilbert's notion of time. "So, let me get this straight. Time is directional, for us."

"Yes."

"And time is *meant to be* directional. We're not meant to be shoved into the past or thrown into the future."

"Yes."

"And if it's possible to break this unspoken rule, people like you come in and fix it."

"…Yes."

"So the *Castle* broke the rule."

"Yes."

"And you're attempting to…fix the problem?"

He had the grace to look vastly less certain. "…No."

"I give up. Let's move on to point two. The water said that the reason you're here—and now—is because it's the only moment in which there was a break, or a space."

Gilbert's eyes narrowed—all three of them. "The only moment?"

"Yes—and I don't think it's a coincidence that you yourself said when you arrived here, you could no longer see time. Something's happening here. Or it will happen, soon. Something is broken for only a very small window of time—our version of time." Her thoughts raced ahead of her ability to express them. Or retain them. "If you notice big breaks, big things that are wrong, then this must be something that you can't or haven't noticed. Maybe you don't see *us* because our lives are too short and too slight—"

"You think this break is something that we would not have noticed."

She nodded. Hesitated. "Do you *know* what happened? The *Tha'alaan* is going to be lost. Part of you was there, in the future in which it disappears. Do you know *why*?"

"My perception of your life is filtered through the Tha'alani. It is why I can speak to you and understand you as well as I do." The water lowered her head. "Ybelline is attempting to find an answer to your question. She cannot...move...through time. She knows that something is coming. She may know...when."

"Severn?" Kaylin asked.

He came forward to join her.

"Gilbert, you'd better come with us. I think you...destabilize...the Garden."

Gilbert nodded. The water, however, asked, "Why do you have that child with you?"

Kattea shrank into Gilbert's chest, trying to look smaller.

"He needs Kattea to get back," Kaylin replied.

The water's frown etched itself into Kaylin's vision. "Is that what the child told you?"

"It's what Gilbert told us." Kaylin felt the water's grip on her hand tighten. "You don't think she's in any danger from him?"

"This is not perhaps the safest time in which to introduce a mortal," the water replied. It wasn't an answer. There wasn't going to be an answer—at least not while Kattea was present. Kaylin decided it was a provisional "no." No, Gilbert did not intend to harm her, and yes, there was danger regardless.

But it couldn't be worse, at this point, than death by Ferals. Clinging to that thought, Kaylin said, "Evanton, can I use your mirror?"

★ ★ ★

Bellusdeo was with the Arkon when the mirror connected. She took one look at Kaylin and her eyes darkened to the orange with which Kaylin was becoming increasingly familiar. "We're fine," she said quickly. "But—there's a problem."

"We spoke with the Keeper." Which was, strictly speaking, true. "And the elemental water. Gilbert *is* here because of the water. Kattea was right about that. But the water didn't choose a specific time and place—it brought him here because it was the *only* option available. This was the only time to which Gilbert could be moved."

The Arkon pinched the bridge of his nose.

Kaylin failed to mention the Tha'alani, weighing the options. The Emperor forced the Tha'alani to work on interrogations—and it was a work that twisted and broke them without extreme care. It damaged the entire race. She didn't want the Tha'alani exposed to any more Imperial scrutiny without a damn good reason.

But if the death of their race didn't count as a good reason, she would never be able to come up with one. She cleared her throat. The Arkon looked even more irritated. "For a member of a short-lived race, you have a propensity to waste time."

"Sorry. You always get angry if my explanations are 'inadequate.' I'm just trying—"

"To waste more time." His eyes were still open, but only barely.

"The elemental water brought Gilbert and Kattea here. Through an underground tunnel. Into large, stone halls underneath a basement on the Winding Path. The *reason* they're here is because it was possible to bring them."

"And?"

"Sometime in our immediate future—the future that Kattea is ostensibly part of—there's some sort of disaster that apparently destroys Elantra—or at least the parts of Elantra that are not the fiefs."

"You think it has something to do with the murders," Bellusdeo said, when the Arkon failed to find words.

"The maybe-murders," Kaylin said.

"Pardon?"

"Gilbert insists that they're not actually dead." She hesitated. She needed to stop doing that, because Bellusdeo's eyes narrowed until they matched the Arkon's. The Arkon let out a small stream of smoke. "But...Gilbert said that he thought all the previous attempts to cast magic in that particular basement were an attempt to speak certain words."

"Please repeat that slowly," the Arkon commanded. The mirror's image shifted, cutting Bellusdeo out of the frame.

"I asked Gilbert to inspect the bodies, because he sees things I can't," Kaylin said, resigning herself to the longer explanation. "To *me*, they're dead. I've seen corpses. But...they disappear if I view them through my familiar's wing. I thought there was some chance he'd see a dimension to the difficulty that would explain *why* they disappear."

"Continue."

"When we descended into the basement, Gilbert looked at the sigils left by other casters. He—" She grimaced. "He pulled words out of the sigils that *I* see when I detect traces of prior magic use. He did so in such a way that they were visible to everyone present, even Gavin."

"Did the Sergeant capture these words for Records?"

"Not while we were there—Gilbert thought there was a significant danger that the mirror network would be compromised." She shook her head. "*Compromised* is the wrong word. He thought it would be a total disaster. It wouldn't be the first time magic caused problems via the mirrors.

"But—the night before the murder, Gilbert's house was visited by four men. One of those was an Arcanist. Gilbert did not, according to Kattea, react *well* to the visitors—but Gilbert has no recollection of a conflict."

"Was he injured enough to sustain memory loss?"

"Not exactly." Kaylin thought explaining Gilbert to a very cranky Arkon was the definition of "career-limiting."

"Teela and Tain headed out to the Arcanum—or the High Halls—without the rest of us. If there's any information, they'll dig it up. Oh," she added, "there was one detail. The Arcanist in question was apparently wearing a tiara with a diamond in its center."

The Arkon's eyes slid from orange to something very, very close to red. "This theoretical Arcanist visited Gilbert."

"Kattea said Gilbert was angry; to Kattea's eyes, magical hostilities were exchanged. I'm not certain Gilbert sees this as conflict. And no, before you ask, I don't think Gilbert in the Palace is a good idea. Do you recognize what a diamond-wearing Arcanist entails?"

"I have work to do, Private."

Kaylin surrendered. "The water of the future blended—somehow—with the water of right now. The *Tha'alaan* resides, in great part, in the elemental water's core. It brought some of the memories of the future *Tha'alaan* with it when it arrived." She exhaled. "Every Tha'alani in their quarter dies. The experience of each and every death has been dumped into the *Tha'alaan*; it's uneven, and I think the Caste Court is attempting to mitigate the obvious damage that'll cause.

"But Ybelline is aware now of how significant this is, and she is examining the memories of the last few deaths, to attempt to give us more information about what caused it."

"Very well. I wish to have the visible words examined. I also wish to have the basement beneath Gilbert's house examined. I am not in a condition to examine them personally, and even were I, Tiamaris was as close as we come to an expert in ancient buildings and writing. He does not, of course, have my wealth of experience—but he has a particular focus.

"He is not, however, likely to be available. I will therefore send Sanabalis." He turned to glance off-mirror; he spoke, but the mirror did not convey the sound of his voice. "I expect a full report of any relevant information gleaned from either the Tha'alani or Tiamaris."

"I can interrupt you?"

"You may even do so safely, for the duration."

"I think he's going to send Bellusdeo with Sanabalis," Kaylin told Severn. She glanced at Gilbert. He had no difficulty keeping up with the two Hawks. Kattea had flagged, which was fine; Gilbert was carrying her. Kaylin suspected he would carry her anywhere, for as long as it was necessary.

The water's silence made her uneasy. She could not believe that Gilbert intended to hurt Kattea—but what constituted harm, for Gilbert, was probably not even translatable into Elantran. Or any other language Kaylin knew.

"If," she told him, as they continued their very brisk pace, "you see any other buildings of significance, let us know?"

He nodded. He had said very little since his encounter with the water's Avatar, and seemed—for Gilbert—less confused and more grave. He stopped well short of the guard post occupied by the Tha'alani, and Kaylin thought it best to ask Ybelline's permission—through direct mental contact with the guards—to dispense with the usually thorough inspection. Kattea flinched when one of the guards bent down to touch Kaylin's forehead with the stalks that grew out of his own.

The guards themselves were not especially eager to touch the thoughts of an outsider, but knew their duties; they waited until Ybelline granted permission for Kaylin to enter the quarter.

One of them wore the tabard of the *Tha'alanari*—one who was capable of guarding their thoughts, or the thoughts they took in, from the rest of the *Tha'alaan.*

It was he who escorted them to Ybelline's home.

The streets of the Tha'alani quarter were never empty; today was not an exception.

Kaylin had not visited while in possession of the familiar— and like Nightshade's mark, small and flappy had become so much a part of her daily life she could almost forget he was there. To anyone who hadn't yet seen a tiny, translucent dragon—which clearly moved on its own—the familiar was a delight and a curiosity.

Small children gathered by the side of the narrow road that wound its way through the oddly curved, rounded contours of the dwellings the Tha'alani favored. They were openly curious, and some, bolder than others, attempted to touch the strangers in the Hawks' tabard. Some stepped back, clearly nervous.

"They don't see a lot of outsiders," Kaylin told Kattea, who had stiffened in Gilbert's arms. "So they're curious."

Kattea clearly had the usual fear of the Tha'alani mind readers. Kaylin tried not to resent it, because she'd once felt that fear herself. But she did pause to let the bolder children touch her extended hands, and she did allow one hesitant child to brush her cheek—he was too nervous to truly connect—with the stalks on his forehead. If she'd once been as frightened as Kattea, she wanted to make clear that the fear was groundless, and there was no better way.

On the other hand, the small dragon was the star of the show today; all of the telepathic questions the children transmitted were about him. He was well enough behaved that he allowed them to touch him—but not with their slender, immature antennae. The children radiated delight and wonder so strongly, words would have been superfluous.

But Kaylin had come here for a reason, and if spending the day amusing small mind readers was actually a happy thing, it took up time they didn't have. Their escort understood this, and the children melted away, some with obvious reluctance. No words, however, were exchanged. They weren't necessary.

Ybelline was waiting for them. She wore very simple robes—yellow, fringed with purple—that flowed loosely down her shoulders and arms; the sheen of the fabric caught the sunlight, which reminded Kaylin that it was not actually that late in the day.

Ybelline's jaw was tightly set; she smiled—because she smiled so often, it was practically her default expression—but her color was bad, and her eyes were darkly circled. Kaylin, who often hugged her, hugged her now for entirely different reasons. Ybelline's stalks brushed Kaylin's forehead and settled there.

Kaylin told her everything. Ybelline was *Tha'alanari*. What she saw in Kaylin's thoughts, she could—with effort and discipline—keep out of the *Tha'alaan*. She showed Ybelline the three corpses that had been the start of her involvement; she showed Ybelline Gilbert, Gilbert's basement and her attempt to heal him. She showed Ybelline the elemental water and told her what the water had said.

Her conscious memory was nowhere near as good as the memory Ybelline now touched, and Kaylin was perfectly willing to let the Tha'alani castelord rifle through all of it. She had no fear at all that Ybelline would judge her.

"Come with me," Ybelline said, as she withdrew.

Kaylin hesitated, and Ybelline marked it. "I'm sorry. I want to introduce Gilbert and Kattea. Gilbert, Kattea, this is Ybelline—the castelord of the Tha'alani."

Gilbert set Kattea down and offered the Tha'alani woman a very deep bow. It was not, strictly speaking, a Tha'alani greeting, but Ybelline interacted with enough people that she recognized it as a gesture of deep respect, regardless. Kattea's stiff nod was less admirable and far more skittish—but this was something Ybelline understood, as well. Kaylin's annoyance was deeper and lasted longer.

Then again, some of it was with her past self, and no one could get as angry with Kaylin as she herself could.

Gilbert offered Ybelline his hand. Kaylin stepped between them a shade too quickly. Ybelline, however, shook her head. "It is all right, Kaylin. It is a risk I am willing to take."

"He's not—"

"Yes, you've told me. But I have...done as I must. I have experienced my own death." Her smile was slightly gray, but the resolve beneath it, unshaken. "Experiencing death is not, in the end, as terrifying as it seems at a remove; it is not fear, but fact."

"Ybelline—"

"If you are not mistaken, he will help us. And if I am not mistaken, it is Gilbert's help we now require."

"It's the 'me not being mistaken' part I'm worried about," Kaylin replied.

Ybelline's answering smile was deeper this time. "It is because you are young. If you do not trust yourself, that is...how do you say it? Not my problem."

"That's pretty much how we say it, yes." Kaylin exhaled. "Gilbert, I'm not sure if you know the Tha'alani, or know about them."

"Kattea fears them," Gilbert said, which caused the younger girl to blanch. Then glare. "You do not."

"No, I really don't. If we could all communicate the way

the Tha'alani do, I'd be out of a job. You will not find kinder or more understanding people anywhere, ever."

"But you are still worried."

Kaylin exhaled. "I am worried *for* them. When they speak to you, when they read your thoughts, those thoughts become part of what they know, and what they know is part of the *Tha'alaan*. Healing you…made it clear that you're not like us. But if you're different in the wrong way…"

"You are not castelord, Kaylin," Ybelline said firmly. "And I am not a child to be protected when the future of my people—and yours—is imperiled."

"I am not worried," Gilbert said—to Kaylin. "It is frustrating; it is hard to make myself understood to your kind. What she knows—what she can know—cannot hurt me."

"And if she touched your name?"

"That is not the way it works" was his quiet reply. He almost sounded regretful. He once again extended his hand; Ybelline took it. She hesitated.

"The functionality is within the stalks?" Gilbert asked, correctly identifying the hesitation.

"Not entirely—but yes. They are not always necessary for the Tha'alani."

His smile was slender, but genuine; she'd amused him. She certainly hadn't amused Kattea. Kaylin placed a staying hand on the younger girl's shoulder.

"You let her touch you," Kattea whispered.

"Yes, I did. The thing about Ybelline is this: she can see *everything* about you—all the things you hate, all the things you regret, all the things you would never tell anyone—" with each phrase, Kattea's body stiffened slightly "—but she doesn't judge you. She will never hate you, even if you hate yourself. I know it doesn't make sense to you," she added. "But I'm not worried for Gilbert."

"You're worried for *her*?"

Kaylin nodded. "Not because I think Gilbert will try to hurt her," she added. "But I'm starting to think that people—like us—aren't meant to understand people like Gilbert. I mean, we're not even built so we *can*. I think there are whole parts of him that make no sense to us, and will never make sense to us. We can think about him on the outside until it's exhausting, but—we're not *inside* of him."

Ybelline stiffened, in a much more obvious way than Kattea had; Kaylin crushed the girl's shoulder, realized what she'd done and apologized.

"Gilbert's like us, in one way," Kattea surprised her by saying.

"Oh?"

"Or maybe he's only like me."

Paying attention to Kattea was easier, at the moment, than watching Ybelline. If Kaylin had thought her wan and pale before, it was nothing to the color she now became. But Ybelline was right. Kaylin was a *private*. Ybelline was castelord.

"How is he like you?" Kaylin asked, forcing her eyes away from the Tha'alani and Gilbert.

"He's lonely."

"I don't think Gibert gets lonely the way we do."

Kattea folded her arms, her fear turning to annoyance. She radiated anger at what she assumed was condescension—and to be fair to her, it kind of was. "I think I know Gilbert better than you do."

"You've known him for what, three weeks? Maybe four?" Kaylin bit back more words. "I'm sorry. I'm worried, and I'm cranky. Gilbert isn't human. No, more than that, he's not like *any* of the races you know. From what he's said—and you've heard him say it—he was built for a purpose."

"So?"

"What kind of crappy god builds loneliness into something that doesn't *need* others to survive?" Her brain caught up with her mouth and shut it down.

Helen had been built with a specific purpose. Some of that purpose, Helen no longer remembered. Helen had never described herself as lonely, in the years—or centuries—before Hasielle, her very first tenant, had arrived. She hadn't used the exact word, no. But she'd been drawn to Hasielle because Hasielle was the type of person to *make* a home of wherever she lived. To bring warmth or light or life to the space, just by being in it.

To *keep* Hasielle, Helen had destroyed parts of herself. She wasn't, hadn't been, in *love* with Hasielle—but the yearning for her had been visceral.

For how long had she observed Hasielle, without even speaking to her? For how long had she noted Hasielle's cleaning and humming and cooking?

Kaylin looked at Gilbert's profile. Gilbert might have been a cleverly painted statue. For how long had Gilbert been aware of Nightshade, in the dim recesses of an ancient building in the heart of the fiefs? At the beginning, he hadn't even been *aware* of Nightshade.

But at some point in Nightshade's captivity—and Kaylin could think of it in no other way—Gilbert had chosen to speak with, to communicate with, the fieflord. To do so, he'd had to invert himself. What inversion meant, Kaylin still didn't know. She understood only that it was risky and voluntary.

She closed her eyes.

Gilbert is lonely.

Yes, only idiots would create something that got lonely. But…weren't the idiots in part created *because* something wild and ancient and world-devouring…had been lonely? Maybe it was part of the essential nature of anything in the universe.

Nothing existed in isolation. And maybe nothing *wanted* to. Not if it could think, move, feel.

Helen had observed Hasielle for a very small fraction of Helen's overall existence. Thirty years? No. Less. Her decision to damage herself, to cut off her figurative limbs, had been arrived at without consultation with Hasielle. She had not, in any obvious way, revealed her presence, her sentience. She had gambled everything on Hasielle, on the hope that she could become the home in which Hasielle *wanted* to live.

Gilbert had actually spoken with Nightshade. He'd done so continually for three or four decades—if that was even accurate. And Gilbert had found Kattea; had rescued an orphan from the fiefs. A little girl whom he had not been built to even *see*—all because of that time with Nightshade.

"I'm sorry, Kattea," she said—meaning it now. "I think you might be right."

Kattea was young enough—barely—that the genuine apology made up for Kaylin's earlier doubt. Kaylin turned to Gilbert, and the feelings of guilt evaporated as Ybelline's knees buckled.

CHAPTER
21

She was there to catch the castelord; Gilbert hadn't moved an inch.

It was hard to remember that they had anything in common; for one long moment, she wanted to deck him. But she didn't have more than two arms and needed both. "Ybelline," she said, urgent, her hands brushing the Tha'alani's forehead.

Gilbert blinked. Well, he blinked with two of his eyes. The third eye, which had been more or less closed, snapped open.

"Yes," he said, to thin air. "I see."

Ybelline's eyes were almost always gold; it was easy to think of them as normal—or normal human, at any rate. But when her lids fluttered open, they revealed irises of hazel. Kaylin could not remember what hazel meant in the Tha'alani; she imagined it wasn't good. "I am...uninjured, Kaylin. Help me stand."

Kaylin did so. Severn helped unobtrusively; Gilbert continued to stand, unmoving, as if people generally collapsed in his presence as a matter of course. Ybelline was not steady on her feet; Kaylin shifted position, sliding an arm under her arms and around her back, to brace her. Although she didn't always notice this, Ybelline was not small.

"Come with me," the Tha'alani castelord said. By default, this would have happened anyway, given that Kaylin was most of the castelord's locomotive force at the moment. "Gilbert," she added.

"Yes?" He didn't actually look at her. Kaylin wasn't certain what he was looking at, but whatever it was, he stared at it intently. The small dragon whuffled, apparently unconcerned.

"We're leaving."

"Yes?"

Kaylin snorted and looked to Kattea, who nodded and caught Gilbert's arm. Gilbert blinked as she tried to move him—and failed. Kattea was not, however, a quitter. "Gilbert—we have to *go with them*."

"We don't," he said, looking confused.

Ybelline turned to Kaylin and touched her forehead. *He is not human.* She used the broader word, the old Elantran one.

No. I—I trust him, though.

I think trust is almost irrelevant, Ybelline replied. *But I will thank you for bringing him.*

Given Ybelline's collapse and continued shakiness, Kaylin had severe doubts that those thanks were deserved.

I am grateful. She was. *It was so difficult to understand what I was seeing or hearing that it…removed me from the immediacy of so much death and so much fear. I am still…uncertain…that I understand what Gilbert attempted to tell me. I am also uncertain that he understood me.*

He thinks he did.

Ybelline nodded. *I do not think I will make that attempt again in the very near future. But oddly, it is safer to have Gilbert touch the Tha'alaan than it would be to have your Barrani Hawks touch it. Gilbert's thoughts and beliefs would be very like a poorly structured dream—and we have those in the Tha'alaan, in number.*

Where are you taking us?

To the long house, the caste hall. The Tha'alanari will meet us there. I have asked them to do what I have done. If I can touch the experience of death—and I can—I cannot examine it with the care we now require, not at any speed. At leisure, when this crisis is behind us, I may return to it. She meant it, too. *But not now. We cannot, I believe, direct our future selves; their memories are much like our own: they are resigned almost instantly to a past we cannot change and must simply accept and understand.*

If Kaylin adored Ybelline—and she absolutely did—she didn't adore the other Caste Court officials even one tenth as much. In general, officials were the last people Kaylin was sent to speak with; they made her feel instantly defensive, and defensive Kaylin offended the officials. Things generally went downhill from there.

Ybelline, well aware of Kaylin's discomfort, shook her head. "They are more hardened in their suspicions of outsiders, but they are aware that you are capable of touching the *Tha'alaan* on your own, and they have seen what you desire for, and of, it. They find you...ill-mannered and hasty, but they respect what you have done in the past.

"And regardless, they are the men and women who are willing to visit—and revisit—their own deaths in an attempt to make sense of what occurred."

"Did Gilbert have anything helpful to add?"

"Not intentionally." She glanced at Gilbert. "And perhaps I am also too hasty. But—and I'm certain this will not shock you at this point—I believe the Arcanist in his memories may have some light to shed on the difficulty."

"You didn't recognize the Arcanist?"

Ybelline fell silent, in all ways. Kaylin was genuinely surprised. "Ybelline—"

"I believe I have seen that man before. Or one dressed very like him."

"In real life?"

"No, Kaylin. In memory. In the memories that we are forced

to invade, and of which we are allowed to speak only in the presence of Imperial court officials. I will speak with those officials when we are done."

"I think Teela has some idea of the man's identity. Or at least of the tiara's significance."

"You wish me to leave this to your Teela?"

"I'd just as soon you spent as little time with Imperial officials as possible."

"Even the Hawks?"

Kaylin grimaced. "Maybe especially the Hawks." Because it was through the Hawks, for the most part, that the Tha'alani "interrogators" were summoned, and through the Hawks that the Tha'alani were exposed, consistently, to the *worst* mankind had to offer.

"I understand why the Hawks were created. I understand their purpose. If it were not for the Hawks, we would never have met, and I would consider that a great loss on my part." She straightened and pulled away from Kaylin, testing her legs for strength. They held her up, but she wasn't going to be running anytime soon.

Kattea had managed to drag Gilbert in more or less the right direction; he still looked unfocused and inattentive. Kattea, however, looked more frustrated than worried.

Yes, Kaylin thought, the child had only known him for a handful of weeks. But she was right: she understood Gilbert better than Kaylin did. Maybe necessity had forced that understanding on her.

"Should Gilbert go, too?" Kattea asked. Gilbert's reaction to being touched by a Tha'alani had eased the younger girl's fear in a way that Kaylin's interaction with the younger children hadn't. And of course, that made sense: children were not powerful, or not more powerful than Kattea—but Ybelline, adult, was.

Gilbert finally noticed where he was. Or at least that he was somewhere that wasn't strictly on the inside of his own head. "I am not certain that will be necessary," he told Kattea. "Or that I would be welcome; I may cause...confusion."

Ybelline actually laughed. She was careful not to touch Gilbert, but she did not look at him with worry or dread. "You will certainly cause that."

"What is your preference?"

"I am torn—my people share thoughts and experiences, but we are not all of one mind, and we bring different knowledge to those shared experiences."

"I can attempt to contain my thoughts."

"I rather think that would be beside the point" was the castelord's gentle reply. "They are waiting."

To Kaylin's surprise, Draalzyn was present. Draalzyn was seconded to the Hawks, but worked for the most part in Missing Persons. He was older than Ybelline, his hair streaked with gray, and at the moment, he was just as pale as Ybelline, although this wasn't always the case.

His eyes did narrow when he caught sight of Kaylin.

Kaylin nodded.

"Private Neya," another man said. Scoros. Of all the *Tha'alanari*, Scoros was the least intimidating, if one excluded Ybelline.

"You've grown a beard."

"I am making the attempt, yes. It is supposed to make me look more mature, and therefore more worthy of respect. You don't like it?"

"It's...different."

He chuckled. "My family is not enamored of it, either; Eladara says it is uncomfortable, and my son detests it enough that he tried to shave it while I was sleeping." At Kaylin's expression, his chuckle became a laugh—and his laugh, like Ybelline's, was one Kaylin loved. But it faded as Gilbert entered the room, Kattea clinging to his arm.

"Corporal Handred is not of the *Tha'alaan*," Draalzyn said.

"No. Nor are our other guests." Ybelline emphasized the last word very slightly. "But in this, they are all intent upon preserving the city. You have seen some part of what we have only barely managed to contain; you cannot imagine that the deaths coming to Elantra will occur in our quarter alone."

Draalzyn nodded slowly. He never looked precisely happy, and his beard framed his face in such a way that his pallor was the second thing you noticed, if you noticed anything at all. "Your point is taken. Have you spoken to Private Neya outside of the *Tha'alaan*?"

"Not in any great detail. Will you speak with her directly?"

Draalzyn looked as if he'd rather kiss a hundred toads. Which was fair, because Kaylin would rather kiss two hundred. They both shut up.

"Scoros?"

"It is as you know. We will retreat to this building and open the interior gates. Those who flee through the tunnels will not survive; they perish first. Those who remain to defend and guard their retreat perish shortly thereafter."

"What attacks the quarter?"

"It is still not completely clear to us," Draalzyn replied. The stalks on his forehead were weaving in a graceful way that was at odds with everything else about the man. "The deaths are not instant—but they are quick. Some are crushed. Some are, we think, beheaded; some are torn apart in a matter of seconds. Some feel the pain of fire—but only briefly. They are panicked. They are in their homes or in the streets; there is very little warning."

"They don't *see* anything?"

"No, Kaylin."

"So—whatever kills them, whatever slaughters them, is *invisible*?"

Ybelline answered before Draalzyn could. "There are tactile impressions, but these are also confused. Yes. I would guess that the deaths will be the same across the city. In this possible future, I reach the mirror," she added softly. She hesitated. "We manage to secure a safe area, a barriered hold. But activation of the mirror—" She inhaled sharply. "It summons death into our chambers."

Kaylin's hands were fists.

"Don't," Ybelline said, reaching for those fists and forcing Kaylin's fingers to unbend. "It is a mercy. For all of us, it is a mercy; the pain and the fear of our people's deaths have driven us all to the edge of madness."

"Or over it," Scoros said quietly. "We have attempted to piece more together. I believe it is Draalzyn who suggests the barrier."

Draalzyn nodded, his lips twisted. "I have gained some knowledge among your Hawks. It is not, in future, enough. I do not cast the spell in question." He didn't say who did. Kaylin didn't ask.

"Can you tell me what kind of barrier? What is it meant to protect you against?"

"It is an inversion," Ybelline replied, "of a summoning spell."

"A summoning spell?" Kaylin felt like a parrot.

"We have, prior to this, summoned water. And fire. It is a specific spell that requires the names of those elements. The barrier is comprised of that knowledge and the attempt to drive them out."

"But—but why?"

"Draalzyn?"

Draalzyn looked as if he'd swallowed a rat that wasn't quite dead. "Ybelline, must I?"

"If you prefer, I can visit the memories of your death and the hours before it occurred." Her eyes, as she spoke, were gold.

Draalzyn grimaced. "You think I would spare you that pain when I have had to endure it myself?"

"Yes, actually, I do." She smiled.

He threw both his hands up in disgust that was only partly feigned. "This," he told Kaylin, "is what you must watch out for when Ybelline knows you too well. She will twist you around her finger; you will do what she wants you to do because you can't bear to cause her pain. Even," he added darkly, "when you wish to strangle her.

"The concept of a magical barrier exists among the mages. It was of interest to me, and of interest to my kin. It was not a priority, because it does not prevent actual *people* from crossing its lines. The barriers exist in a particular form; they exist as a counter to other magicians. There are many theories about magic—its use, its origin—and therefore many theories about the counters that can be put into play.

"The barrier was one such theory. I suggested it to Ybelline at an earlier stage in her education. She considered it with the same care she considers many foreign things." The implication was not lost on Kaylin.

"The barrier works, in the future?"

"Yes."

"Wait." Kaylin held up a hand, although Draalzyn didn't seem to be in a hurry to interrupt her. "You—you don't think it's the *elements* that destroy the city?"

"We *do not know*," he said, drumming the table at which he sat. "We do not speak with the elements. We speak into the *Tha'alaan*. The *Tha'alaan* is part of the elemental water—but it is a small part, at odds with the whole. It is inconceivable to us that the water itself would destroy the city—but I am told I, at least, suffer from insufficient imagination." This last, he said in a very sour voice, with an expression to match.

"It is, in theory, possible that magic as our mages currently understand it has its underpinnings in the elemental forces. Frankly, this makes sense to me, if we accept that the world itself is derived from those forces."

"There's no way the elements go to town if…"

"If the Keeper is still in control of his Garden," Ybelline finished for her.

"If he *wasn't*, the fiefs wouldn't be standing in the aftermath. The fiefs are part of *our* world, right? Whatever happens here—or to the rest of the city—doesn't destroy the fiefs. They're still standing."

Kattea cleared her throat.

This caught Kaylin's attention immediately.

"I was alive when the city across the bridge disappeared. I don't remember any of it—I was too young."

This caused a predictable fuss, but in keeping with the Tha'alani, it was a *muted* fuss, and it was resolved in relative silence. Kaylin wished she could be on the other side of that silence, but held her peace. All eyes in the room turned to Gilbert, and from there, found Kattea.

Forehead stalks bobbed, eyes shifted color, people rose.

Ybelline, who had not yet taken a seat, seemed to stand at the center of a silent storm. Kaylin wanted to be her umbrella, but knew she didn't actually need one. "Gilbert," Ybelline finally said.

Gilbert nodded, his eyes slightly narrow, as if he'd followed the entire silent discussion. He probably had, but didn't yet know what to make of it.

"If it is acceptable to you, Scoros wishes to communicate more directly."

Scoros rose as Gilbert nodded. He apparently had some questions of his own to ask. Gilbert was silent, however, and became as still as he had when Ybelline had made contact with him the first time.

Because Scoros was prepared, he didn't collapse the way Ybelline had, but he stiffened until he appeared to be almost as rigid as Gilbert, and when he withdrew, he was visibly shaken. He didn't turn to Ybelline; instead he turned to Kattea, who had surrendered Gilbert's arm. She made no attempt to take it back—she couldn't. She'd taken an involuntary step—or three—away from Scoros.

Scoros immediately raised both of his hands, palms out, and stopped moving. "I do not intend you harm," he said quietly, "and I will not touch you at all without your explicit permission or a direct command from the Emperor."

"They don't particularly *want* to read our thoughts or know our secrets," Kaylin told the younger girl. "They find our fear suffocating and our lives difficult. If it weren't for the Emperor's commands, they wouldn't interact with us at all—not the way they interact with each other, anyway."

Kattea said nothing.

Scoros stepped back, found himself a chair and sat heavily. He looked at Kattea. "Please. Tell us what you remember. Or tell us what you were told."

Kattea left Gilbert standing to one side of the room; he was, once again, unaware of his surroundings, his two eyes blinking rapidly, his third staring at nothing anyone in the room could see. The familiar on Kaylin's shoulder lifted his head, looked at Gilbert and snorted. He then lowered it again and closed one eye. Kaylin thought he would sleep, but he lifted his head once more, grumbling, and stretched his wings, smacked Kaylin—

possibly accidentally—on the cheek with one and pushed himself off her shoulder.

He flew *to* Kattea and hovered in front of her pale face. He didn't land; he did squawk—quietly, for him—while he hovered.

"Put out your arm," Kaylin told the younger girl, gentling her voice as she realized Kattea was rigid with fear. Kattea blinked. Her eyes widened as she looked at the familiar, and some of that fear—though not the bulk of it—lessened. She put her arm out, and the familiar—complaining quietly the entire time—landed on her forearm, then inched his way up to her small shoulder.

She giggled. It was part nerves and partly the effect of his small claws; he didn't dig in, but they tickled.

"We will not touch you without your permission," Scoros said again. "Fear," he continued, in a very conversational voice, "is difficult for any of us to deal with. You think adults don't feel fear—but you are wrong. We all feel fear. It is part of being human. Secrets are harder for my people. Children don't have any; they have not yet learned how to keep things from their kin. But because they can see the experiences of the rest of us, they understand that their fear, or their sense of shame, is not unique—it is natural. For your kin, the shame and the fear grow far deeper roots; they become larger and stronger.

"It is not so with the Tha'alani. There is nothing that you have felt that we have not felt. There is nothing new in it, for us; it is new to you because you have nothing to compare it with. But we understand that your secrets are necessary to you and the way you think and live.

"In your world, which is our world in the near future, almost everyone who lives in the city has died. In our world, which is our present, that future has not happened—yet. It is to prevent that destruction that we ask you now to consider allow-

ing us to see parts of your life. We don't know what destroys
the city. Any clue—any information that your parents might
have given you, anything that your neighbors might have said
to your parents when you were too young to understand the
words—might help us."

The small dragon nuzzled her cheek—and then bit her hair.

"No," Kattea said.

The small dragon squawked.

Gilbert failed to notice any of this. Kaylin wondered what he
had heard in the *Tha'alaan*; he didn't hear what she'd heard, to
be so frozen in place by it. She wondered, briefly, if all thought
had…dimensionality; if there were parts of thought itself that
she couldn't grasp, even if they *were her own thoughts*. She didn't
particularly like where this was leading.

Kattea shook her head again. No.

And Kaylin wanted to shake the girl until her teeth rattled.
Which was wrong. She *knew* it was wrong, but they had so
little information that *any* might prevent the looming disaster.

"Yes," Ybelline said quietly, as Kaylin startled. The Tha'alani
castelord was standing so close to Kaylin they should have been
touching. They weren't. "But that is the shadow fear casts, always. Kattea's fear. Our own fear. But we cannot be you. We
cannot be Kattea. What we can justify in the heat of the moment, we must live with forever; it becomes part of not only
who we are, but who our people are. Every action we take
shapes and defines us.

"And there is enough darkness at our roots. We have struggled for generations to lift ourselves out of our past. We will
not go there again."

The small dragon squawked; it was a softer sound and reminded Kaylin of crooning. With edges.

Kattea started to cry. The tears trailed down her cheeks, but
didn't give way to sobbing; her breath wobbled, but she held

herself upright. Sleeves dashed tears away almost angrily. "My dad was a Sword," she said, spitting the words out as if only force would eject them. "A *Sword*."

She had said that before.

"Most of the Swords died. Some of the Swords were ordered over the bridge—two bridges—and they *made* people follow. My dad was one of them. It was his job, he said. He was supposed to keep the city safe. He was supposed to be there to stop fear from turning people into—" She stopped.

"Animals," Kaylin supplied. "The Swords patrol. The Hawks investigate. When something big goes down—raging fire in the city, for instance—the Swords are sent out. They're trained to lead. They know how to make people listen. They can stop panic from becoming as much of a danger to people as the fire would be." She swallowed. Turned to Ybelline and almost knocked her over.

"There wasn't enough room, in the fief. It was crowded. Dad said—" She swallowed. "Dad said—" But she choked.

"Was the Emperor in the fiefs?" Scoros asked. "The Emperor is really the commander in chief of both the Swords and the Hawks."

"No. He—he died."

Silence.

"All the Dragons died. Mom said you could hear them roaring for a day after the clouds moved in." She swallowed. The still tears now threatened to become ugly tears. Ugly tears, on the other hand, were practically the only tears Kaylin could cry. "I want—I want to make a deal. With you." She didn't say this to Scoros.

She said it to Ybelline. Ybelline nodded, but didn't move from Kaylin's side.

"If this is *really* the past, if this is really *our* past—"

Kaylin knew what Kattea wanted then. Knew it before the words left the girl's mouth.

"If this is our past, if this is my past, if this is what the city was before—before the gray—it means my mom and my dad are still alive."

"Kattea, no. I have told you." Gilbert spoke. Gilbert not only spoke but moved, becoming part of the human landscape again. His third eye shuttered as he approached Kattea. She actually stepped away, and he stopped. "My apologies," he said, to the room at large.

"I didn't understand," she continued, refusing to meet Gilbert's eyes. "When we came here, I didn't understand what it meant. But I understand it *now*. I want to see them. I want to see my parents."

Those ugly tears? They threatened to fall right now. In their wake, anger followed. Kaylin wasn't remotely certain *who* she was angry at, either. She was angry at Kattea, yes. Kattea might—just *might*—have information that could save Elantra. If the Emperor knew of it, he'd order the Tha'alani to do what they were not willing to do otherwise: read her mind. Sift through her life. Pick out the useful bits.

Kaylin wasn't even certain she'd *want* to stop him.

"If you let me see my parents, I'll let you—I'll let you read my mind." She folded her arms, crossing them a little too tightly around her upper body, as if by doing so she could hold herself up.

"Kattea," Gilbert said again. "I told you—"

"I *don't care*, Gilbert."

"They won't know you. You are not their child. The parents who raised you are dead, and you cannot go back to them. Nor can you bring them back. If you save these people, they will not be *your* parents in future. It is not the way time works. It will only cause pain. To you."

And it was pain that they *didn't have time for.* Kaylin opened her mouth, and Ybelline's palms cupped her cheek. Both of her cheeks.

Do not resent her.

How can you not? *If I were her—*

Would you not wish to see your mother, even now?

I don't remember my mother.

That is not an answer, Kaylin.

It wasn't.

Do not judge her. Not one of us do, or will. She is frightened.

And when had that mattered in Kaylin's life? Oh, it was an ugly, ugly thought. In answer, the *Tha'alaan* joined her. They did not deny the ugliness; they embraced it as if—as if it were natural, normal. As if it were something they were certain would pass, because ugly thoughts, just like graceful ones, were part of life.

If you think it will break her, deny her; if you think it will help us, accede. Do not judge the desire. If I were her, I would have it. Even if the world were ending around me. If the last thing I could see were the parents who loved me—I would find them.

Kaylin realized that this was why Ybelline had come to stand beside her. Severn had, as he so often did, fallen silent, moving away from the conversation and the personal elements it contained until he was almost invisible.

Would she want to see her mother?

Yes. But not if it threatened the entire city.

And Kaylin was an adult. The loss of her mother wasn't new; it was a fact of her life. Kattea's loss was fresh, and the consequences of that loss, fresh, as well.

"...Here's what we'll do," she heard herself say.

Kattea turned instantly.

"We don't have the time to see your mother. I'm sorry—but we don't. I can't explain, to your mother and father, that you are their child from the future."

Kattea nodded. Kaylin realized the younger girl would agree to *anything* that would give her a glimpse of her parents, and she despised her own resentment. "So I can't guarantee that we can see your mother.

"But I can guarantee that we can see your father. I work at the Halls of Law. If he's a Sword, so does he. It's going to look odd—me bringing a lost child to the office—but I can *do* that. That's the best I can do," she added. "On very short notice."

Kattea appeared to be holding her breath, but her eyes still worked; they flicked to—and away—from Gilbert. "Yes."

"Yes, that'll do?"

"Yes. I won't—I won't tell him who I am. I won't talk *at all*. I just—"

She needs to see him, Ybelline repeated. *If she does, she will have an incentive that her own life cannot, at the moment, provide. You, of all people, should understand this.*

Of course she did.

CHAPTER 22

Ybelline Rabon'Alani accompanied them to the Halls of Law. Scoros offered; Kaylin, attached to Ybelline, and therefore aware of the *Tha'alaan*, heard him. Draalzyn also offered, and his offer made more sense: he was accustomed to the Halls of Law, and he had an actual desk within the missing-persons division of the Imperial Hawks.

But Draalzyn looked like a grizzled veteran of innumerable battles. Of all of the people in this room, he was the one who most terrified Kattea.

They didn't make Kattea choose. They chose. Ybelline smiled at Kattea.

Kattea managed to smile back. It was very, very hard to be terrified of Ybelline. The small dragon remained on Kattea's shoulder for the time being, and they left the long house in single file. Walking out of the Tha'alani quarter was never fast, but the children were held back by their minders, and only the very young let their resentment of this be known. Loudly.

Gilbert trailed behind Kattea, looking confused. Confusion appeared to be most of his natural state, but there was something in it that worried Kaylin; she couldn't say why. Since "why" was effectively her job—as well as "how"—she mulled it over as she walked. Sadly, thoughts of this kind led to walking the way patrolling Hawks did. Ybelline was fine; Kattea was straining. Gilbert was falling behind.

"What was your father's name?"

"Corporal Krevel."

Kaylin glanced at her partner. "I'll talk to Jared," Severn said. Jared was the equivalent of Caitlin; he served the Swords, not the Hawks, but he was nothing like Caitlin in personality—then again, almost no one was. He kept the Swords running, and he kept the Sergeant of his particular office more or less calm. The important fact, however, was that it was in his office that the duty rosters were posted.

When Clint caught sight of Kaylin, she almost lost her nerve, his expression shifted so suddenly. Tanner, by his side, mirrored his expression.

"Where have you been?" Clint demanded.

Kattea slid behind Severn and peered out from behind his back. Severn, Kaylin noted, was not on the receiving end of what looked like outrage.

"What's happened?"

"Ironjaw's been trying to get hold of you, is what," Tanner replied.

"I can't—"

"There's been a problem on the Winding Path."

"I wasn't there. I was in the Tha'alani district."

They both stopped, as if only now recognizing the Tha'alani castelord. They shared a glance. "This is not going to be the day for polite, diplomatic visits," Clint told her. His tone did not match his words; it was a touch too warm. "If you need a favor from anyone in command in the Halls of Law, now is the wrong time to ask for it."

Ybelline nodded, her expression grave.

Kaylin forgot about Kattea's father and Jared and pretty much anything that wasn't Angry Marcus and Emergency. If Kattea had not caught her elbow, she would have sprinted up the stairs and down the halls that led to red-eyed Leontine. But Kattea did grab her arm.

"They're with me," Kaylin said, nodding in the direction of Ybelline, Gilbert and Kattea.

"They don't want to be, today."

"Teela said she'd informed the office about the reasons for my absence."

The two duty Hawks exchanged another glance.

"Teela's part of the problem." Clint was grim. "Teela, Tain, Lord Sanabalis and—"

"Bellusdeo."

"Lord Bellusdeo, yes."

Against their better judgment, Clint and Tanner let the entire party pass into the Halls. Kaylin sprinted into the office, stopped at Caitlin's desk, introduced Kattea and Gilbert in a breathless rush and then abandoned them both; it took less than two minutes. Two long, endless minutes, while fear sank roots in every thought she was capable of having.

Teela, Tain *and* Bellusdeo.

She wasn't even concerned that the Emperor would reduce a useless private in the Imperial Hawks to ash—a very real possibility. Teela and Tain had gone to the Arcanum. Sanabalis and Bellusdeo had gone to the Winding Path. They weren't in the same place.

Something in the future would destroy the Tha'alani quarter. What if it had *already started*?

She came to a skidding halt in front of what remained of Marcus's desk. It looked as if someone had taken a very large ax to the desktop. The papers that generally littered the desk in various piles had been removed. Or rather, they'd been cleaned up; one or two had clearly fallen beneath desks and hadn't yet been retrieved.

Marcus had grown about three inches in every dimension, he was bristling so badly. Kaylin didn't need to meet his eyes to know that they were red. She did need to be able to understand Leontine to catch his first words—which she would have heard even if she'd taken the time to plug both ears.

She exposed her throat instantly.

The office was almost silent, which was what generally happened in the presence of an enraged Leontine. Kaylin's fists clenched; she managed not to close her eyes. Or move anything but her chin.

Marcus's claws were fully extended when he reached for her throat.

Kattea screamed.

Marcus hunched and wheeled in the direction of that scream, snarling. Kaylin knew better than to grab Marcus when he was in this state, but she shouted—in Leontine—to get his attention.

He spun again, inhaled, exhaled and forced himself to speak Elantran. "Where...have...you...been?"

"Teela told you—"

"Teela told us that you were convalescing in a house *on the Winding Path.*"

Kaylin nodded. "I was."

He growled. He turned and barked the word *Records* in the direction of his desk. Which no longer had a mirror *on* it. Caitlin's quiet voice repeated his command, and as she hadn't trashed her desk in worried fury, her mirror shivered to life.

Gilbert, however, shouted "No!"

Under other circumstances, a man with three eyes shouting in the office might have gone south, but Ybelline took the opportunity to intervene. She stepped in front of Gilbert before Marcus reached him, raising a hand in front of the Sergeant's face.

Marcus came to a full stop before any part of his body connected with that hand. His breath was a growl—but he couldn't, at the moment, help that. "Private. Explain yourself. Now." He turned to face her.

Kaylin risked her life. She answered with a question. "What happened on the Winding Path?"

"I was about to make that clear. Who is this man—and *what* is he?"

"His name is Gilbert. It was his home I was convalescing in. If something's happened to it, he wasn't there—he's been with me the entire morning. Marcus—what happened?"

Ybelline said, to Caitlin, "It is best that the mirror network not be utilized at the moment."

Caitlin, noting Kattea, nodded; she did not look well pleased, which surprised Kaylin.

"Tell us *why*, Castelord," Marcus said. His voice was much quieter, which was actually a bad sign in Leontines.

"There is some sort of magical difficulty in the city, and it is being in part driven by—and expressed through—the mirror network. I believe—Gilbert would be the expert, not I— that use of the mirrors increases the danger."

Caitlin blanched.

So did Kaylin. "There's no way to shut down the mirrors— not instantly, and not without at least using them once. Mirrors get used by almost everyone. Even people who can't afford a private mirror use the public ones in the markets."

"*Private.*"

"I don't know, Marcus. Ybelline does. We've had mirrors malfunction before—you remember, the mirror greeted everyone by name in that cheery, cheery—"

He growled. "You're *certain*?" It was Kaylin he asked.

She swallowed. Remembered how Ybelline had said they died. Nodded.

"Fine. Perenne!"

"Sir!" Perenne appeared from around a pillar—the one advantage to a junior desk was its distance from Marcus.

"Run upstairs to the Hawklord. Tell him what Private Neya just said." He turned to her. Of course. "You had better be right."

Marcus's eyes dimmed to a reddish-orange; his fur settled into more or less normal height, except around the ears and possibly the back of his neck. Kaylin couldn't see that, and didn't try. He barked commands, and the office once again returned to a semblance of normal—but it was a shadowed normal; anxiety fluttered beneath the surface of every spoken word.

"Castelord," Marcus said, bowing.

She smiled and inclined her chin, as if she hadn't, minutes before, been confronted with raging, animalistic Leontine. She did not step entirely out of his way. Kattea came out from behind her. She was shaking, but she wasn't cowering. Which was good, given Marcus's state of mind.

"I'm Kattea Krevel," she told him.

"Marcus Hassan," Marcus replied. "Sergeant Marcus Hassan. We need to inform the Emperor—" He stopped. Growled. "Shojii!"

"Sir!"

"Tell the Swordlord and Wolflord what's happened."

"The Hawklord—"

"Now."

"Yes, sir."

Marcus turned back to Kattea. "Krevel. Krevel. Corporal Krevel? Are you related?"

Kaylin froze. Kattea didn't. "Yes. I'm his—his cousin."

"And this man is a friend of yours?"

"Yes."

Marcus sniffed the air. Leontine sense of smell was acute, no surprises there.

"Marcus—the Winding Path?"

"We're not certain what happened," he said. "Something big. Half of the street—the middle half—is no longer visible."

"What do you mean, not visible?"

"Exactly what I said. There's a very large gap—a circular gap—where the middle part of the street used to stand."

"That's not invisible."

"People don't fall off the street into what looks like a pit. They keep walking. They vanish. They don't appear on the other side. We've cordoned off either end of the spherical space—but it's growing. The Swords are mobilized; the Aerians have been sent to patrol." He cursed in Leontine. "The sky above the sphere operates the way the area on the ground does—but it's harder to see."

Kaylin stopped breathing for one long moment.

"Yes," he said, although she hadn't spoken. "That's not theoretical."

Kattea, listening, said, "That's how it started."

Marcus frowned. He wasn't as tall as the Barrani, but when he looked down at Kattea, he seemed to be doing it from a much greater height. "Private?"

Kaylin exhaled. "We should head up to the Hawklord's Tower," she replied, "so I don't have to repeat myself."

The aperture to the Tower was open when they arrived, as were the doors. Kaylin was grateful; the door wards of the

Hawklord's Tower were, with the exception of the Imperial Library, the worst magical door wards in existence.

Lord Grammayre's eyes were almost black, they were so dark. That left no room for worse, which meant they didn't change shade when Gilbert walked in behind Kaylin. Kattea was in front of him, Ybelline behind; Marcus was leading the way and Severn pulled up the rear.

"Teela and Tain headed out to the Arcanum. At least that's where they said they were going."

"They mirrored from the Arcanum."

"Then—"

"They went, in haste, to the Winding Path. Teela said the man to whom she wished to speak had been resident in the Arcanum; he left, in colloquial words, a lot of corpses. Among those corpses was one that was not quite dead. They mirrored to request that backup be sent to meet them on the Winding Path at the scene of the investigation." Marcus growled.

Lord Grammayre bowed to Ybelline.

"But they—"

"They wanted *you*."

"Oh."

"You went to Evanton's."

"Yes."

"And the Tha'alani quarter was on the way?"

"…No."

The Hawklord lifted and lengthened his wings, as if testing them. They were, had always been, beautiful. And they could also be deadly. "The Arkon sent word. We will not be able to respond in the usual way, but the Aerians have agreed to serve as emergency messengers until this crisis has passed." He exhaled. "Gilbert lived in the house across the street from the murders?"

Kaylin nodded and began to speak.

★ ★ ★

She managed to make it through half of the story—at least as she perceived it—before the Hawklord stopped her and looked up, to the open aperture. Shadow darkened the floor—the skies were not exactly clear. But the shadows caused by this cloud didn't pass, and in the end—

In the end, they resolved themselves into a familiar, draconic form. Kaylin thought—for just a moment—that the gold meant Clint had been mistaken about Bellusdeo, because the Dragon was gold.

But it wasn't Bellusdeo.

She had never watched a Dragon shift form in midair before. This Dragon, however, obviously considered the interior of the Tower too small for a safe landing—at least for the people currently beneath him. He shifted, golden scales blurring and reconfiguring as he descended; his wings shifted shape and size before they at last folded—literally—into his back.

The Dragon was the Arkon.

"You're not supposed to be flying," Kaylin told him, because surprise had loosened her jaw. And her brain, clearly.

"I have come in search of your Gilbert" was his rumbling reply. His eyes were orange. Of course they were. "And it was decided that his presence within the Palace at this time constituted too much of a danger." His nod to the Hawklord was perfunctory, and Marcus might as well have been invisible; he did offer an extended nod to Ybelline.

Ybelline said, "I must return to my own kin." She offered the Dragon Lord a much deeper bow than Kaylin felt he warranted, and turned toward the Tower doors.

It was Kattea who stopped her.

To Kaylin's surprise, she stopped her by grabbing the Tha'alani castelord's arm. This shocked Ybelline enough that she stopped moving; she looked, with concern, at the two shaking hands on her sleeve. Kattea swallowed and tightened her grip.

"You're leaving because of me."

Ybelline did not deny it. Kaylin seldom used the word *love*; it was a word she felt was meant for babies and young children. But as she realized Kattea was right—that Ybelline was, in fact, leaving before she could be ordered to examine Kattea against the younger girl's will—she resented, deeply, the lack of an *adult* word that was equivalent, but less embarrassing.

Ybelline smiled sadly at the girl. "We have not yet fulfilled our part of the bargain."

"You won't. You won't be able to. He's out there—he's in the streets, on the Winding Path, trying to keep people from panicking. That's what my mother told me. That's what he did—because *this is when it started.*" She swallowed. "I don't know anything. I was a baby. I don't remember.

"But they talked. They told me things. If you—if you can find things in my memories that I can't—" She swallowed again. "My dad lives. He's going to live. My mom, too. But he hated that so many people died. He felt like he'd failed. Like they'd *all* failed. The Swords. The Hawks. The people whose job it was to protect everyone.

"Maybe that's *why* I'm here. Or why Gilbert is here. I don't know." Tears welled in her eyes. "I was mad at my dad. When he left. When they left to look for whatever it was they were looking for. I—I didn't say goodbye. I wouldn't talk to him. He wouldn't take me with him. And I knew—he was just *going to die*. I just—" She fought back tears. "I was a terrible daughter. If I could go back—if I could change one thing—I would say goodbye. I would tell him that I loved him. I would tell him.

"…But I can't. Gilbert wasn't afraid of you. Kaylin's not afraid. If—if you can find something in me that can help… do it."

★ ★ ★

Kattea was almost white, and white did not look good on her. Neither did red-eyed terror. But she held her ground, looking back to Gilbert only once, as if she needed his approval. Given that Gilbert wasn't even passably human, and that Kattea knew this very well, this said something to Kaylin.

Breathe, Severn told her.

She reddened.

Ybelline knelt. Kneeling, she was shorter than Kattea. She opened her arms, but held them wide, to either side of the girl, and waited.

The Arkon rumbled. Kaylin desperately wanted to give Ybelline as much time, as much space, as she could, because Kaylin understood the effect Kattea's fear would have on the older, wiser woman. It was a type of poison.

It was a poison Ybelline accepted, because in the end, she had little choice; if she did not do it, another member of her caste would be forced to it.

Kaylin walked over to Gilbert, caught him by the arm and dragged him over to where the Arkon stood. The Arkon's face, hair and eyes were familiar, but he had chosen to wear the armor available to all of his kin in their mortal form. It was either that or nudity.

"This is Gilbert," she said. "Gilbert, this is a Dragon known as the Arkon. I'm not sure what that means, since he *has* a name. But—call him the Arkon unless your name is Bellusdeo."

The Arkon, in golden plate armor, raised a brow at Kaylin. Gilbert looked confused.

"Bellusdeo, as you are aware, filled me in on many of the details of the past few days."

Kaylin nodded. She had expected rage. The Arkon's eyes

were orange, but he was, unlike Marcus, his usual self otherwise.

"I do not hold you responsible for Bellusdeo's disappearance. The Emperor may, but he has not—yet—chosen to fly. Sanabalis is vastly more competent and resourceful than you are, in general, as is Bellusdeo. They are together. If they have not been instantly obliterated, it is left to us to find and retrieve them. I believe it is possible your Gilbert may be of assistance."

Gilbert said, "I must go to the Winding Path."

"Yes, that was my thought, as well." He glanced at Ybelline and Kattea; they were now locked in an embrace—but Kattea had stopped trembling and appeared to be leaning *into* the Tha'alani woman. And, from the sound of it, sniveling. Kaylin could only see her back. "Is the child necessary?"

Gilbert said "Yes" at the same time as Kaylin said "No."

The Arkon, predictably, was annoyed. And just as predictably, he was annoyed at Kaylin. "Do not let sentiment blind you. At this juncture, we cannot afford it."

"Sentiment? I barely even *know* her!"

The Arkon ignored the comment; he spoke to Gilbert.

Gilbert replied.

Neither used a language she understood. She thought it might be the same language that the Arkon had spoken to Mandoran in the library. "Time is of the essence," the Dragon told them. "Castelord, I regret to have to interrupt you, but I require the young woman's presence."

Ybelline did not appear to hear him.

The Hawklord however, placed a staying hand on the Arkon's shoulder. "She will require some minutes, yet. Kaylin, please fill the Arkon in on the details of the rest of your day while he waits."

★ ★ ★

The Arkon's eyes had shifted toward gold as he listened, although the predominant color was still orange.

"You are from a different *time*? And so is the young girl?" He threw a narrow-eyed glance at the Tha'alani castelord as he asked.

Gilbert hesitated. Hesitation was his most frequent conversational tic. "Kattea is."

"And you are not?"

Gilbert turned to Kaylin, of all people, as if she could somehow answer the question the Arkon had just asked.

The small dragon lifted himself off Kattea's shoulder, pushed himself gently into the air and then squawked. Loudly. Had he been sitting on Kaylin's shoulder, he wouldn't have bothered to put distance between his mouth and her ear.

The Arkon frowned. "That is hardly an answer," he said to the familiar.

Squawk.

"Very well. Kattea is from the future as it exists if the present continues. Gilbert is a question mark. What happened with the Keeper?" When Kaylin failed to immediately answer, he said, "You are aware that the Keeper is under surveillance. It is… unusual…for rain to fall only within the Keeper's storefront."

"I was getting to that part."

"My apologies for the interruption," he replied. Not that there was any chance this would stop him from interrupting her again. She continued, speaking about the rain in the store, the flood and her eventual discussion with the elemental water.

"The water is *aware* of the time shift?"

Kaylin nodded.

"Kaylin—"

"I think it's only aware because of the *Tha'alaan*." As she said this, she realized it was fundamentally true. "I'm not sure the fire or earth or air notice—or care. But the *Tha'alaan* exists the way the rest of us do, because it's part of the way we live. I mean—it's like organic Records for the race itself, so it's built of our lives."

The Arkon seemed surprised, but nodded.

"What I don't understand is why the water was raining on the inside of the store. The water does lose its temper from time to time, but—it's usually confined to the Garden."

The Arkon's nod was slower to come this time, and his eyes shaded to a much stronger orange by the time it had finished.

"Do you think whatever's eating the city eats the Keeper's Garden? I mean, in the future, where the water comes from?"

"Thank you for adding a worry I had not considered to those already on the table." The Arkon turned to Gilbert again.

Gilbert said, "...Yes. I think that's likely. I believe I must return to the Winding Path." He glanced at Kattea. "Will you take care of her?"

"You're not leaving here without her."

"Kaylin—"

"I mean it."

"You do not have much time left."

"We don't even know that it started there—has anyone been to the Arcanum?"

"Lord Diarmat and Lord Emmerian are currently at the Arcanum," the Arkon replied.

That seemed backward to Kaylin. "You're probably the Dragon with the most knowledge of ancient magic—why didn't they come here?"

"Because I am, as you state, the most learned. I am going to the Winding Path. I am apparently going to the Winding Path without the benefit of mirrored information."

"Do you understand *why* the mirrors are so integral to the problem?"

"No. The Imperial mages are now considering the difficulty. Because of the water, you chose to visit the Tha'alani directly."

Kaylin took the hint, picking up the very interrupted thread of the story. By the time she'd finished, he was no longer glaring at Ybelline. "Please plug your ears," he told her. He lifted his voice and repeated this request.

Kaylin had a good idea of what he was about to do, but covered her ears anyway. Covering her ears never really stopped Dragon roars from being deafening.

Her instincts were right: the Arkon roared. It was not a *short* roar, either.

He had the grace to wait until the roar had stopped echoing before he spoke again. "I am confirming, for the Dragon Court, that the mirror network's usage can—or will—be deadly. I have also passed word about the shielding the Tha'alani used to some effect in their last stand. The latter, I feel, will buy us essential time."

"Any idea what the Arcanum was trying to do?"

"The Arcanum is composed of men and women with great ambition and power. They seldom work in concert. It is highly unlikely that individual members are aware of the full extent of the research of their various colleagues. Those that survived the internal difficulties of the morning claim ignorance; I am inclined to believe them. At the moment, the Arcanum is attempting to preserve the city—which they happen to reside in. They will not sabotage our efforts."

This was not an answer. "If we understood what they were attempting, we might have some chance—"

"Thank you for stating the completely obvious."

Kaylin shut up. Gilbert, however, did not. "If possible," he said, to Kaylin, "I think your Mandoran and Annarion might be of assistance in a way that none of the rest of you can be."

Kaylin nodded.

Stopped.

Nodded more emphatically. If mirrors were not forbidden, Kaylin would have been on them *instantly*. Severn understood why. If Teela had died, Mandoran and Annarion would *know*. If she hadn't—and she had been pushed forward or backward or sideways in time, they would only know that she'd disappeared.

Just as Nightshade had disappeared.

"Private," the Arkon snapped. "Your fidgeting makes me almost motion sick. Be *still*."

The Hawklord gave her a Look, which implied that she was embarrassing the entire force in public, and she stopped rocking on her heels. "How do you think Annarion and Mandoran will be helpful?" she asked, to distract herself.

"They see in a way that you can't. They see in a way that I can't—or rather, they see less, and see it from a different vantage. I do not understand the whole of what is, or is not, inimical to your kind. Kattea has taught me much, but she is not aware of everything I do, and some of what I have done, she considers hostile."

Kaylin frowned. "The Arcanist visited you, the night before the murders."

"That is what she maintains."

"She saw him. You…didn't." Kaylin's frown deepened. "The night after the murders, he came again. That time, you saw him, and she didn't."

Gilbert didn't reply; he was now as silent as Kaylin couldn't be.

"It's like the corpses or the stones, isn't it?"

"It is not," he finally said, although his frown had deepened. "I could see the corpses in question. I could see the three stones."

"You could see the words. You—" She turned to the Arkon. "Did Sanabalis manage to get that information to you?"

"No." He turned to Gilbert. "It is, in part, to speak of these so-called words that I came."

Squawk.

"Ah. I am not certain that I can duplicate them."

Squawk.

"I do not see *how* it is skirting the rules. They have been seen. Their presence was not revealed by you. I am not certain you were aware of them at all."

SQUAWK.

"He has a bit of an ego," Kaylin said. "What does he mean by rules?"

"I believe he expects you to understand what he means; it is irrelevant. I am not...as he is. It is difficult for me to manifest the words I see in a way that makes them accessible to your kind," Gilbert said.

"He means anyone alive in the city," Kaylin told the Arkon, "not mortals. And frankly, I'm not certain it would be a good idea to have Gilbert attempt to re-create what he saw."

"Why?"

"I don't think he'd do anything to harm us deliberately— Kattea's here, if nothing else. But I don't think he's always *aware* of what might cause harm. Kattea seemed to feel there was actual, magical conflict; Gilbert seemed to genuinely feel there wasn't. He's not an Arcanist. He's not trying to live forever or rule the universe or whatever it is that drives the Arcanists.

"I just don't think he truly understands what life *is*. Our lives, anyway."

"I will take that under advisement." The Arkon spoke as if he meant it. "But at this point, I do not feel it is Gilbert who is responsible for the state of our city, and any information is not only relevant, but urgently required. I am therefore willing to have that risk taken."

Kaylin turned to Lord Grammayre, who nodded. The

Arkon was not, in theory, in the chain of command—but theory could be stretched in emergencies.

Gilbert glanced, once again, at Kattea. "Very well." He lifted his hands slowly, held them in front of his body, at elbow level, and turned them, palms up, as if he was carrying something no one else in the room could see.

His eyes began to glow.

CHAPTER 23

Kaylin was accustomed to seeing eye colors change; glowing was another thing entirely. When Gilbert's eyes glowed—as they were glowing now—it looked as if his head had been hollowed out and was being used as a lamp. It was not a comforting sight.

Kattea was still wrapped around Ybelline; if warning needed to be given to—or about—Gilbert, it wouldn't come from her. Kaylin opened her mouth and closed it again as the familiar came to sit on her shoulder. His claws dug through her tunic. Clearly she wasn't the only one who was nervous.

"I don't suppose," she whispered to the familiar, "you could tell me what he's doing?"

Squawk.

The glow of Gilbert's eyes brightened so much, it was hard to look at his face. The Arkon's inner membranes rose, and he lifted a hand; Kaylin felt a wash of unpleasant stinging settle across her arms, her legs, the back of her neck—anywhere that was marked. She even approved of it, although she gritted her teeth.

The light seeped out of Gilbert's eyes, as if it were crawling. This was very disturbing to watch. He was apparently in control of its destination, though; it fell into his cupped palms, curling in and around itself as if it were a dozen small snakes.

Could have been worse, she told herself. Could have been cockroaches.

Squawk.

"I know. Sorry."

The snakes began to separate, and Kaylin watched as they hardened and shed parts of themselves. She looked up to Gilbert's face; his eyes were once again obsidian. They did not reflect the glowing light she could clearly see taking shape in the palms of his hands.

The Arkon's expression stiffened as the runes took form. They were not, to Kaylin's eye, true words, not the way the marks on over half her skin were—but they seemed similar. She frowned and approached Gilbert. She saw magic's aftereffects as sigils—usually blue, and usually much larger than these. But she had seen such sigils as dark shadows, dark smoke, before.

These were similar, in the end, to those, although they were much more solid.

"Arkon?"

"They are not," he said, "a language I recognize."

"Not true words, then?"

"No." He replied without obvious disgust, which was unusual. "Do they look like your marks, to you?"

She shook her head. "They look—this is going to sound strange—"

The Arkon coughed.

"Sorry. They're brighter and more consistent, but—they remind me of the sigils left behind in the Leontine quarter."

"When?"

"When Marcus was accused of murder." It felt as if it had been years ago. It hadn't; objectively, it had been months. *Maybe* a year. "Someone tried to kill us—Severn and I—and a black, smoky sigil rose in the wake of the spell."

The Arkon's expression shifted, and not in an entirely natural way. "Does this aperture widen?" he asked the Hawklord.

"It is in its widest configuration at the moment."

Exhaled smoke was most of the Arkon's answer. "We will need to exit by the stairs. There is only barely enough space here to land—and I am not young, anymore."

Which was entirely irrelevant to immortals, as far as Kaylin knew. She kept this to herself. "I'm not saying it's the same."

"No—it wouldn't be. But it implies two things, neither of which is in any way positive."

"And those are?"

He stared at Ybelline, but answered. "Sigils are representative of the *caster's* magical power. It is why they are unique."

She knew that, and tried not to resent his explanation of the obvious. Maybe someone in the Tower didn't. Like, say, Gilbert. Or Kattea, who couldn't listen at the moment.

"You will perhaps note—or perhaps not, given your training and education—that the same sigil has different styles of presentation, depending on the school of magic utilized."

This was less obvious, to Kaylin. In general, she didn't notice the style of, say, everyday handwriting—only the legibility.

"You feel that these runes are similar to the sigils you found in the Leontine quarter. Sanabalis has seen those sigils—he does not interpret them the way you do, of course, but that is a matter for later. The sigil, at the time, you described as black smoke."

Kaylin nodded.

"What is the similarity, then?"

Kaylin wasn't quite certain. The problem with the Arkon's questions was that he expected good answers, and he was short on patience. Fair enough. They were short on time.

"While you are gathering your thoughts, we will descend."

"Private Neya," the Hawklord said, as the Arkon headed toward the Tower doors. "The Arkon is the voice of the Emperor for the duration of this crisis. You will obey his commands as if the Emperor—or the Lord of Hawks—had personally issued them. Before you leave the building, visit the quartermaster."

The situation was dire enough that Kaylin didn't even think to flinch.

"Take flares. Also," he added, "take a portable mirror."

"We can't *use* mirrors—"

"At the moment, there are no connections to the mirror network, and it is just possible that it is the network that needs... adjustment."

"Gilbert, do you think it's safe to have one on hand?" Gilbert looked up. He didn't answer; Kaylin wasn't certain he could hear her.

"Gilbert!" Kattea said, in mild disgust. Kaylin saw that Ybelline had released the girl. The girl, however, had not released Ybelline; she was holding on, tightly, to the Tha'alani's hand. "He gets like this," Kattea told the castelord. She let go of the hand she'd gripped so tightly with obvious reluctance, and walked across the room to where Gilbert, a pile of golden, glowing words in his hands, stood.

Reaching out, she caught his wrists in both of her hands. "Gil-bert. Gilbert."

"Why is he called Gilbert?" the Arkon asked her.

Kattea said, "He needed a name."

"And he chose that one?"

"No, I chose that one. Is something *wrong* with it? *Gilbert.*" She sighed. She followed that sigh with a single word that was nothing like a name. It was nothing, in the end, like any of the other words Kattea was prone to speak. The air crackled around its syllables. Even the Arkon looked surprised.

Gilbert, however, blinked rapidly. The words in his hands

dissolved; he shook them as if they were liquid, and his hands, wet. "Ah, Kattea. Have you finished your discussion with Ybelline?"

"Yes—because no one else could get your attention."

"I am sorry. I was attempting to read the words."

"Is that a smart idea?" she demanded. "I mean—doing it *here*?"

He blinked. "It is only reading. I did not attempt to invoke their power in any way. I do not think they have power, independent of their original location." He looked up at Kaylin. "I am considering your Arkon's question. I did not see the sigil you speak of. But I understand differences in style and presentation.

"What was the purpose of the spell that caused the sigil to be written as smoke and darkness?"

Kaylin frowned. "At the time? It was meant to kill me. To kill us," she added, nodding in Severn's direction. She cursed the lack of immortal memory; it made her job much harder. Teela never had this difficulty. "The sigil didn't look like a sigil to me, not at first. It really did look like black smoke. But the smoke formed curves, loops—cursive elements of actual writing. They had dimension. Usually sigils don't. They're kind of splashed across walls or floors or physical objects that happened to be in the blast radius."

"And is that the similarity?"

"I don't know. The smoke never stopped moving. By the time it had stilled enough, Sanabalis had dragged me out of the wreckage. I couldn't read it, but I didn't get a better chance to study it."

The Arkon exhaled. "The street," he said grimly.

"Did Sanabalis not tell you?"

"I will have words with him when this is over."

★ ★ ★

The quartermaster was grim. Kaylin was not, and had never been, his favorite person; he considered her young, feckless and grossly irresponsible. Giving her a flare was not a problem; giving her a portable mirror *was*. Had she not had the Arkon literally standing over her shoulder, he would have refused; she hadn't had time to wait for Hanson's requisition order.

Though he always made a point of following strict procedure when dealing with Kaylin, he was clearly not willing to play that game with a member of the Dragon Court.

He was stickler enough that he demanded the Arkon's signature, though. Kaylin, given the orange of the Arkon's eyes, wouldn't have dared. This was probably why she wasn't the quartermaster.

The halls, as they walked swiftly through them, were silent—mostly because they were empty. It was likely that the Hawks had joined the Swords on the Winding Path. It had only been three weeks since the ancestors had attacked the High Halls; only three weeks since over a dozen Hawks had been buried. For the Swords, the losses had been higher; the Swords had been trained to deal with panicking crowds.

You didn't send untrained men into those crowds and expect good results, although you could pray.

If the Halls of Law felt deserted, the streets surrounding them were not. And the thanks Hawks and Swords would get for putting their lives on the line in an emergency boiled down to invective, resentment and very harried compliance.

Some days, Kaylin hated people.

The Arkon appeared to dislike them even more than she did. If she wanted to kick them or curse them—and sadly, she did—she *didn't* want them to wind up on the wrong side of angry Dragon breath. They were just as afraid and just as ignorant as she was, on bad days, and she didn't feel she deserved reduction to ash, either.

People screamed and got out of the way when the Arkon, with no warning, transformed, the plates of his armor opening and falling, on invisible hinges, toward the ground. Kattea was one of those people. Gilbert scooped her up and took one step to the side as the Arkon's wings exploded from between human-seeming shoulder blades. His neck lengthened. His tail appeared. His head expanded. This last made Kaylin snicker.

"We are going to your abode," the Arkon said, without looking back. "Now. You can climb up on my back. Sit between the ridges. Or I can carry you in my claws."

No one took him up on the latter, although Kattea was fearful enough that she might have been forced to, if not for Gilbert. Gilbert, holding her, leaped up. She turned into his chest, threw her arms around his neck and buried her face in his shoulder.

Ybelline's hesitance was purely physical. None of it reached her face. She clearly wanted to go back to the Tha'alani quarter, but she didn't ask. Anything that needed to be said to the other members of the *Tha'alanari*, she could say from here. Or from anywhere in the city.

Kaylin was only barely seated when the Arkon roared and pushed off the ground. She settled her hands against his back; Severn caught her waist and held it.

The Arkon had been injured three weeks ago. Injured enough that Bellusdeo had been—and still was—very worried. But she knew the Dragon would probably bite her arms off if she tried to heal him. Dragon bodies weren't like mortal bodies; they were a duality. Kaylin wondered if she could sort of...sneak healing in while he was preoccupied.

"I will drop you," the Arkon said loudly. "And if you'd deserve it, Kattea doesn't."

Which was a no. "Will you land in Helen's tower?"

"I will land in the street."

"Our tower's bigger than the Hawklord's—and Helen is safer."

The Arkon growled. But to Kaylin's surprise, he took her advice.

She hadn't lied, but she hadn't exactly been truthful, either; Helen could shift the interior of the house to accommodate any guest. The tower's aperture opened as the Arkon approached it from on high; it was wide enough that he could—with caution—land. He did, but the landing was heavy, and he was silent while his passengers disembarked.

"Welcome," Helen said. Or rather, Helen's voice. Her Avatar had not yet reached the tower. "We've been waiting. Mandoran is very upset."

Kaylin remembered the revelation she'd had back in the Hawklord's Tower. Movement returned in a frenzied rush as she raced for the door, yanked it open and took the stairs four at a time. Helen would see to the guests.

For some reason, the dining room had become the gathering spot for Helen's inhabitants. The parlor was in theory more comfortable and more homey—but it was only used when there were guests. The fact that there were guests didn't change the venue this time, however.

Mandoran and Annarion were seated at the dining room table.

"Teela?"

Mandoran nodded. "We can hear her. Barely, but we can hear her."

"Tain?"

"She says he's alive. More or less. She's pissed off at him, if that helps."

"Not really—it just means he's more injured than she is, probably because he was trying to do something stupid, like protect her."

"Got it in one."

Kaylin exhaled. She closed her eyes. Eyes closed, she could more clearly hear Kattea—which meant Gilbert was close. She inhaled deeply and opened her eyes. Small and squawky was seated on her shoulder, wings folded, eyes alert. Ybelline was a yard behind Gilbert and Kattea.

"Does she know what happened?"

"This would be a *lot* easier," Mandoran said, "if we *had your name*. Or if you had ours. I get that you don't want to let yours slip—but—" He subsided because Annarion had kicked him. "She says to tell you this is yet another attempt to gain immortality."

"The Arcanist was *Barrani*. He already *has* immortality!"

Mandoran gave Annarion a *look*. "This," he said, rising, "is *stupid*."

Annarion rose as well and stepped in front of him.

"I *mean it*."

"He gets that," Kaylin said. "And we don't—we don't need to do this. Helen can hear you. Helen can translate."

Helen's Avatar appeared in the far door. "I cannot translate well," she said half-apologetically, "and I confess I do not understand your reluctance; it is your name and should be your choice. Kaylin, however, is hesitant. She considers it dangerous."

"Why? She's mortal. She'll die in a handful of years."

"Because she is Chosen, and she doesn't understand what that means. Your Teela is correct, in a fashion. Immortality is the translation—it is an ancient Barrani word, and it does not have meaning in Elantran as it is currently spoken.

"You have had—Teela tells Mandoran—some experience with the Barrani who seek…freedom? From the shackles of their names. That freedom exists in the mortal; it does not exist in the immortal. It does not exist for either myself or Gilbert. Once I would not have understood the desire; it would have seemed tantamount to suicide.

"But I have come to understand it, with time."

"Would you destroy your name?"

"I have already destroyed parts of it, as you know. But no, Kaylin. That is not exact. I have cut off limbs. I have closed eyes. But the core of my name is still transcribed by, proscribed by, words—and I do not resent them. They gave me life. But there is persistent belief that freedom from words conveys limitless power to those who were created to contain words.

"To my eye, it does not; you were not created to contain words, and you are limited in ways that your immortals are not. But I have never been ambitious."

"Mandoran—what happened in the Arcanum? Why did the—whatever it is—start at the Winding Path? Teela went to the Arcanum, didn't she?"

He nodded.

"And then she went to the Winding Path?"

"No."

"So *where is she?*"

"She doesn't know."

"Is it a room? Is it—"

"She doesn't know, Kaylin. It's dark where she is. She's injured. Tain is injured. She's carved out a small space—"

"Tell her—tell her to use elemental shielding, if she can." Kaylin had no idea what Teela's magical abilities were. Beyond the implication that Teela had once belonged to the Arcanum, she knew nothing about Teela's magical past. Teela had never volunteered the information. But Kaylin had only asked once.

"She wants to know what you mean by elemental shielding."

"The Tha'alani used it—will use it—in future. It seemed to stop the spread of—of whatever ends up killing most of the city."

Ybelline lifted a hand. She was frowning. "You have your own *Tha'alaan* between you, yes?"

Neither Mandoran nor Annarion had been part of this city when it had become a city; they had very little familiarity with the Tha'alani—probably a good thing for the Tha'alani. They looked at Ybelline.

"No," Kaylin said, before anyone spoke. She caught Ybelline's shoulder. "You do not want to do this."

"I have touched Gilbert's thoughts without ill effect. I believe your Teela can do what we did, but much more effectively, if rumors about her past are true. What you tell her of what I've *said* will take time."

"Mandoran is not a normal Barrani—"

"I know. Which is why there is some chance that he will allow this. My communication does not require knowledge of his name. And you will not have to take it, either."

Mandoran said something colorful in Aerian.

Ybelline's eyes narrowed instantly. Clearly, the castelord had a working knowledge of Aerian.

Mandoran walked around Annarion, who was stiff and wary, and presented himself to Ybelline. "This doesn't hurt, does it?" he asked.

"Not unless you fight it, and even then, the pain is not physical."

"I would not do that." The Arkon had arrived.

★ ★ ★

If Mandoran was willing to listen to his cohort and the Chosen, he was absolutely *not* willing to take advice from an ancient Dragon—a Dragon who had, no doubt, existed at the time of the wars of the flights. He practically grabbed Ybelline by her shoulders and yanked her toward him. The castelord stumbled; Kaylin had to suppress the very strong urge to knock Mandoran off his feet.

Ybelline righted herself, lifted her hands and placed them on either of Mandoran's shoulders—not his cheeks, as she had done with Kattea.

The Arkon exhaled smoke.

It was very hard to ignore an angry Dragon when he happened to be standing at your back. Kaylin managed, turning to face Annarion, as Mandoran was now busy. "The Tha'alani had an experimental magic that seemed to protect them from whatever it was that will destroy this city. I don't know if everyone dies—but the Tha'alani quarter perishes. Teela is alive—"

"Is she anywhere near Bellusdeo?"

"No," Annarion said quietly. "She is not certain where Bellusdeo is."

The Arkon's eyes couldn't get any more red, but he seemed game to try. He glared at Kaylin. She didn't take this personally because he was glaring at everything, at the moment. "She has Maggaron with her."

"And Sanabalis." The Arkon exhaled. "With luck, he will actually listen to her. Bellusdeo's tone can be difficult, but she is not, in general, reckless. And she has lived with Shadow and its subtleties for centuries."

"I'm not sure this is *about* Shadow."

"And you feel it is not? Given the sigils and their similarities?"

Kaylin glanced at Gilbert. "I'm beginning to think that we

don't understand nearly enough about what we call Shadow. Gilbert lived in Ravellon. There are elements of Gilbert that we would classify as Shadow—but I don't think he means to absorb, devour or transform us. Or kill us all," she added, just in case this wasn't clear. "Gilbert was the one who first warned us against mirror use. It was only when we spoke to the *Tha'alanari* that his warning grew teeth."

Ybelline pressed her weaving stalks gently against Mandoran's forehead. Ybelline knew Mandoran's mind was not Barrani, although it had once been. She knew that he was not immortal in the way the Barrani and the Dragons now were.

Her eyes, which she'd closed, widened; her entire body stiffened. Kaylin was behind her instantly, set to catch her if she fell. Mandoran, however, caught her waist, bracing her. His eyes were blue—but it was not the shade that meant danger or death. It was a pale, sky blue.

She had never seen that color in his eyes—in any of their eyes—before. She had seen it in the Consort, in the West March. She glanced at Annarion and was surprised to see that his eyes, while the regular sort of blue, now rested in a face that was bordering on crimson. So. Sky blue meant what she probably thought it meant.

Ybelline did not blush. She forced herself, slowly, to relax. It occurred to Kaylin that this was something Ybelline had probably encountered in the Imperial dungeons, and the thought made Kaylin nauseous. Severn touched her shoulder; she jumped. But after a long, slow breath, she leaned into his hand.

Annarion frowned. Whatever Mandoran was passing on, he was listening. "Kaylin."

She nodded.

"You said it was raining in the Keeper's *storefront*?"

She hadn't—to Annarion. Clearly, Ybelline was explaining everything that had led to this point.

"Teela wants to know why, or how."

"Tell her to ask Evanton."

"She wants me to smack you and repeat her question."

"I don't know. It makes no sense to me, either—the water, the force of it, is contained *by* the Keeper, in the Garden.

"Evanton was in a room upstairs," she said, speaking—and thinking—slowly. "I think he was *trying* to contain the water's spread in the store."

"Confine it to the store?"

"No—not exactly. I think there's got to be some sort of fail-safe there, some way of speaking to the elements when it's no longer safe for even Evanton, the Keeper, to do so."

"You are certain?"

"I can go back to Evanton's—after we've at least got some idea of what's going on in the Winding Path. Does Teela think that's where she is? Yes, I know she said she doesn't know. But Teela thinks in her sleep. There's no way she's sitting on her butt in the dark not trying to figure things out."

"She thanks you for your confidence. And asks you to shut up."

"Why?"

"Because," Annarion said softly, "Ybelline is speaking now. She is describing the exact steps taken to cast the spell that might have preserved the Tha'alani for some hours before they were also destroyed."

The Arkon was absolutely unwilling to join the *Tha'alaan*; he was not unwilling to listen to Annarion. Annarion, aware of the Arkon's intent stare, spoke of the similarities between summoning and repulsion. Both required knowledge. Both required—to Kaylin's surprise—an openness, an awareness, a centering of the elemental *name*. Repulsion was not, as Kaylin had first assumed, an act of destruction or rejection. It was a barrier erected with the complicit acceptance of the summoned element; it was a marker they agreed to overlook, in its entirety.

Mandoran didn't speak. He had managed to loosen his grip on Ybelline's waist, and he had closed his eyes.

"Teela says she understands enough now," Annarion finally said. "She is going to try it on her end." He hesitated and then added, "She is profoundly grateful to the castelord. Ybelline, she is in your debt."

Kaylin winced. The Barrani had peculiar and unfriendly ideas of debt. "Are they anywhere near the Winding Path?" she asked, again.

"They were in the Arcanum. Teela found a crack in a wall there."

"Is that code for something?"

"Yes. The Arcanist in question—who has been missing for some time, due to the machinations of the Imperial Wolves—left research notes, instructions and apparently bound followers. One of those followers destroyed the necessary research."

"Voluntarily?"

"Teela doubts it. She points out—to Mandoran—that this is *how* names are traditionally used. The enslaved Barrani had enough time to give Teela warning—but not enough will to subvert the command. Teela and Tain survived. The others in the room did not."

"So...they should be *in* the Arcanum."

"That's what Tain thought. The destruction in question—Teela thinks it was meant as a...test."

"Test *of what*?"

"She is uncertain. She is familiar with the Arcanum; she says that is not where they are now."

"What, exactly, occurred?" the Arkon demanded.

"An explosion of the type an Arcane bomb would cause. It

was not an Arcane bomb. It appears to have caused displacement."

"She's not ahead in time, or behind," Kaylin said.

Gilbert, however, frowned. "Why are you so certain?"

"Because we can talk to her."

"No, Kaylin. Mandoran and Annarion can speak with her. Had Annarion been keeper of his brother's name, I believe he *could* have heard Lord Nightshade. They are not what you are. They are not what Lord Nightshade is. But they are not entirely separate. I may be mistaken, but I do not think Teela is precisely here and now. But there are multiple perturbations and I do not understand the whole of them."

"Teela thinks it's the same day," Annarion said.

"Teela is sitting in the dark, possibly in a dungeon—how the hell would she know?" Kaylin snapped.

But Mandoran said, "Her voice is thin. It's weaker or quieter than it usually is. Gilbert might be right."

"And he expects you two to somehow be able to ignore time?"

Gilbert said nothing.

"Teela says we need to speak with the Keeper."

CHAPTER 24

"Does Teela still have the portable mirror in her pocket—and did you tell her not to use it?"

"Yes, and no. Don't make that face," Mandoran added. "Ybelline made it clear. I passed it on." He had to shout the last phrase because the Arkon was also conversing. This would have been difficult, no matter what, but they were on the Arkon's back. It was crowded.

Mandoran and Annarion had not been exactly *delighted* with the prospect of climbing on a Dragon back—and specifically on the Arkon's. The Arkon, however, insisted, and he was in full Dragon mode. They chose the better part of valor.

Mandoran complained more, though.

The Arkon did not insist that Ybelline accompany them, but did not offer to transport her to the Tha'alani quarter, either. He insisted that Kattea remain with Helen. Kattea insisted otherwise. She did so from behind the safety of Gilbert's back, as Gilbert didn't seem to be intimidated—in any way—by the presence of a giant golden Dragon giving him the evil eye.

Gilbert insisted that Kattea be allowed to choose.

Kaylin, who *had* an opinion, struggled to keep it to herself. Yes, Kattea was an orphan. Yes, she was a child. Yes, she was making decisions based on fear and air and hope. And yes, someone responsible should be making the hard decisions *for her.* But if she had a guardian at all, it was Gilbert, and Gilbert felt that she would be safe. He made clear that the Arkon could carry Kattea—with Gilbert—or that he and Kattea would make their way to the Winding Path on their own.

The Arkon agreed to carry Gilbert.

The streets near Helen were empty.

The streets a few blocks away were not. The Arkon muttered something about breathing to clear space. Kaylin kicked his side. Her familiar squawked—a lot.

"It is *gallows humor*," the Arkon replied. "Or at least that is what I am told it is called."

"People need to laugh for it to be considered humor."

"And if they do not laugh?"

"Not funny. Humor is supposed to be funny."

"*I* find it amusing."

"Fine. Tell it to the other Dragons!" She regretted this about two seconds later, because he resumed his booming conversation. To her ear, he sounded angry, but she couldn't see his face and couldn't judge by eye color.

Squawk.

"Yes," Kaylin told him, almost inaudibly. "I see it."

There was a very large crater in the center of the slope of the Winding Path, or at least that was what it looked like at a distance. Kaylin could see the sharp edge of the street; she could see what she assumed was the brown of the dirt that underlay what had once been road. She could see the edges of the homes two streets over—and the homes at either end of the crater. Raising her voice, she said, "Do you know if it's gotten bigger?"

"It has expanded, yes," the Arkon replied. "If the castelord is correct, we may be able to halt the expansion."

"Did it work for Teela?" Kaylin shouted.

"I'm *not* mortal," Mandoran shouted back. "I can hear you if you're not screeching!"

"Just answer the question!"

"Yes. Wherever she is currently confined is affected by the shield."

Kaylin hesitated. The marks on her arms were not glowing. She squinted, swiveling on the Arkon's back to get a glimpse of Elani Street. The familiar squawked, loudly, in her ear.

"Arkon!"

The Arkon roared.

"I think—I think we need to find Evanton."

If turning Hawks to ash had not been illegal—and difficult, given she was on his back—Kaylin would have been smoldering. At best.

Mandoran and Annarion weren't fond of the idea, either—which was, in Mandoran's case, perfectly understandable. "Why?" the former demanded. Loudly.

"It's the elements," she replied. "I don't understand how—or why—they're involved. I *know* the disturbance is centered on the Winding Path. But—something must happen to Evanton, or his Garden—in the future. Which is probably really, really close."

"The Tha'alani quarter is not destroyed for an hour and a half," Mandoran told her. "From now. That's all the time we have."

"I *know that*," Kaylin snapped—although technically, she hadn't. "But the water was *outside* of the Garden. Yes, it was confined in the Keeper's abode—but it shouldn't have been able to rain in the store." And worse. "I think—I think the water that came from the future and merged with the water *here* wasn't confined in the same way in that future.

"If the Keeper was dead, there *wouldn't be* a fief. Or seven."

This was true, given everything Evanton had ever said about the Garden. Or anything the elements had said about themselves. But she couldn't let go of the notion. "Ask Teela."

"Teela is preoccupied at the moment—" His words cut off as the Arkon banked sharply. Kattea shrieked, and Kaylin let the Arkon know just how useful fancy flying maneuvers *weren't*. "Teela says the equivalent of *what*?"

Kaylin laughed. "In Leontine, right?"

"It's a remarkably flexible language."

"Yes, well. If she—"

Annarion said, with vastly more distaste, "She has almost finished indulging in Leontine metaphor." It was amazing to Kaylin that he and Mandoran could be so close, could have spent all of their lives in each other's pockets, and be so very, very different. "Arkon, she asks that you honor Kaylin's request." This last was said in very formal High Barrani.

The Arkon, however, was already on it.

Kaylin knocked with almost enough force to stave the door in. "Evanton!"

Grethan opened the door, his eyes wild; they were almost brown. The stalks on his forehead were weaving frantically. "Kaylin!" No rain fell in the store at his back, and the floor looked dry. This should have been a comfort.

"What's happened? Where's Evanton?"

"He's in—I think he's in—the Garden."

"We need to talk with him. It's—" She started to say *an emergency*. Grethan's expression, however, made it clear that he knew.

"I can't reach him."

"What?"

"I can't—I can't enter the Garden." He reached out, grabbed

her shoulders, dug his fingers into her arms. She let him. Had he been older there was a very real chance she would have broken his fingers or one of his arms—but his fear was so strong she couldn't, for a moment, see him as adult. As a threat.

Grethan was Tha'alani. His forehead stalks, however, were decorative. He could not join—or touch—the *Tha'alaan*, as the rest of his kin could. The only way for Grethan to reach it at all, the only way to alleviate the isolation that was almost unknown to the Tha'alani, was through the elemental water.

"Slow down," she said, forcing herself to do the same, although she had no time. She could practically feel the Arkon breathing down her neck. "Grethan, slow down. Where did you last see Evanton? He's not in the Garden?"

"There is no Garden."

Kaylin headed—sprinted—toward the rickety, narrow hall on the other side of the kitchen. She wasn't certain whether or not Grethan followed, and at the moment, she didn't care. She made Teela's Leontine seem tame as she skidded to a stop.

"Grethan…"

"I told you. It's gone."

The hall with which Kaylin was most familiar was no longer a squeaky mess of narrow boards, made even narrower by overstuffed shelving. It hadn't transformed into a grander hall, and it hadn't, as halls did in Tiamaris, remade itself to better accommodate the actual number of visitors.

It had simply ceased to exist.

Squawk.

"I know," she whispered. "We've got a problem."

The Arkon surrendered draconic form when Kaylin returned to the street. Gilbert, Kattea, Mandoran and Annarion slid off his shrinking back before they ended up in a pile atop his human form. Grethan held back, his toes on the threshold, his hands gripping the frame of the door.

"What is happening?" the Arkon demanded.

"The Garden—or at least any way of *reaching* it—is gone."

"Gone, as in the door has disappeared?"

Kaylin swallowed. "Gone as in: miniature version of the Winding Path." She turned back to Grethan. "I don't know if you heard, but—part of the city is doing the same thing as your back hall. But on a much larger scale."

To her surprise, Grethan nodded. "Evanton heard. Evanton—" He swallowed. "He went to the Garden."

"How did he hear? Did he use the mirror?"

Grethan nodded.

Kaylin cursed. "Can you hear the elements *at all*?"

The boy shook his head. The presence of a Dragon and two Barrani calmed him a bit, as did the two Hawks.

"You said he went into the Garden before it disappeared?"

Grethan nodded again.

Kaylin considered the wisdom of bringing Mandoran and Annarion into the store. But Mandoran hadn't set off any alarms or fail-safes; he hadn't caused problems until he'd been introduced to the elemental water itself. If there was no Garden, this was less likely to cause problems. She hoped.

"Gilbert—when you went to speak with the water—"

Gilbert nodded. He tried to set Kattea down, but she clung to him tightly.

"Did you make it to the Garden?"

He frowned. Kaylin led him to the start of what was no longer a hallway. The edge of the floor curved in a circular shape, as if someone had dropped a giant stone ball into something much squishier. To either side, she saw what she would have expected to see if a large spherical chunk had been removed from a building.

Beneath this sphere of absence, she could see stone halls.

Squawk. A translucent wing rose instantly to cover the upper half of Kaylin's face.

"Teela demands to know what you see *now*," Annarion said.

"Teela is definitely feeling better. Tell her I see the hallway."

"Pardon?"

"I see the Keeper's hallway. I see the door that leads to the Garden. I see his packed shelves and his threadbare runners. He's there." She poked the familiar. "Show Grethan."

The Keeper's panicked apprentice stepped back to stand beside Kaylin, and the familiar sighed and lifted his other wing. He dug claws into Kaylin's shoulder, in theory for balance.

"What do you see, Grethan?"

"I see—" He ducked out from under the wing. Rose again. Ducked. "I— The hall is there."

"Yes. Via dragon wing, it's there." She ignored the Arkon's cough.

"Can I— Is it real?"

Squawk.

"Gilbert, what do you see?"

"I see the hall that I walked this morning. The floor will hold Grethan if, and only if, he does not lose sight of it. Grethan, you said the Keeper was in the Garden?"

"Yes," Grethan replied, once again looking through the small dragon's wing. "Can we go there?"

"Arkon?"

"If the Keeper is having difficulty, I am not certain adding Private Neya will make his life any easier."

"Which means…no?"

"Which means: hurry."

Gilbert reached out and caught Kaylin's shoulder. "It is possible," he said grimly, "that without the familiar, your Grethan will be lost."

She hesitated. "If the Garden itself is in the same state as the hall—or the corpses—we're probably doomed anyway." She slid an arm around Grethan's arm. "It's up to you. Do you want to join Evanton, or do you want to wait?"

"I want to go to the Garden."

Annarion coughed.

Everyone—except Grethan—turned to look at him.

"What do the two of you see?" Kaylin asked.

They exchanged a glance. "Do you have a rope?" Annarion asked Grethan. Grethan shook himself, ducked out from under the familiar's wing and disentangled his arm. He walked back into the kitchen and made the noises people made when they were looking for something they were mostly certain was there—somewhere.

He came back with a length of rope. Annarion took it, tied one end to Mandoran's waist, endured Mandoran's criticism of his ability to tie a knot and then tied the other to his own.

"I see a hall," he told Kaylin, when this was done. "But there's something off about it. Does it strike you as odd when you have your familiar's help?"

"Only in that I need his help to see it," she offered. "To be honest, I'm slightly more concerned about the basement."

Silence.

"The basement?" Mandoran asked.

"The stone halls beneath this one. You can see them where there should be floor."

They exchanged another glance.

"Please tell me you can see them."

"We can see the hall, but it is…transparent. We can't see what's below it. Severn?"

Severn said nothing.

"Kattea?"

"I think I see dirt. It's kind of dark."

Kaylin fished a flare out of her kit. "I don't suppose you have another rope, Grethan?"

She tossed the lit flare down into the basement she could see without her familiar's wing, taking care to avoid following it.

The light illuminated the hard sides of walls, and the rope seemed to sink forever; the flare didn't actually reach the floor on the first two attempts. "Can you see the walls now?"

Silence.

"Okay, tell me what you guys *see*."

Mandoran said, "I think I see what you see."

"You think?"

"The walls are old and crumbling, to my eye. If the street is built over this, it's a wonder it hasn't sunk."

"They're not crumbling, to my eye. They look almost new." She frowned. "They look…" She turned to Gilbert and Kattea. "They look like the walls in your basement." She paused. "They look *exactly* like the walls in your basement.

"Gilbert—"

But Gilbert had come to the edge of the hall that the rest of them could see—or rather, the edge of space where the hall had been. "Yes," he said softly. "You are right."

"Share," Mandoran said, in exactly the intonation Teela would have used.

"Gilbert's basement is a giant hall, or a series of halls. There are doors, which imply rooms—but Kattea said—"

"The rooms move," the girl said. She glanced at Gilbert. "Gilbert has a room. Sometimes it's hard to *find* the room."

The Arkon's very orange eyes fixed themselves on Kattea. "How do you find the room without getting lost?"

"There's a mark on the door. Gilbert's name."

Silence.

"When you say Gilbert's name—" Mandoran began. Kaylin stepped on his foot.

"The rooms…move," the Arkon said slowly. "But you find them. How long does it take you to find them?"

"Not very long. Well, once it took hours."

"And you said the water carried you to the basement, and you found the house above it?"

Kattea nodded, uncertain now; she looked to Gilbert for confirmation. "We found the stairs," she said. "And they weren't like the rest of the halls. I mean, they were more… normal. So, we climbed those."

"Where did you think they would lead?"

She glanced at Gilbert again. He seemed to be interested in the answer; Kaylin wanted to scream with frustration. Time. Time. Time.

"Somewhere safe," she said quietly. "Somewhere on the other side of the bridge." More silence. "I thought… I thought maybe I might find my dad."

Kaylin said, "Grethan, I think you should join Evanton."

He blinked. "Do you really see stone halls?" he whispered.

"Yes. But I think Evanton might need a bit of help. It's just a guess. I can't hear or see him." Which was probably a mercy.

Grethan, having found more rope, nodded, and slid an arm around Kaylin's again. The small dragon complained but lifted a wing. Kaylin walked Grethan down the familiar hall to the familiar door. "You guys can see us, right?"

Silence.

Severn?

No. There is some panic, but it is muted; Gilbert believes he can see you, and the Arkon has chosen—barely—to trust him. Hurry.

Mandoran? Annarion?

I am attempting to keep them in one place. Annarion is worried.

Worried?
His eyes are almost black. Mandoran's are the regular blue.
Don't let them follow.
No. But, Kaylin—hurry.

The door opened into the Garden, and to Kaylin's surprise, it didn't open into torrential storm or mudslide or raging fire or windstorm. She could hear the relief in Grethan's breathing. "Evanton!"

The Keeper was nowhere in sight.

Kaylin, clutching Grethan's arm, told the familiar to drop his wing. The wing folded; Grethan's arm was still attached to Kaylin's. The apprentice, however, froze in place, his eyes widening, his stalks doing the panic dance while attached to his forehead.

There's a problem, she told Severn. And there was. She had thought—she nudged the familiar—that the Garden existed; she assumed it was just the hall that was a problem. But Grethan couldn't see the Garden without the familiar's help. And Kaylin was afraid to let go of Grethan because she wasn't certain she would be able to find him again if he moved.

"We're switching places," she told the apprentice. "Do not let go of my arm unless you want to lose me forever."

"What—"

"I need to know what you see when you're not looking through his wing." Before he could reply, she said, "Keep an eye out for Evanton. I think we're going to need him."

The familiar raised his wing to cover Grethan's eyes again as Kaylin slid out from behind the other. He bit her hair and smacked her face—twice—to let her know just how smart he thought this was. He also tucked his tail, tightly, around her neck. "Grethan didn't fall through the world when you removed your wing," she reminded the squawky pest. "And you're hardly likely to be able to stop me from falling at *that* size."

She regretted the words the minute they left her mouth, and pretended they hadn't. Grethan was calmer, but true calm was not going to return until they had at least found Evanton.

"What—what do you see?" he asked her.

She was asking herself that, as well. She had walked the gray space between worlds before. She tried to remember the experience, because it was a lot like this—and yet, *nothing* like it. Nightshade had torn a hole in the world—a literal tear—to free her before she was eaten by the thing the gray space contained.

"Kaylin?"

"Still here," she said. But she had no idea where "here" was. The ground—if it was ground—felt slippery but hard, like wet mud. She couldn't see it. She couldn't see her own feet. She couldn't see the shrines, the grass, the braziers; she couldn't see the path that led to the small stone hut that could be the size of a mansion—on the inside.

She couldn't see the shrouded gray of nowhere, either. The air was oddly luminescent. There was no horizon, no landscape. Even the light, folding in on itself like short auroras of color, did not suggest distance or geography. This was not where Teela and Tain were.

"We need to find Evanton," Kaylin said. She could feel Grethan's arm in hers, but wasn't surprised to note that she couldn't see him. "I think you're going to have to take the lead here."

If Grethan answered, she couldn't hear him. Then again, she wasn't certain her words had reached him, either.

"Why," a familiar voice said, "are you just standing there? Teela says hi, by the way."

Kaylin turned toward the sound of Mandoran's voice. She wasn't particularly surprised to discover that the Barrani, at least, was visible.

"Teela's about ready to give up," he added, with so much cheer Kaylin knew she wasn't giving up on survival.

"Your name?"

"Got it in one. She hates the idea—but she hates the idea that she has no other way of reaching you more. I suggested she give you her name, but she said it would be a conflict of interest."

"What?"

"She's a Hawk, she's not going to give up her job and she's your superior."

"If she gave me *her* name, though—"

"She doesn't think it would make much of a difference. She'd still be the one in power."

Barrani arrogance made Kaylin want to scream. "Why are you *even here*?"

"I could see the hall. I could walk across it—but not easily. I didn't expect the Garden to just let me in—but Grethan didn't close the door, and apparently, unseen doors don't work the way the normal ones do."

"What do you see now?" she demanded.

"You. Clearly. I mean it. You look exactly the same as you always look: dirty, cranky and clumsy. Emphasis on *cranky*."

"Where is Annarion?"

"He's on the other end of the rope, theoretically. It's not a *long* rope."

"Fine. Can you see Evanton?"

"No."

"More looking, less talking."

He snapped a pretty sharp salute, and Kaylin didn't bother to tell him all the ways in which the gesture itself was incorrect.

★ ★ ★

She didn't understand time. She didn't understand space, not as it applied to layers. But it was clear to her, as she followed Mandoran, that the space she was now in was layered in some way; that she could see layers of it, depending on how she looked. No one else could see them without the help of the familiar. But the world itself still existed. Somehow.

Kaylin?

She missed a step. Since she couldn't even see her feet, this shouldn't have been surprising.

Nightshade? Nightshade, is that you?

She felt faint disapproval—blending with condescension—which was answer enough. Turning to Mandoran, she said, "I can hear Nightshade!"

Mandoran did not react with excitement.

"Tell Annarion?"

"I did. Gilbert is on his way."

"Pardon?"

"Gilbert thinks he understands what the difficulty might be. He's on his way."

"He can't bring Kattea with him. Tell him."

"You're going to have to tell him yourself," Mandoran said, turning. Kaylin's grip on Grethan's arm tightened as the entirety of the landscape went dark. Gilbert, apparently, had arrived.

Kaylin said, "What do you see?" to the Barrani beside her.

Mandoran frowned. "I see Gilbert. You?"

"Shadow." And it was. The faint iridescence of moving chaos had become embedded in a growing darkness. Kaylin had seen this before. She had never seen it from the inside, but she had seen what it had done to people who had.

Every instinct in her screamed to run—or fight. The small dragon smacked her, hard, with his wing. It was purely to get her attention; he didn't leave the wing over her eye. And to be fair to him, it worked: he got her attention.

Mandoran's eyes, she realized, were like the rest of the surroundings. They looked like…liquid Shadow. She couldn't tell if this was just a reflection of the environment, but she doubted it. Strongly. She knew he could be an impulsive, feckless, *condescending* idiot—but she wasn't afraid of him. She wasn't certain that she could be.

Severn—I don't think Grethan can hear me.

He can't.

Can he hear you?

Yes. He is shouting for Evanton. I suggest—

Got it.

"EVANTON! *EVANTON!*" She stopped. "It just occurs to me—if he's actually alive and he's not trapped and he's doing something finicky, that's going to piss him off."

"Too late."

Angry, cranky Evanton was the definition of No Fun Whatsoever—but the relief Kaylin felt at the pinched irritation of his voice made the risk of actually encountering him up close and personal seem tiny.

"Evanton?"

"I heard you the first time."

"Can you—can you see me?"

"I can see something moving, yes."

"Great, keep talking. We're kind of walking around in darkness here."

"She's walking around in darkness," Mandoran said, correcting her.

"Mandoran. Kaylin thought it was a good idea to bring you *here*?"

"Actually, technically, Gilbert wanted us to tag along, and

the Arkon brought us here because Kaylin insisted on visiting you before we went to the *actual* disaster."

It was hard to forget the visceral fear that had driven her here when her friends were in unknown trouble. She pushed them out of the way—barely—and said, "The water shouldn't have been able to rain—or flood—your store." As she walked in the direction of his voice, the dark outline of the Keeper finally resolved itself, as if he were simply part of the Shadow that had chosen to solidify.

"Yes."

"I think the water—the water that brought Kattea and Gilbert here because it *could*—exists in a place where there is no Garden. In the future that Gilbert and Kattea come from, the water wasn't confined."

"You have spoken to the elemental water outside of this garden before."

She nodded. "One of those places was beneath Castle Nightshade—which is where Kattea and Gilbert met the water. But... the water brought something of itself from Kattea's time, and I think that something is the reason containment of water has become...difficult?"

"*Difficult* is too mild a word. The water is attempting to communicate something to me, and I am clearly unable to translate."

"Did the water do this?"

"No."

"Then what—"

"I did it," Evanton replied. "If you refer to the phasing here, it's a choice I had to make. There is something that is attempting to attack the foundational stability of the Garden in ways you cannot perceive."

Gilbert said, "I can."

"I thought," Evanton said, "you might be here." There was

a thread of very, very dry humor running through his colossal understatement. "Is Grethan with you?"

Kaylin answered. "I've attached myself to his arm; he's probably having circulation problems. If I—if I let him go, will he be where we are?"

"Where does he think he is?"

"In the Garden. The normal Garden. I can see it if I look through my familiar's wing—and that's what he's doing now."

"Are you certain?"

"I was, when I walked in." She poked the small dragon; he snapped at her finger, but not hard enough to draw blood. His annoyance didn't prevent him from lifting his spare wing and setting it against Kaylin's upper face, however. She saw Evanton, standing in the rock garden, his apron askew, his robes of office absent. Mandoran vanished, as did any evidence of Gilbert and his innate darkness.

"Grethan, can you see Evanton now?"

Grethan's entire body relaxed. Answer enough.

She asked the familiar to lift his wing from Grethan's view. The Tha'alani tensed again.

"Now?" Kaylin asked.

He squinted. "...Yes. Yes, I can see him now. He looks like a shadow." She then asked the familiar to let her see without his wing, and he folded it in silence.

A pale Grethan stood by her side in a dark and almost featureless landscape. The only thing the two views had in common, beside some variant of Evanton, were the stones of the rock garden. But not *all* of the stones.

Here, there were four, like little monoliths. Kaylin walked Grethan to Evanton; the older man caught the younger man by the shoulder and moved him into a position that was central to the standing stones. She asked the Keeper one question. "Is there a reason you're in the rock garden?"

"Yes."

"Do you have time to explain it to me? I think—I think it could be important."

If he did, the explanation would have to wait. "Grethan, you will not be able to return if things do not go well here. I am not," he added, "expecting that things will go well. I believe there would be a home for you in the Tha'alani quarter—"

Grethan shook his head, his face flushing.

"Yes, there will be anger. There are always consequences for ill-considered actions. But the *Tha'alaan* is aware that you saved that child's life. If there is anger over the part you played in her kidnapping, there is also gratitude. I believe Ybelline would accept you into the *Tha'alaan*; she would become your water in the outside world."

He shook his head again. "I learned to hear and remember and experience life in a way that Tha'alani don't. It's too late—and I don't want my life to be part of theirs. I think it would hurt them."

Kaylin shook her head. "They have the lives of *warlords* in their past. There's nothing you've done that compares to the pain of those memories."

Evanton cleared his throat. "If, however, you are determined to remain, come stand where I'm standing and *do not move until I tell you to move.*"

Kaylin, however, understood. "He wants you to leave," she said quietly. "He wants you safe. You found the Garden on your own. The Garden let you in without Evanton's permission. If something happens to Evanton here, you can find your way in again."

But Grethan shook his head, his eyes dark and shadowed. "There will be no Garden," he said. "The water said that the Garden will be broken and lost."

CHAPTER 25

"Grethan!"

Grethan jumped at the change in Evanton's voice. He moved to Evanton's side. "You see the stones," he said.

So did Kaylin. There were four in all. Not three, as there had been in the basement of the house on the Winding Path. "Is the number significant?" she asked.

Evanton frowned.

"The number of stones."

"These have words," Evanton replied. "At their base. And before you ask, no, I am not turning them over for your inspection." Instead, he spoke, his voice low and resonant; it might have been a Dragon voice, given the way it carried.

Words appeared in the air above each of the four stones, and Kaylin recognized them instantly, although she only knew two: *fire* and *water*. The other two, *air* and *earth*, she had never attempted to use. She understood the purpose of these stones.

No, she thought, that was wrong. "Evanton, why do you have these stones? I mean, why are they here and why couldn't you hear or see us until we were practically standing on top of them?"

"They are the foundation of my garden," he replied. "They are…tent pegs, driven into the fundamental layer of reality in which we live. They are not cages," he added, "but containers; the words at their base are words given willingly, and written by the elements. Water as you drink it, water in your wells, water when it is not summoned, exists. It exists as part of the world, and it is not sentient. The glass of water you drink doesn't think. The water with which you bathe doesn't think.

"The fire over which you cook, the earth over which you walk—they are part of the elements. They are like—like fingernail cuttings, or the dead skin you scrub off. Within my Garden, the elements are sentient. They are also contained—but understand, Kaylin, that they are ancient, ancient forces. They do not exist in one simple fashion; there is water here. There is water where the familiar guides you to look. There is water in the past and water in the present and there will be water in the future; it persists.

"We persist in a similar way until our deaths—but only on the narrow path of 'world.' Pretend the world is like a very fine, many-layered cake. We cannot exist on any layer but the top. Or the bottom. The limitations on our perceptions, the limitations of our physical forms, demand it. There are stories—old stories that perhaps even your Arkon has forgotten. During the time of creation, many creatures were made.

"But many of them could not survive. Just as fish need water, men—and in this, I count all the races that have ever lived in Elantra or beyond its borders—need solidity. They need a fixed place, a living world.

"Worlds were made. They were made like the cages small rodents live in. They were made larger, of course, and the bars were meant to be invisible.

"But the elements you see and touch and summon can live in any layer of existence, and do. What they are in the other layers is—should be—irrelevant to us, here." He hesitated.

She marked it. In general, Evanton's hesitations were a sign of growing temper—but this was different.

"Mandoran does not live the way Teela lives, although he is trying. He can walk, speak, think, in dimensions to which he was not born. It is why the water reacted so poorly when he visited the Garden the first time."

"It's not doing that now."

"No. It cannot see him now."

"I don't know what you've done to the Garden, but we need to know how it works."

Evanton, in shadow, could still somehow stare a hole through her. "Do you think this is something I do regularly? Perhaps you are unaware of the term *emergency*? Perhaps—"

Grethan caught his master's arm.

"Your Garden isn't the only place in the city that's functionally disappeared. A space like this—very like this—exists in the center of the Winding Path. And it's growing. We need to stop it." She hesitated. "The water told you what happens in the future. The city is destroyed—or at least the Tha'alani quarter is. Gilbert is here—no, *Kattea* is here, from the future after that destruction.

"I have no idea where *here* is," she continued. "But...I can hear Nightshade. He's alive."

"You could not hear him until you entered this space?"

"No." She hesitated. "Does this mean we're somehow outside of...time?"

Kaylin.

The voice was stronger. It dispelled doubt. It was Nightshade.

What...is happening? Where are you?

Look, she told him.

I am. I see darkness. I see...shadow. My brother?

He's somewhere safe. Well, safer. Do you know the date?

Silence. She filled the silence with a furious rush of information. Nightshade didn't interrupt her; he had no need. What her words couldn't convey, her thoughts did. But she felt his growing uneasiness.

Kaylin, who is Gilbert?

She froze. *Gilbert. You met him in Ravellon.*

I am not foolhardy enough to enter Ravellon unless at great need.

Silence then. It took Kaylin a moment to reorient herself. Or Nightshade. *Where are you?*

I am in my Castle. It is…difficult to maneuver here.

Andellen?

I…do not…know. Nor, at the moment, did he appear to care. *Who is Gilbert?* he asked again.

She told him. Or tried to tell him. His frustration grew. Whatever she was telling him, he couldn't understand. She tried again. She tried to visualize Gilbert as she'd seen him when she'd healed him. She *knew* she was speaking, knew she was thinking, could visualize it herself. But Nightshade couldn't hear her when she did.

Nightshade was no longer uneasy; she thought he was afraid.

"Evanton, are we outside of time?"

Gilbert, however, answered. "You cannot be outside of time," he replied. "Were you, you would be very like your fish out of water. You would die." As he spoke, darkness condensed until it resembled a silhouette of Gilbert. He looked much like Evanton did, to the unmasked eye.

"Would it be instant?"

"Very close. Perhaps the fish analogy is incorrect." He approached Kaylin, Kattea in his arms. Kattea, unlike Gilbert or Evanton, looked like her normal self. She was pale but silent, and her fingers, where they gripped Gilbert, were white-knuckled. She looked through Kaylin, her eyes blinking rapidly.

"Kattea?"

"She cannot hear you," Gilbert said gently. "I do not have the gifts that your familiar does. She is...safe, with me. But she perceives only darkness. She does not speak, and she doesn't see or hear."

Kaylin could see nothing in this darkness as clearly as Gilbert's eyes. There were the three he'd been left with when she'd healed him.

And there were the dozens that she had gently closed. They surrounded him like a swarm of moths might surround the fire that would kill them.

She'd thought that this darkness, this shadow, this swirl of gloom and fog, were familiar. She now knew why. They reminded her of Gilbert's rooms. Of Gilbert's endless rooms. They reminded her of the darkness in which she'd found— and closed—his eyes.

She had called it healing. But when she'd finished, she had no better idea of what Gilbert actually was. She didn't have that now, either. But she watched as Gilbert's eyes—the ones not immediately attached to his face—began to open.

"Gilbert—don't—"

He smiled. The light from his embedded eyes revealed his familiar face, although the rest of his body remained in darkness. The unattached eyes did not stop opening; lids curled up and vanished. This was not comforting.

"I believe I understand some part of what has occurred here. Keeper, we have disturbed you in your very necessary work."

"But—"

"No, Kaylin. This choice is not the choice your Keeper would have made had it not been for the recursion of the water. It is a choice he *must* make if your city is to have any chance of survival. But you—and I—have other tasks. I understand now."

Kaylin wasn't certain if it was Nightshade's fear or her own that made thinking difficult. She *hated* fear. What good was it?

If Evanton's Garden was—tenuously—in Evanton's hands, the *rest of the city* wasn't. While Evanton tended to the Garden, in whatever form it currently existed, the Winding Path waited.

And time. Time had passed. *Breathe, idiot.* Time had passed, but if Gilbert was right, what Evanton was doing now bought them more of it. The regular, garden-variety version that Kaylin actually lived in.

"Evanton, how do we get to your basement?"

"My *what?*"

"Your basement. The hall is gone. I guess it's here, wherever this is. But beneath the hall I could see the basement—and it's not much of a basement."

Silence.

"There are halls—there are stone halls. They're a hell of a lot wider than your actual hall, and you could probably ride an army through them without threatening the stability of the floor."

More silence.

"Grethan, tell him."

Grethan, however, was silent, as well. His silence, on the other hand, didn't last. "There—there were no halls. I mean, I didn't see them."

Figures. Kaylin poked the familiar. The familiar pretended she didn't exist. "We're leaving—if we can. But if you've got some sort of mirror access here, *don't* use it."

"Is there difficulty with the mirrors?"

"Severe difficulty, actually. And no, before you ask, we have no idea what it is. But in their future memories, Ybelline and the *Tha'alanari* made a last stand in the long house. They cast a barrier spell of some sort—one meant to repel elements—and it worked. It was the use of the mirror that killed them. Something came through the mirror, which was on the inside of their defenses."

"Noted."

"We're leaving Grethan with you."

Gilbert's eyes continued to open, but they opened slowly. "Are you sure you should be doing that?" Kaylin demanded, in as much of a whisper as she could.

"I am not certain to what you refer."

"You're opening all your eyes."

Squawk. Squawk.

Gilbert smiled. It was the wrong kind of smile. "It is necessary, Kaylin. We must find our way back to the store."

The ground still felt like mud beneath her feet. "I can reach Nightshade here."

"Yes. That is not necessarily a good sign."

"Gilbert..."

"Yes?"

"...I don't think he knows who you are."

"Yes. Come, Kaylin."

"I'm following, but I don't understand—he thinks he's in his Castle."

"Yes."

Understanding, when it came, was fractured. "You think— I'm speaking to him before whatever emergency occurred that caused the Castle to expel him."

"Yes."

"But—"

"He was not meant to live in Ravellon; not as it is currently constituted. There was a time—" He shook his head. "But no."

"But you said you were trying to find a way to *bring him back*."

"Even so."

"Gilbert—you wanted to help him because he became your friend."

"Yes."

"I don't understand."

"No, you do not. What confuses you now?"

"If we can reach Nightshade *now*, he'll never go to Ravellon. He'll never meet you. You'll never—"

"Yes. Yes, Kaylin. The only way back, for your Nightshade, is now. If we resolve the difficulty before it engulfs your city, the Castle will release him. He will be, as he once was, Lord of Nightshade."

"And you?"

"I do not understand your question."

It was Mandoran who answered. Of course. Kaylin understood only half of what he said.

"I will return to Ravellon."

"But he won't be there."

"I do not know."

"You're lying."

"Yes. The Arkon is impatient."

"The Arkon is *always* impatient." She picked up the pace, trusting Gilbert.

Mandoran kicked her ankle; she turned to glare, and he whispered, "He knows what he's doing. He's made his choice. No, it's not a *happy* choice—but immortals are accustomed to that. All of us. Leave it?"

She opened her mouth.

Annarion—who wasn't even *present*—added, "Please." The desperate tone of his voice hit her, hard.

She closed her mouth. Next topic. "Why do you look like Shadow?"

"I do not know what you see when you look at me. I am certain that what I see of you is not what you see of yourself. When you speak of Shadow—or when Kattea does—she refers in large part to what she calls Ferals."

She would.

"But, Kaylin, the Shadow of which you speak exists in you, as well. It is not so large a component as exists in me, but it is unfettered."

He must have seen her expression with one of his floating eyes, because all she could see was his back and he didn't have eyes in it. "The Shadow in *you* is slight and unrestrained. In me, it is contained, confined. It is a necessary component of my existence. It gives me...flexibility."

"But the Towers were created to guard against Shadow."

"Yes."

"And the Shadows in Ravellon—"

"Yes. It is complicated. Shadow as it exists in me has no will. In you, it has no will; you are in control of most of your actions. You require sustenance. You require rest. You do not classify these as particular weaknesses. If, in sleep, a differing sentience arose, you would. Change is a fundament of your world. If you could not change, you could not exist. Time is the allowable axis around which that change revolves."

Time. Again.

"Change was revered, before I, and my kin, were created. What you classify as Shadow is ancient. It was the work of many and its existence, the cause of many debates. Perhaps you would call them wars, if you could witness them at all; I do not think you could."

"Could we?" Mandoran asked.

"It is possible you could perceive it. You are not as Kaylin is. But it is not relevant, at least not now. The malleability of Shadow was considered a gift; it was a medium in which much that had been impossible became possible. It was not, itself, sentient. But in the way of things, Shadow itself could alter what could not otherwise be altered."

Kaylin frowned. After a pause, she said, "The words?"

"Yes, Kaylin. The words. The words that gave life, even to those who were of Shadow. They could not destroy the words, of course—but they could, with time, alter their construction, and in so doing, change the meaning. I do not believe this was the intent of their creators, and at first, it was not seen as a threat; it was...new. Unexpected. A surprise. Not all such surprises are pleasant.

"I was created long after. I was not meant to police the Shadows, or even to guard directly against them; that was not my function. Only where their actions crossed my directives did I seek to destroy them. Kattea has said she hates Shadow."

"Who doesn't?"

"I do not. It is what it is. It is, in the end, the sum of its experiences. Does it destroy? Yes. But so do the Towers and the Guardians. It is not personal."

"And are Shadows involved in this?"

"No. Not directly, and perhaps not at all."

"Then what *is*?"

"Shall we see?" He took one step forward, and as Kaylin followed, the world reasserted itself. Annarion, Severn and the Arkon waited. Annarion gave her a tiny nod of acknowledgment; his eyes were blue. Blue and...gold. It was a very striking combination.

"We found Evanton," she said—to the Dragon. "And I think we need to take a different road to the Winding Path."

"What exactly does that mean?"

"See those halls?" She pointed to the spherical absence that had once been worn, wooden flooring.

The Arkon frowned.

"We need to go there."

She lost Nightshade when she regained sight of the rest of the world. She noticed his absence instantly. "I don't understand time."

"No. But you are not meant to understand it except in one way. You follow time; you are captive to it." This was not the usual variant on the inferiority of mortals; Gilbert didn't seem capable of genuine condescension.

Kaylin nodded. Severn fell in beside her. "We're looking for stairs," she said. "Down."

"My function is not to preserve you or your kind. That is, perhaps, the function of what you call the Towers."

"The Towers don't—"

"They have their limits and their instructions, yes. Within the confines of the Tower—as with Helen—they are...elastic. They have enlarged functionality. But their confines are very, very strictly drawn, very strictly contained. It was not always so," he added. He looked as if he would say more, but fell silent as he glanced at Kattea.

Kattea said, "I'm better at finding stairs than you are."

"This is true."

"Put me down."

"I do not wish to lose you, Kattea."

"*You're* the one who gets lost all the time." She squirmed her way out of Gilbert's arms, and he let her go. She then took off for the kitchen and paused to grab something from the table before heading out into the mess of a storefront.

"She's eating your cookies," Severn observed.

"Hey!"

The Arkon coughed. "They're probably stale, anyway," Kaylin muttered. To Gilbert, she said, "So...back to your function."

"My function is simply to preserve the structural integrity of time."

"Is that why the water was afraid you would destroy her?"

"Yes."

"But you're not going to destroy her."

"No."

"Would you have?"

The Arkon exhaled smoke.

"Would you like to take over the rest of this conversation?" she demanded.

"Yes. There will be fewer interruptions of an entirely pointless and frivolous nature. You," he added, "may help Kattea find the stairs."

There were, as it turned out, no stairs. Kattea, however, found a trapdoor. She stepped away and Severn pulled it open, using the hook built into the handle to hold it in place. "Stairs?" Kaylin asked.

"Not exactly. I think there's a ramp."

"Think?"

"We're going to need some light."

Light was found—Evanton's store had lamps with varying levels of oil—and Severn was proved correct: there was a ramp. It was, however, made of wood; sliding down was out of the question unless one wanted a backside full of splinters. The Arkon looked about as amused at the idea of ramps as Kaylin was at the idea of a backside full of splinters.

Mandoran and Annarion went down first.

Gilbert followed; when he was halfway down the ramp, Kattea leaped onto his back, which nearly sent him tumbling into the Barrani. The Arkon was pretty much steaming at this point. He glared dubiously at the ramp. "Private, Corporal, you go first."

Kaylin opened her mouth.

"I do not believe the ramp will sustain my weight."

He wasn't wrong. Although he looked—for the moment— like an armored old man, his weight was closer to the draconic end of the scale; the ramp snapped when he was halfway down the incline. Fortunately, the rest of their party had already cleared the area.

"Have you considered the significance of these halls?" The Arkon asked, after he'd picked himself up and dusted himself off.

"I consider them pretty significant," she said, after a pause. "But—Evanton wasn't aware of halls beneath Elani, and I would have bet real money that they didn't exist before Gilbert and Kattea made their way here."

"Do you think they were created by the water?"

A good question. "No."

"But the water found Gilbert and Kattea and moved them—two people who were not, originally, from our time—here?"

"Well, yes—I don't think Kattea was lying."

"And Gilbert?"

"Gilbert doesn't understand enough about our way of life to be a good liar. No. I don't think either were deliberately falsifying events." She hesitated. Gilbert had forbidden the use of mirrors. And mirrors existed across the city—even in the fiefs. Except for now.

Now the fiefs were off the network; they could be reached by foot, but not by the magic that powered mirrored communication. "Has anyone heard from Tiamaris?"

"Yes."

"Did Tara knock the fief off the mirror network?"

"Yes." The Arkon glanced at Kaylin with obvious surprise, which was slightly insulting, and approval, which should have been, but wasn't.

"And the fiefs exist post-disaster, whatever that disaster was." She turned to Gilbert. "Are these halls a reflection of the mirror network?"

Gilbert said, "I believe so, yes. Helen believes that the underpinning magic of that network has been extant for far longer than your Empire. The magic is used, and channeled, but it is not well understood by your kind."

"Or by yours?"

His smile was slight. "Or by mine. I believe the halls, as you experience them, are an instability in the underlying magic. As such, we can enter almost any building to which the network itself has been granted access. I do not believe it is sentient," he added softly. "But it responds to sentience."

"Not to ours," Kaylin told him.

"No, perhaps not. To the water, yes, in some fashion."

Kaylin nodded.

"I did not recognize immediately what it was. My apologies. But I recognize it now; follow, and it will take us where we must go."

"How are you so well acquainted with these halls?" the Arkon asked.

It was Kattea who answered. "Gilbert lives here." She was once again perched—as if she was weightless—in the curve of his right arm; her own arms were around his neck. It made her seem much younger. She yawned.

"It is better," Gilbert said, "that Kattea sleep. She will remember this as a dream or a nightmare when she wakes."

Kattea lifted her head and shook it. "I'm not sleepy."

"No, of course not."

"I don't want to leave."

"You are not leaving."

"Will you save the city?"

"I will save the city."

"Will you take me with you?"

"Hush, Kattea. I cannot see past your voice." It was an odd thing to say, and it seemed to Kaylin that Kattea was struggling to keep her eyes open. Given the circumstance, this was surprising. Or maybe not. She glanced at the Arkon; his eyes' inner membranes were high, but they were a steady orange. He nodded in answer to the question she didn't ask.

Magic. But not a magic that caused Kaylin's skin to ache. While they walked, the Arkon turned to Kaylin. "You said there were traces of six different mages along the wall in the basement that led to the corpses."

She nodded. "There are no records of similar murders, not in the Halls. If this has happened before, it was never reported."

"Or it happened before Records were kept." He shook his head, murmuring softly. This time, Kaylin's arms began their almost comfortingly familiar ache. "Gilbert does not see those corpses as dead."

Kaylin nodded.

The Arkon directed the next question to Gilbert. "How do you see the living?"

"Kattea speaks. She eats. She breathes. So does Severn. They both...move. They respond." It was growing darker in the tunnels; the light cast by the lamps seemed dimmer, somehow. The light cast by Gilbert's swarm of eyes, however, was brightening.

"In what way did the three on the Winding Path seem like Kattea or Severn?"

"They speak."

"They don't speak in a way that the rest of us can hear," Kaylin argued. "They don't move in a way the rest of us can move. They don't—I'm sorry—bleed."

"Is bleeding necessary?" Gilbert asked. "You are not bleeding now."

"Well, no—I haven't been injured."

"Ah." He stopped. "Can you not hear them?" he asked her. "They sleep. They breathe. They murmur."

"Not to us."

"They are exactly like you, Kaylin."

Since they were male and, well, dead, Kaylin felt under-standably frustrated.

"They are exactly like you would be if you existed outside of time."

"What do you mean, outside of time?"

He glanced back; Kaylin squinted in the light of a thousand eyes—or what felt like a thousand eyes. "They have been re-moved from time."

"Kattea—"

"No. Kattea exists in time. At the moment, she exists in your time, for want of better words; she is here. She is present. I told you, you were created in such a way that you are like fish; time is your water. Removed from it, you will drown in air. They have been removed. They will die. But they are not yet dead. Time does not move for them the way it now moves for you."

She struggled with this, and found she could almost accept it. What she didn't understand was why. "Why did someone take them out of time? I mean—how is that even possible?"

"I am uncertain as to the mechanics," Gilbert admitted. "But there is a schism here. A break in time. Something has tunneled into the structure; there is a crack, a fissure. It is what destroys you, in the end."

"The fiefs—"

"The Towers protected the fiefs, as you call them. The break was infinitesimally small. We would never have noticed it under normal circumstances."

"The *entire city is gone.*"

"Yes. But time moves to that point and past it. It is continu-ous. The only reason we are here at all is because of that break. I do not lie, Kaylin. It is possible for me to travel. It is not pos-sible for me to interact with you while I do so. You are...so much a part of time you can hardly be seen. To my kin, the loss of your city—the loss of your world—would not register. It is only because of the inversion that I could speak with your Nightshade. When I left in search of a pathway that could return him to his home, I did not choose to surrender that inversion.

"But it is not natural, to me. It is not...simple."

"Then why did you do it?"

"I was...curious."

Kattea lifted her head. "Because," she said, "he's lonely."

CHAPTER 26

Gilbert did not deny Kattea's simple statement. Kaylin wondered if he understood what it meant.

But she thought of Tara, and her long search for—in the end—Tiamaris. She thought of Helen, and her patient wait for a tenant who would value her and—yes—love her for everything that she could, and wanted to, give. She thought of the Hallionne Kariastos singing a lullaby in the quiet of a West March night. She thought of the Hallionne Bertolle, whose brothers she had woken from their figurative graves, and his gratitude for it.

And she thought, in particular, of Hallionne Oberon's Avatar, cradled weeping in the arms of the Lord of the West March.

Not by any stretch of the imagination were these buildings—and they were buildings—mortal or normal. And yet, they all understood loneliness.

She wondered if being lonely was part of the base state of existence. Hadn't the Devourer been lonely, in the end? Was it really so hard to believe that Gilbert was lonely?

No. No, it wasn't.

Was it impossible to believe that Gilbert could want—could make—friends? That he could come to feel friendship with Nightshade strongly enough that he felt moved to help him?

Kaylin exhaled. No.

Nightshade was still *in* his Castle. He had been pushed ahead to *this* time, weeks after the first disruption. Kaylin was pretty damn certain that what was happening on the Winding Path was the disaster that caused his Castle to throw him into the heart of Ravellon.

But if they prevented the disaster that caused the Castle to send Nightshade into the heart of Ravellon, Gilbert would not meet him.

Yes, she thought. *Yes, Kattea. You're right.*

But there wasn't a damn thing she could do about it.

By the time Gilbert came to a halt, the underground was bloody cold. It was also…wet. Water lapped around the edges of their boots and continued for as far as the eye could see. Gilbert's many eyes provided illumination that was simultaneously disturbing and welcome.

The water had carried Gilbert through the halls before.

"Yes," Gilbert said, although she hadn't spoken. "We are close. Be cautious here; the water is not consistently deep. There are unexpected—what do you call them? Wells?—beneath the surface. They are not wide, but they are also not," he added, "easily navigated. Mandoran, please watch your step."

"We can see them," Mandoran replied. He was nervous.

Kaylin was nervous as well, possibly for the same reason. She wasn't particularly surprised when the water grew choppy, and six inches began to swell into something closer to midthigh. "I want a boat," she said to Kattea, who had continued her struggle to stay wakeful.

"If we—if we fix things, if we save the city, can I meet my parents?" she asked. She asked in the same tone she might have used to ask if she could have wings. Kaylin knew. She'd asked both questions, in her distant childhood—even when she knew the answer was, and would always be, no.

"Yes. You can meet your parents. Or at least your father."

She nodded into the crook of Gabriel's neck. "I don't *want* to sleep," she murmured. "You'll just leave me behind."

"He will not recognize you," Gilbert said gently. "He will not know you."

"I…I know that."

"You cannot apologize to him."

"I know. I *know* that."

Gilbert's eyes—about half of them—turned to Kaylin. "I do not understand this."

But Kaylin shook her head. "Yes, you do. You left the *gardia*, and home, to free Nightshade. He won't remember you. He won't be grateful. You will be no part of his life. He's not the most trusting or friendly of men—he couldn't be, and still be fieflord. Even if you wanted to make friends with him again, it wouldn't happen. He was willing to be vastly more open with you than he is with *anyone* because he had nothing to lose.

"You know that you'll lose that, but you came anyway. Kattea wants to see her father in the same way. Just—to see him. To know that he survives, and that he has a life, and that eventually he'll have her. She wants to see her mother for the same reason. But…"

The Arkon caught her shoulder and gripped it tightly enough that she fell silent.

Kattea lifted her head. "Why are you stopping her?" she asked, in a bleary tone. "She's not saying anything I don't know. Gilbert's Nightshade won't exist, if we save people. And that means I won't exist, either. The city won't be lost. My parents won't flee across the bridge. Their daughter will live in Elantra. She'll grow up here. Maybe she'll become a Sword. I don't know."

"Is that—"

"I was going to die anyway. I was going to die. Gilbert found me. Gilbert saved me. But in my future, in a future without Gilbert? I'm *already* dead. And it hurt." She shook her head. "There's no future for me, no matter what I do. I get that. But there's a future for my mom. There's a future for my dad.

"I wasn't a great daughter."

"You don't think your father understood that you loved him?"

"It *doesn't matter.* I told him—" She buried her face. "It doesn't matter. Just—promise I can see him, if we all survive."

"I promise."

Gilbert led them, at last, to his room. The halls appeared to travel the length of the city; they branched in multiple places. There were no doors that Kaylin could see, but there were places that appeared to be almost entirely underwater.

"Yes," Gilbert said, again as if she'd spoken out loud. "If you take this stretch, you will find yourself in the Tha'alani quarter. I do not believe the water will drown you." He glanced at the Barrani and added, "That applies purely to Kaylin. It is not safe for the rest of us."

"And you know this, how?"

"The water is speaking," Gilbert replied. "It is…angry, but sane. It is here that the water will remain while it retains its human sentience."

"Does the water kill the Tha'alani?"

"If you do not know, I cannot answer; I cannot sense their deaths. I am not in the moment of those deaths."

"Gilbert—you said when you arrived here you could no longer see time."

"Yes."

"Can you see it now?"

"No. But I can sense it now. I am not certain what will happen to you if you ascend the stairs," he added. He had come to stairs. Kaylin even recognized them. "Kattea, wait in my room."

"No."

"Kattea—"

"*No.* I'm not gonna say goodbye. I'm not. This time, *I'm going, too.*"

Gilbert looked—well, a swarm of eyes did—to Kaylin for support. She wanted to give it to him. Kattea was a child. She was an older child, true—but there was room for her in the Foundling Halls, and Marrin would see that she was both safe and fed.

Kaylin meant to say as much. She opened her mouth to say it.

But from a remove of years—and years—she could see Kattea from the inside of the girl's life. She could feel the want—and the decision—as if it were her own. How old had she been when she went to work for Barren? How old when she'd learned a dozen ways to kill? How old when she'd killed?

Kaylin, Severn said.

I can't. Don't ask me. I can't.

"Kattea," Severn said, "I am neither Gilbert nor Kaylin; I am not a Dragon and I am not Barrani. I'm not certain I have much to contribute beyond this point—will you wait in Gilbert's room with me? We have much in common."

Kattea looked at Severn, really looked at him.

"I'm not certain I have much to contribute; I may distract Kaylin because she'll be worried. You may distract Gilbert for the same reason. He's asking you to remain behind because you'll be safe."

"But you're her partner." Kattea was the daughter of a Sword. An officer of the Halls of Law. She knew how partnerships worked.

"But she's Chosen."

"What does that even *mean*?"

"She can cheat. She can use powers the rest of us can't—not even the mages."

"So…you're like the lame duck?"

"Yes."

Severn—don't lie to her.

"You'll stay with me?"

"Yes."

"Gilbert, you promise you'll come back for me?"

"Yes, Kattea."

Kaylin had very, very mixed feelings about leaving her partner behind, but very clear feelings about what he was now doing. "He will keep you safe," she told Kattea. "He kept me safe for years. My mother died when I was five, and I never knew my father. I just had Severn and the streets of the fiefs."

"Teela's not impressed," Mandoran whispered.

"Tell her not to report me. If we actually manage to get out of this in one piece, I could finally make corporal."

"Not leaving your backup behind, you won't."

Kaylin cursed but kept on walking. Gilbert found the door to his room. It was not in the same location it had been when Kaylin had come to heal him—if healing was even what she'd done. But as she crossed the threshold, her arms began to glow. Kattea's giggle made it clear that her neck was doing the same; the girl thought it funny because Kaylin had a soft halo around her head.

Severn settled down at the desk; Kattea sat cross-legged on the bed. "Can you read?" she asked.

"I can—any book in particular?"

It was the last question Kaylin heard as she closed the door.

"My thanks," Gilbert said to her. "It is difficult to do what must be done while Kattea is so close. I fear to injure or break her. She is delicate, her connection to life so tenuous. Will she be stronger when she is older?"

"She won't be Chosen, if that's what you mean. And she probably won't become Severn without a lot of trauma and training."

"It is odd. She is like Nightshade, and yet, unlike Nightshade. It was the work of decades to become attached to the sound of his voice, the tenor of his very quiet thoughts. Kattea has none of his power. If Kattea had been pushed into Ravellon, she would have died before her voice could wake me. The air might kill her. The night. The wrong morning mist. She is loud and she feels both pride and shame; she is constantly in motion, even when she sleeps.

"Many were the discussions I had with Lord Nightshade; many were the topics we discussed. I learned the history of the Barrani; he learned the history of my kin; he explored the *gardia*, where it was safe to do so. I saw wonder in him, and through him, wonder at things that had never moved me before.

"I felt peace when he spoke of his brothers. No, I felt peace when he spoke of Annarion."

This couldn't fail to get Annarion's attention.

"He was subject to time as you were meant to experience it," Gilbert said to Nightshade's younger brother. "And you were subject to a type of freedom that you were never meant to have. You did not expect your brother to change. He finds it uncomfortable to be judged by you, because you haven't changed in ways that are clear to him. What you want and what you believe—of honor, of justice, of duty—he once believed. He does not wish you to see him as he sees himself. He has a very ferocious pride.

"But I wander. Nightshade's mind is sharp, as is his curiosity. If we did not understand each other immediately, we learned;

he asked questions that remain with me now, and I will have the answer, although not soon.

"Kattea is not like Nightshade. Her temper is quick to light, and her tears, quick to fall; she sleeps, she eats endlessly when given opportunity, and she asks no questions that I understand." He lifted an arm and pointed; the arm seemed like velvet obsidian to Kaylin's eye. The lamps reflected off wet floor, but not off Gilbert.

The stairs hugged wall.

"What do you mean?"

"How does the sun work? Why do the moons exist? Why are there dogs?"

"Those seem like perfectly reasonable questions to me."

"Do they?"

Kaylin frowned. "Your room—it's waterproof, right?"

"Yes. It is proof against any element; it cannot be pushed out of phase."

"Good. Get up the stairs. Move. Move move *move*."

The Arkon was less equivocal about these stairs, although they appeared to be wooden slats; he went up first, quickly followed by Mandoran, Annarion and Gilbert. Kaylin, at the foot of the stairs, turned to face the water as it lifted itself from its bed of ancient stone floor.

The water emerged in the shape of a woman with hollow eyes; she wore a dress that literally flowed down shoulders and arms, its hem blending with the inches of water that remained on the floor. "Kaylin."

Kaylin nodded.

"Chosen."

She nodded again, aware that her marks had continued to brighten; they were not as sharp a light as Gilbert's unattached eyes cast, but they were the same color. Two watery hands rose in a swift snap of motion that ended with...eyes. The water then took those eyes and inserted them into her own sockets; golden light was absorbed by the water, changing every element of its color.

In a face of water, the two eyes looked almost natural. "The Keeper is holding the fundaments in place. The only element to escape—to be forced out—is water, for reasons that must now be obvious. Nor is it all of the water—but the part of me that exists in another story, another ending, cannot merge with the containment. I hope your Evanton survives.

"Mine did not."

"What was done—what's *being* done—it breaks the Keeper's Garden?" Kaylin asked. It seemed the only germane question, because the water might actually know.

"The Keeper's Garden exists in time; it requires time. We do not, not in the same fashion. It is only in our interactions with you that it is a necessity. We are part of your life. You are part of ours. Someone sought to emulate the Garden itself; they did not understand the construction required. The Keeper's stones are not stones, except to your eyes. They are names, Kaylin. They are the force of the truth of fire, water, air, earth."

"There's more than one truth."

"There is more than one interaction, and we have loved the stories you tell us of our import to your kind. But those stories are not truth as we understand it. They are not," she added, her voice darkening, "truth as others understand it; the small moments in which you take joy are not...joy to them. Perhaps once they were.

"The Keeper's Garden has proved unassailable without internal aid."

"But—"

"Come. I have seen death, and loss, and it is fresh in me

because it is part of me. The greater part of me that sought to preserve you was most tightly wed to the *Tha'alaan*—but that is not all that I am. We must find your bodies. We must find your stones."

Kaylin frowned. "The stones in the Keeper's Garden are meant to contain the elements?"

The water said, "Yes, and no. While we retain a thread of attachment to ancient vows and containments, we *will not* harm him if he stands thus."

It was, Kaylin thought, a variant of Ybelline's protective barrier.

"Why stones?"

"I do not understand the question."

"Why four stones?"

"They are not precisely stone. But they are anchors, Kaylin. They are the heart of an ancient vow. While they stand, the Keeper stands. While they stand, the attachment to world and time and your kind also remain."

"And he needs the anchor."

"The world as you exist in it requires them. The lack of those anchors will not harm us, and it will not destroy us; it will destroy some small part of what we are."

"And the Arcanist needs anchors." She spoke the words slowly, as if testing them.

"There is a problem," the Arkon said, from the top of the stairs.

Of course there was.

"What is it?"

"There seems to be no house."

"You expected that." It wasn't a question.

"In some fashion, yes. Mandoran?" To Kaylin's surprise, the Arkon's tone implied that he considered Mandoran a *peer*.

The Barrani hesitated. It was Annarion who said, "The inside of the empty sphere that's eating the city is not empty."

Kaylin snorted. "What, exactly, is at the top of the stairs?"

Squawk. Squawk.

Gilbert's many eyes widened. "I understand," he said, voice grim. He pushed his way to the top of the stairs, and given the width of the stairs, this took time. "Chosen." The single word was almost a command.

Kaylin would have followed anyway—because his many eyes had come to rest around her like a swarm, and they appeared to be attempting to adhere themselves, through cloth, to the runes on her skin. If she hadn't been afraid of squashing them, she would have brushed them all off.

Mandoran caught her arm as she moved past him. "Teela's voice is much, much clearer."

"So...we're probably where she is."

"Yes. For some reason, this is pissing her off."

"Can you *try* to use High Barrani?" Annarion said.

"Why? Kaylin never does. It's about *communication*, brother."

"Has she moved at all?" Kaylin said, hoping to stem the tide of a different kind of brotherly interaction.

"How did you guess?"

"If nothing's broken, she hates to stay in one spot. Did she find Bellusdeo?"

"...No, sorry." At Kaylin's reply, he turned back to Annarion. "See? Completely colloquial."

"She's not Barrani."

Mandoran shrugged. "Popular wisdom says neither am I."

"Chosen," Gilbert said, demanding attention that should never have been diverted. Kaylin made it the rest of the way up the stairs.

The elemental water reached out with a single hand. She said nothing, but Kaylin understood what the gesture meant. Before she had learned to hate the world, it had been one of hers. After she had learned that the world was not only pain, disgust and death, she had struggled to learn how to do it again. It was harder, the second time—but maybe it was just as necessary.

Without a word, Kaylin took the water's hand. The water didn't have the same trouble negotiating the cramped stairs that Kaylin—and everyone else—did; she simply followed by Kaylin's side, as if she could walk on air. This was wrong, of course: she rose, the water on the ground her elongating pedestal.

There was no small hall. There was no parlor door. There was, however, a front door, if by door one meant a structure that looked as if it had literally been created by a four-year-old with a crazy assortment of chalk. Or fifty four-year-olds, all vying for the same few yards of space.

"Look ahead," Gilbert warned. "Look *only* ahead."

She could hear voices to her right and her left; they sounded like mortal voices. Elantran voices. She froze. She had seen her share of conflict; she knew what battle sounded like. There was fighting—and dying—to either side of this primitive stretch of ground. She turned to the right—or tried. The small dragon smacked the bridge of her nose with his head. Hard.

He followed it up with complaints. Since it was Kaylin whose eyes stung with the force of the blow, she felt this unfair.

"They are echoes. They are not real. Do not *make them* real."

"How the hell do I make something *real?*"

"Obey Gilbert," the Arkon said. His voice was a great deal louder than the voices to the right and the left. It came from behind; he might as well have picked her up and shaken her until her teeth rattled, because the syllables reverberated throughout her entire body. Even the eyes clinging to her shirt seemed to wince.

"Should you even be up here?"

"Someone has to keep an eye on these two," he replied. "Do *not* look back."

"He means us," Mandoran said. Annarion, predictably, said nothing.

To the water, Kaylin said, *Can you look?*

Yes. But I understand what Gilbert fears; I consider his advice wise. You will not make things real, *as he states—but you will be drawn to them; they will be like gravity, and you, like a person who has taken steps off a very high cliff. They are possibilities, Kaylin—but you exist in a world of constant possibility. To look—left or right—is the equivalent of making a decision, of acting on it, yes? The action decides the course you follow; reality asserts itself around that choice. Your reality.*

But people are—

Dying. Yes. And they are being born. And they are loving. And hating. And weeping in sorrow or joy. They are pleading. They are screaming. They are singing. Those are the sounds of your lives. She smiled as she spoke, but it was not a happy smile.

Kaylin nodded, exhaling. "We're walking between possibilities."

Yes.

"And if we choose one, we'll fall off *this* path."

Yes.

Fine. It made sense, in a strange way. To the Barrani, Kaylin said, "Do you guys see a door ahead of us?"

"If you call that a door, yes."

The Arkon's magic made Kaylin's skin itch. As they walked, itch transformed to pain. She didn't ask him what spells he was attempting to cast, because she was certain he felt they were necessary, and his was the voice that counted here, according to the Hawklord. But she was very grateful Kattea was no longer with them, because Gilbert…was losing solidity as he walked.

No, not solidity, exactly—but form. The darkness of his silhouette spread and thinned, and as it did, she could see the moving squiggles of opalescent color she associated with chaos, and only with chaos.

The small dragon squawked loudly and then, to make a point, exhaled.

He exhaled a stream of silver that was flecked with the same opalescence. Kaylin froze, and because she had, the Arkon walked into the back of her feet. "Private?"

"My familiar just exhaled."

"Yes, and?"

"I've seen that breath destroy Ferals from the inside out, and I'd rather not get a face full of it."

Squawk. SQUAWK.

"I believe you have insulted your companion," Gilbert said.

"Not intentionally." She straightened her shoulders. "Fine. I apologize for my instinctive and very reasonable reaction." She closed her eyes and continued to walk. The air smelled of wilderness and forest and…cinnamon. When she opened her eyes, the particulate mist had not cleared; if anything, it had thickened. But it didn't sting her face or her eyes.

"Does this count as you helping me do something I can't do on my own?" She knew the price he had demanded for it the last time she'd asked, and she was not any more willing to pay it now.

No, her familiar replied. She recognized his voice instantly, and felt both gratitude and fear. Any place in which she could hear his actual words was never a *good* place. *No, Kaylin, it does not. It is a variant of what your Arkon is attempting to do.*

What, exactly, is he attempting to do?

Survive Gilbert.

CHAPTER 27

Survive Gilbert?

Look at him, Kaylin.

I've been looking at pretty much nothing else. Given that his eyes were part of him, this was mostly true.

You have not, the familiar said, with some exasperation, *seen him.*

She looked, and she saw it now: Gilbert was Shadow. Gilbert was darkness.

The halls beneath the city had reminded Kaylin of the High Halls because the ceilings were so tall.

Gilbert filled them. Not only in height, she saw that now, but in width. He was a moving cloud—a dense cloud, but one that implied spaces and gaps. His eyes were part of that; they weren't, as they had appeared on first—or fiftieth—glance, separate. They existed on the end of shadow tendrils, and they moved around Gilbert as if he were some kind of Shadow octopus, but with more tentacles.

She had no idea *how* he had carried Kattea on his shoulder or in his arms, because she couldn't see that he actually *had* either of those things.

Had she been standing on the border of Tiamaris, she would have tried to kill him.

No, actually, she would have accepted that she *couldn't,* and she would have retreated, a fancy word for "run for her life." She felt a moment of very visceral fear, but the fear was double-edged. The expected fear—of Gilbert—she accepted. She had no choice; it was there, rooted deeply by every other experience of Shadow she had ever had. But the unexpected fear, that *maybe* those other Shadows *had been* like Gilbert, and she had done her level best to kill them—that one was new.

And hadn't she feared—and hated—the Tha'alani in exactly the same way? Hadn't she viscerally, forcefully, made this clear *every single time* she mentioned them?

And hadn't she been wrong—so very, very wrong—in the end? But she hadn't *killed* the Tha'alani. She'd hated them, but she'd never killed them.

Shadows, she'd killed.

Yes.

Was I wrong?

Kaylin, it doesn't matter. If Gilbert—for reasons of his own—attempted to kill you now, and you stood still and reasoned with him, you would die. The Shadows may have their reasons; they may have motivations that you could—with effort—understand. But they would devour you whole if you did not flee or destroy them. You faced the Devourer.

I didn't hate him, though.

It doesn't matter. Hate him, not hate him, he would have destroyed not only this city, but the world in which it is situated. Sometimes motivation doesn't matter when survival is immediately at stake.

Gilbert's eyes glared pointedly at her. "What?" she demanded. "I'm still moving!"

She was, but it was hard. The badly drawn door didn't seem to be getting any *closer*.

"Gilbert," she said, to take her mind off the multiple fears that were all screaming for attention she really didn't want to give them, "you said it was your job to fix time, right?"

"A vast simplification, but yes. Why?"

"How do you *know* when it's broken?"

He stared at her, or rather, his eyes did. At this point, he was dark enough, amorphous enough, that she had no sense of which direction he was facing, and had to take it on faith that it was forward. "Ask the water, Kaylin. The water feared that I would destroy it."

The water was easier to talk to, in all ways, than Gilbert. *Do you understand it?*

Yes. I hold the Tha'alaan *within me, but it is not the whole of what I am. When I returned, some part of me was not bound by the Keeper and his Garden. The Garden is gone.*

But—the world exists because of the Garden.

Yes, Kaylin. Yes, and no, as you must now understand. The fiefs exist because the Towers could contain those living within their boundaries. But the fiefs of Kattea's experience are dangerously unstable. She has not spoken of all of it; I am not sure she is even aware of the differences, although she will grow to be so. There are four stones in the Garden.

Yes.

There are five cages, in your time.

The Devourer.

Yes, Kaylin. But he, too, is not what he was. He has heard our voices, and Evanton's voice. He sleeps. When he wakes—and he will wake—the Towers will not be proof against him. It was always, and only, a matter of time for the small pocket of your world that remains. For Kattea and her kin. For the Barrani. She hesitated. *The worlds the Devourer destroyed were all part of your world, in some fashion.*

Kaylin's head began to hurt.

The way in which they were connected is through time. *But time, for many beings, is flexible. It can be manipulated. Such manipulations are not guaranteed to destroy. Think of creation as a vast plane. It seems endless. It is endless. You cannot see its beginning; you cannot see its end. You can dig. You can build. You may build a city. A country.*

But you cannot take the whole of the plane and fold it.

...

The Keeper's Garden is built on a foundation of elements and emptiness. Out of this, the natural order arises in this world.

Other worlds have different—

Yes, of course.

Even the ones that are part of that plane?

Yes, of course. When the plane is folded, it wakes—or once woke—Gilbert and his kin. He flattens it. It is what he does. He can see the plane as it extends through layers of time—but each layer must be distinct, its own. The layers do not contain him; he can pass between them, at need.

If the perturbation is concise, distinct, if it does not materially alter the shape of the plane, it is possible to ignore or overlook. Or to miss. But that is not, I think, what occurred here. What occurred here did not fold the plane—my appearance did.

What occurred here? Kaylin paused. Stopped. Thought about three non-corpses, three stones which must have been meant as anchors, and Arcanists. She hated Arcanists. The familiar—still in his most common form—bit her ear. Clearly, this was not the time for ranting, even if she kept it to herself.

"They didn't fold the plane," she said aloud, which probably caused some confusion to everyone who wasn't the elemental water. "They just cut a chunk out of it. Or they tried to cut a chunk out of it—and they're trying to anchor it, somehow. The chunk."

"Yes," Gilbert replied. "That is what I believe occurred. I do not know the *reason* for the attempt. Perhaps it is not about immortality as you define it. Perhaps it is…more."

"What was this building *supposed* to do? Do you even know?"

The Arkon said, "I think that largely irrelevant."

"But if we know what it was supposed to do, if we understand how it was supposed to work—"

"Private, your grasp of subtlety is nonexistent. It is almost a negative. When I say *irrelevant*, what I mean is *forbidden*."

"Forbidden?" Mandoran asked, voice cooler.

"By Imperial Decree."

"You're the Emperor now, are you?"

"I am the keeper of the archives; things ancient within the boundaries of the city are my responsibility, by *Imperial Decree*."

Gilbert said, as if the Arkon had not spoken, "We have assumed this is a matter of time. I do not believe this is necessarily accurate, given the lack of overall disturbance. But there are other factors involved in this plane you call your world. There are actions the Ancients could take that you cannot take. You are Chosen, but you are confined, in all ways, by the limits of your state.

"The Ancients were not. *I* am not. You see me, now, as I am—but you cannot see all of me. Nothing I could do to you would permit it. Mandoran and Annarion can see more—but it is that ability that makes their existence so tenuous in your world. They are trying...to invert themselves. Do you understand?"

"You mean—invert themselves the way you inverted yourself to talk to Nightshade?"

"Yes."

"Uh, that's not how we see it," Mandoran cut in.

"No?" The eyes—even the ones on Kaylin's arms—swiveled to try to get a glimpse of Mandoran.

"Definitely not."

But Kaylin said, "Do you think that someone like me—or Teela, or the Arkon—is trying to invert themselves in the opposite direction?"

"I fear that is very much the case. I do not know how Annarion or Mandoran came to be who, or what, they are, but it is not, in my opinion, something that you could survive. Not even as Chosen."

"So…the person who did this is probably dead, and we're left with the disaster?"

"I do not know. I do not know who did this. I can make guesses as to why—but it is my supposition that they sought to be free of all confines."

"Which means?"

Mandoran snorted in derision. "They wanted to be gods."

Kaylin, looking at the eyes on her shirtsleeve and the swirling Shadow tendrils that seemed to be the whole of what Gilbert now was, said, "I bet it's overrated."

"I don't know. We're not gods. We have trouble being whatever it is we now are. Gilbert?"

"Yes."

"The door's not getting any closer."

"No. No, it is not. Please brace yourselves."

The Arkon grunted.

The familiar said something in a language Kaylin didn't recognize. The meaning, however, was plain. *Just use Leontine,* she told him. *That's what the rest of us do.*

It does not come to me as naturally. Forgive me any pain I cause you.

Kaylin had time to brace herself, but only barely. Many things seemed to happen in a frenzied rush, but they were each distinct enough that she could catalog them.

First: the water *roared.* The sound was similar to Dragon roaring, but it resonated in a different way. Possibly because the water was in her ears. Literally. The Avatar lost form and shape as it rushed up Kaylin's arm to surround her in a moving pillar. Kaylin didn't even have time to hold her breath.

Second: Gilbert reached for the door. He reached with a multitude of tendrils, each of which ended in an eye. Kaylin could see the eyes dissolve, and wasn't squeamish enough—barely—to look away or close her own. It was as if the door was exactly what it appeared to be: a chalk drawing on cobbled stone. Flat and unreal.

Gilbert's eyes were crushed; Kaylin swore she could hear them squelching.

Third: the door *moved*. Under the locomotion of tentacles of creeping Shadow, it moved—directly toward where Kaylin now stood. *Protect the Arkon!* she thought desperately to the elemental water.

The water expanded. It expanded to encompass him, just as the door hit with the force of an Arcane bomb.

Kaylin was very, very, *very* grateful that Severn had chosen to remain with Kattea—because if he hadn't, Kattea would be here. She would be at the heart of the explosion, because that was where Gilbert was.

She would be at the very center of the expanding wave of something that was like Shadow, but paler, brighter and harsher. Water streamed away, as if the column that had protected Kaylin from the impact was wounded badly. Kaylin's arms were glowing a brilliant gold. She hadn't released the water's hand; her own still clutched it as if it were still in that form.

She instinctively tried to heal the water.

The familiar squealed in her ear. He didn't speak, but clearly she was about to be so stupid she didn't deserve actual words. She cursed him in gurgling Leontine and held on to the water as if her life depended on it.

"Remind me," the Arkon said, his voice very watery, "that I am never to be involved with one of your excursions again. It makes me angry."

For once, Dragon anger was not the biggest threat in the room. And *room* was entirely the wrong word for it. It was a space, yes—but it wasn't confined by walls or ceiling, or even a visible floor. Nor was it empty.

Kaylin, the familiar said. *Close your eyes. Now.* Before she could—and honestly, closing her own eyes should have been simple—he reached around her face with his wings and covered them.

The wings did not instantly ease the pressure of sight. Around her in a swirl of motion were faces, bodies, crowds; she could not pick out a single person because they moved so quickly that they were a blur. But even as a blur, she could recognize basic shape, basic form. She could see wings, eyes, skin color, limbs—even fur. She could gain a basic sense of height, of age; she could *hear* a plethora of voices, some raised, some muted.

And she realized that this was what had existed to either side of the strange corridor they had been walking. She had been told not to look. She wondered if looking now would have the same effect as turning would have had then; it would be so easy to be lost here.

But the water was in her hands, the familiar on her shoulder, the sound of an extremely disgruntled Dragon at her back. Something touched her gently—gently enough, carefully enough, that she didn't react violently.

"Kitling."

"Teela!" She turned then. Or she tried to turn. The small dragon's wings were *incredibly* strong; she couldn't move her head.

Mandoran cursed. In Leontine. "Grab Tain!" he shouted. Kaylin could hear his voice so clearly that the sound of the moving throng—the continually moving, dizzying crowd—was almost silent. She clung to the sound of his voice.

"I can't— He can't *hear me!*" Annarion's voice.

Kaylin was suddenly very, very afraid for Bellusdeo and Sanabalis. Because she suddenly understood that they must be here, as well.

Kaylin, close your eyes.

Bellusdeo and Sanabalis were here, among the hundreds. The thousands. The tens of thousands, even. They were here in every second of the whole stretch of their lives, compressed and overlapping. She had the sickening sense that she had to grab them. But she could only grab one of them, one each, and there were *too many*.

Kaylin. Your eyes.

And she understood, then, that these were the layers of which Gilbert had spoken; that every time, every second of time, was in some fashion its own discrete identity. That she existed in all of them, but that she could not live *aware* of each and every one. It would destroy her. She couldn't see past the blur; couldn't hear past the noise. She couldn't move without colliding with someone or something.

And she understood, as well, that in this throng, if she concentrated, she had to find *one* Bellusdeo. One Sanabalis. One Maggaron. And they had to be the ones that belonged where she belonged, in the same when, the same now. But it was worse than that. Because more than just Bellusdeo and Sanabalis and Maggaron were trapped here.

Teela. Tain.

Anyone who had lived or worked on the Winding Path. Most of those people were people she did not know and had never met. Most of those people were not yet aware of where they were or what had happened—but as she watched, as she failed to close her eyes, she realized that they were becoming aware. They didn't see as she saw—but they saw *something*. The tide of voices turned to confusion, and from there, to panic.

Panic was never good in a crowd. And this crowd was endless, eternal. It went on forever.

She wasn't sure when the first death happened.

She wasn't certain when it spread. But it *did* spread. She could see blood. Could hear screams. Could only stand, helpless, while the world spun and spun and spun.

Kaylin.

Severn. Severn's voice. And Nightshade's. They overlapped—but each voice was singular. It was not a crowd of voices. It was not multiple Severns or multiple Nightshades. They were on the outside. They were the people she had known. They were not every possible person she might know or could know at every stage of their lives or her own.

They were the people with whom she had a known history. She wanted to weep.

Can you see it? she asked them. *Can you see what I see?*

Yes. Again, they answered in concert.

Nightshade said, *The disturbance has not spread to the fiefs. I am, however, unable to use the mirror network within the Castle.*

She nodded. *I think—I think we've been walking in the mirror network.*

Doubt, from Nightshade.

Cautious, surprised agreement from Severn.

What did Gilbert do?

I—I'm not sure. I think he may have collapsed the network completely. I don't understand how, or why, but—something was done to the network and its power, and I think… Gilbert could make halls or paths out of it.

The world around her became silent as she spoke.

She opened her eyes. She couldn't remember closing them; she could remember being nagged *to* close them. She almost closed them again. She stood in the streets of her city. The street itself, the cobbled stones, had a curious, blurry quality. The bodies did not. They were stacked; they overlapped; they should have been a mountain of corpses. And they were, but they occupied the same space.

There was no clear path from this street to the house in which the theoretical murders had taken place, and Gilbert made it clear that he intended to climb over them.

Kaylin had seen corpses before. She had never seen a battlefield.

"Mandoran?"

"Here." She turned, or tried to turn; the familiar bit her.

"Oh for hells' sake, you stupid—" She bit back the words, because she could, once again, see Gilbert—and she decided that she did not *need* to see Mandoran and Annarion. Gilbert, in the great, carved halls beneath the city, had looked like the epitome of a one-off Shadow: tentacled, walking death. In the streets of Elantra, now, it was worse.

He didn't climb over the bodies that littered the streets in uncountable numbers.

He *ate* his way through them. She could hear every bite, every swallow. Her hands were on her daggers; her arms glowed. So did Gilbert's many eyes, because the damn things were *still attached to her.*

She looked at the eyes while Gilbert's very disturbing meal continued. One part of her brain told her to calm the hell down: the people were *dead.* They couldn't feel pain, and they didn't care what happened to their bodies. It wasn't as if they could use them for anything, anymore.

The other part of her brain was actually working.

"Gilbert," she said while she looked at one of the many eyes. "I need you to find my friends."

"Your friends?" he said. He swallowed. She really, really wanted to be sick.

"Bellusdeo. Sanabalis. Maggaron. I think Mandoran has Teela. And I think Teela has Tain."

"And the rest?"

She said nothing for one long breath. "And the rest. But I *don't know* them. I can't tell you who to look for."

"No, Chosen." The eye to which she'd been directing most of this conversation began to blink rapidly. "But it is not necessary. I am not what I was when you first encountered me."

He certainly wasn't. The creature that he had become couldn't *fit* in his house, for one. "What you did for me, as Chosen, was necessary, and I thank you." The eye rose from her shirt. So did the rest of the eyes. "But what I must do cannot be done while I am so confined."

As he spoke, he rose, and rose again, until the skies were all of Shadow, and eyes. He descended upon the house in which the murders—the non-murders—had taken place. And he froze part of the way there, in midmotion.

"This...is not good," Mandoran said, from behind her.

The Arkon roared. There were words in it. Kaylin turned, and this time, the familiar did not attempt to prevent it.

A golden Dragon reared its very large body in a street with a lot fewer corpses, and roared again.

And another Dragon answered.

"Bellusdeo!" Kaylin shouted. The bodies that had been a mountain and a nightmare were sparser now. Kaylin could see the house in which the three men had first been discovered. The front of the house was irrelevant; the Arkon breathed, and fire turned it to ash and melted stone almost instantly.

"Arkon—stop—"

He roared again. Kaylin said, to the familiar, "Stop him from destroying the house—"

Stop him from attempting to enter it, Kaylin.

Her brows rose in outrage. The Arkon was full-on Dragon; she was full-on Kaylin. She couldn't stop him from walking across a *street* when he was in human form; she had no chance—at all—of stopping him if he decided to go on a rampage.

Stop him; it is not safe.

"For him or for me?"

For any of us.

Bellusdeo is there—

Yes.

Kaylin nodded. "Arkon! Bellusdeo is in the house; if you destroy it, we'll *lose her*!" She wasn't actually certain that this was true. But she was certain it was the *only* way to catch his attention. And it worked. Of course, this meant she had the full attention of a red-eyed, raging Dragon.

"Gilbert?"

Silence.

She looked at her hand. It was wet, but the water was now absent. All that remained of what had been a pillar was…two eyes. She could no longer hear the water's voice. She could no longer hear the voices of anyone who wasn't actually standing in the street beside her. Well, plus Severn and Nightshade.

The two eyes the water had taken had not returned to Gilbert. They floated at roughly eye level, as if they were still part of the nonexistent element. As she repeated Gilbert's name, they swiveled to look at her.

"Were you trying to destroy the house? Or preserve it?"

"One question at a time," Mandoran suggested. He walked to where Kaylin was standing. Teela was by his side—literally. It looked as if her leg was broken or badly sprained, which was almost enough of a shock that she forgot to think. Annarion was carrying Tain. He was in worse shape.

But he was certainly well enough to open an eye and growl at Kaylin—in mewling Leontine.

"Fine. Suffer. It's not like we actually need backup that's useful and mobile."

Teela snickered. Tain growled again.

Now that she looked at them, neither Mandoran or Annarion were looking all that great, either. They weren't physically injured, but she had seen dead Barrani that had healthier color.

"He was trying to crack the house open," Annarion said. It took Kaylin a moment to realize that he was answering the question she'd asked the disembodied eyes. "The house is where we have to go. Gilbert has—arranged things in a way that won't destroy you."

You. Not us.

"He can't make it all safe. He's—he's placed us all in the same layer of time. But he requires power and he can't make it stick for long—something is pushing against it."

"In the house."

Annarion nodded.

"When you say 'you' and not 'us,' does that mean—"

"We can see...more." His smile was strained.

"I can hear your brother. He is very, very clear now."

Annarion seemed to sag, as if something had been cut. "I don't imagine he's saying anything repeatable."

"Not really—but some of it's Barrani, so it might be useful later."

Mandoran managed a weak grin. "What kind of Barrani? Ouch!"

Annarion hadn't touched him.

"We need to enter the building. I guess the Arkon made

it easier; it's not like the walls are going to keep us out. The Arcanist was doing something with the three bodies. They were laid out as if they were part of a ritual. I'm guessing," she added, staring up at the frozen shroud of darkness, "that ritual is almost complete, and that Gilbert is buying us time." She picked her way over the few bodies that remained; there was no smell, here, which made it easier. Or rather, there was—but it was cinnamon. Evidently the familiar's cloud was still protecting them.

Mandoran and Annarion hesitated.

"Stay here," Kaylin told them. "I'll go with the Arkon."

Teela said, "They are not staying here." Her eyes were a murderous blue, and her lower lip was swollen. "And I'm not, either." She pulled herself away from Mandoran. Sprain, then.

"Teela, I don't think it's safe for them."

"And you think it's safe for you?"

"Chosen, remember?"

"You don't even know what that means."

She is not wrong, the familiar said.

Do not foolishly insult her, Nightshade said. *An'Teela is known for both her cunning and her ability to nurse a long grudge.*

Severn, on the other hand, said nothing. It was a comforting nothing; an acceptance of things he couldn't change.

She looked at the floating eyes. "Can you keep them coherent? Can you keep them safe, here?"

Gilbert didn't answer. The two of his eyes that had once been set into the water's Avatar floated away, gaining speed as they approached the two Barrani. Mandoran raised his hands to swat them away. Annarion, on the other hand, had an armful of Tain to deal with.

Regardless, the eyes gained enough speed to ram into the foreheads of both Mandoran and Annarion.

Mandoran had developed very, very impressive Leontine.

Annarion, Kaylin decided, was just one of those people to whom cursing would never come naturally. Which was a pity; Kaylin would be swearing herself blue in the face had one of those eyes attached themselves to her actual forehead.

Both the Barrani now had a third eye—an open third eye that was the wrong color—just above the bridge of their noses, between their brows. Their natural eyes blinked rapidly; the borrowed eyes did not.

When Annarion fell to one knee, Kaylin ran toward him. It surprised her—and his older brother—when he didn't wave her off. Instead, he allowed her to slide an arm beneath his arms and take some of his weight while he regained his footing. "My brother can see all this, can't he?"

"…Sorry."

"Not as sorry as I'm going to be." He inhaled deeply, exhaled and said, "Thank you, Gilbert."

Gilbert didn't respond.

"Does it help you to see?"

"Yes. It helps me to see only one thing. It helps Mandoran, too, but he's more vain. He really dislikes the *look* of the extra eye."

"Gentlemen," the Arkon said, in the testiest of voices. "You are all incredibly unattractive to *me*; the extra eye makes no difference. Shall we?"

Both Barrani had the grace to redden, which added welcome color to their faces. Nightshade was *not* impressed.

"What should we do with Tain?" Annarion asked.

"Give him to me," Teela demanded. "I'd wait outside, but I don't think outside is going to be any safer."

CHAPTER 28

"What do you see with the extra eye?" Kaylin asked. The Arkon's breath had gotten rid of the stairs that led to the front door—which was fine, because they'd also done away with the door. At the moment, Kaylin's primary concern was what remained of the first-story floor in the wake of Dragon breath.

The Arkon wasn't worried about the flooring or the possible fall, but he *was* a Dragon, after all. Kaylin, however, couldn't expect to fall through a crumbling floor and land without injury.

He pushed Kaylin out of the way and pretty much stomped in. "Where is the—" He froze.

This was *not* promising.

From her position directly behind the Arkon, Kaylin couldn't see what had caused him to freeze. "Arkon?"

"I do not care what the Emperor says," the Arkon said. "If we survive this, I am going to burn the Arcanum to the ground."

"You'd have the full support of most of the Halls of Law," Kaylin told his back. "What are you staring at?"

He moved to the side, and she entered the house—or tried. Standing in front of her, with a very dubious expression, was... herself. "Is this a mirror?" she asked the Arkon. "Can you see your own reflection?" She couldn't see his reflection—only her own.

"It's more complicated than that, but yes." He snorted in disgust, and small flames lapped the edge of his beard. The Arkon drove his fist into the mirror; the mirror didn't shatter.

To the familiar, Kaylin asked, "Can you do anything?"

Silence.

"Mandoran? Annarion?"

The answer was a resounding no. They saw exactly what the Arkon and Kaylin could see: images of themselves. Only Mandoran seemed to find this disturbing.

The Arkon chose to share his disgust in loud draconic. Kaylin lifted her hands to cover her ears, as his speech was *not* brief.

Bellusdeo replied. Her voice was thinner; it lacked its usual resonance. Kaylin told herself that this was because it lacked her usual *anger*, but couldn't make herself believe it. And only an idiot wasted time trying to believe their own lies.

"Is Sanabalis with her?"

"Yes. He is…injured."

"Maggaron?"

"He is—understand that this is Bellusdeo's phrasing—'stupid.'"

Which meant alive, but not in great shape. "Is she in the basement?"

The Arkon spoke again. This took longer. So did Bellusdeo's reply. "Yes. She recognizes it from Records. She cannot hear you, by the way; she can hear me. I do not think she can hear Annarion or Mandoran, either."

The two Barrani were conferring. They did so in silence, although Mandoran's expression made it clear that it wasn't an amusing conversation. "We think there's a way in," he finally said.

"Good," the Arkon replied. "Find it."

Mandoran approached the mirror. To Kaylin's surprise, she could now see his reflection as well as her own; the Arkon's was still absent. He reached out, placed his palm against the center of his own reflection and pushed. The reflective surface, which had showed no sign of reaction at all to a Dragon's weight and momentum, bent. It didn't break; it stretched.

Mandoran then moved a yard to the side and tried again; Annarion did the same in the opposite direction. Here, the lack of most of the front walls helped. But if the putative Barrani weren't as confined to *this* existence as Kaylin or the Arkon, it didn't matter. To their hands, the reflective barrier was not as solid, but it wasn't permeable. Nothing they did could bring it down.

Bellusdeo roared. This time, the Arkon did not respond.

"What—what did she say?"

"She is tiring," he replied.

"Does she say what she sees? Is there *any* clue at all?"

He didn't answer, and she was never going to be desperate enough to grab him by the shoulders and shake him. Not the Arkon.

Not Mandoran or Annarion, either. She backed away from the house and turned toward Gilbert—or what remained of Gilbert. He was frozen now, like a wave in motion—but with tentacles and a million eyes. He might have been the nightmare version of a starry sky. Or the monster version, if monsters told stories to their offspring.

And Gilbert was not a monster. Gilbert had saved Kattea. Gilbert was willing to save them all.

"Mandoran. Annarion. Come here."

"What have you found?"

She shook her head. "I think—I think I might have a way in."

They stared at her. She fished around in the small satchel of things-that-must-not-be-lost-on-pain-of-quartermaster and withdrew the very expensive pocket mirror the Hawklord had insisted she requisition. She wanted to stay in the quartermaster's good books. Or at least his mediocre books. Or even his minor-pest books—instead of his public-enemy-number-one books, which was where she often resided.

But in the close call between pissing off the quartermaster and pissing off the man responsible for her job, she'd chosen the quartermaster.

"That's a portable mirror."

Kaylin nodded.

"That you're not supposed to use."

She nodded again. The Arkon joined them. His eyes brightened visibly—which meant they became orange, rather than the bloodred they'd been stuck in—at the sight of it. "You mean to use the mirror network to get in."

She hesitated. "Not exactly."

"Not exactly?"

"I mean for Gilbert to use the mirror network to get in."

"There's a slight problem with that," Mandoran said. "Gilbert's not moving."

"I *know that*. But he's not dead, either. If he were, you wouldn't have eyes. I mean, you wouldn't each have a third one. And the third eye *is* moving, even if the rest of Gilbert isn't. I think he's—I think he's stuck like that on purpose."

"Because of the eyes."

"Yes, because of the eyes."

"She's going to strangle you," Teela told her friend. "And I might consider helping, even in my diminished state."

"Fine. What exactly do you propose?"

Kaylin handed Mandoran the mirror. The third eye widened. It looked as if it were trying to *expand*, and that was more disturbing than its continued existence in Mandoran's forehead. Annarion immediately came to join him, which had the same effect. Both of their eyes—their natural eyes—rounded.

"Or maybe I'll strangle Kaylin instead," Teela said.

Mandoran coughed and said, "You're the Chosen."

"Well, that's just *great*."

Kaylin rolled up her sleeves.

They don't even give instructions, she said to her familiar.

No. But, Kaylin, having observed your life for some small time, they don't give you instructions for living, either. Life happens.

Not everyone who is alive has marks like these.

No. And not everyone who has borne them hated or feared them.

Kaylin walked over to Gilbert, or to the part of him that she could actually reach, none of which involved his eyes. She touched the extended Shadow that was his body. It felt surprisingly like the mirror barrier that prevented entrance into the house, but it reflected nothing. This made sense. She didn't expect to see a reflection of herself in Gilbert, because in the end, he wasn't human. Or Barrani. Or Dragon. She could spend her entire life studying Gilbert, and she knew she would never understand most of him; she probably couldn't conceive of what most of him was.

He looked monstrous, to the eye.

But people who looked dazzling could be monstrous. She had some experience with that. And whatever Gilbert was, he had saved Kattea's life. He had not lied to Kattea about what he was. He had not promised anything.

He promised he would return to her.

Yes. But that wasn't a lie. Not yet.

He understood loneliness. Or maybe he didn't *understand* it. But he *felt* it. He was ancient, but in some ways, it was impossible not to think of him as young. It was the lack of practical experience. It was the open confusion. Gilbert had not learned to hide his weaknesses. On this plane, he didn't appear to even understand many of them.

"Gilbert, can you hear me?" She glanced at Mandoran; Gilbert's eye moved. "I—we—can't use the mirror network the way you've used it. Or the way I think you've been using it. I'm not sure it's even safe for us—"

The eye rounded.

"—without you. But we can't get in. I understand that you're buying us time—*our* time, our version of it—but the time won't matter if we're stuck outside." As she spoke, the light of the words on her skin dimmed. "Can you use the mirror network to build us a passage?" *And build yourself a mouth*, she thought, trying not to let anxiety tumble into frustration.

The eye in Mandoran's forehead narrowed.

"Can you hear *anything*?" she asked him.

"No, sorry. Don't give me that look—I'm trying. This is nothing like the heart of the green."

The words dimmed again. Kaylin held out a hand, and Mandoran dropped the portable mirror into her palm. "Records. Winding Path, basement."

Portable mirrors were considered conveniences for relaying information *to* Records. The small glass surface was not considered useful for studying that information, except in a pinch—which this was. Kaylin wasn't certain what the mirror would show and was almost disappointed to see a small, hand-sized version of the basement as she had first seen it, what felt like months ago.

"Records: bodies."

The image in the mirror moved exactly the way it would have moved on a normal day. She felt disappointment deepen and panic grow.

"Do not drop the mirror," the Arkon told her. His voice,

however, had lost the sharpness of edge. "Put it down, Private. Put it down carefully."

"But it's not—"

"Put it down."

She swallowed, nodded and bent at the knees, placing the mirror's nonreflective back against uneven stone. That done, she stepped back.

Shadow fell like a silent tidal wave. She stood beneath it, raising her arms to cover her face—which was both instinctive and less than useless. But the Shadow didn't hit her, didn't crush her—and didn't sweep anyone away. It didn't break stone or fence or lamppost.

As if the mirror were the very bottom of an impossibly large funnel, the Shadow condensed to a point, its height vanishing as the mirror absorbed it. The eyes that Kaylin always found so disturbing did not likewise fold themselves into the mirror; they remained arrayed around the group, encompassing Teela and Tain, as well.

Kaylin was knocked off her feet as she turned toward the two Hawks. She covered three yards, maybe four, as she tucked her shoulder and rolled, drawing daggers as she gained her feet. She turned.

The Arkon was in full draconic form.

He stood in front of something that looked vaguely like a mirror—if mirrors were made of polished obsidian. The street to either side of that obsidian surface was no longer visible.

"Next time, could you give me a bit of warning?"

"I did not think it wise for you to stand in the middle of the mirror as it transformed. I may have been mistaken. This is, I believe, Gilbert's version of a mirror." If it was, it was taller than the Arkon in his draconic form; it easily dwarfed Kaylin. "What do you see in it?"

"The…basement."

"Good. Stand aside."

Kaylin shook her head.

"Don't argue with a Dragon, kitling."

"Fine." Kaylin didn't waste her breath; she conserved it and sprinted. She leaped into the mirror, trusting Gilbert not to kill her, eat her or send her somewhere she couldn't afford to be, trusting him to somehow preserve her, as he'd somehow preserved Kattea, a different orphan from a fief that would—if this worked—no longer exist.

She thought she could hear his voice, although she couldn't understand his words. She *definitely* heard the Arkon's, reminding her that he had been designated her commanding officer. She didn't sit still in time to *hear* his command. Nor did she try to explain why she had to go through first, because she couldn't. In theory, a Dragon was a better advance force than a mortal. Everyone in this group was a better advance force than a mortal.

But she could see the net of Gilbert's eyes tightening around them; she could see the way their rounded surface reflected runes: her runes. She could see, as she moved through this passage, eyes that extended into the distance, and they seemed infinite. But they formed runes. Words. Hers.

Because Gilbert, as he was now, couldn't speak.

No. That probably wasn't true. Kaylin, as she was, couldn't hear him.

Be ready, Kaylin, the familiar said.

She burst into the basement and nearly tripped over a body.

The body was Sanabalis. He was in mortal form, he wore gray Dragon armor and he appeared to be bleeding. He also seemed to be wheezing. Bellusdeo, almost in mortal form, was encased in armor the same golden hue as the Arkon's; she was on her feet and armed with what appeared to be Maggaron's weapon. Her eyes were bloodred.

Kaylin couldn't see what she was fighting. Whatever it was, it drove her back; the sound of metal hitting something was loud and clear. Beyond the combat, Kaylin could see three men. They were no longer laid out in a row against the ground; they stood at three points of a carved stone triangle, facing in toward its center.

Kaylin landed and leaped instantly to her right; the Arkon came crashing down in the spot she had briefly occupied. He roared. The floor shook.

Mandoran and Annarion followed, and behind them came Teela and Tain, both of whom were on their feet. Kaylin felt magic's edge; she knew how they were on their feet, and she knew it wouldn't last. Tain, at least, found a patch of convenient wall near Sanabalis and braced himself against it.

Teela intended to fight.

What she intended to fight wasn't clear—at least not to Kaylin. She couldn't see it. Maybe the Arkon could. Maybe Mandoran and Annarion could. She could take care of herself in most of the fights her job made necessary—but this wasn't one of them. Let the immortals do what they did better.

To the familiar, she said, *Hide me.*

It is already done, but, Kaylin, be wary. What you face here is not a Feral or its distant, more powerful cousin.

She headed directly for the three men, who were—as Gilbert had said—not dead. Something whistled past her theoretically invisible cheek. She felt the sting of a cut and raised her hand; it came away bloody. She didn't swear—she headed straight for the center of the triangular formation and stopped.

There were three stones where the three living men were standing. They existed in the same place as the men, although the men didn't appear to be made of stone; the effect was disturbing. The men seemed to be breathing, but slowly, as if air was scarce. The stones appeared to be faintly pulsing in time to their labored breaths. Kaylin didn't have time to examine them more carefully. Or at all; something struck her arm, her right arm, and this time she could see the welt that crossed it, and the blood that followed.

She couldn't dodge what she couldn't see. And clearly, whatever attacked her could see her. The advantage in this space was not hers. The Arkon breathed fire; Bellusdeo did not. The fire didn't appear to hit anything; even the stone that made up the basement—and stone was not generally proof against focused Dragon fire—failed to melt or char.

And yet, the female Dragon's sword hit something; Bellusdeo could sense what Kaylin couldn't see.

Yes. She is not you. See what you can see.

I can't—

And her eyes opened.

Her eyes, that was, if she'd had a hundred of them.

It was not like being trapped in the maelstrom that had greeted her on the Winding Path. For one long moment, she could see, and she could process *everything*. Every iteration of Bellusdeo, of the Arkon, of the rest of her companions, fit together, overlapping in a way that felt right and made *sense*. Each image was distinct; there was no blur.

Yes, Kaylin. Gilbert's voice. It was a whisper of sound, a thin thread; it belonged to no one in the room.

I...cannot do more. It is here, it is in these layers, that you must find the aberration.

You can't?

Silence. Bellusdeo's sword flashed. The Arkon breathed again. Teela threw something—two dozen times—that looked like a spell. She could see Annarion and Mandoran; unlike every other person in the room, they had a certain solidity, a singular, uniform presence; their movements, their actions, were perfectly in line, perfectly synchronized, as if they existed across all possible slices of time in exactly the same way. There was no flickering; there was absolute uniformity. The only thing she couldn't see in the room was herself.

Mandoran turned toward her. His eyes widened as they met hers, and narrowed as he spoke—and she could *hear* his voice. She might not have been trapped in this strange state at all.

"Move it, Kaylin!" He was armed with daggers; Annarion had a sword.

So did their opponent, who might have been a ghost, the visual impression of his existence was so vague. She could see the pale, luminescent form of something that might once have been Barrani; it was amorphous, but sharply lit and strangely compelling. The only thing about him that appeared solid at all were his eyes. They were Barrani eyes, except in one regard: they had no whites. Where whites would have been, there was Shadow and the edge of chaos.

"Kaylin!" Annarion's sharp, clear voice.

Kaylin turned once again to the three men, to the stones and to the center of the triangle they formed. Like Annarion and Mandoran, the men were sharp, singular; they did not have the range of motion or action that anyone else displayed. They didn't sit or stand or slump—or bleed. She walked into the center of the triangle, hoping to find the answer to the problem there. It was just stone floor. It didn't glow. It didn't contain some sort of magical pillar.

It *did* contain the faintest trace of a caster's identifying sigil. She adjusted her vision, effortlessly looking out of different eyes. The sigil grew brighter and clearer as she worked her way through each viewpoint. Each eye offered a slice of event, a moment in time. She only had a hundred. She could have had a million. More.

The sigil grew brighter, and brighter still. She stepped slightly back, glancing again at the three men. And she realized that there were not three men. The three she recognized were the strongest visual image—but superimposed on them were other faces. Bodies she hadn't seen and didn't recognize. This was not the first time men had been laid in this circle. Not the first time this had been attempted.

But the other faces were made...of stone. They were somehow anchors for the person who had cast this long and complicated spell.

Gilbert said, *I cannot do what must be done without destroying everything this room contains. If I do what must be done, I will destroy you, this building, the entire mirror network.*

"And what about your rooms? Kattea?" Kaylin was afraid for the child.

Severn, by remaining behind, had given her a singular gift: he had lessened the one fear he *could* lessen. It wasn't a gift that he could have given so many years ago.

And he said, *You would have stayed with Kattea. But, Kaylin: you're the one with the marks. I'm just...*

Severn.

And he was.

Chosen. Kaylin. She nodded and turned away. Or turned toward; there was no away in this room. Every eye saw something slightly different. Every eye opened on a layer of...time. The events that destroyed the city occurred here. She only needed to find the right time, the right moment.

The eyes that were open would not close—not without help. Even this, she understood: they would not close without help. They had not closed the first time without help. She'd closed them then.

She could close them now.

It had taken hours, the last time. Gilbert could exist at any point, at any time—but Kaylin couldn't, and she didn't have hours. She frowned. She couldn't see herself. She couldn't see every iteration of herself that must exist. She was grateful to Gilbert then.

As she stood above the trace of sigil, the proof of a cast spell, she closed the eyes that did not lead to the beginning of the spell. She closed the eyes in which the Barrani—for he was that, or had started out that way—was nothing but a ghostly impression. She didn't need to touch the eyes to do this—she knew how to close them, having done it once, before.

She'd done it once so that he could function properly at her speed, in her time, with Kattea. She hadn't realized then what she was doing, and knowing it now changed very little except the fact of it: she could close the eyes. She could narrow the view.

She could find the moment in which the spell itself was taking shape and form. She didn't need to understand the spell. She only needed to stop it. To unwind, rewind and *find* the right moment.

"Mandoran!"

He looked up, his eyes widening, and nodded. His leap took him across the room; his landing, less graceful, almost knocked Kaylin off her feet.

Annarion moved to intercept; of the two, he was the better fighter, and if he carried the brunt of the battle, he didn't carry it alone. But he could see, blindingly clearly, what the others could only barely follow.

Kaylin understood how Bellusdeo had come to be injured. How Maggaron had almost lost his arm. How Sanabalis— ouch. She could see it all, as if each moment were captured in Records. And she could see the moment at which the three men in the circle lifted their heads, opened their mouths and spoke.

Their voices were louder than the Arkon's; they were almost on a level with angry Bellusdeo and angry Emperor. The edges of sound trailed from one eye to another as she followed it back, and back again, and froze.

She was almost there now; almost at the moment of the spell's culmination—and she suddenly realized it was *not* where she wanted to be. She wouldn't survive it. She would be pulled from the here and now of Kaylin Neya into whatever plane awaited the Barrani Arcanist.

She didn't even understand how the Barrani Arcanist remained trapped, if barely, in these ones.

Oh. Yes, she did. Gilbert.

She needed to shift her view to a different eye. She needed to stop the linear backward progression—and she was running out of eyes.

Yes. I am sorry, Kaylin. I borrow the power of the marks of the Chosen—but they are not infinite, as you are not infinite; I have tried to…isolate…the exact event in this location. This type of precision is not, was not, ever demanded of me. The Ancients wished to preserve the possibility of life—but the fact of life was of less concern.

She nodded. He wasn't offering a guarantee—but life didn't. It offered chances.

She hesitated; Mandoran turned his back toward her, bending slightly into his knees. Waiting and watching. "Can you see it?" she asked him. Her voice sounded wobbly and stretched.

"Yes." His didn't.

"But you can't reach him?"

"No. Not yet."

She didn't ask how he could see the Arcanist without being able to interact with him—especially not when *interact* meant kill. She needed to close or at least narrow the remainder of

Gilbert's open eyes, because it was becoming harder and harder to focus. Harder to find the moment in time—because there didn't seem to *be* one.

Gilbert—

"Kaylin!"

She stumbled.

"Kaylin." Mandoran's voice was beside her ear; one of his arms was under her arm, shoring her up.

"How long? How long ago was it?"

Mandoran's answer made no sense. Literally. It did not resolve into syllables. She wanted to cry; she felt as if she was fumbling the only chance she was going to get, and the cost of that fumble, the *cost* of it—

No. No. *Think, damn it. Focus.*

She tried. She moved viewpoint, moved vantage; she looked through every eye that remained. The Arcanist *would not* resolve. The center of the triangle, which contained the very real nucleus of a magic that made her entire body scream in pain, would not solidify in *any* of Gilbert's remaining open eyes.

Breathe, Kaylin.

Severn.

Breathe. Gilbert couldn't see what caused the break. He can't see it now—it exists outside his sphere of influence.

She knew this. She didn't resent hearing it. Severn's voice was calm, but not distant. She felt his concern, his worry—but there was no fear in it. Not like her fear.

You can feel the magic. You can feel it strongly enough. You're almost there. And he believed that she would get there; there was no doubt in his voice. She stood on that belief, because she had none of her own, and it helped. It gave her space to think. Again.

The voices of the three men were becoming stronger. Stuttering between them, other voices joined in. Kaylin pulled herself up and away from Mandoran, which took a great deal of effort. She turned—and this took effort, as well. It was almost as if she was becoming fixed or frozen; as if time was hardening around her and anchoring her in place.

And it wasn't the right place. Not yet.

The other voices drew her attention, because she couldn't see who was speaking—if the staccato sounds could be called speech at all. She turned, stumbled again and this time righted herself with the nearest object that wasn't Mandoran's arm.

It was stone.

It was stone that felt warm; it was stone that was in motion, vibrating as if struck.

It wasn't stone at all.

Across town, Evanton was attempting to use the stones in his Garden, or what remained of his Garden, as an anchor for… reality. She wondered if those stones were like these: these were almost like bells. Resonant, when struck, the sound growing louder before it died into stillness or the silence of the city— which was never truly silent.

Yes, her familiar said quietly.

The Garden's stones resonated with the names of the elements.

These stones didn't. Couldn't. But they spoke with the voices of…men. Of mortals—

Not all.

—of people like Kaylin, or Teela, or Bellusdeo, or Maggaron.

Why these three?

Three were needed, the familiar replied. *This is not the Keeper's Garden; the three were meant to anchor one small space for one brief moment.*

But why not immortals? Why not the Barrani whose name he owned?

The Wild Elements agreed to the cage of the Keeper's Garden. The three who are here chose to be here. Those whose name he might have known would almost certainly not.

She turned then and threw her arms around the stone she'd used to shore up her weight. Her teeth rattled with the vibration she both absorbed and muffled.

The light in the room shifted. Kaylin didn't turn to look at the triangle's center. But she didn't need to turn: she had Gilbert's eyes, and she could see everything.

CHAPTER 29

Mandoran's eyes widened. He abandoned his daggers, abandoned his position and—to a lesser degree—abandoned Kaylin. Kaylin grimaced. She didn't have Mandoran's True Name, or the True Name of any of his cohort, but she could practically hear Teela scream at him. She knew why he was there.

He threw himself around the second stone, just as Kaylin had thrown herself around the first one. Throughout, the men in the triangle stared straight ahead, as if they lacked solidity. As if they were simple illusions.

But nothing was simple.

The room shuddered again; the pain caused by magic increased. Kaylin clung tighter, not to still or muffle the vibrations, but to stop herself from screaming. She bit her lip, tucked her chin and cursed in slow, deliberate Leontine. It helped.

There *was* something in the center of the triangular formation after all.

She couldn't tell Annarion to hug the bell. He wouldn't survive it. She opened her mouth and closed it with a snap, but not before a single word managed to escape it. "Teela!"

One of her oldest friends—in all senses of the word—heard her. Or maybe she heard Mandoran. She flickered as she crossed the floor; she didn't close the gap in any consistent way. She ran; she walked; she vaulted; she edged around Annarion. All of her possible movements were traced across the air and across Gilbert's remaining open eyes, because each of his eyes could see her, and she wasn't exactly the same in any of them.

But she was Teela in *all* of them, and she understood exactly what needed to be done.

The Barrani Hawk reached the third stone, skirting the sides of the implied triangle, and threw her arms around it. Kaylin heard her grunt. She heard it clearly. But she was no longer looking at Teela. She was looking at the center of the room.

A dense, almost sparkling haze was beginning to form there. It implied shape, form and solidity without possessing any of these things. It made Kaylin's eyes ache.

No, not her eyes. Gilbert's eyes. Gilbert's eyes hurt. Gilbert's eyes watered.

Kaylin opened the two she'd been born with. She couldn't remember closing them, and it was very, very disorienting. Her two eyes saw less than any single eye of Gilbert—but they saw what they saw more clearly. Kaylin's back was toward the other two stones, but she could see Bellusdeo, the Arkon, Annarion. Behind them, Maggaron, Sanabalis and Tain. She couldn't tell if Sanabalis was still alive—not with her own eyes.

Gilbert's could see Sanabalis so clearly she might have been standing beside him—but Gilbert's eyes couldn't check a pulse. They couldn't touch anything, but they could, apparently, feel pain—and they could transmit that feeling to Kaylin, who was already in enough of it.

Grinding teeth, cursing in Leontine, she kept her hold on the stone, but shifted, turning her body, and therefore her head, her physical eyes—not Gilbert's—toward the center of the triangle.

Standing there was a Barrani Arcanist. He was striking because his hair—like the Consort's—was a white, long spill from head to midthigh; it was not the usual Barrani black. His skin was pale; he looked almost alabaster. His lips, his cheeks, the contours of his closed eyelids were so *still*. He wore a circlet much like the Arcanist Evarrim's. Kaylin couldn't tell what color the gem had once been. Now? It was scorched, cracked. She had seen this happen once, to a ruby, in the circlet of a different Arcanist.

Gilbert's eyes couldn't actually see the Arcanist. Kaylin's now could. But Annarion and Bellusdeo continued to battle with someone or something Kaylin still couldn't see clearly.

"Mandoran, Teela, can you see him?"

Teela lifted her head; her eyes narrowed. "Yes, kitling."

"Can you—"

"He's not corporeal," Mandoran said.

"What *else* do we have to do?" Kaylin shouted. She had to shout to be heard over the growing noise of stones, people, combat. She had to shout to be heard over her own fear.

"Gilbert has to *see him*!"

And Gilbert couldn't. But Mandoran could.

"Look at him!" Kaylin shouted.

"I *am* looking at him!" the Barrani who was not quite Barrani shouted back. Two of his eyes were blue; one was a golden orb.

She understood, finally, as she met its lidless stare, that the thing that shed light at its heart was a word.

A true word.

"Mandoran, *look at him* with *all* of the eyes in your head!"

"I can't—" His blue eyes widened.

Kaylin turned the rest of Gilbert's open eyes toward the Arcanist they couldn't see. Mandoran turned the single, foreign eye in the same direction, at the same time.

Light blinded every one of Gilbert's eyes that Kaylin could use. It might have blinded the one in Mandoran's forehead;

she didn't know. She couldn't see out of that one. She couldn't see out of the one Annarion carried, either.

But the voices of the three stones converged into a single, resonant voice: a high cascade of syllables that sounded almost like the notes of a song. She nearly joined it, it was that compelling. She could *feel* it as much as she could hear it—probably because the entire front of her body was now plastered against the oddly warm stone surface. She couldn't mute it in any other way.

Almost, she didn't want to. Almost. But her familiar bit her ear. At this point, she was almost numb—his teeth couldn't compete with the pain the magic was causing. Or they shouldn't have—but he wasn't just a translucent lizard.

Kaylin lifted her head; she'd tucked her chin, the way she always did when pain was harshest. Tears trailed down her cheeks. She was certain that blood also trailed down her ear, her neck. It was a different kind of pain; it braced her.

Arms shaking with both tension and the vibration of the stone around which her arms were wrapped, Kaylin understood that when the stone stilled, when this eerie, unintelligibly beautiful song faded, it would be too late.

She wasn't the Arkon. She wasn't an ancient Barrani. She wasn't Gilbert or Tara or even Helen. She had straightened the lines and shapes of true words; she had touched them, intuiting meaning slowly and with effort; she had held them together. She had carried them—and was still, in some fashion, carrying them now. She had even spoken them.

She had never spoken them without the aid of someone who was an ancient, powerful immortal standing almost literally over her shoulder and speaking them into her ear. The small, ancient, powerful immortal sitting on her shoulder was only biting at the moment.

It was possible that Gilbert was trying to speak. It was possible that he was standing over her shoulder and screaming in her ear—if he could even *find* it, right now.

She met Mandoran's borrowed eye, swallowed and spoke the word that gave it its light.

Or she *tried*.

Kaylin understood that this word, this word at the heart of Mandoran's borrowed eye, could be spoken because she had seen Sanabalis do it. She had seen the Arkon do it. True words tugged at her memory. They always sounded familiar; they sounded like something she should recognize, should be able to repeat, should understand.

But her own fledgling attempts to speak them had always been a fumbling disaster. It had taken months to be able to think and hold the name of fire for long enough to light a bloody candle. She didn't have months now.

You do, Kaylin. It was the familiar. *If you require them, you do.*

I don't have time.

No? You don't understand where you are or what Gilbert has done. You have *time. You have all the time in the world.*

What?

You have time, Kaylin. The path that makes your minutes and hours is—was—broken here. It is twisted and stretched. And...it is now a contained anomaly.

What will it cost?

She felt his approval and hated that it made her feel better. She wasn't a child, anymore. She shouldn't *need* approval.

To succeed? You have all the time in the world. They do not. To take the *time, you will have to do what the Arcanist has done: step out of time. Uproot yourself.*

What if—

Yes. Think of the life you live now as a cloth. Your Arcanist has slashed it. There is a long cut, but it can be stitched or mended. There are two sides from which you can mend it. One requires speed, and one does not. But if you mend it while you are entirely uprooted, you will not be able to return.

But won't I—

Cause the same disruption as the Arcanist? No. There is a difference.

She swallowed.

Gilbert is here now. Gilbert is aware of you.

She did not want Gilbert to destroy her.

He will have no need. You will be adrift from the thing he is meant, and was created, to safeguard, and there will be no tear. What happens to you after is not his concern. Understand what he said, Kaylin: he could repair what has been broken here, as can you. But you are needle and thread. He is torch and sword. He will destroy anything that is dependent upon the cloth, and he does not wish to do so. He is trying to preserve you.

Why?

Because Kattea was correct. Find a way.

Something hit her in the face. She didn't lift her arms, because the stone was still vibrating; it was only the muffling that suspended or stretched the moment itself. Her cheek stung. It burned.

Yes.

It was Nightshade's mark.

Your brother is going to be so pissed off.

He laughed. The laughter was wild, loud—it was almost the type of laugh she was used to hearing from Mandoran. *You stand on the very precipice, and that's what you think of? That my brother will be angry with me?*

She thought her cheek would blister, and she held on to the sensation. She had always been, and remained to this day, afraid of Nightshade.

Yes, Kaylin. Nightshade understood the value of fear. *I will not allow you to do this.*

Don't, she told him, weary now. *Help me, or leave me alone.*

Help you?

Yes. She could see the cold expression on his perfect face; she could see the color of his eyes. She couldn't touch him, but… he was here. She accepted it. She felt the pain recede. She was right, too: her cheek was going to blister.

But she understood what she had to do. She called Ynpharion, the Barrani whose ambivalence was one part gratitude, one part disgust and three parts resentment; he was the only one whose True Name she held against his will.

Lord Kaylin!

I know. I know. I'm in the center of the storm, and I need your help.

He was instantly wary. Instantly cautious. The High Halls was mobilizing around him, but he had frozen, and when he moved, he moved toward the Consort. *I am never far from her now.* He said it with pride, with yearning and with—yes—a tingle of fear. The Barrani did not trust. *What help do you command?*

Just—stay here. Stay here. Speak to me.

He was confused. He was suspicious. He was, however, willing. He didn't fight her at all.

She then reached farther, to the West March. *Lirienne.*

Kaylin? She could see, in the distance, the exterior of the Hallionne Alsanis. *Yes. The Hallionne has summoned me. Sedarias is…concerned, and the Hallionne cannot calm her. What has happened?*

Mandoran, Annarion and Teela are with me, and we're—

She gave up on words; she let him see.

He didn't ask what she wanted or needed. He didn't ask what she commanded; if she held his name, it was, in the end, with his permission. All of the power she had over the Lord of the West March was theoretical, and they both knew it.

This annoyed Nightshade. For once, he kept his criticism to himself.

The Lord of the West March smiled; she felt the warmth of his expression. *When*, he asked, *will you visit?*

Not right now.

The smile deepened. She held on to it as she reached for the last of the names she knew, the last of the things that were true and prickly and binding.

High Lord. His was not a name she called. It was not a name she approached. On most days—good *or* bad—she buried the knowledge as far away from conscious thought as she possibly could. Lirienne had chosen—as Nightshade had chosen—to gift her with knowledge of his name. The High Lord was more complicated.

She felt his eyes open and look inward, and they burned like green fire. He did not seem surprised.

No.

She wanted to apologize for bothering him, even given the circumstances. She wanted to let go of what she'd touched and back as far away as possible. The only person who agreed with this choice was, of course, Ynpharion.

But it was too late.

Show me. The words were a command, and she obeyed instantly; had started to obey before she'd really registered the silent words. His touch was not gentle.

My sister will be angry, he told her, *if I lose you.* She saw him so clearly she thought he must somehow be here. In this room. In this fight.

Ynpharion was annoyed. Annoyed and awed. *You feel the presence of the High Lord.*

Yes. But she felt the pull of all of them. She felt their weight. It was a weight she had taken on in ignorance the first time; it was a weight she had required to save a life; a weight she had given, willingly; and a weight she had taken without permission.

She held on to all of them. She wove them together. They were her tether.

She turned to Mandoran once again, and she looked at the word that he carried. It was not part of him, but at the moment, it was not separate.

She listened.

She listened to the voice of the stone.

She listened to the sound of Annarion's sword, of Bellusdeo's sword; she listened to the crackle of the Arkon's fire, the Arkon's magical focus.

And then she cut herself off from each, one at a time, concentrating until the only sound that remained in the room itself was the quiet, constant hum of a single word. She strained to hear it, because she couldn't move—and neither could Mandoran.

Her voice was thin, weak, when she lifted it. It was hesitant, which annoyed at least three of the people whose voices she could not—and did not want to—silence. She *knew*. She knew that hesitance was very much like silence; it was like the wrong word, the wrong language. She strengthened her voice. She began to struggle with syllables, with stringing them together in a continuous shift of sound. With speaking as if the spoken word *had* meaning.

And this annoyed only one man.

Shouting, he said, *is not a sign of strength. It is a sign, perhaps, of bravery or foolishness—but not strength.*

You *say it*.

She felt his annoyance. It was bad. But she understood, as well, that the High Lord couldn't *see* the word. He could see what she saw, but only to a point. It was like Teela and Mandoran or Annarion. They were willing—sometimes eager—to explain, to let her see, but their explanations made no sense to her. Teela couldn't process them.

She let panic go. Of all the weights she carried, it wasn't one she could afford. She looked through Gilbert's eyes—the ones that were open. Gilbert's eyes couldn't see the word there, either, which made no sense.

It is your word, Kaylin, the familiar said. *It is a word absorbed from you.*

The word hung in the air, at roughly the same height Mandoran's forehead had been from the ground. She listened again. She strained to bring the sound closer. The word drew closer instead. In shape, in size, it seemed simple, but as it approached, she saw that it was more complicated than it had appeared at a distance. The single line that underlay the whole wasn't actually a line; it was a composite of strokes, of lines that appeared to move in the same direction.

Closer, she could hear it. It was like a chorus of sound. She had one voice, and she faltered again. She could not repeat what she heard. Not all of it. Not all at once, if ever. But…if this was like a chorus, there had to be a melody. And that, she thought, she could follow.

Kaylin. Severn's voice. It was thinner, quieter, than it normally was. All of their voices were. She wanted to tell them to shush, to let her listen. She didn't, because Kaylin realized that was where it would start: these were the voices that connected her, in some fashion, to a world outside of Gilbert's eyes and Gilbert's power. If she lost them, she would never find her way back.

They couldn't see what she saw. They couldn't hear what she heard. But they could see some part of her, and at least one of them could see it more clearly than she could see it herself. She willed them not to let go of it.

She couldn't see cloth, as the familiar had described it, and that made her task harder. But she looked at the word, and only at the word, and she felt her panic recede. The marks on her arm were visible, even though her eyes were closed; they were the only other thing she could see.

No.

No, that wasn't true. She could see the Arcanist. His eyes were closed; he looked waxen, graven, a thing of stone. She wouldn't have said he was alive, because she could see no hint of breath, no motion at all. She could see no sign of life in him.

This was significant. Had she been able to feel the beat of her own heart, it would have been fast. But she felt oddly disjointed now, as if her own body was no more alive than the Arcanist's. Her eyes were closed, of course. She shouldn't have been able to see him. Yet his image filled her vision—as did the glowing marks on her skin.

But she had always been able to see words.

How had she taken Ynpharion's name? He hadn't chosen to expose it or offer the knowledge of it to her. She hadn't carried and completed the name that would define both his place in the world and his power in it, as she'd once done with the High Lord. She had taken it because she could *see* it. She could touch it. She hadn't had to speak it at all.

How had she preserved the one rune from the Lake of Life that she had given, in the end, to Gilbert?

She had grabbed it. She had held it. She had placed it on the only easily exposed skin available: her forehead. The words she had forced herself to speak, with Tara as a crutch, had never been hers. The words that she had placed in the core of Helen were not words she'd *spoken*. They were not even words she had her own words to express.

She had a thing or two to say to the Ancients, none of it particularly polite. Why had they chosen someone to speak the remnants of their old stories when that person *couldn't speak the language*?

Because, she thought, speaking it wasn't necessary.

They were simultaneously her words, and yet not. She was part of their telling, but they were not, had never been, her story. She didn't need to be anything other than what she was—whatever that was now. She fell silent, staring at the Arcanist. Loathing—and she really did hate Arcanists—fell silent, as well. She did not understand, and would probably never understand, the *why* of what he had attempted to do.

And it didn't, at this moment, matter. She understood her own "why." It was in this room: Teela. Tain. Bellusdeo. Maggaron. And yes, Annarion, Mandoran. The Arkon. Sanabalis. It was Severn and Kattea. Lirienne. The High Lord. Nightshade.

Even Ynpharion, although he despised her.

Beyond them, the Halls of Law. Marcus. His *pridelea*. Caitlin. Joey and the mother she felt she knew, although she'd never met the woman. The Hawklord. Marrin and her foundlings. Evanton. Helen.

The Emperor. Diarmat. She didn't even grimace, thinking his name.

All the things she loved. All the things she hated. All of the people.

She reached out and caught the floating word at the heart of Gilbert's eye in both of her unseen hands. If she understood what had happened, it was one of her words, anyway—one of the ones she carried as both responsibility and bane. She felt its edges as sharp, painful things; she felt the whole of its weight.

And then she turned toward the Arcanist, made hollow by his own action. Fractured by it, so that part of him was fighting Annarion, and possibly killing Dragons, while he somehow remained here. She whispered Severn's name, over and

over, listening for him. Listening for him as she'd listened for
him for eight years of her childhood.

Hearing him in echoes, in fear, in hope. The other voices
were there, but so muted, she could barely touch them.

It is different, the familiar said. *You gave Severn your name.*

She placed the word she carried against the forehead of the
Arcanist. In the darkness of her closed eyes, the word seemed to
melt into his forehead; its golden glow spread from there across
the surface of his alabaster skin, changing white to something
warmer, something that might actually be alive.

Kaylin! No!

She felt Severn's panic—a sharp tug, an insistent, almost
overwhelming pull.

Not yet. *Not yet.* It was gone before she had to fight it.

The Barrani Arcanist opened his eyes.

Barrani had beautiful eyes. She thought this without desire, without warmth. The length of his lashes, the color like
a dusting of perfect snow; the width of his eyes and the shape
of them; the placement across the bridge of an unbroken, perfect nose.

They were beautiful. They were nothing like her eyes.

And they were a shade of purple Kaylin seldom saw. Purple
was the color of loss, of funereal grief; the Barrani offered it
to very, very few.

Grief.

As his eyes widened, as his face took on lines of expression,
they darkened as well, becoming a much, much more familiar
midnight. She might have taken an involuntary step back—in
part because it was the only smart thing she could do—but he
began to fade from view almost before the color of his eyes
had fully made the transition.

★ ★ ★

Kaylin. She felt the same visceral pull she'd felt the first time, but this time, she obeyed it. She had nothing left to fight with, and even if she did, she had no desire at all to fight.

She couldn't see. She couldn't see, and if she'd had the strength, she would have panicked. But Severn's voice—no, all of the voices she'd gathered and touched—came rushing in, to fill the void left by darkness.

She could hear.

She felt heat above her upturned face; she felt stone—suspiciously warm stone—against her arms and chest, and remembered the stone bell. It was still now. It did not vibrate. Nor did she hear the oddly staccato voices of the three men.

She heard blades clashing, and then she remembered.

She remembered the eyes of the Barrani Arcanist. He would die here, no matter how powerful he was; she was certain of it. If he was forced to actually face the people in this room— the least of whom was exhausted to the point of diminished vision and apparently clinging blindly to a rock—he wouldn't last five minutes.

But his grief—grief, not rage—cut her. She *knew* what would have happened had it not been for Gilbert, but she thought that maybe, *maybe*, the destruction the Arcanist had caused was unintentional. And maybe, if his only desire was to somehow be free, if he had somehow met Gilbert on his own, he might be at peace.

It was a stupid thought, and pointless, because he'd be at peace now, regardless.

"Kaylin."

She tried to speak, but apparently she'd been screaming, because her throat felt raw and scraped, and she could barely hear her own voice over the rest of the almost overwhelming noise in the basement.

"Kaylin, you need to let go." She recognized Annarion's voice.

"Are my eyes open?" she asked him.

"...Yes."

"I can't see you—"

"Let go, Kaylin." Pause. "Your *cheek*."

She smiled. "Yes. Your brother is...in his Castle." She groaned as Annarion apparently attempted to remove her arms—or her skin.

"You need to let go. The Arkon says we need to break these stones."

She looked, tried to look, at Annarion's face, which she assumed was in roughly the same direction as his voice. And she saw one thing: Gilbert's eye. Gilbert's only remaining eye; the others, she could no longer use. She couldn't really see out of this one, either, and realized that it was probably still embedded in Annarion's forehead.

He lifted her. He carried her. She cried the whole way because her skin hurt so much. She wished she'd removed all her clothing before she'd arrived in the basement, which was not technically legal.

The eye began to move. She could see no word in it; it was a simple, and small, golden orb, with a pupil that seemed to have depth; it reminded her, in a tiny way, of the small pond at the heart of the Keeper's Garden.

She tried to speak, but failed. She closed her eyes. She wanted to beg Annarion to put her down, but before she could, he did—and she watched this lone part of Gilbert, whose Shadow, whose presence, she couldn't otherwise see, move to what she assumed was the exact spot on which the Arcanist had been standing when he'd cast his spell.

She didn't know what Annarion was doing. She'd have to ask him, later.

But the sound in the room grew sharper and more distinct—which was not, in her present condition, a gift, exactly—as Gilbert's remaining eye grew less distinct.

She could hear Dragon roaring. She'd learned to differentiate between "discussion" and "argument" while living in the Palace. Most native draconian spoken in the Palace, on the other hand, was the latter.

And she thought, with increasing confusion, that one of the two voices—three voices—raised in argument was the Emperor's, which made no sense.

It was the last thought she had before she slid into a very blessed unconsciousness.

CHAPTER 30

Afterward, she heard the rest of the story, because she didn't really make it back in a condition to witness it for herself. The Arcanist had appeared in the center of the room. The fighting nearest the stairs stopped instantly, which did *not* mean that the fighting had stopped entirely. Given the other occupants of the room, the rest of the fight wasn't particularly long.

It was Mandoran who told Kaylin that Gilbert's eye—the one remaining eye, in Annarion's forehead—had left Annarion. And it was Annarion who told Kaylin that he thought Gilbert had used what power he could summon, through that tenuous connection, to patch the rend in time. To change the things that had happened. To bring the *rest* of the city back.

Annarion very deliberately ignored Kaylin's face for twenty minutes—or longer—of their first visit. When he couldn't keep that up, his eyes were drawn instantly to her cheek. Which was blistered and puffy. Nightshade's mark was, of course, still there—and Annarion understood exactly *why* her skin was blistered, and it reminded him of the very core of his anger at his brother.

Since his brother was actually alive, worry had given way to the usual resentment. The two of them were going to have to talk, but Annarion was unwilling to risk visiting Castle Nightshade again.

"I called him," she said quietly. "I needed his help to keep myself...here."

Mandoran said, "That's better than your usual attempt at lying. Half of it is probably true." When she winced, he added, "You're not going to make anyone believe that he burned part of your face at your request. Except maybe yourself. The rest of us are actually Barrani. We know how it works." She realized, with some surprise, that Mandoran was almost as angry as Annarion.

Tain had cracked ribs and a pierced lung. It was Teela who passed that news on. Tain was apparently recuperating in a building that wasn't sentient and didn't also contain Mandoran and Annarion.

"Did I really hear the Emperor?" Kaylin asked the Barrani Hawk.

"I'm certain even the dead heard the Emperor. That's a yes, by the way."

She wilted. And fell asleep.

She slept on and off for three days.

During that time, Helen visited frequently with food. Marcus's wives, led by the indomitable Kayala, visited, Marcus in tow. It was always funny to see Marcus surrounded by his wives; he was like a kitten. She was never stupid enough to *say* this in his hearing, though. Moran visited while Marcus was present, chatted amicably with his wives and gave Kaylin a very, very thorough medical inspection. She treated the burn on Kaylin's cheek, as well.

Since she was not actually in the infirmary when she did this, Kaylin had hopes that her demeanor would be substantially different. Clearly, exhaustion had made her stupid. Moran told

Kaylin—and Helen—in no uncertain terms what she *expected* of Kaylin's convalescence. Kaylin didn't pay much attention to most of it, but Helen certainly did, and Kaylin tried to remember that she had *wanted* Moran to live here.

Caitlin visited, with food. And flowers for Helen, just because. The Hawklord did not visit. The Arkon did not visit, either, but that was probably for the best.

Kattea, drawn and silent, her expression the forced smile of a child who has nowhere else to go and knows it, visited; she came in with Helen and left with her. Helen informed Kaylin that Kattea would be staying temporarily. Well, technically, Helen *asked* if Kattea could stay. But she asked in a tone of voice that made it clear there was only one acceptable answer.

Since it was the answer Kaylin would have given regardless, this was fine. Kattea, however, was not—and Kaylin could not force herself to stay awake for long enough to do anything about it. She did ask Kattea about Gilbert, heard Helen's *very* sharp intake of breath and let the matter drop.

Bellusdeo came by with, of all people, Sanabalis—who was not dead, but looked almost as if death would be a mercy, his color was so bad. Bellusdeo's eyes were a shade of orange that shifted perceptibly to gold when she saw Kaylin. "This is the first time you've been awake while we've been here," she said, by way of explanation.

Kaylin deliberately didn't ask her about the Emperor. She did ask about the Arkon, and both of the two visitors winced.

"Lannagaros is not, perhaps, in the most social of moods," Bellusdeo said. "I am sure he will recover. Lord Diarmat inquires after your health." Her smile was slightly edged as she added, "His concern almost appeared to be genuine."

"He just wants us back in class."

"Of course."

★ ★ ★

Severn didn't visit, and that was worse.

On the morning of the fourth day, she had a visitor she hadn't expected.

You should have, he said, standing on the steps leading to the front door.

Yes. Maybe she should have. The mark on her cheek was no longer quite as puffy and sore. All the rest of the pain caused by magic faded when the magic itself did. Trust Nightshade to be an exception.

She was more or less on her feet. Although Marcus had told her not to come into the office for a week—with pay, even— she was restless, and therefore chose to dress for work. If work clothing wasn't exactly lounge-around-at home clothing, she took comfort in it anyway. And it wasn't as if Helen was going to judge it.

"I should hope not." Helen's voice was not accompanied by her Avatar.

I do not think I will be allowed entry without your direct intervention. Which made it pretty clear where Helen's physical representation actually was. Kaylin moved, crossing the floor and the halls to reach the stairs almost before she took the time to think. The small dragon flew from the left side of the pillow— his de facto perch for much of Kaylin's convalescence—to her shoulder; he wrapped his tail lightly around her neck.

Squawk.

Her home was not a place she'd ever expected to see the fieflord. Home wasn't a place she'd ever intended to *invite* him. But she didn't want Helen to reduce him to ash or send him to another dimension, either. They'd gone through a lot to actually bring him home.

Which was not, of course, his experience of events. He had

lost a month to the defense mechanisms of Castle Nightshade. He had not lost decades—if, indeed, Gilbert's approximation of the time they had spent together had been accurate—in the heart of Ravellon. Whatever had happened in some future, it was gone; it was in the past. And that was ironic.

She wondered if that was what had happened to Gilbert, but shook her head as she looked down the stairs. If Gilbert was gone *because* things had been changed, Kattea wouldn't be here. And Kattea was here, waiting for Gilbert with increasing impatience—which everyone expected—and diminishing hope. Which was heartbreaking.

Helen was standing in the doorway. The door was open, but Helen hadn't actually moved aside to allow Nightshade entrance. Kaylin could see her back. She could see the delicate lines of shoulders that were not *quite* elderly; she could see the stiff, straight fall of Helen's arms.

"Helen."

Helen didn't turn.

Kaylin came all the way down the stairs. She intended to join Helen, or to at least stand beside her—but Helen lifted an arm to prevent this from happening.

What did you say *to her?* Kaylin demanded.

I merely told her I wished to pay my respects to both you and my brother. There was a glimmer of dark amusement in the words. That and anger.

"Helen," Kaylin repeated. Even when the ancestors had attacked them all, she had never seen Helen behave quite like this.

Helen turned her head—only her head. Her eyes were jet-black. Her face had lost most of the lines that implied smile or laughter.

Is that really *all you did?*

Helen turned back to her clearly unwanted visitor.

I am not unwise enough to attempt to cause harm in a building of this type. I was perhaps under a misapprehension about the building's exact nature, as all of my knowledge comes—indirectly—from your first encounters with it.

Her name is Helen.

Silence.

Kaylin folded her arms. "Helen, please. He is not going to hurt me. He's not even going to try."

Helen did not appear to hear her.

"Annarion lives here. Nightshade is—as far as I know—his only surviving family."

"Did I not tell you," Helen replied, relenting enough to speak, "that I would not allow those who intended you harm across this threshold?"

"Yes. Yes, you did. But he has had *plenty* of opportunity to cause me harm in the past, and he's failed to take advantage of any of them. I don't know what he's done—"

"You do not understand the nature of the harm. Would he kill you? No. He would no more destroy *Melliannos*, his sword. Both you and the sword are of value."

Nightshade stiffened; his eyes were as dark as Barrani eyes could get.

"I do not intend to destroy him," Helen continued. "I do not wish to hurt Annarion, and his anger with his brother stems, at its base, from attachment."

"Annarion can't visit his brother in Nightshade."

"I fail to see how that is my problem."

"It'll be *my* problem if Annarion leaves the house. He's been able to move freely only when I'm physically *with* him. If you want me to see less of Nightshade, this is the safest place for *me* to be. I don't ask that you let him do whatever he wants solely because he's a guest." Which, to be fair, Kaylin knew would never happen. "But you're *here*. There's nothing you're not aware of.

"And he did help me," she added.

Helen's eyes narrowed as she glared at Kaylin's blistered cheek.

"...We had different ideas of what I was supposed to be doing during the confrontation."

"And his ideas were clearly of more value to him than yours."

"...Helen, he's *Barrani*. He's a Barrani Lord."

"So, if I recall correctly, is your Teela."

"You didn't see Teela when I was in training."

"It is in no way the same, as you are well aware," Annarion said from the top of the stairs. Kaylin had no idea how long he'd been standing there. He spoke in very stiff High Barrani, and his eyes were as dark as Nightshade's, if for entirely different reasons.

Kaylin placed a hand on Helen's shoulder. "Helen, please."

Nightshade was, if anything, more annoyed. *Do not beg a building such as this. You are Lord here, or you are prisoner. Choose.*

"That's not the way Helen—or I—work. It's not the way we *need* to work."

Then you are subject to its—

Her.

...her *whim*. His eyes narrowed, and he turned away from the door. *This was an abominable idea. I have no idea why I am here. I almost cannot believe the centuries I spent attempting—in some small way—to retrieve the brother I could not believe was dead.* He headed down the stairs.

"Helen, *please*."

Helen exhaled. It was a sound that was vaguely reminiscent of Dragon.

"Nightshade!" As he continued to walk away, she said, "Calarnenne." She spoke without force, as if it was merely a mortal name. He stopped.

Annarion had come down the stairs; he'd reached the doors. Helen's ability to shield his presence extended to the fence line, but he was understandably reluctant to test this. Kaylin glanced at his expression. It was nowhere near as shuttered as Nightshade's, and yes, there was anger in it.

Anger, she thought, and bewilderment.

"They need to talk," she told Helen. She spoke very quietly, but without hope that either of the two men would fail to hear her.

"Then perhaps it would be best if they used the Twilight Room. I do not like this, Kaylin. I understand that you accept certain attitudes as inevitable cultural behavior. But Lord Nightshade is unlike the other Barrani you have invited as guests."

"I am not more of a danger than Lord Teela," Nightshade said, voice sharp, eyes narrow.

Helen's eyes rounded. They were still obsidian, but the expression itself was more human.

"Lord Teela," Helen replied, in a voice that was about as soft as her eyes, "does not trouble herself to hide her thoughts when she enters Kaylin's home."

"My thoughts," Nightshade said, "are not your concern."

"No. But Kaylin is." Before Kaylin could move, Helen reached up and gently touched the mark Nightshade had placed on Kaylin's cheek.

Kaylin was surprised. It no longer hurt, and she didn't resent it nearly as much as Annarion, Mandoran and Helen did. "No, you don't," Helen said.

At least teach your Helen that she is not to reveal the thoughts you are wise enough not to put into words.

"But none of our anger is as deep as Teela's." Helen shook

herself, and as she did, she resumed the most familiar of her forms. "Annarion? The Twilight Room?"

Annarion nodded grimly.

"Will you require refreshments?"

"I'm not sure, yet."

"Should I inform Mandoran that the meeting will be private? I believe he is...concerned."

Nightshade's anger turned on edge—and gave way to a bitter amusement.

"Yes," Kaylin answered, before Annarion could. "Tell Mandoran exactly that. It's not like he's not going to know if Annarion needs backup."

Helen led the way.

Her voice, however, remained behind, and when the Barrani and her own Avatar had cleared both the foyer and the visible upper hall, she said, "He feels that he owns you."

"He can't own me. For one, it's illegal. For two, he's wrong. I'm not responsible for how he views me. I can't change it. I'm responsible for how *I* view me, and I'm telling you it doesn't matter."

"He does not have friends, Kaylin. He has lieges and servants. He does not understand family as even Annarion understands it. What you want will never be of value to him in the way that what he wants is. I cannot read him," she added. "But he is powerful, and that attitude combined with power is not...safe."

"No, probably not. But—he *did* spend centuries trying to find a way to reach, or free, his brother. And I actually really like his brother." She exhaled. "I don't know how he feels about his brother *now*, but...he's capable of more than you fear. I know he is."

"Perhaps. But you are not his brother. I do not like this,"

she added, belaboring the obvious. "But I have grown fond of Annarion, and Annarion *is* his brother."

The discussion wasn't over by dinner. It wasn't over by the time Kaylin went to bed. Nor, apparently, was it over when Kaylin woke the next morning.

It wasn't over when she'd finished breakfast, either, and Mandoran, her only company at the table, was distracted by it because he couldn't hear most of it.

"Helen can," Kaylin reassured him. "Annarion's not in any danger."

"Not physically, no." He exhaled and changed the subject in a particularly Mandoran way. "Moran's not going to be happy that you're walking around the house like that."

"I didn't break a leg," Kaylin replied. "There is nothing— besides a small burn—wrong with me."

"That's not what she thought."

"Believe that I know what she thought." Kaylin grimaced. "But I'm well enough." She stood.

"You're going to see Kattea?"

"Yes. I don't suppose Gilbert showed up while I was sleeping?"

Mandoran shook his head. "The Tha'alani castelord did, though."

"Is she still here?"

"No. Where are you going?"

"We promised that we would do one thing for her if she would help us," Kaylin replied. "And I am going to do that one thing if it kills me."

The wing of the Halls of Law occupied by the Swords never looked as messy and cramped as the Hawks' office. The choke point was a desk—a very tidily kept desk—behind which Jared sat. Jared was a giant of man, shoved into a chair. Time had made him balder and a little wider; it hadn't made him more patient. This was because patience was his single saving grace, and he couldn't possibly contain any *more* of it and still be part of reality.

She cleared her throat when he lifted an inquisitive brow. "We're hoping to speak with a Corporal Krevel."

"Corporal Krevel? You mean Krev?"

Kaylin nodded.

"Idiot broke his arm in the panic. His left arm. He's in the back writing reports." Jared frowned. "Heard you'd done yourself an injury, too. What're you doing in?"

"I'm avoiding Caitlin—and Moran. Mostly Moran."

"So you're not on duty today."

"No." Kaylin lifted her right hand, and Kattea's arm came with it. She'd taken hold of Kaylin's hand when they'd entered the Halls of Law, even though she felt self-conscious about doing so. She was ten, not four. "I'm taking a friend on a tour of the Halls of Law."

"What did she do wrong?" Jared asked, smiling. Most of the smile was for Kattea. Kattea smiled back at him, but she continued to hide behind Kaylin.

"He doesn't bite," Kaylin told her.

"Much," Jared added. "Sets a bad precedent in the office."

"I've got a Leontine for a sergeant. Biting is pretty much standard operating procedure. Do you mind if we look around?"

"Does it matter?"

Jared's patience was not immediately obvious to people who didn't know him or hadn't worked behind his desk. He wasn't particularly *gentle*, and his kindness was of the gruff variety.

"Not a lot, no. I promise I won't break anything."

"Don't."

"What?"

"Don't make promises you can't keep. And I hope you're good at ducking." To Kattea, he said, "Most of the Swords here today are sitting at their desk until they've finished writing out their reports. We had a bit of excitement in the city last week, and they'll use any excuse they can to avoid the paperwork. It makes them cranky."

"If everyone already knows what happened, why do they need to write reports?" Kattea asked. Kaylin was a bit surprised, but as it was a bloody good question, she let Jared handle it.

"Because the Lord of Swords is not a patient man, and he can only be in one place at one time. When the paperwork *isn't* done, *he* gets cranky. I'd rather deal with cranky rank and file than cranky Lord of Swords."

"But why does—"

"Because if the Lord of Swords doesn't have those reports when he makes his own report to the Emperor, the Emperor gets cranky."

Kattea nodded. No one, no matter their rank or lot in life, wanted the Emperor to get cranky.

Given Marcus and his visceral resentment of paperwork, Kaylin was surprised to see that Jared's remark was true. The desks here were occupied by people who—while frustrated or grim—were writing. All of the Swords had been mobilized during the incident. The reserves had been called out, and shiftwork had been abandoned.

But the Swords—like the Hawks—were down in numbers.

Almost no one who worked on the force resented being called up in an emergency. Emergencies caused panic, and the Swords were trained to contain it and to insert themselves as de facto leaders into any group large enough to turn mob without warning. Almost no one, however, enjoyed it when paperwork was considered that emergency.

In other words, if there was a bad day to bring Kattea to the office, this was it. Kaylin drew Kattea aside and said, "I'm not sure this is a good day. No officer I know is in a great mood when they're chained to a desk with a non-life-threatening injury and being forced to write reports."

Kattea nodded as if she'd actually listened to—and heard—the words. But her hand tightened around Kaylin's, and Kaylin correctly interpreted this as *there are no bad days*.

Corporal Krevel was maybe fifteen years older than Kaylin at first glance; then again, his shoulders were hunched, and his hair looked as if he'd tried to extract chunks of it in frustration and had mostly failed. Kaylin started toward his desk, and Kattea's hand tightened. She stopped and turned to look at the girl.

And then, seeing her eyes—which were watery, but still managing to keep tears in the right place—she looked away. She hadn't rehearsed what she'd meant to say—which would have been smart—and found even the basics of general introduction had deserted her, because she was thinking like Kattea.

She was thinking of what she might have said to her own mother, if she'd somehow had a chance to go back in time to a point when that mother was still alive. She inhaled, exhaled and walked over to Krevel's desk.

Krevel looked up when her shadow darkened the paper on which he was, admittedly resentfully, writing. His fingers were ink-stained; his nails were short. His slightly narrowed gaze wasn't hostile; he recognized Kaylin's tabard. He didn't immediately recognize Kaylin, but seemed to think he should. After a moment, his eyes cleared.

"Private Neya," he said, abandoning the paperwork with almost palpable relief. Any excuse that didn't involve more death was going to be grabbed with both hands if it tried to escape.

"The same."

"Rumors of your demise were greatly exaggerated?"

"Evidently." She smiled, held out a hand; he shook it. She introduced both Mandoran and Kattea, and continued, "Caitlin says you've had some recent good news?"

He smiled broadly; the smile shifted the lines of his face, and possibly also explained the dark circles under his eyes. "Yes. Three weeks ago, actually—but in keeping with my wife's family traditions, it won't be public knowledge for another year."

"Why?"

Kattea said, "Because so many babies die early. It's bad luck."

Corporal Krevel looked surprised. "I'm sorry. My manners are appalling." He offered Kattea his hand; there was a moment's hesitation before she took it. To Kaylin, he added, "Missing Persons?"

"Missing Persons wasn't much help," Kaylin replied.

Kattea said, "No one is looking for me." She tried to smile. It took just enough effort that she lost control of her eyes— a control that had been shaky to begin with. Tears began to stream down her face as she forced her hands to her sides, where they balled in helpless fists.

Krevel frowned. "Are you all right?" he asked the girl. He lifted his gaze to Kaylin, which was a silent repeat of the question he'd asked. Kaylin had nothing to give him. She wanted to explain—and given the recent events, with large chunks of the city disappearing—she might have made the explanation stick. But...then what? According to Caitlin, they already had a child—a newborn daughter named Kattea.

Kattea nodded. She didn't speak for a long moment. "Can you tell me what you saw?"

"What I saw?"

"When the city disappeared?"

Kaylin threw him an "it's your job" look.

But Krevel, frowning, nodded. "You might want to grab a chair," he added. Most of them were filled at the moment.

Kaylin left to find a chair and was surprised when Kattea accompanied her. "He liked to tell that story, sometimes," she whispered. "I've heard it all my life."

Not exactly the stuff of bedtime stories, in Kaylin's opinion.

"He loved being an Imperial Sword. It was what he *did*. He said it was important to know what you stood for. He would tell me stories about being a Sword. I thought maybe I could be one, when I grew up." She paused in front of an empty chair, one of four against the wall nearest the Swords' duty roster.

"But...there was no Emperor. There were no Swords left." She smiled brightly, or tried. "I wanted— I know I can't hug him. I know he can't hug me. I know I can't apologize or tell him that I always loved him. Or tell him that I understood why he left.

"And I want to do all those things. But he's *not* my father. He will be. But he's someone else's father now. We're strangers." She exhaled and then turned, leaving the chair to blindly throw her arms around Kaylin. "I love him. But he doesn't even know me."

Kaylin held her.

"And it has to be enough to know that he's still alive. When the Halls of Law were lost—he said it broke something in him."

"He said that to you?"

Kattea snorted. "Not *to me*. He was never that honest with me. He treated me like I was a kid."

Kaylin did not point out that she was, technically, a child. She also didn't point that eavesdropping was rude, because rude or no, it was pretty much human nature. "Help me with

the chair," Kattea said, voice momentarily muffled. "I can't—
He won't—"

Hugging her tightly, Kaylin said, "Do you want to leave?"

Kattea shook her head. "He loved his job."

"Doesn't look like he loves it much right now."

That got a small laugh out of Kattea, which was probably as
much as she could manage. Kaylin disentangled herself from
the girl and helped move the heavy chair to where the corporal was waiting. Kattea brought it in close and crawled into it.

As it happened, Jared interrupted them before Krevel could
start.

"Bad news for the private," he said, waving Krevel back to
his report writing.

"Oh?"

"Moran wants to see you."

"I'm going to kill Clint." She turned to Kattea and her father and said, "Can you wait here for a few minutes? Moran's
annoyed language isn't suitable for children."

"Or anyone, really," Krevel agreed.

As she walked away, Kaylin could hear Corporal Krevel
answering a young girl's questions with growing excitement
and pride in what he did. It wasn't a bedtime story. It wasn't a
hug. It wasn't a declaration of forgiveness, and it wasn't—and
couldn't be—a homecoming.

But it was all she could get, and Kattea wanted it desperately.
A story about the end of the world that she'd heard so often
growing up, it was probably memorized. A story about the
end of the world that *wasn't* the end of any world but her own.

Moran's eyes were ash-gray, which was not the color Kaylin had been dreading when she entered the infirmary. She
motioned toward the chair the Hawks privately dubbed the
Torture Mill, and Kaylin meekly sat in it.

"You didn't come here alone."

Kaylin shook her head. The small dragon squawked. Moran frowned in the general direction of the noise.

"Kattea is with her father?"

Kaylin was surprised. In retrospect, she shouldn't have been. Moran *was* living with them, after all. Of course she knew.

"Helen was worried," the sergeant explained. She examined Kaylin's cheek. "Marcus is worried."

"I've avoided the office."

"And how did I know you were here?" She took the much more comfortable chair opposite Kaylin's. "What are you going to do with Kattea?"

"I don't know. Marrin would take her, but the Foundling Hall is always crowded and it's always short on funding. And we *have* room…and Helen would never let anything bad happen to Kattea."

"What does Kattea want?"

"I don't know. She won't say." Kaylin exhaled. "She's waiting for Gilbert. My guess is that she thinks, if she doesn't make a choice, there's still a chance he'll come back."

"What do you think?"

Kaylin examined her palms. "I think Gilbert's not human. Or Leontine. Or Barrani. Or even Helen. I think he had to injure himself, possibly profoundly, in order to spend time with us at all. I think—" She exhaled. "I think Gilbert, or something like him, was probably responsible for what happened to our city in the future we didn't reach. All the deaths, the absence, I mean.

"I don't believe that Kattea would be—could be—happy with Gilbert."

"But?"

"But it's what *she wants*. And if I was certain that she couldn't be happy, that she couldn't survive—"

"But you're not."

"No. Gilbert kept Kattea alive. He found her. He brought her here. His time with Nightshade—time which will no longer exist—had a profound effect on him. I think there's a possibility she could."

"She's too young to know what she wants."

"Then we're *all* too young to know what we want. We don't know how things will turn out. We don't know what will happen in the future. But—he was there when she needed him. She had no expectation that he *would be*. She thought she was going to die. She didn't.

"And she was right. I mean, she was wrong, but she was right. Gilbert did need her. Or rather, *we* needed her to be with Gilbert. I think—I think he kept her as a reminder of what would otherwise be destroyed."

"But Gilbert has not returned," Moran said quietly.

"…No. Until he does, if he does, she'll stay with us."

Moran nodded.

"So you called me in here—"

"To give Kattea some time alone with a man who thinks she's a stranger, yes." She wrapped her arms around her upper body. "I envy her. I envy her, and I almost pity her." She shook herself, adopting a harsher expression that was more at home in the infirmary—where it was admittedly necessary.

Kaylin rescued Corporal Krevel an hour later, and hated to do it. She watched from a distance as Kattea continued to pepper the poor man with questions. She was sitting almost unselfconsciously close to him, but she was young enough that he didn't appear to notice.

"Kaylin!" she said, when Kaylin approached. "Corporal Krevel's daughter has the same name as me!"

"I hope she grows up to be a tenth as lovely" was the corporal's gallant reply.

"I'm sure she will," Kaylin replied. She held out a hand. Kattea hesitated briefly and then took it; her grip was both shaky and strong.

EPILOGUE

Kaylin didn't see Severn again until she resumed her regular duties. She tried—once—to reach him in other ways, but he was silent and withdrawn. So she paused to dump her bracer into the Ablayne on her way to her first official day back in the office and on the beat.

The duty roster was up, and she was penciled in—on her regular Elani beat—with Severn.

He made it with seconds to spare and met her eyes for the time it took to blink—which was to say, she almost missed it. The walk to Elani was beyond awkward. Kaylin had a million questions she wanted to ask, but settled on one at random.

"Where have you been?"

He glanced at her. After a long beat, in which she thought he wouldn't answer at all, he said, "Is there a way for you to take your name back?"

She missed a beat. She didn't miss a step. "Killing you."

"That seems a bit extreme."

She shrugged, fief shrug. "It's a Barrani name. What did you expect?"

That pulled a smile across his mouth. "Nothing short of death?"

"Not that I know of, no. I've asked. The Barrani aren't famously good at divesting themselves of power. Why are you asking?" But she knew. She knew then.

Squawk.

"Oh shut up, you." She stopped walking. Severn slowed and turned; people passed by them and between them as they locked gazes.

"This is because you tried to use my name against me. When I was fighting the Arcanist."

His gaze dropped away from hers.

"So—you've been *avoiding me* because of *that*? *Seriously?*"

His silence was pretty much a "yes."

"Severn—I know you were afraid for me. But you *stopped.* You stopped before I even had a chance to fight you off. I don't— I wasn't angry that you tried."

"I am."

"Fine. You go ahead and be angry at you—but don't take it out on me." She stomped down the street.

He followed. "Kaylin."

"Not speaking to you right now."

"We're on patrol."

"Seriously not speaking to you right now. We don't need to talk to patrol."

"The last time you were in a mood, you kicked Margot's sign over. She reported it."

"Fine."

"Kaylin—" Severn caught up, reached out and grabbed her arm.

She yanked it free. Stomped forward. Stopped, wheeled and almost ran into his chest. "How," she demanded, "was that different? How was grabbing me by the arm different?"

"Kaylin—"

"I mean it! How was that any different than using my name against me?"

"You know why it's different."

But she didn't, not really. "If I knew why, I *wouldn't be asking.*"

"It's different because when I grab your arm, you yank it back. It's different because you have a choice, in that. It's different because I know I can—" He stopped.

Kaylin folded her arms. "Listening," she said, as if listening took colossal effort.

"Kaylin—I hear you all the time. If I listen. If I don't. I hear you when I'm sleeping. I hear your worries. I hear your anger. I hear your hope. I—hear you."

"Yes, and?"

"You have some chance of beating me in a fight if we go all out right now—if I don't use your name to control you."

Her arms tightened.

"All right, not a *great* chance—but better than none. When I—when I use your name, if I use it *that way,* you've got no chance at all. I *do not want* to lose you. I do not want you to walk senselessly to your own death. I don't care if that's your choice.

"But it's been made clear to me that your choice has to count for something. My choice can't be your life. And I—" He exhaled. "It's— It was too hard. I don't know that I have the self-control for this."

"And if I trust you?"

"Do you?"

All of the past stood between them now, although they were practically touching. She looked at Severn. At his scars. At his brow, at his clear, clear eyes. They looked almost gray, an effect of the early-morning light. A hint of a smile turned the corners of his mouth, but it was a bitter smile.

"I trust you with my life," she said and looked away.

"It's hard enough," he told her. "It's hard enough without the constant…"

"Constant what? Danger?"

His laugh was low and short. "No, Kaylin. Not danger. Not magic. Not chaos. Not the possible end of the world. Ever since you left Nightshade, I've faced that one way or the other." He lifted his chin, looking skyward; he slid a hand to the back of his neck. She watched the tension ease out of his jaw, although it remained in the corners of his mouth and eyes. "I'm sorry."

"Without what?" she said, in a softer voice.

"Desire." When she failed to answer, he added, "You asked."

She had.

"And now you're panicking." The rest of the tension left him then. It flooded into her instead. "I don't want to frighten you."

At thirteen, she would have said, *You don't scare me.* She was old enough now that she didn't bother with bravado. "I'm not— You're not—" She exhaled. "I'm—"

"I know." He lowered his hand. "I will not say I'm waiting for you. I'm not *waiting.* You're my partner. You're my backup. My life is in your hands."

"Mine is in yours."

"Yes." He hesitated. "But you're the only person I see when I look toward the future. That may change. It may have to change. But regardless, you're my partner."

"Except when you feel guilty and ignore me?"

"Except then."

"I knew," she said quietly.

"Because of the name?"

"Partly. I don't want—"

He lifted a hand, pressed a finger against her open mouth. "I know. But here's the thing: you have to know. Whether it's yes or no. You have to know."

She nodded. Closed her eyes. "Next time, tell me? I mean,

if you feel guilty, apologize—that's what most of us do. But don't—don't just disappear."

He didn't tell her that she knew where to find him, because that wasn't the point. He didn't tell her anything else, not in so many words. And the truth was: she was afraid. She was afraid of being wanted by Severn. She was afraid that she couldn't reciprocate. She was afraid that *she could*. She was afraid that things would change.

On the one hand, she was unlikely to be able to break his jaw if she froze or panicked, and that was something.

You have to know, Severn told her. *You have to know that this is something you want, and not because I want it. Not because what I want overwhelms what you want.*

When they reached Elani Street, he knocked over Margot's sign before Kaylin could.

Helen was waiting for Kaylin at the end of the day. She nodded at the familiar, draped across Kaylin's shoulder.

"Have they finished?" Kaylin asked, as she removed her boots.

"I am not certain they will finish before the end of the week, if you refer to Lord Nightshade and Annarion."

"But they're both still alive? That's something."

"The only person who has lost his temper—so far—is Annarion. It has caused negligible damage." She seemed much more relaxed than she had when Nightshade had first entered.

"I am, dear. I do not trust him where you are concerned—but he feels a very strong attachment to Annarion."

That stung a bit, which was stupid; Kaylin let it go.

"Annarion feels a surprisingly strong attachment to *you*," Helen continued. "So does Mandoran, but I believe Mandoran blames this on Teela. Teela—"

"Yes, I know. She still thinks of me as a child in need of protection."

"Barrani children are not often protected in the way mortal children are," Helen said, correcting her gently. "Bellusdeo has also had one visitor."

"The Emperor?"

"No, dear. Lord Sanabalis."

"And Kattea has had one visitor. I am afraid," Helen continued, voice soft, "that I have been forced to confine him. He accepts this."

"Have you told Kattea?" Kaylin asked, looking up the stairs. In answer, Kattea appeared, clutching the rails at the height of their rise.

"Is it—is it—" The name wouldn't leave Kattea's mouth.

Helen smiled, although the smile was troubled.

"That's a yes," Kaylin said.

If they expected to be led to the parlor, they were mistaken. Helen walked to the kitchen, and from there, to the doors that led down. Kaylin had always had a particular dislike of basements, but it had definitely grown stronger in the past week or two.

The stairs, however, did not contract or expand under her feet. No doors magically popped into existence. Helen held a lamp, and the lamplight cast perfectly normal shadows.

"Did he—did he do something wrong?" Kattea asked, her voice echoing.

"Not on purpose," Helen replied.

"Is he in a dungeon?" This was asked with less dread.

"Yes."

Kattea's eyes widened. She glanced up at Helen, but there was no fear in her expression; there was a little bit of wonder. Kattea had clearly never seen a dungeon before.

★ ★ ★

Whether or not Helen had transformed the hall to which the stairs led to better conform to Kattea's bright imagination, Kaylin wasn't certain—but the hall certainly looked like a storybook dungeon, replete with flickering torches. There was a barred gate at the end of the short hall.

Fingers were wrapped around two of those bars; they looked like mortal fingers, normal hands. But they were very clean and very unblemished, and anyway, they weren't the thing that caught attention.

The eyes were.

Kaylin thought she would recognize those eyes anywhere, even when there were only three of them.

"Kattea," Gilbert said. His voice echoed far more than Kattea's had, and for longer.

"Can he come out?" Kattea asked Helen.

"Not safely, dear—I'm sorry."

"Can I go in?"

Helen was silent.

Gilbert's hands loosened. "Tell her," he said.

Helen nodded. "Gilbert's presence here is destabilizing. What the Arcanist failed to do, Gilbert might do by accident, as he is now. If he adopts the form with which he was created, he will cause no damage—but he will not be able to interact with you."

"I told you I would come back."

"But—but when you were here," Kattea began. She faltered. Helen said nothing.

"Helen, can't you do something?" Kaylin whispered. Kattea had normal hearing, after all.

"I am doing everything I can," Helen replied gently.

"Is it safe for Kattea? Is it safe for her to enter?"

"It will be safe for Kattea, yes."

"What are you not saying?"

Helen exhaled. She knelt beside Kattea, whose eyes had not left the bars behind which Gilbert stood. "Gilbert is here because he promised he would return. He wants you to know that you saved this city. You saved the Swords. Because he found you, because he remained with you and because he listened to you, he could hear everyone, and everything, else. He understood how very, very little room he had to maneuver in if he did not want to destroy the anomaly in the usual way."

"Why can't he tell me that himself?" she asked. She was still looking at Gilbert.

Gilbert's eyes closed.

"He wants to see you," Helen replied. "And so, he is here."

"Gilbert," the girl said, shaking her clenched hand free of Kaylin's almost numb one. She propped her hands on her hips. "What did I tell you?"

"You told me that I am lonely," Gilbert replied.

"And *what else*?"

He smiled. "That you would never leave me alone."

Kattea nodded.

"If you come with me, you won't be able to visit any of the friends you've made here. You won't be able to visit your parents. Or your city."

"They're not my parents," Kattea replied. "They're not my parents anymore, anyway."

Helen, silent, waited. Kaylin frowned.

But Kattea said, "I shouldn't be here, should I? I shouldn't still be here."

Gilbert did not answer.

Kaylin stared—at Helen. "Helen—"

"If I understand everything that has happened, Kattea should have been swept away when the damage was repaired," Helen replied. "She should have ceased to exist. I am not Gilbert; I cannot speak with certainty."

"But she *is* here," Kaylin said.

"Yes, dear."

"And she is *staying* here."

"I think," Helen said quietly, "that that decision is not yours—or mine—to make."

"No," Gilbert said, as if no one else had spoken. "This is not where you should be."

"I should be in the streets of Nightshade. With the Ferals."

He nodded.

She was afraid. Anyone with half a brain would be afraid. Kaylin started forward; Helen caught her shoulder in an iron grip.

"I should be dead."

"If I understand events, yes," Gilbert replied. "But...I do not want that. I can see no way in which your lack of death causes instabilities."

"Because it doesn't, or because you don't want it to?"

Helen exhaled. Her grip on Kaylin's shoulder tightened, which Kaylin would have bet was impossible; there would be bruises, later.

"What happens if I stay here?" Kattea asked quietly.

Helen said, "If you remain within the house, no material damage should be caused. You would be contained—in an entirely different way—as Mandoran and Annarion are contained."

Helen was lying. Kaylin could tell, although she wasn't sure what the truth was. On the surface of it, the words seemed reasonable. Even believable.

Kattea hadn't noticed. "Will Gilbert be able to visit again if I stay here?"

"No, dear. It was very, very difficult for Gilbert to arrive here at all; I am uncertain how he did."

But Kaylin thought she knew. A very small part of the many, many words that constituted Gilbert was of this time. It was a Barrani True Name.

Kattea turned from Gilbert behind bars to the woman who was, effectively, his dungeon. "I'd like to go in now."

Kaylin opened her mouth. She thought Helen would break her collarbone, but she forced the words out anyway. "Kattea, you don't need to go. You can speak to Gilbert here. Gilbert's not human. He can't speak with you without injuring himself or limiting himself. You don't—you don't belong with him."

Kattea turned back; her eyes were wet. "I don't belong any-where else. I would be dead, if not for Gilbert. Gilbert found me—us—a home." She was pale, some combination of white and green that made her look the very color of fear. "I was alone. I was alone, after my father left. I understand why he left—I *truly* understand it now. I understand what he lost, be-cause I've seen it."

"You haven't—you haven't seen your mother yet—"

The tears fell. "I can't. What I want—what I need—she can't give me, and *I can't ask.*" She swallowed, reining the tears in. "I'm grateful that I saw my dad. But…he already has my mom. He already has…me. They don't need me, they don't want me, they don't even know I'm lost."

"I could—"

"Tell them?"

"I'm sure—" Sure of what? That she could make the cor-poral and his wife believe her?

Kattea's answering smile was tremulous, thin—but like a knife's edge. It cut. "Gilbert," she said quietly, "is lonely. You have Helen." She looked past Kaylin to Helen and said, "Thank you, Helen."

Helen's smile was warmer, fuller. In response to Kattea, the cell door clicked audibly.

"Kattea—" Kaylin said.

"Thank you, Kaylin. Can you—can you say goodbye to the others?"

"You don't *have to do this*."

"I know," she said. "But the only person who needs me now is Gilbert."

Kaylin understood, because she had been where Kattea was standing—emotionally, at least. She had been alone and without purpose or value. She had made a life for herself as enforcement for a man she *hated*, because the only alternatives were to become a corpse or a victim. A different kind of victim.

And it had seemed to that Kaylin, the desperate, broken girl of years ago, that she would never, ever have a family again. That there would never be a place for someone like her. She would have no friends, no purpose, no reason for existence.

And she wanted to tell *this* girl, this Kattea, who had not sunk to theft and blackmail and assassination, that years from *now*, she would have friends and a home and purpose again. That life, even the worst life, didn't have to remain forever shrouded in darkness and fear and loss and self-loathing.

"No," Helen said. "But you had no one who needed you after the deaths of your girls. Or so you thought. And Kattea is correct. If we—Gilbert and I—were not created to be as free-ranging as you and your kind, we live. We breathe, in a fashion. And we know loneliness and even despair when our lives become devoid of purpose. I do not know what has happened in Ravellon. I do not know why Gilbert chose the long sleep—if indeed he so chose.

"But he said himself that he had not expected to wake again. And yet, he did. His Nightshade is not your Nightshade, but the memories remain—for Gilbert. And memories are precious, Kaylin, for ones such as us. But they are not fully sustaining, in the end.

"Kattea understood that Gilbert was alone. She herself was alone, and if those states are not materially the same, there is enough overlap. Kattea was not, *is not*, wrong." She released Kaylin's shoulder, which was good, because her arm was now numb.

"Kattea—" The familiar, silent until now, bit Kaylin's ear. She turned to glare at him. "You don't understand!"

Squawk.

Kattea ran back, threw her arms around Kaylin and hugged her ferociously. "He came back for me," she whispered. She was trembling, yes. And afraid. But beneath both of these things there was another truth. "He *came back*."

Kaylin returned the girl's hug.

The small dragon warbled at Kattea, leaning down until their noses touched. He then exhaled. Kaylin had no time to move, no time to eject him, no time to shove her hand between the girl's face and the small dragon's breath. She tried, anyway.

Kattea, however, did not seem to be harmed by the silver mist she inhaled. Kaylin watched in shock—in anger—as scintillating particles of color blanketed in gray disappeared into the girl's mouth and nose; she watched in horror as they emerged, slowly, in the very normal brown of her eyes.

She turned to Kaylin, and her eyes widened; the fear left her face because there was no room for anything but wonder. She spun and stared at Helen, her eyes widening farther. Whatever she saw when she looked at Helen delighted her, and Helen returned her smile.

She turned, last, to Gilbert, who waited, his knuckles white where his hands gripped the bars of a door that was no longer locked. Her smile reasserted itself, but it was wider, brighter.

She walked toward the cell door and struggled to open it.

Kaylin moved forward, but Helen lifted an arm and Kaylin froze. "You want what's best for Kattea."

"Kattea's a child."

"You were a child when you made the decision to flee to Barren."

"It's not the same, Helen."

"No, it is not. Kattea's death might well have been yours, but her life from the moment of its prevention has not. You think to prevent her from making a mistake, and that is commendable. But Kattea is not you, and her life, not yours. In this, she has the right to choose. She is not a babe-in-arms. She is not a child who can barely walk, and stumbles constantly. She is not, you will say, adult. But she understands what is happening.

"Respect her choice."

Kaylin swallowed the rest of the words. Kattea was walking into the unknown, yes—but she saw a home, a family of a kind, in the multiple veils of the darkness that were Gilbert. There was no certainty that she'd survive—but there was no certainty that she wouldn't, either.

"Gilbert," she said.

Gilbert's third eye—the middle one—rose to meet Kaylin's; the other two were focused on Kattea as if nothing else in the universe existed.

"You'd better keep her safe. You'd better keep her happy."

Gilbert smiled. "That is a threat, yes?"

"Kind of, yeah."

Kattea had finally managed to pull the door open. Gilbert released the bars; he could not cross the threshold.

"No," Helen said quietly. "He can't. In truth, it is not quite safe for him to be here at all. He can only be here because—"

"Because Kattea is," Gilbert said. "And because I promised." He knelt, in form and shape very much the man Kaylin had first met. He opened his arms.

Kattea ran into them.

Kaylin had watched Gilbert carry Kattea as if she were weightless—and she probably was, to Gilbert. He lifted her now as if she were precious. "Thank you, Helen. Thank you, Chosen. I do not think you will see us again."

"Where—where will you go?" Kaylin asked.

Gilbert smiled. "Home, I think."

She would have asked him where home was, but the Shadows he cast grew thicker, darker; they rose above his shoulders like the arch of wings, and like wings they snapped open; when they folded, they folded gently around Kattea, until Kattea could no longer be seen.

She could be heard: she was giggling. "That tickles, Gilbert."

"Apologies." It was the last thing he said before he dissipated, taking Kattea with him.

★ ★ ★ ★ ★